DANCE ON SATURDAY

DANCE ON
SATURDAY

STORIES

◆◆◆

Elwin Cotman

◆◆◆

Small Beer Press
Easthampton, MA

Small Beer Press
150 Pleasant Street #306
Easthampton, MA 01027
smallbeerpress.com
weightlessbooks.com
bookmoonbooks.com
info@smallbeerpress.com

Distributed to the trade by Consortium.

Library of Congress Cataloging-in-Publication Data

Names: Cotman, Elwin, 1984- author.
Title: Dance on Saturday : stories / Elwin Cotman.
Description: First edition. | Easthampton, MA : Small Beer Press, [2020] |
 Summary: "Dance on Saturday is a collection of stories about
 transformation, loss, and human nature. Church-going immortals tend
 life-extending fruit. Swarms of deadly wasps engineered by a polymath
 sorcerer battle killer snails. Geese take human form and must survive
 juvenile detention. A high school, high-stakes volleyball game turns
 demonic. Heroes and monsters people these exuberant, magical tales"--
 Provided by publisher.
Identifiers: LCCN 2020006213 (print) | LCCN 2020006214 (ebook) | ISBN
 9781618731722 (paperback) | ISBN 9781618731739 (ebook)
Classification: LCC PS3603.O868348 A6 2020 (print) | LCC PS3603.O868348
 (ebook) | DDC 813/.6--dc23
LC record available at https://lccn.loc.gov/2020006213
LC ebook record available at https://lccn.loc.gov/2020006214

First edition 1 2 3 4 5 6 7 8 9

Set in Bembo STD. Titles in Flood STD.

Printed on 30% PCR recycled paper by the Versa Press in East Peoria, IL.
Cover art "Actaeon" copyright ©2020 by Christopher Myers (kalyban.com).

For Antwon Rose II. For the dead. For the living.

CONTENTS

DANCE ON SATURDAY

Upgrown from the tilled soil, the vines grew thin as old memories. They thickened as they twined six feet up the trellis to bloom in a panoply of grapes, raspberries, passion fruit, kiwi, and blackberries that shone on the chapel walls like many-hued jewels. Fruit in a church would look odd anywhere, let alone the Garfield neighborhood of Pittsburgh, but in every other way this was a normal ministry: a podium, a choir section closed off due to lack of parishioners, an organist and drummer to the right side, and two squares of gold-filigreed bars on both walls framing the altar. They may have been air vents or decoration—no one had ever known. The Fruit of Jehovah Baptist Church was a red brick building that had swelled with amens since the Northern Migration, and, for the first time in recent memory, black-clad mourners filled the pews to capacity. Riley Brown was dead. Standing four rows from the mahogany casket, Teetee reached out to pluck a kiwi. She bit through the skin, and her gums turned to a battlefield between sweet and sour. On the dais the All Nations Presbyterian Divine Choir clapped and sang "I'll Fly Away," four unified voices rolling over the mourners and out the double doors to flood the summer sky.

Verse after verse had Teetee dancing on her toes, wishing the song would never end, in contrast to Warmell at her left hand, the picture of stoicism. He fanned himself with the pamphlet that said "Homegoing for Riley Brown" in gilded calligraphy underneath a slipshod Xerox of the departed that made his face resemble a jigsaw piece. Positioned among the mourners were the Fruit, a term known and used only between themselves. There were fourteen of them, counting Teetee and Warmell. While the men wore black suits, the women adorned their colossal church hats with feathers and sequins and leaves, the rocking of their heads like a galaxy of swift-moving planetoids. She spotted two-thirds of the trio known as the Hallelujah Crew: Sister D, short and round and beautiful; Sister E, taller yet equally rotund, her face wide and lavishly wrinkled. There was Murray, a tall and strapping man who'd taken to wearing women's clothing. For the funeral he'd debuted a smoke-gray dress, black sequined shawl, and a crown that looked like a disco ball. On the dais sat five deacons sat in high-backed chairs, somberly nodding. They had ponderous titles—one was the Divine Servant of Strawberries, another the Lord Gardener of Granny Smiths—and were known for their weighty personalities. In appearance they ranged from a young woman to a sixty-year-old man with hair in his ears. All had dark and endless eyes.

The pastor at the podium was a rotund and youthful man with silver at his temples and square spectacles. Organ blasts sounded every time he paused for breath. He said, "Let us give thanks to the Lord for the fruit that sustains us, gives life, and holds memory." This he reminded them of every sermon; as their memories changed to fit new circumstances, they trusted the earth to be constant. His new blue eyes had Teetee guessing—Blueberries? Grapes?

"There is no greater loss than that of a loved one," he continued in his baritone voice. "But we must remember this life is but a doorway to the eternal life Jesus promised us. If there was one thing to say about Brother Riley, it was that he loved Jesus. And *he* knew one day he would finally meet his Lord. I would ask you to rejoice—for that day is come."

She began to cry. Were she a vulgar woman, she'd have cussed out Riley in his casket. This funeral felt as wrong as the selfishness of him for letting his pancreas ossify. He was dead. Damned dead. Present and absent, flesh and air. His choice offended her—how could anyone alive *not* be offended? (Let alone someone like her, who lived forever.) It seemed as if the waxy face in the box was mocking her.

Out of them all, Riley had chosen to experience the twentieth century. It happened under their noses, in the time it took to scratch your nose; his aging from a child who smelled of bananas to a man who smelled of knee-socks and tax reports, then his rapid fade to an elder who walked with elbows bent like a grasshopper. He filled his decades with super-highways and rock 'n roll, with cancerous air, with black rights given then stripped away. *Maybe he chose suicide to cure the loneliness,* she thought. Though she knew loneliness—which, unlike most ailments, had no cure—she resented him all the same.

He could have talked to us about it. Because he wasn't alone, not with fourteen brethren. Still, even they might have been unable to sway a choice he'd had centuries to dwell on. Despite her anger and disappointment, she knew this could not be the first time one of the Fruit had unlocked that moss-furred door between here and the afterworld. She just couldn't recall. Being of the Fruit offered her incalculable biological advantages, but her brain functioned more or less like any other, best capable of storing the most recent information while older knowledge melted to sludge in the basement of her subconscious.

After the reading of Paul's letter to the Romans, Riley's twelve-year-old goddaughter sang "Amazing Grace." Next came a member of the jazz band he'd played with in Homewood, a lanky man who shared Teetee's high yellow color and gray eyes. He fluted a somber melody that rustled her bones.

Family and friends gave tearful eulogies. As the remembrances rolled on—Riley adopted pitbulls, loved tailored suits, that time in high school he fell out of a tree trying to peep in a girl's bedroom—she found herself touched. (Save the peeping part, which Brother Byron should have known better than to bring up in church.) Warmell squeezed her hand, and she smelled the leafy scent of kiwi off his big knuckles. The walrus-mustached man gazed on the pulpit and clucked his tongue—strawberries, she remembered. His breath smelled like a parfait.

To her shock and delight, a sound of screeching metal filled the nave and Lord Decay appeared from the eaves, his slag metal cloak dragging the oaken floor. She grew dizzy from the voluptuous reek of motor oil she would always associate with the great lord. With a glamor on his true form, most of the mourners barely noted him, other than the suspicion they would normally reserve for a white man with a three-piece suit and three chins come to a black funeral. No doubt they assumed him some muckity-muck, a superintendent or city councilman.

The Fruit, on the other hand, saw a man with the head of a deer. Soft and reddish fur coated his diamond-shaped face, and he stared from the pulpit with eyes like ink. His armor showed its age, the heraldry on his breastplate battered and faded beyond recognition. To pay respects to a civilian was a princely gesture indeed, as he rarely left his steel mill along the Monongahela. He looked old as rusted machinery, venerable as a priest, deadly as a general, powerful as a storm, and with a tilt of his cervine head hushed the crowd. In a voice deep and elegant, he said that Riley was a dedicated member of the Pittsburgh business community and left behind many who loved him. Those few words left the Fruit saying *Yes!*

But the real surprise came when the girlfriend appeared. She was tall and wide like a sonnet. Teetee noted her narrow hips, large bosom, Atlean shoulders, and sable skin. She wore her close-fitting sleeveless dress belted at the waist, sheer black tights, and a veil drawn down from her pillbox hat. *Black Jackie O,* Teetee thought as the girl took high-kneed stomps up the dais, like her sorrow was a foot of snow.

A hum of gossip rose from the parishioners. Was that his Cleveland girlfriend? The one young enough to be his granddaughter many times over? The one whose kids Riley raised? Teetee looked behind to the loudest whisperer—Sister Mary with her new face, her cherry lips and strawberry nose settled from red to brown. She looked like a haughty thirty-year-old. *Why swap faces if you insist on acting ugly?* Teetee thought with contempt. *In the middle of a funeral, no less?*

Such bougie behavior bothered her more so now that she gazed upon the girlfriend in her magnificent flesh. Yes, her skirt was too short, but children these days had no idea of proper church attire. The parishioners acted like a mistress had come to flaunt her whorish ways, instead of his only woman, guilty of being an outsider.

The girlfriend lifted her veil and Teetee was stunned. Not only was she beautiful, with a square jaw and cheekbones like apples, she didn't look a day over twenty. Hours of effort had gone into her makeup, especially the eyebrows, plucked and painted into a pair of curved spearheads above eyes that on any other day would have looked guarded, even disdainful, but today were at the mercy of grief. Her tears barely allowed her to speak, the accusation with which she stared on the coffin belying what words she managed.

"God is good every day. He was good when Riley got sick. I prayed, 'Lord, spare him. Keep his light with me.' And when he passed, I said, 'Thank you, Lord. For all you have given me. I am nothing without you.'"

"Amen," said the mourners. "Hallelujah. Yes." Teetee felt obscene to witness such pain. Someone could at least offer the poor thing a handkerchief, a courtesy unextended by the pastor on his throne, eyes closed and hands folded in his voluminous sleeves, or the deacons who fanned themselves.

"Goodbye, baby," the girl said to Riley. Her tears got worse. "I know you in Heaven right now, and I'll see you," then she could say no more.

In line to view Riley, Teetee located the girl ten bodies behind her, her hands clasped over her lap. Her Chanel perfume and salty tears stank like musk among the potassium-rich scents of the Fruit. Teetee could smell exhaustion in her body, the near-future of surgeries and syringes and infirmity. She turned back to the casket in time to see Sister Mary kiss Riley on the forehead. *Since when is this a thing?* she thought with a cringe. Sister D, Sister E, Murray, they all smooched his cold skin.

It came her turn. They had gussied up Riley in a suit the color of Lord Decay's fur, a black tie with a diamond clasp, his diamond Alpha Phi Alpha ring wedged on the knucklesome left hand over his chest. In life his gap-toothed overbite had

given him a permanent infomercial grin. The mortician had
sewn his mouth into a skeptical frown. What little resemblance
the sleeper in the box bore to the man she'd known was merely
a strange thing, neither scary nor sorrowful. She nodded to
Riley and whispered goodbye.

A minute later, as she lowered her creaking knees into the
pew, a scream hit the congregation like a war god's sword hitting
the steeple to sever the church in half. The girlfriend sprawled
across the casket. Hers was a true wail, high and undignified,
never changing its hopeless pitch. It made the ladies in the
front row raise their arms like marionettes.

When we all get to Heaven
what a day of blessing that will be;
When we all see Jesus
we will sing and shout the victory

Following the service, hymnal tides carried her into the
foyer, then onto the lawn where the mourners schmoozed.
Unable to recall the last funeral she'd attended, Teetee found
she enjoyed the song and ritual of it all. Of course she didn't
want more, goodness no, but when she stepped into the sun she
felt an exhilarating awareness of the world. She could see planet
Earth with its black suits, football jerseys, rolled sleeves, knees,
tattoos, eyeliner, weeds, squirrels, flies, and flannel, all bloom-
ing with life. The people around her must have felt it too. They
couldn't stop smiling as they assailed one another with who are
you related to, how is so-and-so, every aimless word an affirma-
tion of existence.

They buried Riley in Homewood Cemetery under a boiling June sun. The funeral directors were a gray-bearded father

and two sons, the youngest and handsomest of whom recited a speech. "A flower is born from a seed. It blooms for a time then returns to the earth. On December twenty-fourth, nineteen forty-six, Riley James Brown entered this world. He grew into a beautiful flower that graced our lives for many years, now he has returned to the earth. We wish to thank you all for attending this homegoing service, and for allowing Freeman & Sons to officiate. We hope you will attend the gathering afterward. God bless and keep you."

As they lowered his casket in the hole, she found herself a heathen, an outlaw, a hand over her mouth to stop her involuntary chuckle. Such a Riley thing to do: pick the birthday closest to Christmas, stopping just short of claiming Jesus's day. How almost humble of him.

The funeral procession wound through Point Breeze to the reception in East Liberty, in a sunny garden walled with raspberry bushes. Laden with food provided by the Fruit, the plastic table bent beneath the weight of blueberry pie, apple pie, pumpkin pie, and raspberry peach pie with Belgian pearl crust (to name only desserts). Teetee sampled six dishes but, as she was trying to shed a few pounds, cut herself modest portions that still looked dismayingly diabetic in the puddle of chicken grease. It pleased her to watch the Fruit mingle with Riley's Vietnam buddies and frat brothers, twentieth century babies who carried the years in their crevassed skin and sack bellies. A number of Sister D's ex-boyfriends had come to support her in her grief, which got the gossips whispering. Then there were the children's children playing tag in church shoes, from whom Teetee got her name—having never been a mother, she became everyone's aunty.

As she saw it, black people built their families like sandcastles. A scoop here, a scoop there.

It amused her to see Warmell with the 'Nam vets, because they were men of a certain age, and he a man of certain ethics, all of whom based their impressions on footwear. Cultural pundits made much ado about the value shoes held for young black men, but in her experience whether a kid owned the new Jays or LeBrons merely conveyed his willingness to spend money. For older black men the shoes made them, in their minds, phrenologists. The vets shook his hand as they glanced at his black leather loafers, and he at their shoes, everyone making silent judgments based on toes, heels, wingtips, the amount of karat in the buckles and faux in the faux-leather, the quality of lace. Because no self-respecting man would tread a church floor in busted shoes. Secure in their first impressions of one another, the men proceeded to chat about the funeral, Warmell welcomed fully into their company.

No sooner did she finish laughing at this interaction, Teetee spotted the girl across the garden. Seated on a Grecian bench in the shade of brown pears, she was besieged by six hundred pounds of black matriarch in the form of Sisters D and E. They bombarded her with condolences. Sister D could be heard quoting Bible verse and complimenting every part of the girl's outfit. She asked the girl if she needed anything, and Teetee had to wonder what *anything* even meant. *What if she asks for the stiffest drink possible? What if she asks you to fork over that church crown?* She noticed the girl had trouble humoring people, her *Thank yous* clearly meaning she wanted them gone. Her knees pressed together for a table and a fork in her nervous fingers, she furiously ate pumpkin pie, each slice approaching her lips even as she chewed the last.

Eventually the women excused themselves to find less dour conversation. Teetee wished to offer condolences but it felt improper to bother her, so instead she bothered Murray. She quite liked his gray dress; according to him, his adopted kids were grown and he'd been a father to them. Now he could be a woman. An auburn pageboy wig deepened the shadows in his cheeks—they looked like curtains around his sarcastic mouth.

"Where did you get the dress—" she began to ask, when he lifted his chin and preened. It looked different from last week, more Denzelish. "Oh, is that new?"

"Go and touch it," he said. "Guess what it is."

She put two fingers to his stubbly, makeup-slathered chin. She felt a sharp pain and pulled back.

"Ouch! Thorns? Boy, you better give me a warning next time."

"It's called guayabana," he said. "I had to import the seeds from Nicaragua. Guess how much it cost."

"Too much."

"Damn right. And worth every penny."

"And it still hasn't settled? That's strange."

"You know the exotic fruit takes a minute," he said with a decadent shrug. "I ain't coming to Riley's homegoing looking basic. New chin, new dress. And, girl, what a nice homegoing that was. I'm finna cry all over again."

Teetee liked this liberated Murray best of the Murrays she'd known. The rest of the Fruit met his crossdressing like she would expect of church folks. When faced with his high-heeled strut, they would avert their eyes or find some article of clothing to fiddle with. This annoyed Teetee. After untold life-times, every one of them had to have tried every sexual quirk known to, invented by, or forgotten by man. But begrudging tolerance was the best they could offer Murray.

Charming as he was, she couldn't help but gaze at the girlfriend. She waited for a bolt of confidence to dive like the Tuskegee Airmen and rescue her from timidity. Murray leaned in. "You looking at that young lady like you done seen a ghost."

"Am I?" she asked, chagrined. "Oh. I must look so rude. I just wonder if she's okay."

"Go to her."

He gave her an unnecessarily firm shove in the youth's direction. On the way she wiped grease off her mouth and smoothed her flowing dress. When her eyes met the girl's, Teetee could feel her heart stutter, because those coffee-brown irises held more than the devastation of one who had witnessed death, stunned by the violence and permanence of it. The child had seen her *own* end coming. Whatever traumas she'd survived had imprinted on her in a way that left her hardened, grateful, and fragile.

Teetee sat down on her invitation. Sunlight limned the pears. The girlfriend glanced past her. "I don't know who that bitch think she looking at."

Across the lawn was Sister Mary, bougiest of the Hallelu-jah Crew. Thin, eternally young, her makeup suggesting she'd painted her face with a lollipop. She was giving them the tra-ditional church lady I-see-you-but-I-don't-see-you side eye. Plain inappropriate. It seemed to Teetee that some people simply had a lizard coiled round their hearts.

"That's rude," she thought to say.

"She better not be talking shit," the girl continued. "I ain't come all the way here for that. How you gonna be acting high and mighty in a hat like that? Wearing some fucking duck feathers to a funeral. She tacky like shit."

Mary's hat *did* look like a stuffed duck. Teetee muted her laughter with a hand. Girls these days were so witty. "I'm Jasmine," she said, "but everybody calls me Teetee."

"Deja." They shook hands. The red leather purse on Deja's shoulder gave a muffled growl. "These kids," she said and rummaged for the phone. "They get on my nerves."

"Hmm?" Teetee had trouble hearing lately. She would need a new ear.

"My kids," Deja repeated louder. "They get on my nerves."

"How many?" Teetee asked.

"Three." Deja took one look at the screen and dumped it back in the purse.

Teetee knew their names from the tattoos: Giovanni in cursive on her left breast, Donyelle and Barack on her left bicep, Deja's own name on the right side of her neck. It was rude to stare at someone's bosom, so she tilted her chin just enough to determine, yes, about ten pounds of tissue paper padded the empty space on the right. Her gut told her Riley paid for the surgery. He saved her.

Teetee swallowed a lump in her throat. "I'm sorry for your loss. He was a very dignified man."

"He ain't have to die," Deja said in a small voice.

She chose her next words carefully. There was no telling how much Deja knew about the Fruit. "He did die too young. But we are of the earth, in the end."

"That hand with the ring." She pointed to the grass as if his carcass lay in front of them. "That was a new hand. He just got it months ago. If all he had to do was pull fruit off a vine, why ain't he do it?"

Her voice diminished into mutterings. Teetee kept a blank expression. There was no rule against telling mortals their secret. Certain of the Fruit had gone so far as to raise mortal children over the centuries, though never in large quantity. However, they generally agreed that secrecy was the proper guideline, this moment being proof of why. Knowing he'd chosen death—chosen to leave her—left the girl with agony no one should have to bear.

Teetee took her hand and was alarmed by its dry texture. To her delighted surprise, Deja laced her fingers in hers. It charmed Teetee how their palms were identically white, like two halves of a strawberry cut down the middle. Deja stared up at the pears as if they spoke to her in petally voices. A sob shook her chest. "He said he might even grow one of them for a new pancreas," she said.

"Really?" A sudden thought amused Teetee. "Oh . . . I shouldn't say."

Deja smiled. "Now you got to. No secrets. The Lord don't like secrets."

"It's just . . . most men around here use pears to replace their balls."

By chance the entire reception hushed at the moment she said *replace*. All eyes turned her way. Murray put a hand to his heart. "Why, Teetee," he said in mock affront.

Feeling foolish, she put both hands over her mouth to trap any more crudity and ran to find somewhere private. She could hear Deja chuckle into her wine glass.

She regained her composure in the parlor. When she returned, Deja was gone.

After the reception some of the men went to the bar to celebrate Riley's life, but Warmell told her he was exhausted and would it be alright to go home? They headed from East Liberty to Wilkinsburg in his Crown Vic station wagon, Sam Cooke in the tape deck, his honeyed croon drenching Penn Avenue and all its people in tranquility. Warmell hummed along, his belly nestled so tight against the steering wheel he could have driven with it. Teetee said she wanted coffee so he pulled into the McDonald's drive-thru. The server at the window let her gaze stay on them for an extra heartbeat, and Teetee knew she was curious what about this older black couple intrigued her so. Wondering *Have I seen them before?* People sometimes asked her *Are you kin to* and named the first light-skinned person who came to mind, to which she'd reply with a friendly and affirming *Perhaps.* No doubt a ghost of an idea that was cousin to a truth would cross their brains, but they'd dismiss it out of hand.

Deja—a black name, vaguely French, a mother's desire to give her daughter something special. She remembered a girl she once knew named Taisa who—God be good—had to be forty by now. Faces came and went with such frequency that trying to remember was like reaching to embrace that person, only for their body to dissolve into feathers. Soon Deja filled every corner and closet of her mind. She imagined her in that barbaric downtown Greyhound station, among transients drowning in cable news. Changed into a T-shirt and sweatpants, she'd be hugging her suitcase to her chest and stretching her long legs after hours in the pew. She would be crying.

Once in Wilkinsburg, Warmell's car took up space on Penn like the Macy's Parade, and like a majordomo he tipped his flat cap to friends on Sunday errands. They passed the optical that Riley had managed, closed for his funeral, two homeless cocooned in sleeping bags under posters of bespectacled fashion models. Warmell mused that the University of Pittsburgh Medical Center would buy the franchise before long.

"Riley was the only one of them negroes know a thing about business," he grunted.

At last they parked on a cobblestone street lined with strawberry- and mango-colored vacants. Following centuries of wandering, they were fortunate that Lord Decay had asked them to be stewards. No home had been as safe as Pittsburgh. Sorrow no longer laid his prickly head to rest on their rug. Warmell got out the car, stretched, opened her door, and offered her a hand. She stood with some difficulty. Yes, summer would have to bring new knees. They ascended the crumbling stone steps to their Victorian, which remained standing through a mix of Pennsylvania oak durability and blue-collar irascibility. The windows were boarded; a hole in the awning left the porch strewn in leaves withered to the shape of seahorses. Ivy clung to brick weathered cat-shit-gray. Like an arm from a broken shoulder, a fire escape hung off the gutter by one rusty bolt.

Home.

Warmell moved aside the plywood sheet that served for a door and they entered the living room, the change in time and space like walking through molasses. A casual observer would have seen trash piled three feet deep, remnants of some family forced out after the steel left. They would not have seen the calico armchairs and fleece rug and leather couch, or heirlooms dating to the Reconstruction, like the mahogany hall tree upon which Warmell hung his suit jacket. He settled on the couch with a creaking of cowhide and became one relic among many.

The Hallelujah Crew lived in a graffitied station house on the Southside. The deacons lived in a former Catholic school on Polish Hill that children thought haunted. Lord Decay gave Reverend Goodson an abandoned roller rink. Murray, Larry, and Byron made their nest in a hotel crowning Mt. Washington, a beast of deteriorated luxury with a front door secured by ten pounds of padlocked chain. In former VIP suites lay mounds of rubble and broken glass; electric cords spilled from the ceilings; silence lay thick in stairwells that descended to asbestos bowels—or so it seemed to the thrillseekers and squatters who occasionally snuck inside. In reality the hotel was a series of enfiladed drawing-rooms of the type within which steel magnates once drew social blood with gossip and actual blood with calls to strikebreakers; the suites were arrayed around a central ballroom bedecked in Jazz Age splendor, where Murray often threw parties. From the silk-curtained balconies one could savor the view of downtown Pittsburgh, the skyscrapers a glittering spine for the Y-shaped confluence of rivers.

A grandfather clock chimed two in the afternoon. Warmell settled the funeral pamphlet into the softness of his belly. At the edges of the room lay dark shadows where Lord Decay's spells faltered and time gathered like mold.

"He was a gunner in Vietnam," Warmell said, "on a boat. He must have been scared." Spectacles perched on his nose, he read as if looking for secret codes. "Interesting fella."

Until the day Riley had chosen death, Warmell never found him interesting. Leaving him to his pondering, she walked the purple-carpeted hallway to the kitchen. Bathroom on the left and study on the right. Like the whole front of the house, the study belonged to Warmell; its soothing brown walls were decorated with Horatio Alger and *Tarzan* on the teak bookshelves, bottlecap collections and yellowing baseball cards stashed in cigar boxes on the rolltop desk, model ships and an RCA 86T shortwave radio he would use to pick up trucker talk. Toys of different eras, a smorgasbord of boyhoods.

Her realm was the kitchen. Where most people would see nests of millipedes and pink flooring scars, she saw a fully stocked food lab lined with orange cupboards. A framed poster of Satchmo playing horn at the Harris Grill hung over her pot shelf. Mason jars of mango and nectarine and fig preserves crowded the shelves, with more stored in the steel 1960s fridge that loomed in the corner. Like every day, she set a bowl of apple cider vinegar on the windowsill to catch fruit flies.

There had come a time many years ago when she'd found herself alone, and Warmell had found himself alone, so it seemed natural to move in together. Having no other term for their relationship, she called Warmell her *domestic teammate*. As she saw it, a *roommate* was for college students.

His voice came bouncing off the walls. "Did you know Riley used to sell insurance?"

"Probably sometime in the eighties," she said. It had to be the novelty of his death that fueled this obsession.

Warmell continued, "He ran the nation's second oldest black-owned optical for what? Thirty years? I tell you, they going under without him. None of 'em know how to run a business."

"Times are changing," she said, used to his repeating himself. "Years ago you would've never seen Murray in a dress at a funeral."

"You'd've seen him in a dress, though," said Warmell, disinclined to discuss Murray.

Thoughts of Deja fluttered before her like a crow in her kitchen. Deja on the couch in her apartment, a bottle of scotch in her fist. Filling her glass to the brim and drinking down the blackness.

On the windowsill was a scallop-edged photo of the woman Teetee called mother. Tall and striking in her favorite dress suit, Betty Woods sat on a bench before an Ancient

Greece backdrop, her ankles crossed saucily, her hair smoothed into a bouquet of curls on one side. She had an arrogant smirk that Teetee instinctively mimicked.

Smiling Betty seemed to brag, *I'm still in you.* What was left of the slim-waisted woman who would sit crosslegged on the hood of a Ford truck to watch Fourth of July fireworks redden the sky lived in the folds of Teetee's belly. In the three moles between her shoulderblades was Betty spinning on rollerskates through the rooms of her house. In her long fingers were Betty's blurring ankles as she danced at the Harris Grill.

Warmell had a similar photo on his nightstand. A father, a face, a surname to make him plantable. And within him, as her, a once-person lay in the meadow to stare eternally at the tangerine stars. Before she went outside, Teetee got a glass and pitcher of lemonade from the fridge. She had a powerful thirst.

The backyard had two garden plots and a pleasant cabin built by Warmell some summer ago. It was large and made of timber. Laid in the grass were circular mosaic stepping stones— like gem-encrusted pies—that connected the cabin door to the back stoop. She slipped off her sandals to walk in the grass. Mischievous scents danced under her nose. Spring vegetables grew tall and bright in their bed along the left side fence, but, as always, she was concerned with the fruit that grew in the right corner, in a raised bed ringed with purple sage flowers. The strawberries planted in April had a ruby color. Strung between the leaves were spiderwebs that hadn't been there yesterday— these she proceeded to destroy with apologies to the spiders. She could plainly see that the two trees in the plot, both around fifteen years old and held upright with stakes, would not fruit for much longer. On that sad day Warmell would cut them down and drop them in Frick Park to decompose. One grew lemons that shone like paper lanterns over a Tokyo alley; the other was a fig tree slouched against the fence like a battered pugilist waiting in his corner for the bell to ring.

Teetee took her dry laundry off the line, folded and placed it in the basket, except for a sheer tropical scarf she tied around her neck to feel the warmth of it, then relaxed in her wicker chair beside the fruit plot. She could hear Warmell play the Stylistics as he did motorcycle maintenance out front. As happened this time of year, she felt an urge to regenerate. She became aware of the soft and brittle places in her body that would need replacing. On the fence hung a chalkboard divided into seven squares for Monday through Sunday. It gave her pleasure to look on the untarnished slate that awaited her precise penmanship. She was in what Warmell teasingly called her *gardening mood*. The sun promised a green July moving toward the redemption of August.

She let herself listen to birdsong and think of Riley. What a story! A dignified black man saving his lover's life even as he embraced his end. And under every story, the sad reality. Even with his fancy suits and shiny conk, he did that girl as dirty as anyone could when he died and left her behind. Now that she sat in her chair, little inclined to leave it, she let thoughts of Deja come kiss her idle brain.

Sometime during her reverie she heard a car park in front of the house, startling her, because they rarely had company. She rushed to the gate and saw Murray's orange 1970 Dodge Charger at the curb. Deja sat in the passenger side. All at once Teetee felt her belly curl up, even as a gasp of joy escaped her.

She watched Deja open her door and slowly lower her sandaled foot to the concrete, as if unsure of the earth's consistency. Watched her get out and stretch and scratch her spandexed thigh. She wanted to tell the child that tights were not pants. Besides that unfortunate decision, Deja wore a red tank top bearing some bleached-out decal, and plastic flip-flops, her feet wide and flat and painted with red polish. Teetee liked the shape of them—the feet of a messenger. Her purse hung heavily from her shoulder and dark sunglasses hid her no-doubt-swollen eyes. Her hair was tied up in a black mushroom cloud. Crouched in the driveway beside his motorcycle, Warmell stayed true to his name by warmly greeting her.

"Afternoon, baby girl. I been thinking about what you said about Riley. God is good. For real."

He gave a tight nod to Murray, who had changed to a shirt and slacks, a man once more. Murray took a moment to regard them from the driver seat, one hand on the leather-wrapped steering wheel and the opposite arm slung around the headrest. Digging the scene with a gangster lean, as they used to say. He got out the car with a punch bowl under his arm, dragged his fingertips along the snub-nosed hood as he strutted around, and, upon glimpsing Teetee, summoned her over for a one-armed hug.

"I brought my famous mashed potatoes with mac 'n' cheese!" he declared. "The young madam wanted to come see you, Tee. Wouldn't take no for an answer."

Deja was staring at Warmell's Harley-Davidson, which to most eyes was the frame for a rusted red Schwinn.

"Nice Harley," she said.

It turned out that Riley had acquainted her with the magic in the vacants. That she wouldn't have to explain this was a relief for Teetee. For the second time that day they ate together, at the garden picnic table. Microwaved turkey with cranberry sauce and yams. Two glasses of lemonade. Murray was inside warming up the mashed potatoes.

"I was all ready to leave," Deja told her in explanation, "but I need to talk with you."

"How'd you find Murray?" she asked.

"Riley used to take me to this bar y'all be hanging at. I figured that's where everybody was." Her eyes locked urgently on Teetee's. "How do you grow the body parts? You gotta tell me."

"I—"

"Riley said I could grow a new breast."

What a cruel thing to do, she thought in disgust. To fill the girl's brain with such rot. But was he lying? To think on it, she had a feeling this conversation had come up before. Perhaps the magic had even worked on a mortal. Mountains had worn to dust since her tribe began walking, the only constants an insatiable urge to sow the earth and the knowledge they were responsible for their immortality. That responsibility went beyond physical labor. It required the greater difficulty of belief, celebration and prayer and song to thank the universe for their bounty. Beyond those rules . . . well, anything was possible. Was the power not awesome? Had it not nurtured them through the ages? But if Riley was right, then they should have padded their ranks with Fruit. How had their numbers dwindled?

There seemed no harm in explaining her secret to someone who already knew it. In doing so she was reminded of the amazing life she'd led. Her existence seemed more wondrous and strange the more she described. And though she went over it twice, Deja asked a third time, "They can replace anything?"

"Only if you grow it," Teetee said again. "Only by your hand."

"You mean it'll work for me?" Deja said with a note of hysteria.

Noncommittal responses came to her. *It's no sure bet. I think so. You have to have faith.*

"Yes!" she said. It felt right to do so. That Deja could see past Lord Decay's illusions meant she had to be special. An anointed person.

"Can I show you the scar?" Deja asked with downcast eyes.

The shame in her voice made Teetee frown, since she found herself loving Deja for her ashy black knees that whimpered when she knelt. Wanting to kiss the gray scattered like tinsel in her hair. Maybe it was all novelty for her *and* Riley—this flirtation with death. Seedpods whirled into the yard. Bees made music like violins.

"I understand if you don't want to look," said Deja. "It's ugly."

"I'll look," Teetee said, "but only if you never call any part of you ugly again."

Deja slipped off her shoulder strap. Did the same to her black cotton bra and let tissues fall into her lap. In place of her right breast was a smooth surface from sternum to armpit. Thin as a penciled line and knotted with suture marks, her mastectomy scar made Teetee think of a thistle growing over brown earth. Stretch marks angled down her left breast like tears for its twin. It occurred to her that a big girl like Deja, who had probably developed early, saw her bosom as part of her identity. Impulsively, she touched the empty space. Deja allowed her.

"We chose to become adults," said Teetee, shocked by her words, which had come to her without provocation and sounded like nothing she would say. "Then we chose to be old."

Deja looked scared and confused.

"I don't think it'll be as big as before," Teetee said to change the subject.

"I'm already unbalanced," the girl replied demurely.

"Do you have any fruit allergies?"

"No."

Teetee imagined a breast in her palm. "A cantaloupe might do."

This brought a change in Deja. As they spoke of definites and maybes, her voice rose from dungeon-deep to mountain-top. Teetee tried to avoid condescension. This girl—*woman*, she reminded herself—had borne three children and deserved respect. After a time, Murray entered the backyard, grinning.

"I want y'all to know," he said, "these potatoes were made with love by black people. Y'all best get in on this!"

So they did.

Cantaloupe for breast. Coconut for hair. Cherry for eyes. Sliced persimmon for nose. Strawberry for nose. Fig for vagina. Plantain for cock. Kiwi for skin. Strawberry leaves for eyelash. Orange for kneecaps. Blueberry for knuckles. Cranberry for nipples. Watermelon for ass. Persimmon for shoulders. Grape for teeth. Raisin for teeth. Prune for teeth. Tomato for elbows. Apricot for ankles. Watermelon rind for shoulder bone. Plum for wrist. Banana for spine. Lemon for heart. Pineapple for lungs. Boysenberry for guts. Raspberry for gums. Currant for fingernails. Grape for toes. Date for heel. Nectarine for ear. Citron for fingers. Lemon for blood. Plum for testicles. Lime for forehead. Plantain for fibula. Banana for ribs. Apple for bicep. Peach for tricep.

Life wore the body down. The spine bent and became a rod of pain. When such things happened, they planted new parts into the skin and massaged them down. Death closed one lidless eye on them, and so they lived forever on his blind side.

Though offered the cabin to sleep in, the girl insisted on catching the night bus to Cleveland. Murray drove her to the station while Teetee stayed in the garden, at the table, concerned with her possible dishonesty. *Yes.* She told herself Deja had needed to hear that. Told herself it was a kindness.

She put off informing Warmell until dishwashing time, when he was consumed in the tranquility of moving a drying rag in Archimedean spirals over the plates. After she'd finished telling him, he regarded her for a few moments, his eyes squinted so he looked asleep. Her arms plunged to the elbows in sink water, she waited for him to shoot her down gently; to inform her of a time someone tried and failed to teach mortals about fruit. At last he said, "Might work."

"You really think so?" she asked.

"The Lord is mysterious. If it do, it do. It don't, it don't."

"Don't you think it's what Riley would have wanted?" she replied.

He frowned with his entire face. She could tell her eagerness had him concerned that she might get hurt. Despite his good intentions, his paternalism bothered her. "Don't you like her?" she pressed on.

"She can stay long as she follow house rules," he said. "Back early. No men around. No eating in bed."

All practical rules—save no eating. That had never made sense. Teetee felt like arguing. "She's a grown woman."

He met her with a deadpan gaze. "Grown women don't gotta follow rules?"

"He's a bit of a hard case," she told Deja the next day. "Old school."

It excited her to call someone on the phone after years of using it as a decorative piece for the coffee table. She found herself twisting the cord around her finger like a girl on the line with her Sadie Hawkins date.

"Rules is rules," Deja said through static. "I appreciate old school. I tell my oldest: you don't wanna follow my rules, you can stay with Aunty in Cincy." Teetee pictured her shrugging. "I'ma do whatever it takes. For my kids."

"Do you have friends in Pittsburgh?" Teetee feared she would get lonely.

"All I know about Pittsburgh is Cleveland hates y'all, Wiz Khalifa from there, and y'all had a big rubber duck in the river."

Admittedly, Teetee knew as little about Cleveland. Something about their sports teams never won championships. As she saw it, Cleveland and Pittsburgh were the Montagues and Capulets, too alike in every way to abide one another. Titans in sweatpants and football jerseys staring each other down across the Pennsylvania–Ohio border.

"I forgot all about the duck," said Teetee. "You mean that art installation in the river, right? I thought it was cute."

"Cleveland niggas was laughing at y'all."

A contempt they shared with most Pittsburghers she knew. Shame, she thought, that no other black people found the duck as charming as she did. Dismissed it as the epitome of White People Shit. Then again, she'd heard that Cincinnati, another former mill town, had a rubber duck race along their wing of the Ohio. Maybe this was Pittsburgh trying to outdo them. She couldn't take Deja to see the duck, which had returned to wherever a forty-foot bath toy went, but she grew excited to think they could have picnics. The pool would be open— no, they couldn't go to Highland Park Pool. In summer it got crowded and the water smelled like eighth graders. Lost in thought, she realized Deja still awaited her reply.

"Come over when you can," she said.

"Friday," was her immediate response.

The deadline got Teetee nervously excited. After hanging up she headed down the creaking wooden steps to the basement. Lord Decay had determined that enchanting subterranean spaces was a waste of his time, leaving the air rank with the smell of wet carpet, the ceiling one gargantuan spiderweb fortified with digested fly guts, the floor a tundra of misplaced things so treacherous she hurt her heel stepping on a He-Man action figure. Against the back wall, next to a chopped-up plaid couch, stood her filing cabinet. A kerchief over her nose, she searched the files until she found a notebook marked SUMMER LESSON PLANS in the bottom drawer, burritoed within recipes and church pamphlets and papyrus scrolls detailing Lord Decay's lease agreements. She had written them when teaching gardening to delinquent teens decades ago. It had been an overall rewarding experience, the remembrance of which put her in a happy mood that vanished when she saw her old handwriting—tiny cursive as indecipherable to her as Talmudic script.

It seemed as if her older self intended to sabotage her with scribble-scratch. Undeterred, she tore out the pages and laid them on Warmell's desk, rewrote them word for word in a leather-bound journal. At certain points she needed a magnifying glass. More important than what crops she'd grown, she needed to remember how to *teach*. Stakes this high required a confident instructor. If that meant a few days of seclusion and tedium, she would embrace asceticism.

On Tuesday, Teetee, wearing a pink straw hat to counter the sun, walked to the nearest Carnegie Library for books on melon cultivation. Down Swissvale Avenue to the town of Swissvale, a town that never had a mill but was home to those who'd worked the nearby Braddock and Rankin furnaces. Once the gates closed on the Rankin mill and its cloud-scorching breath forever hushed, the eastern European and Italian workers either died or retired elsewhere, replaced by black people. Teetee couldn't say she missed them, as they'd never seemed fond of her or anyone with her skin color.

In Swissvale, the storefronts were built into squat buildings along broken sidewalks. Victorians lounged sleepily on the sides of twisting and rolling streets. She arrived, tired and sweaty, at the red brick library on Monongahela, comprised mainly of a central high-ceilinged room with plenty of space for dusty metal bookcases positioned around the walls, for the seven flat-screen computers patrons used to web surf. Upon entering she was startled to see the Divine Servant of Strawberries behind the long wooden desk. Dark and blandly beautiful, her appearance somewhere between twenty and forty, thin as the stool she sat on. The Divine Servant wore a cotton blouse patterned with red diamonds and blue clubs, like viewing a deck of cards through a kaleidoscope. Her wire-rim glasses were crooked at the bridge.

"Blessed day, Sister Tee," she intoned. "I trust you gave Him glory this morning and thanked Him for the sunshine."

"And I must have done a good job," Teetee rejoined with a smile, "because he sure delivered sunshine. My word." Or as Warmell had put it: the sun was hotter than Satan's ass crack.

Her attempt at humor dissolved against the Divine Servant's wall of imperious indifference. Over the centuries, she and her four brethren had grown a special connection to the fruit. Though Teetee had little memory of the lean days, she knew those who they called deacons, those solemn shepherds of the earth, had been invaluable in keeping their tribe alive through their skill at planting on inhospitable terrain. When the Fruit settled in Pittsburgh, the deacons distanced themselves from the others. They dedicated their lives to planting and prayer, except for the Divine Servant, who Teetee had forgotten worked a part-time job.

In other words, a sect of monks. It pleased Teetee to know that, among the Fruit, there were those entirely devoted to the spiritual aspect of their unique existence. On the other hand, the deacons had little time for frivolity, their ironclad personality on display that very moment.

"I'm just thinking of trying my hand at melons," Teetee said after a long silence from the Divine Servant. "I was wondering if you had any good books."

"Stacey!" The Divine Servant addressed the bespectacled white teenager shelving a truck behind her. "Sister Tee needs gardening advice. This might take hours, so here's what to do."

"Hours?" said Teetee. "I don't think—"

"Make sure you finish the two trucks. Did you get that? And shelf-read the Romance section. Clean up the Kids' room. Did you get that? Go through the late fees and call every single one. And make sure when Ralph uses the computer he doesn't watch those Japanese pornographic music videos. I won't have any perversion under my roof. Let me write all that down for you."

After writing half a page of instructions on lined paper, the Divine Servant of Strawberries led Teetee deep in the stacks to the Home & Gardening section, where she located no less than five books on melon gardening. "These were written by man," she saw fit to remind Teetee. "The only eternal truth is the Word of God."

They continued to the Spirituality section. A minute later Teetee found her arms overloaded with an additional seven books about the teachings of Christ. The Divine Servant laced her fingers over her lap and Teetee braced for a sermon. For the first time she noticed that the pin on the deacon's breast read DIVINE SERVANT—LIBRARIAN.

"I know about the girl," said the Divine Servant in a low voice.

"Deja?" said Teetee and glanced past her shoulder. They were alone in a corner of the room. She asked, "Who told you?"

"Hush," said the Divine Servant of Strawberries. "It is a blessed thing to take a lost youth under your roof. But if you do not help her find her way to Christ, you have failed her. You fail her *soul*. I have spoken with the divine in my meditations," she rushed on before Teetee could speak, "and He tells me Judgment Day is nigh."

"Or She," Teetee saw fit to say.

"Is the girl Christian?" the woman asked with urgency. "Has she been baptized?"

It saddened her that this fraught and impersonal interaction was the best she could hope for from the Divine Servant, given their shared past. She was seventy-five percent sure they had been pirates together off the Barbary Coast. She adjusted the books in her arms to a more comfortable hold and said, "She seems like a Christian woman. Seemed so at the funeral, at least."

"Only through fellowship will we be saved. The Book of Matthew says, 'Even the Son of Man did not come to be served, but to serve, and to give his life as a ransom for many.' You may think you are giving her a place to get away from whatever trouble she is in, but the Lord has called you to see to her salvation. If you do not accept your role as shepherd, the forces of darkness will fall upon her the moment she leaves your house."

Teetee was annoyed. Already her friendship with Deja had become a bone for that rabid dog, Gossip. Meaning Warmell had told someone and, as these things went, it took only a day before news reached the deacon's implacable ears. Thankfully, it appeared she thought Teetee had taken in a wayward child, the equivalent of a bad girl spending the summer at aunty's in hopes she'd quit acting a fool, nothing to do with growing breasts. The Divine Servant placed both hands on Teetee's cheeks, her face gloomy as a sunken ship.

"Promise me you will lead her to fellowship. Before I check you out these books, you must promise me."

"Yeah," Teetee said.

"Who did you tell?" she asked Warmell after waiting for him in the backyard like a coiled spring. She closed the journal she'd been writing in to calm her frustrations. "I just wrote two whole pages," she informed him. "I may not look upset, but I'm two-pages, single-spaced upset."

Her love of journaling had once excited the other Fruit, particularly Reverend Goodson, whose boyish face lit up to think he might finally have a record of the past. She had had to explain to him that, while Jasmine Woods circumvented her introverted nature by chronicling her life, her predecessor Betty Woods had no such interest in posterity, meaning the journals only went back about forty years.

"I told Byron," Warmell said, hands shoved penitently in his pockets. He wore bluejeans belted snugly under his paunch, an orange shirt from some construction company, and black steel-toed boots dotted with dried white paint. "You know how he get when we're drinking"—he shrugged—"won't stop asking questions till you gotta say something or leave."

"Did you tell him she's growing a new breast?"

"No," he insisted. "Just that she staying over."

"I had an encounter today with the clergy. The more . . . *intense* part of the clergy. I know she means well. All the deacons mean well. But it's a bit much to deal with her," she searched for a word, "*zealotry* when I'm trying to get some books. Warmell," she gave him a serious glare, "we should be careful about Deja's privacy."

He kept his gaze lowered. "I'm sorry."

She pretended to write in her journal. "*His apology was not sincere, but the wail of one who'd been caught and wished to avoid confrontation. Nevertheless, I pitied him.* I forgive you."

"Thank you."

"And would you mind picking her up when she comes?"

In her rush to write a planting schedule, she kept second-guessing herself, every rewrite leading her further from a comprehensive plan. Trying to arrange her thoughts felt like her brain was IHOP at 2 am, she the waitress careening between tables of rowdy drunks. Every night, before bed, she prayed for success. This breached the contract between her and the Lord because she rarely asked him for things. In her opinion God was more than a vending machine that you plugged prayers into until miracles dropped like air-filled Fritos bags. Normally she thanked him for her blessings; however, she found it necessary to pray for Deja's recovery, if only to put the girl's name in His ear.

The anticipation, a mingling of fear and thrill, stayed with her every waking hour, like an itch all over her body. Sometimes she barely felt it; other times she could focus on nothing else and had to open a melon book or redo a day of planning. Come Friday she waited on the porch with a knot in her stomach. As the car pulled up she saw Warmell deep in conversation with Deja. He was laughing. He parked at the curb, got out, and stepped around to open the passenger side. In a perfect world, she thought, they could grow fruit to replace car parts like the lock knob that jerked six times before the door finally opened.

Deja looked rested compared to her last visit. Her shirt read AKRON VALLEY BASKETBALL CAMP '99 (absolutely charming) and might have fit fifteen years ago, the hem clinging to the skin above her navel. Warmell hefted three suitcases from the trunk and Teetee sprang down the steps to embrace her. For a moment she lost herself in the girl, her plumpness, the indisputable presence of her, the strength that rippled like waves from her shoulders and into Teetee's loving palms.

To the unknowing eye, the cabin was a shed half-caved in by winter snows. Inside was a living room, bedroom, kitchenette, and bathroom, windows built into the low ceiling to allow for natural light. The furniture came from a beige vinyl set. On the walls hung collage-style paintings of river baptisms, Yoruba masks, and woolen tapestries depicting orishas, among other afrocentrisms. Overall, a calmly autumnal spot where Teetee often escaped to read poetry or journal. Deja thanked her to see white bath linens on the bed, impeccably laundered. As she unpacked, Teetee admired the efficiency with which she'd folded her clothes. Old clothes—good for gardening.

"Home sweet wreck," Warmell said. He lingered in the bedroom doorway, a timid smile under his mustache. Moments later Teetee realized he'd attempted a joke. He remained standing there for half a minute, wearing a look like the orchestra was playing him offstage, then left the cabin in a stiff-legged shuffle.

Teetee spoke to Deja in her brightest voice. "You can eat anything in the fridge. Giant Eagle grocery's in Edgewood Town Center. About a twenty minute walk. It's good exercise. But Warmell wouldn't mind driving." She gestured to the living room TV. "Oh, and we have videos, if you like movies. But who doesn't like movies?" She laughed for no reason.

Deja set about hanging jeans in the closet. "So you know, I'm a Christian. Baptist Christian. That's all I'm ever going to be."

"Wonderful!" Teetee said with a chill down her spine.

The look Deja gave her was of someone trying to avoid looking too harsh. "In case you do stuff like . . . you know . . . multiple wives or . . . anything with kids . . ."

"Oh, sweetie. We're not a cult. We're Presbyterian. We worship God."

"And God is in the Fruit?"

Teetee chose to ignore the cynical undertone in her voice. "I don't know who else could make us immortal."

With an exhausted grunt, Deja sat back on the queen-sized bed elevated with white comforters. She removed her sandals to rub her blistered toes. She asked, "When do we start planting?"

"Let's start tonight!"

Soft as a moth's wing, "Thank you."

In the house kitchen, Teetee showed Deja five packets of cantaloupe seed on the windowsill. Never touching them herself, she instructed her to pour soil in the biodegradable mini-pots. Count out sixteen seeds. Plant one in each. Happily, she watched Deja water them. In two or three months they would grow huge and yellow and sweet.

Later, at the kitchen table, they went over shade levels and fertilizer. The steely determination with which Deja listened reminded Teetee how badly she wanted this. Losing track of time, she was surprised to read five-fifteen on the clock.

"Dinner should be ready in an hour," she said. "You want some?"

Deja brightened. "Mama gotta eat!"

She ended up taking her plate of microwaved turkey to the cabin, her excuse that she needed to call her kids. Disappointed, Teetee sat in bed with Warmell until lights out, he doing the crossword, she journaling. All night the house creaked and cried around them. Pipes gurgled incessantly.

In the morning she dusted off a boombox and looked through her cassette rack. Grabbed the first three Mariah Carey LPs for maximum positive energy.

She found Deja already outside, waiting by the plot in her sweats. The empty place no longer padded, her cotton tank top sagged from the tip of her remaining breast. Teetee wore overalls, a straw hat, leather gloves, and sneakers. The sunshine got her singing an O'Jays song.

"Ooh, look at you all sing songy," said Deja.

Teetee smiled shyly. "Let me know if it's annoying."

"I love it," Deja said.

Teetee knelt in the fruit garden and sank her fingernails into the warm soil. Images twisted up her fingers, from cuticle to knuckle to cortex to memory. She saw Murray planting seeds and Sister D watering grapes. She wished she could bottle her euphoria, let Deja drink it. Together they uprooted weeds, killed them, cut their rubbery stems at the root.

In dreams she sailed the river, walked through the hills, descended the valleys, scaled the mountains to reach the middle of the beginning, an equator in time before they had words for time. Nothing but bone and gristle, she padded on bloody feet down a tree branch, the width of which called to mind something yet to be invented. What was it? Ah yeah, a road.

Cast in darkness by the branch overhead, she trusted her keen hearing and balance to protect her in the shadows. (To think she'd been so tall and strong!) Her companion's footsteps sounded behind, light as rain on thatch. Two children, vine-belted, the last to remain after everyone else had fallen in exhaustion, to wait in their dozens on the roots below. She made herself ignore the high-pitched voices buzzing about her ears. Accolades could come after the prize was won.

A hitch jabbed her left side. She breathed like she had pebbles in her lungs. When her groping fingers collided at last with the trunk, she spun around to catch breath. Her heart clanked and clattered in her chest. Through slanting bars of sunlight her companion approached with a limping gait. Like her, the other had brown skin, limbs like bramble, and a bald pate. Both were nude save for the belt, a stone knife sheathed against their hips, and across their shoulders a sling woven from their own shorn hair. Both had a gash instead of a worm between their legs. She-who-would-be-Teetee braced her legs akimbo to anchor herself. Her belly and heart thirsted to see the yellow treasure glowing on the branch high above. She lifted a jagged rock from her sling and carefully unspooled the ivy rope tied around it, a nerve-wracking process. Too much force in the swing could send her off the branch. Her companion knelt and hugged her around the waist for added weight. She-who-would-be-Teetee gripped the rope in both hands, gave three big swings that had her shoulders screaming, then let fly into the dark. Twice, the rope wrapped around the branch before it impaled the bark. She unleashed a triumphant yell that her companion echoed. Their cry exploded through the trees, in defiance of every predator who sought their soft throats. A cry against death and hunger. She could taste the fruit on her dry slab of tongue. They knotted the rope in their belts, put feet on the trunk, and climbed.

Wind sang with an alto voice. It kissed her cheeks and turned her sweat to ice. Below, the world was green and purple and brown, a bowl of spilled soup. Her arms ached as gravity pulled at her shoulders, the pain and nearness of death steeling her resolve as she climbed to the mushroom-grown underside. Around her rose the monarchs of the wood, world-trees teeming with life, in whose leaves sounded the movement of a hundred creatures. She saw cocoons stuck to the trunks and imagined the burrowers inside, long-nosed scoundrels dreaming their furry dreams until the white-mooned night they would burst forth as winged nectar-gatherers and snowflake earthward. In exchange for tunnels—shelter when winter came—the children guarded those cocoons. This pact had lasted as long as she'd been in the forest, and she'd been there forever, climbing, reaching as she did now to squeeze the corrugated underbelly of one mushroom and with her pointed toenails puncture another. She walked horizontally up the fungi, careful to balance as she swayed from the rope and slime oozed between her toes. She alighted on the branch, offered both hands to her companion. For a time they lay on their backs, breathing.

Following a brief rest they stole forward, their tread noiseless in a carpet of moss. Needles of pain stabbed her right shin. The branch was narrow enough for three girls to walk abreast. To keep steady, she tightened an arm around her companion (who she realized without knowing why was Murray). Suspended from a vine thicker than her waist, the treasure was twice as tall and wide as they, rotund, oval, gilding the bark with its shine. Knives in hand, they stabbed up into the porous skin and peeled it back; they plunged their hands in the stringy meat to begin filling their slings.

A screech slit the world open. High above, leaves crackled and she looked in time to see a winged nightmare expurgate from their black recess. Suspended on two veiny membranes that each ended with a single claw, it came storming down on them. Its nose looked bashed in and two daggers hung from its black-furred jaw. Its ears were taller than the girls were tall.

For a moment she could see the winged rodent in its entirety, before a colossal falling leaf obscured her vision. She jumped forward and rolled to avoid its crushing impact.

In a fighting crouch, legs braced and arms tensed, she readied for swift and powerful motion. Three strides away the mammoth leaf landed heavily, silently, on the spot where she'd stood. A stench like mud flooded her nostrils. The twisting shadow of the thing entangled her. Armed with her knife, her deadly companion, she had a moment to yell her challenge before winged death struck. A rush of wind, a reek of fur. She stabbed up. Foul blood blinded her.

Fallen on her shoulder, she lifted an arm to wipe her eyes, heard her friend's shrill voice shoot up to the heavens. The wood beneath her vanished and she was falling. She tried to scream but the wind snatched it from her throat like a ravenous fox. Then the rope squeezed her waist to the circumference of a dandelion and she vomited.

Girdled with pain, she hung limp, the forest floor rotating below. She could see her legs kicking pitifully. Craning her neck to look up, she glimpsed She-who-would-be-Murray anchored by her weight to the branch. She-who-would-be-Murray held the leaf above her head as the sharp-winged abomination assaulted her impromptu shield with air and claw and bone. She-who-would-be-Teetee gripped the rope and began the inexorable climb.

They returned to earth with crimson pouring in rills down their legs. There had been no time to heal before other predators made themselves known and forced the girls into a hasty descent. Missing a pinky finger on her right hand, She-who-would-be-Teetee used what strength she had to carry her friend, who had been ripped open down the middle, the wound stanched with blackened leaves. Half her face was a mask of peeled flesh and gaping teeth. The exultant songs of the children changed to horrified gasps. Burrowers came forward to touch She-who-would-be-Teetee's cheeks with blunt and dirty fingers, their compound eyes wet with concern. They stretched their question-mark proboscides to caress her wounds and told her to lie down in a language that sounded like termites scuttling through a log. Heedless of them, she swallowed a bite of golden meat, felt the rush of vigor as her wounds closed from the inside. Laying her friend on the moss, she chewed the sour stuff and spit the juice into her mouth. Her companion couldn't swallow, but She-who-would-be-Teetee kept spitting down her throat. At last light returned to her eye, the bleeding stopped, her flesh knit together. Relieved, She-who-would-be-Teetee held the girl's hand and smiled for her, so joy would be her first sight when sight returned.

Once she knew her comrade would live, she passed meat to the others, who fed gluttonously, juice dribbling down their chins and hairless chests until they were indistinguishable, a sexless race of pulp-smeared beasts. Then she lifted an ovular seed as long as her arm from the sling. What if they planted it and saw what happened? She asked help from the burrowers, who dipped their proboscides in elation.

"Teetee!" she heard a child's voice say.

Wakefulness hit her like a slap to the face. She saw Deja in the garden, crouched like a Klondike pioneer digging gold from a river. Mariah sang from the tape player: *Sent from up above, so much love in my life. I can't get enough of your touch—feels so right.* Teetee found herself in the wicker chair.

"Goodness, child, what?" she snapped.

Deja looked worried. "It looked like you wasn't breathing."

Teetee tried to regain her wits through the fog in her brain. Dream and memory shared the same corner bus station. She saw blood on her lap. She made a fist with her right hand and felt the pinky move. However, when she looked, she saw only a scabbed empty place.

"Oh. How long was I asleep?" She noticed with satisfaction the green stains on Deja's gloves.

"An hour."

How embarrassing! She probably came across a hundred years old. Yet she wondered: Did she really come up with the idea to plant seeds? She? Little docile Teetee? Her impulse was to call Murray and inform him he'd been born a girl. Unfair as it would be for Deja, she wanted to close her eyes and submerge again. The child plunged her gloved hands into the soil like she could wrestle the earth out of shape, and lifted them out with equal force, weeds encircling her arms like green bracelets. These she cast in a knee-high pile.

"I should work," said Teetee, and braced her elbows on the armrests to stand. "You go rest."

"You sure? I can keep going."

Teetee took a watering can to the spigot and filled it half-way. "Never feel obligated to work. You can't just mother other people, you have to mother yourself too. And rest is inherently nurturing." Their gloved hands touched as she passed the can. "Water your babies, then rest."

Later, as Teetee weeded, Deja reclined in the wicker chair and thumbed at her cellphone, a Newport in her teeth. Then she retreated to the cabin and stayed for three hours.

Deja had trouble sleeping. Nine forty-five at night, Teetee would don her purple bathrobe to check on the fruit one last time before bed. She would see the girl through the cottage window, two fans going like the Wright Flyer's propellers to push a cumulonimbus of pot smoke from the living room and out the rear window. Kneeling by the glass coffee table, Deja would pack her weed in a gutted-out Swisher, slip her tongue along the edge to roll a slim needle of a blunt. The first time Teetee saw this she bristled at the disrespect. Then she remembered marijuana had medicinal value, or so they said. Deja had finished chemo just last year; if she looked closely, Teetee could see spots where her hair grew back patchy. Only a tyrant would begrudge her that bedtime joint. Thus she resolved to never tell Warmell.

Sometimes on these nightly excursions, her guilty pleasure, voyeuristic and rude yet strangely fulfilling, she heard snatches of phone conversation: "I'm telling you, she lucky I'm in Pittsburgh. Saying I left my babies? Oh my god, that bitch is lucky.—That is some scandalous shit. Tell me more.—Gio, shut up and put your brother on the phone.—Girl, you will not be*lieve* the crackheads they got here. This nigga was *in* the trash can. I was like, the *fuck?* Nigga, is you Oscar the Grouch or some shit?"

She would watch Deja read from skinny novels with muscular torsos on the covers. Or the girl would curl under the blankets and stare into space, possibly imagining the milk that would pour from her new breast, because Teetee knew by looking at her that she wasn't finished creating life. The cabin light was always on when Teetee left the garden at precisely ten p.m.

Those first two weeks they did an hour of garden maintenance every day. Watering the rows of newly planted strawberries. Fertilizing the tomatoes, cucumber, and radishes that grew diligently in the vegetable plot. Cutting strawberry stolons to keep them from growing invasive.

One day Teetee discovered Deja had killed four flowers by cutting the wrong stolons—a forgivable rookie mistake. But when she pointed this out, Deja jammed her trowel in the soil five times. "Fuck!" she screamed.

Bemused but sympathetic, Teetee watched her breathe heavy until she had no more air and was wheezing.

"I'm sorry," Deja huffed. "That was stupid."

"Please cover the soil back up," said Teetee, who secretly enjoyed the fragrance of overturned soil, the sight of startled earthworms twitching their umbilical bodies. Deja was like a robin flown into the garden: pretty to see and hear, still willing to peck holes in the leaves because those were the terms by which she understood them.

When the strawberries ripened, Teetee made them into preserves she then bottled in Mason jars. The rest went inside Ziploc bags in the freezer. *They look like noses,* she thought amusedly. *Bags of noses.* In the kitchen she would gaze lovingly on the melon sprouts. All were tall with a healthy green color.

Using popsicle sticks, she partitioned an eight-by-five section of garden for cantaloupes. Shame they had no room for a trellis; she adored the sight of melons hanging like rotund trapeze artists from their own vines. Murray delivered a Rubbermaid tub of manure, a concoction he displayed as proudly as his mashed potatoes. He dumped it, along with fertilizer and mulching soil, into a wheelbarrow and stirred with a shovel, careful to pick out any hard bits that might hinder growth. Teetee and Deja took turns tilling the mix into the soil. They wore matching head wraps to keep the sun off their foreheads.

Some days Deja took to her tasks with alarming resolve. She tilled through sweat and fatigue, pruned the trees with grim dutifulness. On other days she took a dozen breaks, which always managed to coincide with Warmell coming in the garden. It made an awful impression when he entered, black stains on his armpits, only to find Deja a yapping, texting, smoking log on the picnic bench. He would say nothing; like a freezer, he kept his cold inside.

"I'm going to the store," he said one day, his shoulders pinched back like a soldier at salute. Sweat bubbles clung to his mustache. "Would you like anything?"

On her knees, Teetee rolled plastic film over the cantaloupe plot. In a week they would plant the sprouts, and she needed the soil warm. She pinned the film under her foot and looked toward the Friday square on the chalkboard, her dinner plans in tiny cursive under the list of tasks. "Cooking oil, please," she told him. "I want to try that new chicken recipe."

Teetee noticed his scowl as he turned away. After his last groaning footstep sounded in the kitchen, Deja stabbed her cig down in the pewter ashtray, which over the week had flourished from zero butts to a three-inch-tall ziggurat. "He really is a man," she said.

"Amen?" Teetee asked, and wished the girl would help with this plastic.

"A man!"

"What do you mean?"

"He making you do all the work."

That needed correction. "I like to do my own work. I don't like anybody getting in the way. Warmell grew enough fruit for himself long ago, so he doesn't garden much."

She relaxed against the lemon tree, her legs wide apart. Under her shirt collar, three buttons undone, a pocket of air chilled the sweat that clung to her chest like candle wax. She had placed a wicker basket of old *JET* and *Ebony* on the picnic table, from which Deja plucked an especially dusty issue with poofy-haired Whitney Houston on the cover.

"He your husband?" she asked as she flipped through, her tone playful.

"No!" Teetee said so shrilly it embarrassed even the figs, who turned their purple cheeks at the touch of an easterly breeze. She breathed to calm herself and explained, "We're domestic teammates. Less than lovers. More than roommates."

"Mmhmm," Deja murmured knowingly.

What was that supposed to mean?

"He gay?" asked the girl.

Somehow the thought had never occurred to her. Depending on what face he wore, he was a rakish bachelor; a celibate warrior-monk; a Barbary pirate whose name spread fear across the Mediterranean, his only love the sea; an old curmudgeon. But homosexual? It certainly made this current incarnation more interesting. "He might be."

"He can be gay," said Deja, "long as he ain't downlow. You say you downlow, that really means you low down. Spreading AIDS."

Teetee wondered if a downlow brother had hurt her once. Even so, that didn't excuse prejudice against all gay people. Wasn't worth that *mmhmm*, as if his queerness were a certainty; in Teetee's experience *mmhmm* should be reserved for moments of absolute truth-telling. Either way, the garden held no time for trifles. Once she had the plastic pinned, she tiptoed around to water the other fruit. Warmell often told her she took politeness to the extreme, meant as compliment and criticism. Now would be the time he would say lay ground rules about lazing in the garden.

But to look at Deja made the word *survivor* buzz through the flowers and Teetee had to allow her small things. Besides, she had no wish to chastise the girl. Given the chance, she would kneel like Jesus to wash Deja's fat young feet until the lifelines glistened in her soles. All she wanted was this girl, this seed on the panting wind, to know the garden as a sacred place. Life never ceased in the marriage of ovules and gametes, in the insects who danced so lustily among the leaves. Wouldn't Deja grow in such a place?

"I know his type," Deja said with a tight smile. "Warmell be Pop Pop. Master o' his domain, yanawmean?"

"That he is."

"Which I guess make you Big Mama."

Teetee smiled. "I'm nobody's mama. And I'm not that big."

She had never seen the inside of a hospital. Never been held captive by pacifying white walls, only ever heard terminal prognoses delivered by gravely handsome doctors on soap operas. She called Illness a muzzled dog in the kennel.

But to wear a plastic bracelet like death's daisy chain.

To tell time by the depletion of IV fluids.

She wondered, when the diagnosis knelled, did Deja worry more for her sons or herself? Did she see healthy people on the mounted TV and imagine a WHITES ONLY sign above them?

On the last Sunday in June, Deja asked to go to church with them. Teetee felt guilty at the request because, in all her garden work, she had forgotten the girl's spiritual needs. The Divine Servant of Strawberries would have been aghast.

"I'm sorry," she said. "I should have invited you—"

Deja took her hands before she could finish. "I'll go get ready," she said smilingly.

Teetee supposed her for the type who would only look her best for the Lord. She would apply her eyeshadow as many times as necessary to make that stubborn right eyelid match the left, and they would arrive to church late. Something of little matter for Teetee, just a humorous thought as she picked which flowing African-print dress she would wear that day. The sun had her feeling ostentatious enough to don her favorite hat: a high-crowned beige immensity with a downturned brim and raven feathers in the band.

To her surprise, she came downstairs at nine-thirty to find Deja waiting in the living room. She was dressed all in white with a silk blouse and pencil skirt. A curly auburn wig brought out the hazel in her eyes. The right side of her chest was padded, perhaps overly so, a strain on the pearl buttons of her blouse. She looked like a woman who loved Jesus and loved herself.

Only a handful of parishioners ever attended service. Teetee counted them in the foyer: fourteen Fruit and a mortal family of five, plus a quartet of tourists in Heinz ketchup T-shirts and Pirates caps who, heavy cameras strapped to their necks, resembled yoked oxen as they followed Sister D through the sanctuary. She regaled them with the hundred-year history of the surrounding bricks.

"The soot from the mills used to get the windows so black you couldn't see through them. Lord, how they scrubbed and scrubbed. None other than the legendary Mahalia Jackson stopped by once to sing a hymn. The late Reverend Haley, bless his soul, says, 'I love your music, Miss Jackson, but we can't have service till these windows are clean,' so she starts scrubbing too. And I have one more story about gospel singers . . ."

When they saw the chapel fruit, the tourists looked disappointed. Clearly they'd expected something more whimsical from the *Weird Pittsburgh* pamphlet under their armpits. Sister D asked for a donation and they did so, unable to withstand her bombast.

Warmell made small talk with Larry and Byron, two corpulent men. Respectively, they dressed in blue, yellow, and burgundy, from their neckties to their gatorskin toes, and looked to Teetee like rays of a sliced-up rainbow. (She especially liked Warmell's powder-blue suit because she could tie its purchase to a date, his wearing it like opening a polyester diary to 1975.) She noticed how people gazed at Deja with curiosity, captivated by her taciturn presence. By her perennially wet eyes, at once haughty and haunted, with which she looked commandingly at the throng.

Then she heard whispering from the vestibule doors. There stood Sister Mary in her blue choir robe, a hand over her mouth as she laid rancid eggs of gossip in Sister E's ear. Teetee wished to slap her.

She and Deja circulated the room until they came to the mortal family: a father, mother, and three Sunday school girls. Aged between ten and fourteen, the daughters wore white dresses and shawls and summertime perms. Good girls. Christian girls. Teetee gave them each a peppermint from her blue nylon handbag.

"Thank you, Miss Teetee," they said and closed their eyes to give silent prayer over the candy.

"They are so respectful," said Deja. "You sure raised them right."

The father touched his nearest daughter on the shoulder. "This one got her friends at school listening to gospel. Soon as they heard the good word, they were done with all that Kanye."

"I hate that music," said the daughter. "Barf."

Deja's fondness for the girls pleased Teetee. Much later, she made the connection to her three sons.

The organ called them to service. They sat in the second row. After the choir finished singing, right as Reverend Goodson strode leather-shoed to the pulpit, Murray came skulking into the pew ahead of her, stage-whispering apologies to no one in particular. Quite the tart, he wore a gold dress with feathered shoulders and sequined chest. That his love handles and shoulders stretched the dress to the limits of fabric and taste was a fact he bore with degenerate aplomb. She remembered him in the tree with her and gave his arm a sororal squeeze.

Reverend Goodson peered down on the congregation, kindly as the moon, dressed in a cerulean robe and kente scarf ironed into two towers on either side of his blockish neck. He did call and response for the Book of Jonah. It amused her how he'd make them repeat the least important facts. "And the sailors said, 'We must throw Jonah into the sea.' Everybody say seeeea!" *Sea!* "For Jonah refused his duty. He was disrespectful to God when he would not preach to the Ninevites. Can you say Nineviiiites?" *Ninevites!* Jonah's superciliousness had the bright-eyed pastor hopping around the pulpit in fury, shaking the deacons on the dais, who sat still as bullfrogs. "He judged other people. And isn't that like so many people today?"

"It sure is," said Deja beside her.

Of all the Fruit, the reverend had most absorbed his current life, being that of a pastor with a shrinking congregation. At times he seemed like any mortal. He brought the topic from Jonah in the whale to the trials of his ministry. "Everyone asks: Where are the people? I was born, raised, and potty-trained in Pittsburgh, PA. And I remember when the church was the place to be. So why will no one come? I weep! I ask myself, how will I pay the bills when I can't even pay my own salary? Everybody say salaryyyy!" *Salary!* "And then I told myself not to worry. God will find a way."

The parishioners murmured, "God will find a way." And He would. Every time the future seemed bleak, and even Teetee needed a lantern to find hope, the powers guided them somewhere new. She thought, *There is no god as benevolent as ours.* She gazed on the three daughters and sorrowed for their generation, who worshipped false gods like money and fame. The collection plate came to her and she happily rid herself of a few dollars, for her and Deja.

In between homilies, the All Nations Presbyterian Choir sang to the rafters. Sister Mary, Sister E, and Larry sang words composed by slaves in the sweating walls of their worship huts, but their voices conjured an older age. Every falsetto a mountain, every tenor a valley, every solo a meadow tortured by winds that swept upon them from the slopes of newborn glaciers. *How many languages have those tongues spoken?* she wondered, in awe at herself and her people. The power of God made her cells pirouette. From her waist upward she swayed to the rhythm. She shook the tambourine. Meanwhile, the Most Humble Devotee of Cherries rose from his seat to offer a wooden bowl of his namesakes to Reverend Goodson, who drew back his sleeves to plunge his fingers in them. When he held out his palms they glowed like fire. Teetee pushed past Deja and into the aisle, sprinted down the burgundy carpet, like the floor was a hot plate, in her mad haste to love the world. On either side of her fruit gleamed so resplendent that no shadow of Hell could touch them. Wielding cherry hands and peppermint breath, the reverend pressed his fingers to her forehead. Struck her with visions of towering trees, of her people traveling downriver in a raft made from a rose petal. Stiff as a plank, she fell into the arms of the Most Humble Devotee, who laid her gently down. Through the leaves she saw Jesus Christ, the lamb of peace, a white-robed warrior against all evil, but then his fingers stretched into sticks, he grew taller, and before her eyes he became a tree. Love consumed her and she spoke in tongues.

In a frenzy the Fruit came dancing down the aisle. Wrinkled bodies, fat bodies, black bodies imbued with the energy of panthers and swiftness of matadors until the pastor struck them and they fell like pinecones. Rather than a release of exhaustion, which their bodies carried little of, to fall was a joyful motion, to roll in rapture, a commune with every plant on the vine.

Falling and writhing. Wailing and chanting.

At the end of service the choir sang "This Little Light of Mine," a joyful noise that stuck in her ears like honey on the lips. A basket of hot towels waited for them on a table by the door. Teetee wiped the cherry pulp from her forehead, and in seeing Deja do the same realized the child had writhed on the floor with her. A surprise at first, even worrisome, followed by cool surety. It made sense that Deja could feel the power. Not as a Fruit—but a companion for their kind.

She had little time for appreciation before the Hallelujah Crew came charging toward them, six eyes shining at Deja like they'd found a quarter on the sidewalk. Collectively they smelled like a menagerie of baby-powdered ceramic figurines unloaded from a dead aunty's room and placed on a shelf at Goodwill. They sallied the girl with hugs and welcome. Sister D led Teetee aside.

"Jasmine, I am so glad you invited her in." Only D called her by her ornate birth name. "Riley lives in her. And a girl like that needs a mother. Mmhmm. Mothers and daughters, that's what's going to cure this world."

"She *is* a mother," Teetee reminded her. "We're more like sisters. Mmhmm. Definitely sisters."

"Do you mind if we borrow her a while? To cook for the homeless. You know Sister D gone treat her right."

She could hear the self-interest in D's enthusiasm and disliked it. Obviously proximity to Deja's youth had her feeling more like a woman and less like a river, more sky than dirt. Teetee felt a pang that she knew for possessiveness. Since God don't like ugly, she said, "That sounds wonderful!"

Like hell it was. They shouldn't overwhelm the girl like that. Even kindness could be a curse if applied like a hammer. Teetee watched them gather around the monstrous stove in the sticky-floored kitchen, sirens to its rock. They soon had scrambled eggs sizzling atop the fire-breathing skillets. Mary sliced up apples from her garden. What Teetee never understood was why they didn't garden the whole meal, instead of mixing it with high fructose artificially flavored chemicals that turned black people's blood to cheesecake. *None of my business,* she reminded herself. Deja unbuttoned her pearl cufflinks and rolled up her sleeves, started whipping grits. Sister Mary sidled next to her, ruby lips shining as she shared gossip about parishioners. Teetee decided to leave before her discomfort grew worse.

A few hours away from Deja's company allowed her to get sleep remedies. Dewigged and dressed like a man, Murray drove her to the Hill in his nail-polish-red 1956 Cadillac, one of eight vintage cars displayed in his ballroom.

"Thank you so much for asking about the tea leaves," she told him.

"Do you know what that girl said to me the other day?" he bloviated.

"Deja?"

"No! My daughter! One we going to see. She say, 'Murray, why is you cussin' so much?' Putting me on blast! She think she the parent and I'm the daughter!"

"That makes sense. We look younger."

"I known that girl since she was zero years old. I might as well have been nursing her."

"Oh, that is just ridiculous."

"Sometimes I don't blame you for never adopting, Tee. Soon as they start showing them wrinkles, they think they the grown one! I told her, 'I am still your father.' Talking shit like she do! How's things with *your* daughter?"

"First of all, she's not my daughter."

"Okay," he said. "Whatever."

"Stop interrupting me! She can get a little off task. But I'm a positive person. We woke up this morning, breathing air. We got to eat breakfast. We got to praise the Lord."

"You know I'm happy for all my blessings. Shit, I know niggas whose balls don't work."

"Shut up!"

"It's true. They need help with that."

"*Shut up!* You are something else."

Wind through the open window stirred his skyward afro that, for his own reasons, he'd allowed to go bald in the middle. No coconut to replace the follicles, an asymmetrical bush that made him look like a queen chess piece. His idiosyncrasies still drew her to him after all this time.

She wondered if they'd ever been married.

They turned up the hill past crackhouses. Over the rooftops she could see the new condos built for white people. With better sleep, she knew, Deja would work harder and feel more confident. "I can't wait until she has her new breast!" she said aloud.

Murray blinked his eyes as if he had dust in them, then stared on the road with a fraught expression. "*That's* why she's staying with you? Did you okay it with the reverend?"

"I don't have to do that."

"What about the deacons?"

"Why would I have to . . ." Before she got herself worked up, she took a calming breath. "Please tell me why you're upset. I'm listening."

Murray took a moment to answer. She noticed how stark he looked without makeup, his bulging eyes and hollow cheeks.

"I think it's asking a lot of the powers to do that for a mortal," he said at last. "We do alright . . ." He slammed the heel of his palm on the horn. Yelled out the window at the homeless man pushing a cart, "Get yo' dusty ass out the road!"

"Fuck you too, nigga!" said the bum.

Murray yelled as he steered the car around him. "Just 'cause you live in the street don't mean you own it! Next time I'ma run yo' ass over." He had both hands tight on the wheel. "Look, Tee. When it comes to the powers, keep it humble. You don't know what could happen."

"What'll happen?" she asked more sharply than she meant to. "You're making me nervous. Has this happened before?"

His Adam's apple was jumping. "No. There's no precedent. You doing the unprecedented and *that* scares me." He took on a blithe tone to ease from the subject. "Whatever, girl. You want to tell the child all this mess and pretend like you ain't just looking for a puppy to take care of, that's on you. I got too much going in my own dysfunctional-ass life to worry about yours."

"Wonderful," she said with a forced smile. "You should come around more often. You should get to know her." Though she knew that wasn't going to happen.

Murray's daughter met them at the door of her townhouse on Center Avenue, ordered them to come in out the humidity. She wore a shapeless nightgown and smelled like an old photo album. She walked with a four-prong cane. "Sit down," she told them. "On the couch."

"Do you remember me, Darla?" Teetee asked her. "I'm Miss Tee. From when you were a girl."

"From when I was a . . ." She shook her head, said *mm-mm-mm*. "Murray, your friends say some strange things."

The smell of herbs permeated wood-paneled rooms air conditioned to the point of discomfort. On TV white people were arguing over five hundred dollars in front of a wisecrack-ing judge. Hung crooked on the wall was a photo of Darla and her late husband, soft-focus, so it seemed that mist enveloped the embracing sweethearts. Teetee took a moment to straighten it. She could hear Darla shuffle through the kitchen, her cane squeaking on the laminated floor.

Murray had a habit, when he got nervous, of acting obnox-ious. "Make sure you pick the right amount," he lectured his eighty-year-old daughter. "We don't got time for no mistakes. You know what? *You know what?*" he repeated louder. "All this hoodoo's too complicated. Just get the girl some Tylenol!"

"Don't be disrespectful," Teetee said. "Geez. Negroes."

She watched the girl pick leaves from one of three potted trees on the dining room table. Sunrays did the limbo under crookedly jammed venetian blinds to douse the plants in chlorophyll. Smell of St. John's wort and periwinkle, barely a scent of Europe off the prickly leaf. The girl came from a line of healers. Her ancestors carried seeds in their hair through salt and sorrow across the Middle Passage.

Darla returned with a Ziploc bag of passion fruit petals. "Serve it with tea."

Teetee thanked her and advised her to take it easy. Murray wrote her a grocery list for his next trip to Giant Eagle. What was intended as a quick visit stretched into an hour of talking, as these things went.

Before they left, Darla called a friend on the rotary phone. "You don't have to get me groceries," she told them. "My son Murray's going to do it. Yes. Murray. The troublemaker."

Teetee could see on his face an old sadness. Insufficient for tears, yet enough to overflow his eyes and swell the pouches below. Years spent raising her in a magical hotel, yes, golden days. Except she couldn't remember being pigtailed Darla carrying daddy's baskets of grapefruit. Who sang gospel in the ballroom for his immortal friends.

The sun was a flaming bauble in the west when Murray brought her home. Before she stepped out he reminded her to be careful with Deja, his voice uncharacteristically cautious. She climbed the front steps, weary from the overlong errand, irritated by his sudden agnosticism. Were she a less classy woman, she might be inclined to point out that time she brought him back from death. She-who-would-be-Murray wasn't questioning the powers then.

She found Warmell and Byron in patio chairs on the porch, playing Crazy Eights on a crate. Byron was a light-colored man with a nose like a sundial and straight black hair. A biker, he dressed in black jeans and a leather vest over a long-sleeved wool shirt, the vest emblazoned with insignia for all manner of masculine brotherhoods. He wore his beard in a braid and a skull ring on each finger. On his invitation she sat and drank an Iron City from the cooler. It pleased her to listen as pontifications gushed like wind from their black-mustachioed mouths.

"Thing about Ali," Warmell said, "he was ours. Even if you wasn't Nation of Islam, you loved Ali. The crazy thing was when the white dudes started loving him."

"'Cause they hated everybody up to him!" said Byron. "They hated Frasier! Hated Jack Johnson . . ."

"They hated Ali, too! I remember what they was saying 'bout Ali when he refused to go in the army. Ran his name through the *mud!* Now that he's old and sick, they say he's their hero? Bullshit. I get mad when I hear white folks talking 'bout Ali was the greatest. I'm thinking, 'He ours! He ain't yours! He the greatest for us!'"

"You know who they really loved? Jordan. They had him in a movie with Bugs Bunny and all kinds'a shit."

"White folks love a winner. Especially a smiley guy like Jordan. But don't get too real. Tyson was *too* real. They put Tyson in jail."

Further proof that Warmell barely remembered his past lives. The mind-pictures, the strange smells and forgotten colors that filled her dreams evaded his. A contemporary man, a sit-on-the-porch-and-bullshit kind of man. Sometimes he lamented this—he would complain that his forgotten lives just *had* to be more interesting than this one.

The grass is always greener on the other side of history, she would say.

"You know baby girl's back?" Warmell told Teetee.

"So soon?" she asked, and stood up from her chair. "Who brought her home?"

"Looked like she took the bus. Tell her to come out and have a beer. All that being inside ain't good for no one."

On her way around back she could hear Byron griping. "You know I tried to use the bathroom at the Greyhound station? And they had the nerve to ask if I had a ticket."

"It's a damn shame!" said Warmell.

"Greyhound used to be the one place a black man could go to the bathroom. Now we got no place!"

She remembered to set a dish of apple cider vinegar on the kitchen windowsill. She entered the open door of the cabin to find Deja at the stove, shoulders hunched over a boiling kettle, fuming.

"That bitch got me fucked up," Deja said without greeting. She still wore her blouse, pencil skirt, and stockings. One shoe lay by the TV, the other on the bathroom floor. "She came to me all like, 'Tell me more about your sons.'"

"Oh," Teetee said.

"Got all up in my business," Deja went on before she could ask who. "'Where they fathers at? Boys need men in they lives.'"

"Oh," Teetee said in a lower voice. "Mary."

"I ain't having none of that. I'm here for my babies."

"I'm sorry that happened," she said with a level tone.

"She don't know shit about me and Riley! No men in their lives? She don't know shit!"

Her heart beating double time, Teetee employed a smile calculated to inspire laughter in the angriest soul. "Whenever I get upset I garden."

"I can't garden today. I ain't tryin'a cause no drama in your house, ma." She blinked away tears. "But I cussed her out. I called her on her shit and she was all like, 'I don't know what I did,' like some white bitch. She sure brought out the ghetto in me. I am a *Christian* woman."

"Just slow down. Take a deep breath."

"Maybe I don't want to calm down."

"We could watch a movie," Teetee said, desperate for a distraction. On the shelf below the TV, she glimpsed *Superfly*, *Lady Sings the Blues*, and *Jo Jo Dancer, Your Life Is Calling*. Crime. Drug abuse. Self-immolation. Black movies—unhelpful and depressing, as always.

The tea kettle whistled. Deja rushed to lift it off the stove, and Teetee watched her glance around in confusion, only to realize she'd set out neither mugs nor teabags. She lowered the kettle into the sink and sat on a stool beside the island, an elbow on the soapstone counter, one opulent leg crossed over the other. "You want some wine, ma?"

Teetee said yes. Deja removed a half-empty bottle of moscato from the freezer and poured each of them a glass. They drank in the garden while Teetee listened to her vent. By degrees Deja relaxed, and unzipped the side of her skirt to let her belly roll into her lap like fresh-baked bread. *That's the place,* Teetee thought with admiration, the flesh where three lives began. Wine could untether her thoughts like that. As she drank she pictured it germinating into grapes inside her chest—two purple bunches where her lungs would be.

Truthfully, she could have cussed both Deja and Mary for this. They were all women. *Black* women. But ego rose above everything, as usual, and common sense took a smoke break as long and useless as the ones Deja specialized in. *Mary should know better,* she thought. Here she was, older than the Appalachians, insecure, a poisoned apple of judgment in the same hand with which she offered friendship.

Teetee called her and said, "That was rude, what you did."

Mary attempted to make her raspy voice sound girlishly affronted. "Why are you defending her when she cussed me out? That girl needs some religion, leaving her kids like that."

"Her kids are at Aunty's. And the next time I see you at church, you better not talk to me."

"Or you'll do what?" She sounded panicked. "Are you threatening me? Long as we known each other, you're *threatening* me?"

"Take it however you will. Goodbye." To demonstrate her calm, she lowered the receiver like a lady offering the back of her hand for a lord's kiss. It settled with a click. "You bougie bitch."

Though a novitiate in melons, Teetee found she enjoyed the diligence of growing them. It was a joyful day when they transferred the sprouts from windowsill to garden. Of the twenty, twelve had survived, a number Teetee welcomed with quiet optimism. She applauded as Deja planted two sprouts in each of six mounds. After she massaged the earth back over them in perfectly round humps, Teetee recited a poem she'd written in their honor:

I like to think I was born a pebble
A shining red agate pressed in the sand.
To grow to a stone would be my life's goal
And all the world would be at my command.

But as I grew older, next to the sea
Other pebbles my companions would be.
Should I be a great stone, I cannot gauge,
But in friendship I have grown great with age.

And she said to the sprouts, "Grow, you princes. Grow!"

Within two weeks, the cantaloupes were budding; however, most of the vines had dry and spotted leaves. She explained to Deja that this happened, that they would lose some plants. She donned a surgical mask and sprayed them with chili pepper insecticide, then a potent fungicide. In the mornings she weeded constantly. She showed Deja how to lay the water hose between rows and keep it flowing at a trickle, for only a few minutes, so the soil stayed moist.

She grew worried for Deja. She could see surrender coming in her frustrated expression. A beautiful child, Surrender. Knobby-kneed and freckled with toast-brown skin, it sang songs and smiled when you called its name. It swerved around you on rollerblades to offer you some of its M&Ms. Surrender stayed at your house all summer and when it left you were exhausted, because it was not your child, but it ate all your food and left a mess in every room.

Deja started coming in the house once or twice a day to pour lemonade or make a sandwich. Then one day, as Teetee set row covers over the melons, she heard a man and a woman yelling in the kitchen. This came as a shock after a casual day in the garden, not too hot, in which she dressed in a bucket hat along with her plaid shirt and jeans.

"Stop arguing!" she heard Warmell say. It set her teeth on edge, because Warmell didn't yell. She sprang across the yard and up the stoop.

Her back to the fridge, Deja shot a glare both defiant and wounded at Warmell, who stood with arms crossed and hip against the counter, a linoleum sea between them. "I don't know what you talking 'bout!" she protested. "That could be anybody did that!"

Neither seemed to notice Teetee, whose bowels twisted in panic. Warmell's scowl was dark like the stains on his work shirt, a gray dress shirt he wore with sleeves rolled to the elbows. "I don't know what it is with your generation," he said dryly, "always trying to obfuscate, shift blame, whatever y'all do. It don't matter if it was you. Clean it up."

"Don't be giving me orders."

His eyes widened. "Don't give orders in my own house? Of all the liberty-taking . . . You wouldn't go up in no white person's house dragging mess on the floor!"

It looked like Deja might sass back. Whatever firecracker sizzled on her tongue, she managed to keep behind her teeth.

"Lord Decay don't like blight," said Warmell.

"Lord Decay?" Deja repeated like it was the most ridiculous name. "I don't even know who that is!"

In the hallway were damage spots on their beautiful hard-wood floors—gray, worm-eaten, warped by water. Apparently scraps of time had been dragged from the corners. Teetee had forgotten that time could catch on your shoe like toilet paper.

Deja breathed like she was nauseous. "I don't know how you can just blame me for something when two other people live here! You sound like the police—"

"I got it!" said Teetee. She yanked a broom from the corner and swept the puddles into a dusty heap.

"You ain't helping," said Warmell. "The child gotta clean up after herself." Deja rolled her eyes so hard the egg-whites showed, then stomped off to her cabin. He gestured at the spot where she'd stood. "See? And you say *that's* a grown woman."

"It was an accident, Warmell! Coulda happened to anybody." They let too much time gather in the house, anyway. Disgusted by it, she swept it into the living room, where she smacked more from the corners, great golf balls of the crap, threw open the plywood to haul back her broom and swing like Tiger Woods. Time went clanging down the porch steps to evaporate in the sun.

That night her gut clenched as she lay in bed. She listened to Warmell shower. Heard him run the faucet for long minutes before he came to bed. For a time he said nothing. Dressed in light blue pajamas, he fit a do-rag over his waves, checked the walls for mouse holes. (He said he could hear them at night.) Fondly, she watched him shine his church shoes, a gesture that in its meticulous vanity reminded her of a woman doing her makeup. He weighted the earth beneath his boulder knees and prayed at bedside. Then he lay beside her, immovable as a barrier reef.

"She can't be showing her ass like she did today," he said in a rumble. Before Teetee could speak, "I'll give her one last chance. But *you* keep her in check."

"I got you," said Teetee. When you right, you right. And he was right.

Six melons flowered between July and August, and something beautiful happened. Deja redoubled her efforts. Teetee didn't need to scold, as she'd feared, because seeing the first green melons filled her apprentice with enthusiasm. Under Teetee's direction she spread fresh fertilizer and propped her melons on bricks. She would look in pride on her blunt and dirty fingernails, on the small weeds flossed between her knuckles.

There were happy days of growth, and sad days in which the fruit struggled, with wine and Philly soul for their balm. Then, one morning, she found Deja standing paralyzed at the edge of the garden, her fists clenched.

Teetee looked past her to the six melons, small and apologetic on their bricks. Mold spots, as big around as nickels and pus-white, pocked their green faces.

Deja spoke in a sob. "Why is they moldy?"

"It's okay," Teetee said instantly. "We gotta prune anyway. We could cut away half of these. If too many grow together, they'll be less sweet."

"I ain't gonna eat it!" Deja snapped. "Why is they moldy?"

To hide her fear, Teetee pretended to ponder the question. Yes, they could replant. But it was early August and frost was looming. Her belly soured to think of Surrender's ugly older brother, Defeat, who appeared on the porch with ten suitcases, a shrieking brat who drank all the orange juice out the carton except that last spitty mouthful.

"Let's think this through," Teetee said in a bright monotone. She spouted horticultural explanations. Maybe something to do with soil and water measurements. Maybe they could spray more fungicide. Maybe they needed more shade, or they could move her fruit further into the sun. The more she talked, the more it seemed ash covered Deja's face, until the girl dropped to her knees. She breathed short and sharp, then she moaned, infant form of the scream from Riley's funeral. Teetee dreaded that scream.

"What am I doing wrong?" Deja said to the earth. "Why, Jesus? Why, Jesus? *Why?*"

Maybe she never had the patience for gardening. Maybe the earth didn't like her attitude. "Pray with me," said Teetee.

"I already pray! I pray every night!"

"We never prayed together." Why hadn't it occurred to her before? The Fruit gathered on Sunday to praise and the power never failed. "I've been alive this long because I *know* the fruit will grow. Call it belief, call it faith, call it optimism. I pray and . . . and I just know good things will happen."

Teetee took her hands and dragged her into the garden, knelt with her over the melons. She heard bees sing. Silken rags of sunlight hung from the lemon branches as if Blackbeard's bride, on the run from her bloodlusting husband, had climbed the decrepit tree and left tatters of her dress as she slipped over the fence.

They prayed for Deja's sons and Riley's soul. Prayed for the Fruit. Prayed for the burrowers. Her eyes closed, Teetee could see the past: the scope of a musket leveled to her eye, an eye she blinked to get the sweat out, the branches above cloistered so tightly the sky became a blue tongue through the canopy. The white man moving parallel to her barrel wore a darker blue, as did his comrades who tramped in a line, muskets over their shoulders and that same quiet emblazoned on their bearded faces. From somewhere a heron shrieked. She pulled the trigger and a red hole blossomed in the blue coat like a tropical fish leaping out the sea. A rush of gritty smoke filled her nostrils. The swamp rang with frog song and gunfire. And when the shooting quieted, she heard unintelligible prayers, dying men calling for their mothers. A child darted among the felled enemy, slitting throats, taking scalps, a death fairy waving a bloody knife above his head. Riley, she realized.

"God bless Deja," said Teetee.

"God bless Teetee," said Deja.

Chance made them black Americans and so they called it God. One day they would call it something else. For all she knew, they were the gods.

Seemingly placated, Deja helped her harvest figs the size of fists, who levitated at the ends of their stems with their own sweet magic. Picking them called for a soft touch, so Teetee left her gardening gloves in the soil to pinch the stems with the same skin she used to ruffle a child's hair or lift a bar of soap. Fig-milk spilled onto her hand; sticky-fingered, she curled her wrist to hide the fruit in her sleeve. She felt very young and a little vain, like she wore a new dress. Excusing herself, because to flaunt her joy would be rude, she padded on bare feet to the downstairs bathroom. On the way she picked up a butter knife. Alone in the trapezoidal room with seashell wallpaper, she cut the fig in half. Pinching the cartilaginous fruit between her index and middle fingers, she propped one foot on the toilet seat and pressed it to the withered flesh of her private parts. It suctioned to her skin and poisoned the near-dead cells. New ones birthed in their wake. Euphoria shot up from her crotch and blasted from her mouth, a molecular orgasm. Swollen, aching, her new vagina beat like a heart between her legs. She spun on a big toe, lifted the toilet seat by its shag cover, and sat with her legs spread. Gathered up the folds of her dress and pissed. It came and came, glorious. She wished it would never end.

None of the Fruit had to work jobs. For one, they lived rent-free. They grew what they ate. Those who cared about money had saved enough to last a hundred years or more. However, the present had a powerful force; it compelled them toward such activities as fit their current lives. On weekday mornings Warmell left for his computer repair shop in Braddock. Larry was a freelance plumber. Byron drove a bus. The Hallelujah Crew woke at seven every morning to waddle down Center Avenue passing out New Testament pamphlets and inviting people to church. Teetee counted herself lucky that, once she'd settled into her new face and body, Jasmine Woods turned out to be a grateful retiree. Far from restricting her activities, this opened up a world of community engagements to occupy her long hours.

For instance, the summer block party on Penn Avenue. The Fruit had made it a tradition that they all volunteered. That Saturday, the sun loomed over a street crowded with black people. The humid air smelled of fried food out the vending trucks. From the shade of her storytelling tent, Teetee watched children run down the street, sparklers in hand, like they were hoisting shooting stars. A KISS THE COOK apron across his sultanic belly, Warmell worked the grill, while Larry, a noted DJ in the Pittsburgh party scene, had Sounds of Blackness spinning all day long. Deja helped watch the bounce house. Teetee noticed her surliness with the children, how she yelled at them if they got too rowdy. It really was disappointing.

She was regaling children with the story of Josephine Baker and the secret documents. For years her group of listeners had dwindled, until it settled at five kids forced by their parents to sit at her knees. They made gestures of theatrical boredom, either yawning like lion cubs or staring into space like an old man who worked a lighthouse on some time-lost strait might stare at the sea. Nevertheless, she worked to keep them entertained. She used to tell African folktales, but the remoteness of the motherland in their imaginations started her turning modern heroes like Dr. King and Muhammad Ali into world-striding, star-footed gods.

"So Josephine Baker gets in her car," she told them, "and she drives through Paris to the meeting point. There are German soldiers everywhere. They are arresting people. And they stop her! And the soldier says, 'I luff your myoo-zeek, Miss Baker, but you must tell us vere you are goin-k.' And she says, 'I am on my way to record a song.' So the soldier is suspicious, and he says, 'Prove eet, else vee vill s'row you in jail.' And what does she do? She takes out the sheet music with the secret message written in invisible ink, and she puts it right in front of his face! She sings, *Blue skies shining at me. Nothing but blue skies do I see.* The German soldiers are so charmed by her voice that they let her go."

"Why did she wear a banana skirt?" a boy blurted.

She took a moment to think up a PG-rated answer. "Why, because she looked very nice in it."

"That's weird," he said.

Suppressing a sigh, she continued her tale, which ended on a moral of believing in yourself. At least the banana skirt boy was engaged. During her story, one girl kept blowing up a latex glove. Another boy left to tell his mom he wanted her iPhone. She slapped him on the butt and told him to apologize to Miss Teetee. *Maybe I should have told a Jesse Owens story*, she thought.

The children dashed straight for other activities once she was done. Forlornly, she thought of how someday, soon, they would become blind and deaf to wonder. Finding her stool too comfortable to move from just yet, she remained in the shade. Sister E came to her with a smile leaping off her face. Her XXXL shirt, adorned with Riley's picture above his "birth" and "death" dates, could have doubled as a tapestry.

"Are you going to D's party tonight?" she asked.

"And what party would that be?" Teetee asked.

"Girl, it's her birthday."

"Her birthday is in the summer, now?" said Teetee, recalling last year's rained-out October barbecue.

"She finally got tired of fall," said E. "I could pick you up, if you like."

Before she could reply, the sound of rushing air drew Teetee's attention to the bounce house. Deja had unplugged it from the air machine. Deflated, it looked like a glob of melted strawberry ice cream. As soon as the children slid out they were confronted with Deja's unamused calves, her tights and tank top, her quivering chest reinforced with rolled-up towel into an indomitable precipice.

"Y'all ain't got no act right," she chastised them. "Y'all act stupid now, you'll act stupid forever. Stupid is for life."

Before long one of their mothers came over. "Excuse me?" she said indignantly. "What did you say to my son?"

Teetee rose from her stool and walked in the opposite direction. There was no role she could play in this tension. With Sister E at her side, she walked until they reached her home. In the backyard she pulled out lawn chairs and they drank lemonade, away from the noise of Penn.

"Where's the party?" Teetee asked.

"Murray's."

"The hotel?"

"No. Different Murray's. Murray's Cafe."

"Murray's Cafe? I hear they have thugs there."

"They do."

"Young or old?" Teetee asked worriedly.

"Both."

"I'm not scared of thugs. Thugs don't mess with Miss Teetee. I will take those thugs and tell them a story. And let them know they're loved. And then they won't be thugs anymore. And if they are, they'll be love thugs. Oh, should I invite Warmell?"

"It's a girls' night."

Usually Teetee avoided joints like Murray's. The days of card cheats and knife fights that birthed her favorite outlaw ballads were gone, and, truth be told, she'd never idolized that life anyway. In the end, bars were loud and smoky dens of misery. But she needed to be social after months staring at plants. It crossed her mind to invite Deja, but she figured a thirty-year-old wouldn't want to spend Saturday night in the company of fogies like herself.

Around seven in the evening she jumped into Sister E's boxy Kia, followed by a short drive to Swissvale. Upon entering the smoky bar she saw the expected crowd of young and old, men and women celebrating the end of another week. Beer scum stuck to her heels. The lady bartender had a pink face and a consternated expression. In the next room over, someone was caterwauling her way through Whitney Houston's "Saving All My Love For You."

"Teeteeee!" Sister D greeted her from her table in the back. Her black-and-red dye job matched the dart board. She wore a Riley shirt underneath a beige fur coat that Teetee found wonderfully soft when they embraced.

"Happy birthday, girl!" Teetee said. "How old are you?"

D barked a laugh. "This time? Let's say forty. A woman can admit when she's mature."

"Where'd you get this coat? It looks old school."

D turned side to side to show it off. "What some call old school, I call vintage, sweetie. I got this at the Goodwill. I am a thrift store queen." She tugged the ends of Teetee's tropical shawl. "And look at you, all Hawaii Five-Oh. Okay, Miss Tee! I see you!"

A shy giggle escaped Teetee. Sister D gripped her by the elbow, the pressure she exerted both forceful and sensual.

"Where is Deja?" she asked. "Is she coming?"

"No. She's, uh, she's sleeping," said Teetee. That D looked disappointed annoyed her, yet Teetee instinctively cast down her eyes in apology, for which she got annoyed at herself. And, seeing another woman missing from the party, peevishly asked, "Where's the Divine Servant of Strawberries?" She felt a satisfying little thrill at her question, passive-aggressive as it was.

"I invited her!" hollered D. "You know how deacons are. Girl just stared at me for a straight minute."

Sister D ordered rum and Coke for herself, Teetee, and E. The drink was brown like the girl back at the cabin. Teetee pictured her in sweats, stretched across the couch, eyes closed, bathed in the light of some bad movie. Sister D guzzled drinks like a college girl. With nimble movements of her fingers, she smoked, extinguished, and lit cigarettes, except for the times she let flirts at the bar light the smokes for her.

Two rums in, D unsnapped her purse to sift through its contents. "Jasmine, I must show you this treasure." She took out a playbill. Dated 1829 and titled *Henry III et sa Cour.*

"*Henry the Third and His Court*," read Teetee, delighted to learn she understood French. "'A historical drama by Alexander Dumas.' Oh my! Where'd you find this?"

"Would you believe under the couch? Do you know what this means, girl? Do you know? I was *in* this play!"

"That's wonderful!" she said, happy for her friend and her found memory.

"Everybody always told me I should be an actress. This is proof in the pudding. Whoever I was, I am sure I had the most memorable death scene. I would have had them all fanning themselves at the Comédie-Française. And I'll bet you I was dancing at the Moulin Rouge."

"Was I there?"

"You were! And so was Mary!"

"For real?"

"I must have been elsewhere," Sister E sadly added.

Self-satisfied, Sister D whapped her knuckles on the playbill. "It all came back to me when I saw it. We were Parisians."

Teetee wondered one thing: "Were we black at that time?"

"Why . . . I don't know. Ha! I hope we were."

Fascinated, Teetee read through the playbill, a ghost of romantic Paris and the beautiful lies they made of history, its paper weighty and its print calligraphic. She finished and handed it back to D, who, a fresh cigarette between two plump fingers, leaned toward her with both elbows on the table, her expression serious.

"So," she said. "Jasmine."

"So. D."

"What's going on with you and Mary? You don't say anything to each other at church."

"Please don't get in it," Teetee said quickly, casting a glance into the other room to find that, yes, it was Mary with neck veins bulging, screaming yet another Whitney song into the microphone.

"Too late 'cause I *am* in it. We're all we've got. You know that."

"She disrespected Deja."

"And how long do you plan on being a monk to only her? Because we got a while." D took a pensive drag. "Deja's gonna be gone soon. It's not fun to hear, I know. But Jasmine, we are *sisters.*"

She spoke the word like an order. Her protectiveness toward Mary, based out of bald tribalism, made Teetee uncomfortable. *Mortals have it easy,* she thought. A girl comes into the world, then another girl, and what conflicts arise over a hundred years are easily released when death wipes away all. The history she shared with Mary was an ocean, they two dolls in a bottle, at the dictates of wind and gravity. To live a planet's age deserved respect.

Teetee downed her rum, ordered two more and went to the other room. She sat with Mary at a small table and they toasted. "To Riley," said Teetee.

That night Mary kept her makeup low-key, purple eyeshadow and lipstick. She wore a Riley shirt and tight bluejeans that Teetee had to admit looked pretty sexy on her. And she wondered, *When will black folks stop putting the dead on T-shirts?* They might as well be dragging around a casket.

"You have *got* to be more open-minded," she told Mary, to not let her off the hook. "Think of all we've done. All we've seen. I don't know why you come at people like that sometimes."

Mary's eyes quivered like robin's eggs about to hatch. She threw a slandered hand to her chest. "I'm just—"

"No, listen. Sometimes we act first, thinking we're doing the right thing. I know you want to help Deja, and you *can* help. But you can't come at her like that. She's my sister too."

"I get it," said Mary, a concession Teetee took skeptically. Whether she would *get it* once she sobered was another story. "I shouldn't have said what I said to her." A pause. "You remember the last time you refused to speak to me?"

"Can't say I do."

Mary finished her glass, leaving a purple mark around the rim. "That playbill D found got me remembering things. It was because of Dumas."

"Really?"

"I loved his books and his plays. He just had so much swagger, strutting 'round Paris like he owned the place. And he had so many mistresses! But you," she lowered her voice, "you thought he was a bit of a fuckboy, pardon my French."

Teetee felt herself smile. "Since when did you curse?"

"That's what you thought! And maybe he was, a little. I wanted to sleep with him, and you said if I did you wouldn't speak to me." She cracked a grin. "I guess I must have, because we didn't speak for twenty years. You can hold a grudge, when you want to."

It took Teetee a moment to digest this. "Dumas really was all up in our business," she said at last. Elbow on the table, she propped her chin in her hand. "I was sure petty, wasn't I? When you said I wouldn't speak to you, I thought it'd be some disagreement over politics."

"You *were* political. You fought with Napoleon!"

"No. Shut up."

"You were a lieutenant or something. I . . . I think you were a man, too!"

She wondered how soon it would be before Mary forgot this Paris stuff, before the memories squeezed from her skull like so many more they had left behind. For now it was clear that her cold-shoulder got the woman feeling threatened, and Mary had done nothing to earn forgiveness. They'd never had much to talk about in the first place. What disturbed Teetee was that she, in the midst of forgiving this sow, this painted narcissist, all for what she thought the greater good, had once held a grudge for twenty years. Once stubborn to a fault, she'd become someone who couldn't bear conflict. It made her a wimp sometimes.

For another week the last three melons soldiered on, grew to the size of a baby's head. Meanwhile, Teetee would invent tasks for Deja. Pick mint and put it in pots. Refertilize the lemon tree. Harvest vegetables and wheelbarrow them to a neighbor's. Cook breakfast in the morning. Deja's frustration filled the yard like the smell of burnt match, and Teetee grew to appreciate their time less and less.

One Sunday afternoon in late August, the work left her so tired she sat in the corner between the fence and the fig tree, and could not have moved if she wanted. To her surprise, Deja sat beside her, and they lay like two porcelain dolls upon a pillow, cheeks together.

"Your hair is so pretty," said Deja. "I wish I had hair like you."

"Oh, don't make me bashful."

"So long and pretty. Princess hair."

"I'm an old gray goose."

"Hell, I know all about Grey Goose," Deja said with a laugh.

Being close to her excited Teetee in ways she couldn't admit. To do so would feel like taking advantage of her, defiling the beautiful thing they'd built these three months. She closed her thighs to stifle the hymn between her legs.

"Can I braid your hair?" Deja asked.

Relaxed in her wicker chair, Teetee let her smooth handfuls of cocoa butter on her locks, wrestle the comb through them until they hung like Spanish moss. Then she braided. Lift the strands. Cross the left over the middle. Cross the right over the middle. Feeing pampered, she let herself dream of her ideal garden. With a raised patio like a bridge surrounded on both sides by green and blue perennials, with benches where everyone she loved could rest, with birdbaths built like gnome houses.

Every so often she opened her eyes to find the sun had edged a little closer to the fence, soon to be gone from sight, and it amused her that people spoke of sunrise and sunset when the sun stayed in one spot, a hibernating bear around which restless cubs tumbled. It was Earth that rose every morning. Deja threaded the hours with stories about her kids. Donyelle, mouthy and a bad student. Gio, quiet and nervous, who she worried about other boys picking on. Overweight and lazy, Barack loved cartoons.

"I did good in school," Deja said, a show of pride to hide her regrets. "Then I had Donny."

Whenever she tightened the braid, it pinched Teetee's scalp, just enough to make her grip the chair arms. "How'd you meet Riley?" she asked.

Cross the right. "Met him at Three Rivers Casino. I was there with my girlfriends and he bought me a Cosmo. And he told me, 'I am thousands of years old.' I thought he was just trippin'. Older men say things, trying to be slick."

"What did you do?"

Cross the left. "I went to his house. And I thought, 'Is he really bringing me to a crackhouse?' I refused to get out. He spent forever just trying to get me out the car. Then he got me inside and I saw it was all true. He told me he was a runaway slave. He said he made his way up north by changing body parts so the dogs couldn't track him. Ain't that something?"

Teetee winced at another hard tug. "Yeah, it was."

"I guess I was being a ho that night. I ain't usually a ho."

There had been a few times Teetee tried romantic affairs. They must not have been impressive, seeing as she couldn't recall names or faces. She remembered the pressure to have children—something she couldn't give men. Better if everyone could self-pollinate like strawberries, or choose not to, and enjoy one another's company without expectations.

"Sex is a beautiful thing," she said.

Deja sighed a bottomless sigh. In its caverns echoed Riley's name, and the names of black boys on gravestones, and breath forced into her lungs by a ventilator. Not for the first time, Teetee felt glad that to bear pain on her body was a choice, like that cold spot on Murray's head.

"The fools loved Riley," said Deja.

"Your kids?"

"That's what I call 'em. Little Fools and Big Fool. Donny got this attitude now. He like, 'Why I gotta go to college? Jay-Z ain't go to college.' I'm like, 'Jay-Z got a little thing called work ethic. You don't.'"

"Isn't he married to Beyoncé?"

"I be telling Donny that. I tell him, don't be going for these fast girls who ain't got no respect for you or themselves. You want Bey, you gotta be Jay. Woman like that ain't messing with no triflin' niggas."

"That's a good philosophy," Teetee agreed.

Deja started the next. Cross the left. "And if you can't be Jay," right, "be Kanye." Left. "And if you can't be Kanye, be Drake. Anything less ain't worth messing with." Teetee noticed she'd stopped saying *fuck* around her. Flattering. But something bothered her.

"Why do all the analogies have to be men?" she asked.

Without pause, "I'm Rihanna. You Mary J."

"That's what I'm talking about." A breeze made yellow leaves twitch on the hard-packed dirt. Autumn was rewriting the garden. "Riley was the last of us to get old," Teetee said. "Even when it made sense for him to get bigger, stronger. He always said he had enough strength, this little boy walking around looking so wise. I thought he'd stay that way forever. Then he stopped replacing his parts. He stopped gardening. But when I think of him, I still see that boy."

"I love him." Deja sounded distant, as if she spoke from the bottom of a river.

By the time she finished braiding, the moon was high. It gathered summer in a pocket and silvered the earth with lullabies.

◆ ◆ ◆

Cross the right.

Teetee ate dinner with Warmell in the dining room. She'd been pondering how to make her case, decided to do so like Obama did with those Republicans—eloquently. Maybe as ineffectively, but worth a try.

"Have you ever thought," she prologued, "that life is like getting your hair braided? It's such a perfect metaphor. Or simile, I guess."

He looked unamused. "Tee, you really gotta just say what you mean."

"I don't know what you got against her," she said.

The scrape of his spoon rang loudly on the plate. "She stopped going to church."

"I don't blame her. After what Mary did."

"I don't know if she said what the girl said she did . . ."

"She said it. Have you seen Mary's fruit?"

Now he looked up, ignorance and indifference mixed on his face like the macaroni and potatoes in his mouth. "Can't say I have."

"Mangoes. Yellow pears. Star fruit. Bananas. A *quince*. She's obviously trying for some Michael Jackson thing."

He shrugged. "I don't get it."

"She thinks she can turn herself white, Warmell. She's ashamed of being black."

"I ain't down for all this gossiping . . ."

"It's true. And it's sad. I feel sorry for her. But somebody with her problems shouldn't be casting judgment on anybody."

"Go to church," he said. "Raise your kids. Who can take off and leave three kids?"

"They're with Aunty." She tired of saying that. "And she's a hairdresser, so she makes her own hours."

"I bet you that ain't the first time they been with Aunty."

"She raises those kids by herself."

"What *by herself*? Riley raised those kids. I'll bet you they called him daddy."

"And he's dead, Warmell. He did a mean-spirited, selfish thing. If he knew he was going to go—if he had his heart set on it—he should have never brought her into it. To think he'd hurt her like that just to have some companionship or sex or . . ." She fought to keep the emotion out of her voice. "She's not alone. And I think we should take her to see some jazz sometime. Riley's band is playing in Homewood tomorrow. It'd be nice for her to see them."

He shook his head. "You've always been like this. You give her an inch . . ."

"And she can take two miles, for all I care. Because all she's ever gotten was that little centimeter. So what if she has some rough edges? I will *not* blame her for wanting more."

"You're making excuses for her taking advantage of you. Just like you do all the work in the garden."

"To hell with the garden." This shocked him. Before he could speak, she went on. "George Bush bombed innocent people for oil. Let's have some perspective." A sense of insidious horror clenched her diaphragm and unleashed words she'd never dared to speak. "You know what the worst part is? Two hundred years I watch black people try to work together. Every once in a while a leader comes, and the white folks kill them or chase them into exile. But *we* are just as much at fault. We can't work together because somebody talks a certain way, or they didn't marry their children's father, or they sag their pants, or they sleep with the wrong people. Because the black hive mind ain't nothing but racism with a beat to it."

He had no response. There followed a quiet that suited them both. They thrived in it, as neither wanted to take it so far that words became swords. In time the silence took on Warmell's quality of calm deliberation, as opposed to her recalcitrance, a feeling like after the storm when leaves skitter on the sidewalk and the earth smells of promise. As they washed dishes, he said they should definitely take Deja out.

Cross the left.

That night, after lights out, the wind through the window brought the sound of male voices. Teetee felt his side of the mattress descend and pop up in a furious clang of box springs. She jumped out of bed so quickly her foot tangled in the blanket and she fell to the hardwood. Only her cry of pain halted his headlong plunge out the door. His gentle hand on her shoulder caused her to gasp, her fear so visceral she gripped his pajama collar to pull him down until their noses touched.

"No!" She could see his mustache bristle over a snarling lip. "Please let me handle it."

"A man ain't gonna be scared in his own house," he said.

"I'll get them out. Just let me do it."

"You got five minutes," said the snarl.

On her way down the hall she could hear him getting dressed. She reminded herself to fear for her safety, because, ridiculous as the thought was, she worried for Deja the most. It was possible the men hadn't asked her permission to come. And if they didn't, what were they doing to her? Holding her bathrobe closed over her pajamas, Teetee made her way to the cabin.

Stupid girl. We were going to a jazz show. He was coming around, you stupid girl.

She knocked hard on the door three times. A fat man opened it and the accompanying fist of pot smoke punched her nose. The man looked wicked in the light of the wall lantern; he had red cornrows and freckles, the black daddy/white mama combo common in Pittsburgh, and his baby kicking gaze crawled down her body to rest on her belly. She tightened her grip on the robe.

"What do you want?" he said smokily.

"What do I want? You're in *my* house."

The corners of his mouth twisted upward. "Man, whatever."

"Get the hell out of my house!"

Laughing, he turned around. "Yo, Day. Lil Ma say this her house."

"Let her in," came her reply.

Besides the one at the door, there was another cooking eggs in the kitchen, and a third on the couch beside Deja, smoking a blunt and splitting his sides at *BET Comic View* on TV. The room stank. Beer bottles porcupined the coffee table. *Does she intend to sleep with them all?* thought Teetee, and hated Deja for giving her such vulgar ideas. Seeing Teetee, Deja took a deliberate hit on the blunt. Afterward she looked disappointed, as if expecting to be more fucked up than she was. Despite her anger, Teetee thought the girl looked gorgeous in her auburn wig with bangs over one eye, black pumps, black pencil skirt, and red sleeveless turtleneck, the empty space stuffed slightly larger than the real breast. She noticed Teetee notice and crossed her arms over her chest, looking shamefaced, then gave a woeful laugh to fake narcotic ambivalence.

"Chill, Tee. They cool. I met 'em at Shadow Lounge."

"Shadow Lounge, nigga," said the one in the chair. He had a neck full of tattoos and a goatee like smudged dirt. "She had some fun."

Since when do no-account negroes go to Shadow Lounge? Last Teetee checked, it was a respectable place, albeit terribly lit. Deja moved her shoulders to pretend music.

"I went out dancing," she said.

"It's late," said Teetee.

"What is it, my bedtime? Shit. I'm a grownass woman."

Teetee felt like she was in some racist white man's nightmare. Sensing the futility, she turned and left to get Warmell.

"Teetee!" cried Deja, but she ignored her. The lantern cast a white plank on the flagstones that helped guide her feet. Not unlike walking a branch. She heard Deja stumble out the door and spun to face her.

"I'm not going to talk to you while you're high," said Teetee. "What's the point, child?"

"I ain't no child. I ain't!" Her protestations came out in a squeak. But the glaciers in Teetee's gaze told her she was, like it or not. She nervously raked her fingers up and down her cheek. "You lied to me. You said you could make me a new one."

"I thought I could *help* you make one," Teetee said. She was tired.

"Fuck you, bitch!" Deja screamed until the last ounce of breath rattled in her throat. "I hate you, bitch. I hate you." Tears fell, and she clapped both hands on her cheeks. "Oh Jesus, why am I here? Why am I here?"

Knowing better than to feed her anger, Teetee remained still as stone and waited on the girl who, knowing she looked weak, tried her best to fix her face in a petulant expression. "I

ain't apologizing to you for shit. 'Cause your husband or whatever he is, he be looking at me funny."

Teetee was sick of her misery, her sad fruit, her low expectations. "You're so lost. You've been told your whole life you
aren't worthy and you believe it. Maybe we can try something
else," she interrupted when Deja tried to speak, "but first you
make those negroes leave."

Exactly four-and-a-half minutes after she'd promised
Warmell, the three men exited the yard, spouting rap lyrics as a
last masculine gesture. There was some "bitch" in Garfield they
wanted to find. Soon she heard them murmuring: "Why is we
standing 'round vacant houses? Nigga, where the fuck is we?"

Such fragile things, thought Teetee, who hardened her
expression as she led Deja to the cellar. She almost feared to
look at her. Afraid that to gaze on her she would see dark
water, and wouldn't be able to tell if the black that erased her
reflection was shadow or oil, the absence of light or putres-
cence of death.

The cellar had two refrigerators, one for fruit and one for
meat. She opened the fruit fridge and Deja's jaw dropped at
the surplus—Teetee's figs, strawberries, and lemons; Warmell's
crops, like pumpkin and squash and kiwi. Teetee saw each fruit
as a year of life, and it did seem excessive, even luxuriant. Deja
shifted from foot to foot while Teetee reached in the back for
a cantaloupe. It had been a gift from Murray's garden on top of
the hotel, and the opposite of Deja's melons—the size and heft
of a rugby ball, orange and ridged, radiant with green veins.

Why didn't you do this before? Teetee could see the question
typed out across her eyes. In truth, she'd always suspected this
was the answer. But that would mean losing Deja's company.
Losing the coconut smell of her hair in the garden.

With a heavy soul, Teetee sat at the picnic table, listening with what she knew for obligation as Deja screamed in the bathroom. Screamed like the city was being bombed. A terrible sound that signaled growth. After several minutes, the shrieks faded and were replaced by the neon voices of night. Deja shuffled into the backyard, dressed in a tank top, arms wrapped bashfully under her breasts. The new one had taken well, only a few green stretchmarks forking the expanse of brown skin.

Teetee clasped her hands with a clap. "Well, that's just fantastic! I knew it would take! And it looks so good on you too!"

She knew her show of joy for a boorish way of telling Deja to leave. This once, she allowed herself to be selfish.

"Thank you, Teetee," Deja said shakily. Her cheeks were dewy. She went into the cabin and kept the light on. In the morning she had a friend drive her to Greyhound.

A month passed. As the summer fruit reached its ripest, a mysterious mold infested the orchards of the Fruit. Quick and spiteful, it struck with white spores on Sister Mary's figs and Murray's kiwi. Sister D's strawberries were born more white than red. Brother Byron's raspberries too. Teetee's lemons plummeted from the branch and split open on the soil, rotted inside like cancered lungs. Branches died on her fig tree and the ants made home in them. Sorrowful, she watched her figs grow spores like shaved ice where the soft meat should be.

The reverend called a meeting at the church. An hour before it began, Teetee sat in the wicker chair, shrouded in evening. Her garden was a tableau of rot that reminded her of her Victorian in the Hill after she'd moved in with Warmell. Lord Decay's spells had lifted from it and, in the time it took to move her luggage to the Crown Vic, the ground floor collapsed into the basement, the copper and wiring vanished, and hordes of ants marched triumphantly up the fungused wallpaper. She unconsciously touched her braids. Deep in remembrance, she was startled when a fruit fly landed on her knuckle, recalled that she hadn't put out vinegar. It felt right to let the sprite lick her skin until it had its fill. These flies lived a month, maybe more.

The meeting began the moment she and Warmell arrived to the basement. Her stomach turned to see the Fruit, these dour immortals, seated around a conference table in the jaundiced glow of a single standing lamp. The room smelled strongly of the cardboard boxes stacked against the wall, alongside a harsher odor. Mold. Her people looked like the patients of an invisible hospital ward. Reverend James G. Goodson. Sister Mary. Sister D. Sister E. Larry. Byron. Murray. The Divine Servant of Strawberries. The Lord Gardener of Granny Smiths. The Fisher of the Vineyard. The Most Humble Devotee of Cherries. The Apostate of Plums. More chairs than people ringed the table, as if set aside for the dead.

We are few, she noted, and felt like roadkill pressed into the concrete.

"Murray told us you were growing her a new breast," said Reverend Goodson. He had a shriveled black pear for a nose. Despite this deformity, he kept an upright and arresting presence.

"This deserves punishment," said the Apostate of Plums. The deacons all sat in a row, five zealots more fruit than human. If it came down to her stoning, they would gather rocks.

Teetee admitted what she'd done. Insisted she'd seen nothing wrong in giving the girl a melon. All the while she tugged the strings of her shawl with the peacock feather design. It had felt necessary to come before them pretty. The Fruit muttered and blustered and accused, until the reverend silenced them.

"We should focus on setting this right," he said, "not on punishment."

"She *should* have known!" said Murray, dressed in shirt and slacks. She cringed to see a spore, half the size of a thumb, atop his left nostril. His were the eyes of an enemy. "You of all people should have known!"

She searched for words. "I–I'm sorry. *You* of all people should know I don't want to hurt anybody."

"Are parts of you molding?" he snapped.

"No." She felt an itch down there that worried her. "Not yet. I hope not."

"Well, isn't that convenient for you?"

"Please, Murray!" She dreaded to lose such a friend. "We have more than enough fruit to last. Missing one harvest doesn't spell doom."

"And what about the next harvest? And the next?"

"That's enough," said Warmell.

"She has to hear this," said Murray. "I want you *all* to listen."

He'd had as poor a memory as hers, he said, but sickness and fear of death had a way of waking forgotten things. Once, there had been a war. He couldn't remember who was fighting or why. But a portion of the Fruit took a side. Led by Teetee, they decided it would be the end of childhood. They allowed themselves to age in order to be stronger allies. They replaced the mortals' severed limbs and filled veins with new blood.

The power that sustained them didn't tolerate it. As punishment, her side lost, and the people she supported became dust, so even the earth didn't remember them. Murray's brows knit darkly over eyes like peach pits.

"And the worst thing is," he said, "the powers weren't satisfied with just that loss. The last burrowers died in *your* war. We lost 'em forever!" Struggling to calm himself, he crossed his arms over his chest in a childish gesture of refusal. "It was none of our business. Never was. Whenever something like this happens, it's always you."

"Selfish," Mary said through tears.

As one, the deacons nodded. Their necks crackled like autumn.

Teetee fought to remember. As the congregation had aged, real arguments between them became few. But she recalled Riley yelling at her, then Mary, about the terrible charter bus they hired to go see *Lion King* on Broadway. For that kind of money, he said, it should have gotten them back to Pittsburgh on time. She wondered: Was that really about Broadway? Or was Riley saying, *It's not our fight*, and her mind stitched the hole with false memories. In the end it didn't matter. Murray hated her now. She felt sick.

"I know I did wrong," she said. "What can I do to fix it?"

The preacher said, "Lord Decay will decide."

"Lord Decay," murmured the others. "Yes."

Warmell put his hand on her back to usher her out the door. Impulsively, she stopped and turned. "I came up with the idea to plant seeds."

"I know," Reverend Goodson said impartially.

"I did," she said louder as she left. "It was me. You were all there and don't *never* say otherwise."

Warmell let her enter the house first. He followed her through the unlit living room, and she wondered if he wanted to touch

her, in affection or anger. Either would have been welcome,
if only to feel another's fragility. Then he brushed past her to
the kitchen, opened the cupboards for a box of basmati rice,
poured it in the pot to start cooking. He lit beeswax candles
so that the fragrance overtook the old house, even the lonely
corners where time asserted its decay. Teetee sat at her picnic
table, windblown leaves cluttering the garden, her emotions
conflicted, until Warmell joined her with two steaming bowls.

He asked if she remembered those days when he'd go play
billiards with the boys. In truth, he told her, he was going to a
coffee shop where he liked the barista. She was thirtyish, just
graduated from community college. He grew addicted to hearing her complain about her weight, or listening to her describe
her anti-circumcision activism. He felt both friend and voyeur.
His eyes soft over the candlelight, he apologized for not telling
Teetee about her. Somehow it felt like infidelity. Or maybe he
was scared she'd start getting close to mortals like Riley and
Murray did. Or she'd think her eternal companionship wasn't
enough for him.

Teetee came around the table and embraced him. "I love
you, friend," she said. "I'm going to make this right."

"Shhh," he said, his hands on the small of her back.

Not long after the clock chimed seven, there came a knock
on the door. They opened it to find Lord Decay on the porch,
accompanied by an owl-headed chauffeur. The lord smelled of
musk and twilight and arrogance. Legend said an evil imp had
snatched him from his cradle as a babe, abducted him to the
woods, and cut his head off. A stumble-legged fawn, who had
accidentally wandered from his family, saw this and charged in
to rescue the lordling. The imp cut off his head as well. Spirits of the Pennsylvania woods found the dead children and,

bereaved at such loss, combined them. Lord and deer, steel and moss, his lifeblood the rust in every train track.

He made his mood clear by flashing oversized incisors. The heels of his leather boots clomped the hardwood as he stepped into the house uninvited. He paced the living room. "What the fuck did yinz do? Why are there so many flies here? Why does it smell like this?"

Warmell approached him. "You gotta understan—"

The lord spun to face them and his antlers knocked down a portrait of a covered bridge. "Understand what? I let you live here! This is my house! Do you know how many rats and roaches would love to live here?"

Unlike other lords she'd known, who prided themselves on their worldliness, Lord Decay cared for little beyond these disheveled houses. A set of keys jangled from his belt loop as he made the rounds, pointing at objects. "This clock is mine. This couch is mine. Piano's mine. I mean, why the fuck do I let yinz live here? I should just let my daughter have the house."

His daughter was half deer-woman, half-coyote. For years he'd said she'd come to fix the plumbing. Eventually Warmell had to do it.

"Now show me the mold," the lord said. They took him in the backyard. Lord Decay sniffed at the white-tufted fruit, flashed his teeth again. "Yinz can't have mold here."

"It just appeared," Teetee protested before she could stop herself.

"Oh, so you don't live here?" he snapped. "This isn't your garden looking like a mess?"

On his order, the owl-man emptied a tube of insecticide onto her plants. "Stop!" she said. "You might kill the bees." The lord ignored her. The backyard reeked.

"We'll clean it up," Warmell said between coughs.

"Oh, I know you will," barked Lord Decay. "*Blight* I will not tolerate." He lifted his black nose to the lemon tree and sniffed the remaining healthy ones. He waved over the chauffeur, who plucked every last one into Teetee's own basket.

"You can't do that!" she said. She felt Warmell grab hold of her elbow. His face was blank but he had a tight grip.

Lord Decay's opal eyes shone darkly. "My house! I'd better get somethin' outta yinz fuckin' up."

The chauffeur lifted Lord Decay's slag metal cloak so he could sit at the picnic table. Were it not for the snot on his nostrils, he would look like a pugnacious plushy. He sounded corporate as he gave instructions. "My people tell me that an apple tree grows in Cleveland. In the black part o' town. The locals eat from it and it helps them know when someone is telling the truth or lying."

"Well, that's a useful skill," said Warmell.

"Not if it's sappin' from yinz, it ain't." A nod to his chauffeur, who reached under his cloak to unloop a long-handled ax from his belt. It was a decayed weapon, the blade constellated with rust spots. He shoved it at Teetee and she gripped the handle, found that her sucrose-infused biceps had no trouble lifting it. "This was forged by my best sorcerers. Chop the tree and it'll never grow again. That way, yinz'll get your harvest back."

"Thank you, my lord." The formalities tasted like rot in her mouth. Silent, she and Warmell trailed him to the porch. He left them with a curt, "Get it done." Then his chauffeur got on all fours so he could step off of his back and into a two-deer-drawn carriage made of broken bus stop benches haphazardly nailed together. The chauffeur closed the door and placed the basket of lemons on the seat beside him, and she watched her fruit depart as the conveyance lurched and rattled in the direction of Rankin and Lord Decay's mill. On either side of the lord rose tottering vacants, his vast and ramshackle fiefdom.

Warmell reached an arm around her shoulders. "It's gonna be okay," he said. "I don't like that they took the lemons, neither."

She breathed deep. "I'm fine. I'm mad but I'm fine." Leaning on the ax handle, she knuckled the tears from her eyes. "What a jerk."

Warmell offered to go with her but she wanted to do this herself. In the morning she caught the first Greyhound bus east of her sorrow. She sat beside a girl who was maybe twelve, large-breasted, who read a *Twilight* novel and looked cautiously at the world whenever she lifted her amber eyes off the page. She seemed pleasant, in her quiet way, unlike the other girls yelling and cussing in their seats.

Teetee dreamed, and the past returned. Dreams of armies, dead bodies, floods, a lover's hair against her cheek. Villains calling for death and heroes rising to challenge them. The selves she'd survived. Black, brown, and red: the color of her people. The glistening skin of the Fruit. Bloody swords and times she'd thought she was dead. The battles, the starvation and toil, the search through miles of hostile land for a single friendly face.

That afternoon she waited in line inside the Cedar-Central Youth Center. She carried a suitcase. All around her proud parents were gushing about their kids. At the auditorium door, a pretty, long-lashed boy sat behind a table, cash box at his elbow. "Five dollars," he said.

"I'm excited for the show," she replied, and almost added *Gio*, because that's who he was. Looked exactly like his mom.

"No, you're not," he said, and took a bite from the bright red McIntosh on the table. He winced, knowing he'd made a mistake by correcting an adult, and said, "I mean, you could be. Maybe you is."

"I'm here to see your mom."

This he knew for truth. "She backstage," said Gio. Teetee paid and took a seat in the middle of the audience, next to a woman who was waving her arms like high speed windshield wipers at the girls in the wings. Were it not for the urgency of her task, Teetee knew she'd be enjoying herself.

A Talent Showcase, they called it. First was a ten-girl dance routine. Then a teenage girl sang a gospel song. Then a scrawny boy did stand-up comedy. Then a rap duo. To the side of the room, she saw a tall teenager readjust a fat little boy's backpack so he didn't fall over. *Donyelle. Barack.*

The MC—a local DJ whom she gave credit for rocking a high-top fade long past the expiration date—announced the next act. Two twelve-year-olds doing a dance routine to "Single Ladies." Half a minute in, the girl on the left got nervous, looking to her friend to remember the steps. She stood paralyzed, feeling the audience's eyes, until she ran offstage in humiliation. Her companion kept dancing. Teetee's heart jumped in her chest when Deja ran onstage with the other girl and improvised moves for her to follow. Deja was light on her feet, smiling. The song ended and the crowd applauded.

The finale was all the children singing a gospel hymn, and during the breakdown someone granted Teetee's wish and handed her a tambourine. She made a joyful noise. After three curtain calls and much whooping, Teetee made her way through the crowded hallway to where she found Deja laughing with some friends. Her lingering affection made her hesitate, not wanting to interrupt, until she remembered her own family in Pittsburgh. Without fruit they would die. Completely, eternally die. The girl saw her coming and ambled with a defeated slouch toward the exit.

"Our fruit won't grow anymore," Teetee told her in the parking lot. "It's your tree. I have to take it down. There's no other way."

Crestfallen, Deja offered no resistance. Their time together had taught her the forces at work were beyond her. Teetee felt something was wrong. "Why are you charging for a kids' talent show?" she asked as she followed Deja up a wooded trail, to the park behind the center.

"It's for Tamir's family," said Deja.

"The boy who was killed by the police." A damn tragedy. Twelve years old, shot down for playing in the park with his friends.

"They filing a civil suit against them pigs and need money for some basic things," said Deja. "Gio was friends with him. He took it real hard."

"How is he now?" Teetee asked.

Her wounded voice scabbed over, hardened. "He don't cry no more. My son's a soldier."

"Children shouldn't be soldiers," Teetee said, more to herself than Deja. Anti-gardeners, these police planted seeds in kids. Death grew from the hole.

The playground had a slide, swing set, and jungle gym, all corroded with rust. The tree spread its canopy over the winos who slept and drank on the benches. It had twelve boughs resplendent with red apples among still-green leaves, ruby refractions in the autumn chill.

"It's helping people," Deja said. "Can't nobody fuck 'em over on contracts no more. Can't nobody say they ain't cheating when they really cheating."

"The fruit never had that power," said Teetee. She wouldn't voice her thoughts—that the fruit had evolved—because she'd come to kill it. "When did it grow?"

"The day I got back." A wino was standing on tiptoes to pluck from the lowest branch. Deja stayed his hand.

"You gotta eat it slow," she told him. "Eat it fast and it'll be too much. Enjoy it, yanawmean."

While this conversation went on, Teetee opened her suitcase on a bench and hefted Lord Decay's ax. She made practice swings in the air. Upon noticing Deja's miserable expression, she bade her sit with her in the grass, in the shade of the tree. The girl put her jacket down so as to not stain her jeans.

Teetee thought, if that poor murdered child was here, he would pick an apple, shiny as the bullet that never killed him. It would tell him the truth: he was young and alive. He was black and beautiful.

"I don't know if I was ever a slave," she told Deja. "But I know I was a maroon in the swamp, shooting colonials. I don't know if I was born black. I might have been born a tangerine and became a person when I hit puberty." She put the flat of the blade to her cheek, caressed the handle. "Once, long ago, my people lived in a forest. It may have been in this world or another. We were kings and queens of the forest. We lived there with our friends called burrowers. And the burrowers taught us the magic of fruit. So we would go to a fruit tree, and we climbed and we climbed and we climbed, and we would bring it down to eat. This way we stayed young. Then, one day, we learned how to plant the seeds. So we made more trees; big, beautiful trees. Ours was a happy kingdom. But one day our forest was gone. So we and the burrowers took our seeds, and we walked and we walked and we walked until we came to a river. We planted and lived there until the river went dry. So we walked and we walked through a desert, and some of us did not make it. We came to a mountain, and there we lived so close to the sky we could touch it, until time blew the mountain away. So we go and we go, looking, searching, finding people and places around the world. A little slower than before, we stumble and we limp and we come to a city of jeweled columns and golden turrets, where sunlight flowed like water through halls resplendent with majesty and memory. We were counselors, sages, and alchemists. And we thought, *This is our place.* That was where we grew up." It became hard to speak, her regret like a hand on her throat. "Then all the people in the city died. The burrowers died. The city became rocks, then less than rocks, until all that was left of it was a wailing in the wind. We had to walk again. Little did we know we had to find the rusted place, where they said nothing grew, and that was where we planted ourselves for good. Of all my blessings, I treasure that the most. The freedom to *stay*." She paused so Deja could digest it all. Whelmed by history, the girl blew out a long breath. Teetee's stomach tightened. "But even that place will go. Every generation, the kingdoms of man grow up sicklier, they die younger. And when they are gone, it will be a time for seeds and growing things. Anyway. My name's Jasmine Woods. Before that, I was her mother, Betty Woods. Before that, I don't know. I do things that hurt people and I don't know I'm hurting them

when I do it. And I . . . I never wanted to hurt you. Maybe
I'm a bad person. Or maybe I've been so many people I don't
know who I am." She met Deja's gaze and was grateful for the
open, neutral look in her eyes. "There was a time I was sad to
be black. I would look around and all I saw was suffering. I
would ask the powers, 'Why do they treat us so bad?' I hated
the powers for what they had done. But I learned the pride.
That I was of a people who could take all the hate and poison
of this world, and laugh, and go dance on Saturday. And my
brothers and sisters weren't just the ones I grew up with. Now
I had many." She took Deja's hands. They felt soft. "My love, I
want you to keep this tree. Maybe my people won't like it, but,
you know what, I'm the one who planted the first seed, so I
get to make a call every now and then. Because sometimes I
tire of life just like your Riley. But I've been black. And this,"
she circled her finger in the air, "this horse*shit* will not be what
I close my eyes on. I refuse to die! Do you hear me? I will live
to see our people renewed."

Teetee and Deja came to a compromise. For six months
out of the year, the tree in Cleveland would bloom. The other
six were for Pittsburgh. Deja's sons brought a stepladder. Gio
and Barack held it steady while Donyelle gave her a hand up.
She lifted the ax over her head and brought it down, severed
the first branch in one swing. The boys gasped in unison at the
strength of this gray-haired lumberjill. She held their shoulders
for support on her way down, then cut the next, repeating until
five branches littered the grass like kindling. The last was too
high for the ladder. She put her foot in Donyelle's hands.

"Careful," Deja said as he lifted her.

Teetee hooked an arm over the branch, lifted her foot on
top of the wood, slowly twisted her hips until she straddled it.

Took a deep breath and exhaled as she swung sideways at the last branch. Apples thumped on the ground. Now there were six. From this day on, her people would be summer people.

Sweaty, she wiped a sleeve across her forehead. "We did it, yinz." She didn't see Deja or her sons below. Her panic turned to resignation as the moments wore on. Though she looked for them, she found them nowhere.

SEVEN WATSONS

If I had the time, I'd tell all kinds of stories bout Pittsburgh Job Corps. But I only got time for one, so it's got to be the Watsons. The rest I'll get to later.

One night in September, I was chilling in the dorm with the buls. Loominati was skinny, Lindsey was pudgy, I was and will be fat. Three hundred pounds since I was little. The buls used to say I looked like a black version of a sitcom dad, especially on nights like that when I was in jeans shorts, a tank, and them reindeer slippers I got for Christmas. Loom lay in his top bunk, shirtless in scrub pants, knitting needles flashing as he worked on a black-and-red blanket. Years in Job Corps and ain't a single RA knew he kept them needles, else they'd take them as *contraband*. Me and Lindsey lounged in bean bag chairs playing Madden on an old tube TV. We had to pause when the RA came in, big orange-haired whitebul called Ortilani, who says we got a new intake. Loom vanished them needles under his pillow.

"I did the last intake," Lindsey told Ortilani.

Real rap, I kept my head down when RAs came calling. Loom said he'd do it. The bul slipped on his flip-flops, scrub top, and red hoodie and shuffled to work. Meantime, I was losing 22 to 7.

"Defense, my nigga!" Lindsey yelled. "Where your fucking D at?" Nigga could talk mad shit when he was winning.

Between the three of us, we had over four years in that building: Lindsey a year and seven months; Loom a year and five; I was coming on a year and eight. Two of them months I'd been a section leader, after Lindsey put in a good word for me. I'll be the first to admit I wasn't the best. During details I let my manz round up the buls while I joked around. Being section leader meant I got an extra thirty-five each payday, and the RAs treated us too, took us to Dave & Busters once a month. We got the biggest room to ourselves: three bunk beds against the outside wall, two wooden desks with cushioned chairs, and six metal lockers painted teal. Three of them beds was for C-Prep buls who rotated out soon as they got they own room. Lindsey ran a store out of there: candy bars, ramen, 'Ports, whatever you need.

Loom returned dragging an adorable little red suitcase by the handle, and behind him came a short bul, five-three at most. He still had that Greyhound stink on him, dressed in a rumpled gray hoodie and jeans puddling round his ankles. Like all the yungbul, he tried to hide how scared he was with a mean mug. I shook his hand.

"Flexo," I said.

"Chris," he grunted.

Lindsey flashed two fingers at him. "Whaddup, Chris. Name's Lindsey."

"Ain't that a girl's name?" Chris asked, amused.

Lindsey rolled his eyes. Loom introduced Chris to the fourth roommate, a big barley-haired whitebul on a top bunk who never bothered nobody. Mostly played puzzle games with the phone up close to his eyes. Chris took the locker nearest the window, had so much trouble with his combo he needed Loom's help.

"Rule number three of Job Corps," Loom told him, "lock up your shit. Niggas here is grimy. You ain't gotta worry about the dudes in this room . . ."

"Cause we have jobs," Lindsey said.

"But some of these niggas you gotta watch out for."

"They will literally steal your dirtyass underwear," I said from experience.

Real rap, the bul ain't have much to steal. He unpacked three shirts, one Sixers jersey, two jeans, five pair boxers wadded in a ball, three pair socks, and a pair knockoff Jays that smelled moldy up close. He emptied his Job Corps "ditty bag," a purple drawstring pouch like Crown Royal came in: a blue toothbrush in the package, two bar Dove soap, a stick of dry deodorant that would crumble like a soup cracker soon as it touched his pit, a comb made for white hair, nail clippers, terrycloth towel and washcloth, a stubby pencil and notepad. He dumped it all on the floor. This got a teeth-sucking sound from Lindsey, who preferred tidiness.

"Second rule," Loom told him as they put his stuff away, "do your details. Ain't nobody tryin'a live in no funkyass dorm, so when you get one, do that shit. No questions asked."

Loom went over the routine. Make your bed before you leave. Breakfast. Classes. Lunch. Sign in soon as you get on the floor, else you get marked AWOL. Fix discrepancies. Free time. Dinner. Evening details. Loom wanted to make sure he got the last point cause he stared the bul down like a cobra.

"And rule number one of Job Corps . . ."

"Don't mess with the Job Corps gals," I said.

"One: drama."

"Two: STDs."

"Three: they fucking crazy."

The bul chuckled like we was joking. Loom got a look of pity on his long, bored face. I figured Chris'd learn soon enough. Sometimes failure be the best teacher.

He got settled in the bunk on top Lindsey, and Loom went back to knitting. 'Cept for me and Linds talking shit, things went quiet till lights out. I thanked God for another day, put on a sleep mask, and lay my head down. Ain't two minutes go by before I hear Lindsey roll off the mattress and land heavy on the floor. He groped round the desk, flicked on a lamp, fumbled his glasses on his face, and knocked on Chris bed three times.

"Chris, you sleep?"

"I'm trying," he groaned, head under his pillow.

Lindsey pointed to the bootleg Jays at the foot of the bed. "You need to do something about them shoes. They funky."

They was woke so I had to wake. Chris sat up, looking put-upon. "Says you."

"Don't you smell that, Flex?" Lindsey asked me.

"I wasn't gonna say nothing," I said. "Ain't no drama with Flexo."

"Well, I ain't chill like him," Lindsey told Chris. "If I got something to say about you, I'm gonna say it *to* you. You need to put them funky shoes in a bag."

"You can't tell me what to do just cause you a section leader."

"Hold up. Slow your roll. Calm down. You living with people now."

"Nigga, I got six brothers!"

"Call me 'nigga' again." Lindsey sounded real dark just then.

Loom leaned out from the bed on top mine. "Fuck all y'all," he said diplomatically. "Go. To. Fucking. Sleep."

"I can give you a bag," I offered too late cause they was in each other face, Fuck you bitchass nigga, I ain't taking shit from no little niggas, I oughta steal you nigga. Repping they cities—I'm from West Philly, Nigga I'm from Cleveland—like every hood ain't the same as every other. It got so heated the bul lifts his shirt to show a scar, like, Yeah I been shot, nigga, and Lindsey says he don't give a shit.

I stepped in. Being wide as I is, I get between two buls, they gots to separate.

"Fine!" Chris yelled. "I came here to get my GED, not fight with niggas over some fucking shoes."

He went to his locker and had such a time opening the lock he cussed at the door. Finally he snatched out some Axe spray, and not only did he douse his shoes, he doused *everybody's* shoes. My eyes turned to balls of stinging wasps. Mucus scratched my throat like steel wool and my nose filled up with boogers so fast it was like I'd inhaled snail shells. Lindsey cussed as he tried to open a window. But none of us got it bad as the whitebul: sleep one minute, bolt upright the next, hand on his chest, wheezing. Loom grabbed him under the arms and helped him out into the hall.

That deodorant got the whole wing fumigated. Niggas was coming out in they boxers, yelling, "What's that smell?" Ortilani had to stay an hour after his shift ended, first to move Chris and the whitebul to new rooms, then open windows in every room to get the rosy stench out. Then he got the lowdown from Linds. Had to give it to him, the bul knew how to talk to authority, that white way of talking. He had Ortilani ready to term the bul right there.

"Tell me exactly what he said to you," Ortilani instructed. "I need to know if somebody's being a threat on my dorm."

"I don't want any drama," Lindsey told him. "But Troy has asthma. He could have gotten real sick. I'm not playing this game."

"You lying!" Chris yelled from an open door. "You started all that shit!"

From outside the RA office you could see down both halls. Look down Summit, you see Chris yelling. Down Phoenix I could see a six-foot gaybul woke from the commotion, voguing in silhouette, dabbing his invisible brush on an invisible compact. Ortilani ordered Chris back in the room with his cop voice—rumor had it he caught bounties on the side. Lindsey asked if he could please go out for a smoke, and Ortilani said yes, so I threw on my coat and followed downstairs.

Outside the featureless center walls, the night was warm and breezy and starry. Rats darted over the concrete and an ever-expanding tribe of wild turkeys was warbling fowl supremacy from the woods we called Camp Green. Caterpillar-chewed yellow leaves lay raked in piles at the edges of the enclosure. Wasn't nothing in the yard but sheds, a rec center, an assembly hall, and the portables where we took class. Directly under the dorm windows was piled plastic cups, plates, and soiled underwear tossed by the nastybuls. All round the center ran a chain link fence topped with barbed wire, with one gate and a booth where a rent-a-cop sat watching sitcoms on a little TV. Through the fence you could just make out Shuman Detention Center. I sat on a brick flowerbed with no flowers, just dirt, while Lindsey paced and spit smoke.

"I don't take disrespect from nobody. How is this little nigga gonna rep West Philly? Tell me, if Philly niggas is so hard, how come they let the white folks throw 'em out? Huh? Ain't no niggas in West Philly no more. Little punk bitch don't wanna see the Cleveland in me."

Talking came hard, what with my lips all dried up like two pieces of pork rind. "It ain't nothing," I said. "He just a yungbul."

Lindsey smirked. "You know Ortilani's getting drunk tonight."

"That whitebul getting *wasted.*"

Sometimes you had to lozenge it like that. Be like, The nigga ain't worth your time, cause none of that fighting did no good. I would hate to see somebody get termed over dumb shit.

Lindsey talked normal round me and Loom but could switch it up with the right people. That made him a favorite with Miss Carter, the center director. She was a perfume-smelling, full-bodied woman who strutted the halls with that bouncy Beyoncé hair. All the niggas wanted a kind word from her, but Lindsey could get one cause he spoke classy. The prestige had him walking the dorms like he wore a monocle.

Like I said, right words for the right people. The fact he came salty at Chris from jump meant he thought the bul was the *wrong* person.

That rubbed me raw, so at breakfast, me and Loom set our trays on the sticky table where Chris and two other C-Prep buls sat picking at they eggs and potatoes, greasy carbs courtesy of the U.S. Department of Labor. We came to squash the beef, and Loom liked to acquaint himself with the niggas he was living with, anyway.

"I'm coming to you personally to say I'm sorry," I told him. "It's two things I know: we all black, and we all here. I don't wanna see nobody get in no shit."

One of the buls told Chris, "Flex be a good guy, Duck."

"Duck?" I asked.

Chris rolled his sleeve to show the tattoo on his right arm: from elbow to shoulder, an oval portrait of a long-neck bird rising from a pond. Wings raised, neck down, unseaming the water as it took off. The portrait frame was drawn with cattails and ivy. I got myself some ink too, but nothing so pretty.

"They calling me Duck," he said, and turned his head to shout, "cause these niggas don't know the difference between a duck and a fucking goose!"

Two tables over the African niggas brayed with laughter. "Hey yo, son," said a Nigerian. "Hey yo, son. Shut the fuck up, my nigga."

When it came to nicknames, everybody got something simple. The big dopey whitebul was Quagmire, like *Family Guy*. The little whitebul Phil we called Fry like Phil Fry on *Futurama*. Nigga from Baltimore was Baltimore. Nigga who looked like Gucci we called Gucci. There was Big DC and Lil DC. I beat them buls to the punch cause I came with my own nickname. Since third grade I been Flexo, when they had us do stretches in gym class, and let's just say I had an embarrassing incident.

Now we was friendly, Chris had one question. "Where you get the weed round here?"

"The weed'll find you," said Loom. "We ain't selling. No no no." He chopped scrambled eggs with the flat edge of his fork. "So you really got shot?"

"Yeah."

"You must be a G, huh?"

"Hell yeah." Boastful at first, he turned humble. Could probably tell stunting ain't impress us much. "I got shot in a bitchass driveby. I ain't even know the nigga."

Loom looked skeptical. "Not at all? You ain't had no heat with this nigga?"

"None."

Loom blew out his breath. "Crazy niggas like that need to get got. Exterminated like fucking Hitler did the Jews."

"Yo, why they call you Loominati?" asked Chris. "You should be called Needles. I'ma call you Needles."

We shook our heads in sync.

"My name ain't Needles," Loom explained, and patted his hip where he kept said needles wedged in the band of his underwear. Seemed hot to me, taking them everywhere he went, but them needles made him comfortable. "They call me Loominati cause I consider myself a scholar on a certain secret organization that runs the world. I'm talking the Thirteen Families."

Chris smiled. "You one of *them* niggas. Always saying Jay-Z in the Illuminati and shit."

"Everybody know Jay's Illuminati. That's why I don't fuck with him—he's too obvious. Most niggas don't know Kobe's Illuminati."

"What about LeBron?" Chris asked with interest.

"LeBron joined this year. You see that last game against the Sixers? He made a signal that showed he renounced God. They all gotta do that when they join."

"You mean he can never get to Heaven?" said Chris, amazed and terrified.

Loom shook his head sadly. "*And* the Illuminati killed Michael Jackson. He was gonna expose them."

Thing was, it ain't sound like horseshit when Loom said it. He had so many dates and events and mysterious coincidences stacked in that oblong head, he even convinced me of some of it. The part bout MJ had Chris looking shellshocked. This was fall '09 and the pain was still raw.

Soon we was sent to class by an electronic honk out the intercom. Buls in khaki and polos went the opposite way down the hall to shops where they learned all that hands-on business. Us in scrubs went to Health Occ, cussing, joking, feuding all the way, not the least that wild nigga Tanje with the face tats who liked to sing R. Kelly in the showers and run round the dorm in his boxers and wasn't into no gay shit, but he would put his junk perilously close to your nose.

He declared, "If any y'all niggas distract me in the Anatomy pre-test, I'm bugging. Real rap—don't fucking test me."

We had class in a long narrow portable, the desktops carved with gang names and area codes and penises. The bald white man who taught Anatomy put on a slideshow bout viral infections. Every picture had yellow rot at the edges, like staring at medical atrocities through a telescope covered in pondscum. We saw a syphilitic nose collapsed under black rot. We saw gums bubbling with pus. We saw a white woman in a red pantsuit posing sexily by the Point State Park fountain. Seconds ticked on the clock, long enough to build the tension before a thunderous click to the next slide—the same woman standing topless, side profile, her forearm so ate with gangrene you could see bone through the black meat. She looked thoughtful. Behind me somebody said he'd still suck her titties.

Sometimes I think that teacher meant to shock us with them gruesome slides. Pretty naïve, in my opinion. What Job Corps nigga never seen blood before? In the 16mm twilight niggas was talking shit and throwing wadded-up paper, but me and Loom took notes, determined to get something out of this.

Them yungbuls got thrown into Job Corps like crash test dummies. Whoever sent them—Justice Department, Health and Human Services, family court, they parents—did so with the intent to teach them a lesson. Sometimes just to punish them. The average age was nineteen, everyone quick to call himself a grownass man. But make no mistake, they was buls. Them first few weeks, when the lonely sank in and they found theyselves living with strangers in eight by twelve feet of concrete, they latched on the first nigga who offered a 'Port and a smile and went right back to breaking they mamas' hearts.

Them's the ones who ended up forming posses and slinging dope. Eventually too many write-ups made it to Mr. Schibetta in Discipline and they got termed. Schibetta was a tall, big-bellied whitebul with beard stubble, his head shaped like a jack-o'-lantern rotting on the porch in November. I ain't get no write-ups so I only spoke with him the one time, when I asked if he'd give my brother another chance. He showed me a folder thick as my pinky, full of Naquan's fuckups. Stealing that lamp out the social worker's office was the last straw, he said.

A month before Chris showed up, Big Jack got termed for standing tall with that big-eared nigga Obama against some Africans. A week later they termed Obama for falling asleep in clinicals. Coop got termed for showing up drunk after curfew. Calvin and Black for fighting. We all liked Malik, good bul, had your back, set to graduate before the whitebul yelled that nasty shit out the window at his gal. Unfortunately for everyone, Malik found the bul.

If they did a trade like Culinary or Heavy Machinery, buls eventually crossed the lounge to the other dorm, Alpha Omega. Ay-Yo, we called it—a scabies-riddled shithole cause the niggas and the whitebuls knew nothing short of a felony would get them termed, so nobody did they details. Real rap, us in Health Occ could get uppity seeing as we stayed in Phoenix Summit. We called it home.

Chris was sixteen years old and raised in foster care. He repped Philly but was born somewhere else. Next two weeks I saw him round, just another C-Prep bul with Band-aids up his arms from getting stuck in Wellness. (Loom said the Illuminati put estrogen in them shots to feminize black men.) I'd see him in the yard during smoke break, hanging with the wrong niggas. Dumb niggas. He'd come in right before lights out, giggling, his eyes like two peppermint candies. Even his fucking up was boring. All them buls smoked weed.

Tuesdays we had to be on the floor for locker checks. After checks we usually got pizza and wings, what I was looking forward to. We tidied our lockers early so we could chill in bed. Loom knit his blanket. I studied a used anatomy book with scratches like mini vampire fangs all over the cover. Then Chris comes in looking horrified.

"Do you know how to knock?" I says.

"I heard they busting dudes for having drugs in they lockers," he panted.

That got my attention cause the RAs hardly never did real locker checks. Made sense, though, Ortilani being a bounty hunter. "Who they bust?" I asked.

"White Chris and Gucci. Said they had dope and coke."

You could hear them needles scraping. Loom said, "We ain't got no drugs here."

"But I do!"

"Shhhhhh!" we both said. And Loom added, "Dumbass."

"Can I hide it in your room?" the bul asked with a crack in his voice.

"Not only no," I said, "*fuck* no."

"They ain't really gonna search yours. C'mon, do me a solid. I'll get you back."

"You better throw that shit away," said Loom.

"I paid ten bucks for it! C'mon, how you gonna do me like this?"

Loom dropped out of bed to go slam the door in his face.

The whole time Lindsey'd been doing homework at his desk, dressed like an accountant in vest and slacks. He glanced up from the textbook. "We really need to start carding niggas before we let them up in here."

Ortilani busted five dudes that night for coke, heroin, and amphetamines. They got termed. I'd known they was running drugs out the Health Occ wing. Why else would they be hanging so close to Shuman in the afternoon? But I ain't no snitch.

You could tell a bul was dirty the moment he showed up. I remember the kingpin of they little group was some white-bul from Johnstown who wore rodeo shirts and had a pair of shoes for every outfit. One time he showed me a photo of his peoples back home—black babymoms, caramel baby, and niggas flashing signs.

"What color is my family?" he says all aggressively.

"A lot of colors," I says to be nice. "It's beautiful."

"My family black, son!"

I ain't cry no tears to see him go.

Worse than the drugs, most of the niggas' lockers looked a mess. The RAs said no chicken and pizza till we straightened up.

Only one who ain't get termed was Chris. Naturally, this got niggas spreading dangerous gossip, and over the next day when I heard that shit I'd pull the nigga aside and say, Really? What makes more sense? That Chris snitched, knowing the type of nutass niggas we got up in here, or the other story you heard, that soon as Ortilani came in he broke down crying and snitched on himself, looking so pitiful the whitebul spared him?

They put Chris on dorm restriction. No weekend pass.

The only niggas you saw on weekends either had no family to visit or no money for Greyhound. I was the second kind. Niggas spent all day in the lounge, a room with an empty fish tank, plastic plants, a couple encyclopedias and Danielle Steele novels spaced like snaggletooth smiles on dusty bookshelves. We kept the TV on all day. Clothes got washed, then forgot, then drifted like icebergs round the laundry room. Boredom kicked in and niggas got up to bad shit. If you ain't see somebody in the dorms, you knew he was out with the buls doing the Job Corps tough guy thing.

Saturday morning I woke at eight, had breakfast in the cafeteria, then slept till two. I went to the lounge, where it worried me when I ain't see Chris. Figuring he must be sleep, I joined Loom at a table by the window.

"Flex," he said, "you know I love you like a brother. But how is you gonna sleep through details, but be the first person down for breakfast?"

"I's a fatbul," I said cheerfully.

We played Speed. By three o'clock the air was thick with trash talk and imitations of the sounds porno gals make. One of the yungbuls rapped for his friends:

I'm so fly can't none a you touch me
Ready for the war when my haters try to rush me
Best get ready cause it's about to go down

"Shut the fuck up and sit the fuck back down," Lindsey said on his way in. He sold frames at LensCrafters and always came home looking fly. Now we could play Spades. He handed me a card with a cartoon witch riding a broomstick, for my daughter back home.

"Don't I always hook you up?" he said.

"You sure do," I said from the heart.

My four-year-old Abacidé lived in Ohio with her moms. I sent a card every holiday. Seeing as Lindsey spent the most time outside, at work or community college, he bought them for me. And when I ain't have no cash, he mailed them.

He opened a carton of 'Ports and displayed them on the table. The buls paid him six bucks a pack and he displayed the crumpled dollars too. Nobody said he couldn't be an asshole.

"Is Big DC playing?" he asked.

"DC sleep," I said.

"What about Lil DC?"

"Weekend pass. Yo," I had a thought, "let's go see if Chris wanna play."

One of the buls on the corduroy couch heard me and perked up. "Duck? He in the bathroom staring at the water."

Lindsey shook his head in contempt. "Weird nigga."

"I'ma check on him," I said. Sure enough, I found the bul in that gray-tiled bathroom, in front of a running faucet, arms crossed over his stomach like he had gastric pain. He wore a wifebeater and neon green shorts, no shoes. Soon as I got near, this nigga wheeled on me with shock and fear. His chest expanded and he rose several inches on tiptoes, then he hissed at me like a cat. His fit lasted a good minute and he ran through every type of vowel. At last, he collapsed against the stall like a deflated balloon. I shut the faucet off.

"You need to go see the nurse?" I asked. I ain't want to say nothing bout withdrawal symptoms specifically, though I was thinking it.

"I miss my brothers," he groaned.

From one of the dorm rooms, I could hear somebody play Lil Wayne. Funny thing: no matter the style or singer, black music always sounds like a bugle charge when played round black people. Makes a nigga feel a little more confident. Buls came through asking if he was alright, and I gestured to say, I got this. I tells him, "I miss my brother too."

"It hurts," Chris said in a trembling voice. "I was living with two of 'em. Then I got popped. They told me Job Corps or jail. Now I ain't got nobody."

"That feeling sorry for yourself ain't gonna work," I said impatiently. "Look, get yo' ass up off the floor and come play Spades."

We made room for him at the table. Chris'd cleaned himself up a bit and put on pants. Saying sorry for the beef, Lindsey gave the bul a 'Port to show no hard feelings.

Come October, Chris was still there and doing pretty good for a nigga who just a few weeks before was in the bathroom hissing.

He joined Culinary but got to stay in Phoenix Summit cause he was ROTC. Started lifting weights in the rec. Started wearing shirts so tight my daughter would of had trouble squeezing in them. This weekly-shapeup-getting-ass nigga would put up the flag every morning and go to class in camo, spine straight as the flagpole. I'd still roast the bul, cause in the halls he played G.I. Joe, but in that bathroom he was taking shirtless selfies.

One day he comes in my room chest first to show me the A on his GED prep test. Sunshine in his eyes, thinking he ain't no orphan no more, that they'd need new words for him. Got so hyped he started talking shit to his old foster dad, an invisible tyrant out the past.

"What you think about that, Mister Henderson? I'm too stupid to live? I'll never graduate high school? Look at me now, motherfucker!"

I was happy for the bul. We all had to go through dark before we saw some light.

Next day, a newbul comes through the front door as we's walking to class. Chris loving smile collided with his and they ran to embrace. I thought they was twins, real rap.

"This my brother, my nigga!" Chris told me. "He finally made it!"

Word must of got out in Philly that Chris was a success, cause after that first one a new Watson showed up every week. It was the damnedest thing. They looked exactly like him only with little differences. One would be an inch shorter, or a foot wider, or have more hair in his mustache. I joked with Chris that it was like Snoopy family. I low they all look like him, 'cept with a hat or something.

"We ain't dogs," he said proudly. "We ducks."

They all got a nickname: Daffy, Donald, Psy, Huey, Dewey, and Louie. And these was some dysfunctional niggas. First off, they always had beef. At meals they'd be snatching food off each other plates and yelling over each other. Second, they always went to Camp Green. Ain't nobody go in them woods 'cept to drink cocktails and fuck them scandalous gals.

One day, one of them came on the floor tracking mud and stems. Chris slapped his brother in front of everybody.

"What I tell you?" he barks. Louder, "What I tell you? Discipline."

I ain't like that one bit. You diss family, you showing every nigga in the place they can diss your family too.

It blew my mind seeing them in the hall—a moving wall of jean shorts and peach fuzz and noise. Out of the seven, I could only tolerate Chris. Rest of them buls ain't have nothing to say. All together they was damn near incoherent.

Nobody liked rooming with them cause they got real protective of they shit. Like that first night with Chris and Lindsey, but worse, six motherfuckers for the RAs to talk down before a fight broke out. I told Chris to check them.

"One of these niggas is gonna swing on your brothers, real rap."

"I know," he said sadly.

"You the patriarch now," I said, "so you gots to teach 'em. Or go tell the nurse to get 'em on some meds or something."

"I know," he repeated, sadder.

They got write-ups, mostly for cleanliness, and Chris was scared they'd get termed. He'd go beg the RAs for leniency and always brought up the foster care thing. Please don't write him up, He ain't know better, This our first time all together.

If one of them ironed clothes, all six had to be in that tiny beige room by the office. At seven o'clock snack time, they'd crowd the office for Pop-Tarts. In some ways they was like no niggas I ever met. In some ways they was every nigga—a collection of rough edges.

Rumor went round that three Watsons took that gal Ivonne up in Camp Green. I felt bad for her—after her brother got shot she started sucking all kinds of cock. Niggas *and* whitebuls. And she ain't care it was getting chilly, leaves flipping off the branches like origami acrobats. She sat her bare ass in the mud and told the buls, Warm me up.

"You really think she did 'em all?" I asked Lindsey over Spades. He was eating a baloney and mayo sandwich with gusto.

"Only three niggas?" he said with a laugh. I could see chewed meat rolling round his tongue. "She slowing down. That gal must be on a dick diet. Ha ha!"

I shook my head. "I'm old school. One man. One woman. No gangbangs. No trains. And with your brothers? Shit!" Me and Loom lost a house. "What do you think, Loom?"

He looked at us with disgust.

"Y'all some ignorant niggas," he said. "I'm tryin'a talk about the Illuminati pushing out the black people in every city. Herding us like cattle. What do you think they're gonna do to us when they got us controlled? The Final Solution. That's what they're gonna do. And you want to talk about Chris dumbass brothers." He played a nine of diamonds. "I hate y'all sometimes."

At breakfast one day, I saw the Watsons all snatch at a biscuit till Chris stuck a fork in it and shoved it in his mouth. "You can tell them buls grew up hungry," Lindsey said.

"All I know," I added, "is there got to be at least one pair of twins in there. Job Corps is sixteen to twenty-four. Ain't none of them buls—"

"Look a motherfucking day over fourteen!" said Lindsey. "Ha ha!"

"They're octuplets," said Loom.

"How many is that?" I asked.

"Eight." One glance at the clock and he started shoveling down food. "They got a sister too."

"Eight!" yelled Lindsey. "They must of broke they mama coming outta there. *Eight?*"

"How you know this?" I asked Loom.

"You ask somebody a question, sometimes they answer."

It took me a moment to process. "Is it even legal to have a whole family up in here? You remember *Saving Private Ryan?* They had to send in the army to get the whitebul when his brothers died."

Lindsey laughed a long time. "The United States Army ain't coming to rescue no nigga from Job Corps!"

"Real rap, Linds. Remember we had that fire last year? Same thing could happen and wipe 'em out. I'm just saying."

The sky turned silver. The oaks shrugged off they acorns. Feeling theyselves kings and queens now the other critters was sleep, the turkeys grew bold. They would post up outside the fence and stare down a nigga.

Chris came to our room one afternoon and sat right down at the desk. He had a new outfit from Wal-Mart—plaid shirt and jeans crisp as a hundred dollar bill. Looked good. He read a letter wrote in pink pen on some loose leaf, stars and frowny faces in the margins:

"Dear Ducky: Every day I think about your cruel words to me. You're not ready? As the song says, *Just when I thought I'd reached the bottom, I'm dying again.* Because we can't be together I feel the sun will no longer shine. You need to think about the pain you're causing me, Ducky. You need to make your choice. Tragically, Keighlyn." In a sobbing voice, he asked, "What should I do?"

Thankfully Lindsey wasn't there to make it more awkward. All through that nonsense you could hear Loom knitting in his bunk.

"He ain't follow our advice," I heard him say.

"Ain't listen to a word," I agreed, secretly wishing a gal would write me something like that.

"She put a Evanescence line in here," Chris said like that explained the whole world. "That's her favorite band."

"Bruh," said Loom.

Chris sounded conflicted. "It's like, if we get serious, I know I'm gonna marry her. A nigga's gotta think about that shit."

"Fuck!" screamed Loom.

"Man, whatever! You ain't got no game, Loominati."

Loom stopped knitting to glare down at him. "I don't need no game. I ain't here for that. You on the other hand is a pussy-whipped, poetry-whipped, thirsty-ass, Chris-Brown-who-can't-afford-toothpaste-looking-ass little nigga. I know for a fact that bitch tryin'a have another black baby, so if yo' ashy ass feel like buying Similac with your fifty bucks a month, that's yo' business."

"I ain't ready to have babies," Chris chuckled.

"That's why I don't fuck with these girls," Loom said. "I'm afraid I'll get one of them pregnant. Real rap—I don't like using condoms."

"I ain't say nothing about fucking her," Chris said dryly, like we was the yungbuls. "I said I was gonna marry her."

This went on for a while. Chris would try to convince us and himself he should get with the whitegal. Then Loom would shit on him. Every so often I noticed Chris lower his eyelids, distracted, sure sign that his brothers had kicked down the door to his thoughts. He was chilling with us to avoid them. It pained me to see him like that, all wound up with love and bitterness.

On weekdays I got in the showers round five a.m. Blame it on food or genes, I gained weight at Job Corps. It took a good while to wash myself, and I got shamed seeing too many faces through the glass, knowing them buls was whispering, "Look at Flexo! Nigga's too fat to wash his balls!"

In my towel and shower cap, I stepped through the bathroom door and into a habitat. Four Watsons stood round in they boxers, hazel-eyed, bul-smelling, grunting and rapping. Water covered the floor cause they'd stuffed up the sinks with toilet paper. Through the glass I could see two of them showering—together. Made me shudder down to my toes. The three at the sink shared a single Irish Spring bar, whittled to a green egg and stuck with black hairs so's it looked like a cheap pet. They lathered they hair into spongy curls before plunging they faces in the sink. The tallest one scooped water and tossed it at the smallest, a puppy-eyed bul curled up in the window.

Bathing together, they looked weirdly innocent—and niggas don't get to be that innocent. Not in this world. My heart turned to a tennis ball knocking back and forth in my ribs. I noticed a whitebul staring at me through the shower glass. His eyes said, Help me.

The fuck did he expect me to do?

A bottle of body wash slipped from my nerveless fingers and hit the grouty floor. All of them snapped to attention. A marshmallow-shaped Watson, maybe Huey, pointed and said, "Chris friend!"

"Chris friend!" echoed the rest, including the two in the shower.

The tallest Watson drew his head from the sink and came anteloping cross the waterlogged floor in three squelching steps. Real rap, I expected him to kiss me. Instead he threw back a yellow curtain and indicated his prize on the drain—a dead mouse smashed in the middle with its little teeth bared in a last gasp, intestines smeared like jelly.

"We had a mice problem," said the grinning Watson. "No more."

"No," I told him. "No no no."

The Watson (Dewey? Psy?) lifted his kill by the tail. Its parts stayed together, two halves connected by a Slinky made of guts. He held it up to my eyes and swung it like a hypnotist coin. The bul had a broad chest and shoulders, his eyes far apart. Otherwise, he was Chris.

I made to leave, but a Watson pressed his hand to the door. He looked like Chris if you stuck him in solitary confinement for a week without food. Bigheaded and hollow-cheeked, he wore a knockoff Naruto headband. Pissed off, I wheeled round and nearly slipped on suds doing so. The two in the shower got out, tied on towels as they came over in a slouching, bow-legged shamble. Antelope, smallbul, ninja, marshmallow, nasty-buls—twelve golden eyes twitching at me in the chlorine glow.

"First off," I told the ninja, "don't get in my face like that again. All y'all: I know what it's like to come up hard. I know safety in numbers. But y'all can't be doing this. And y'all gotta wipe this up before the buls come in. And . . . Shit! . . . Y'all can't be showering together cause the niggas be talking."

For more than a minute I gave instructions and they listened, jaws dropped in dumb reception. Then the door swung open from a heavy blow and Tanje came in. Towel on his waist, he sang, "*My mind is telling me noooooo*—What the fuck?"

The Watsons went off.

"This our bathroom!"

"Stay away!"

"Don't come no closer!"

"Back! Back! Back!"

"Fuck is you doing?"

The littlest one gave an animal shriek.

Tanje was ready to fight them all. I had to push him back in the hall, one hand on his shoulder as I desperately held up my towel with the other.

"I talked him down," I told my counselor the next day. She laughed out the corner of her mouth, which only encouraged me. "I think that whitebul might still be in the shower. He might be eating his meals in there right now."

"That sounds stressful," said Miss Felton. I counted eleven porcelain mermaids among the supplies on her gimpy desk, one foot propped on a book. Paperwork lay in neat stacks round her battle-scarred black Dell. She drank water from a pink-capped clear thermos.

"They had to close that bathroom," I said. "First thing in the morning? The buls was *pissed*."

"You seem calm about it."

"You gots to be." A day removed and I found the whole thing humorous. Still, I left out the part bout the mouse. No sense offending a lady.

I leaned back in the soft-cushioned chair. Her walls was papered with hotline posters. You on meth, call this number. Want to kill yourself, call that number. Miss Felton was light-skin with green eyes that looked soft and stern at once, dotted round with freckles like a carnival mask. Nice figure too, thick, but she ain't show it off. That day she wore jeans and a red pleated turtleneck.

"The thing with foster kids," I went on, "you never know what they been through. I've heard bad stuff bout foster care."

"That's the truth," she said. "So three of them got moved to Ay-Yo?"

"I told Ortilani to do it! Straight up told him you can't have a whole family in one wing. Course they wild out. Counselors be thinking they know everything but . . . You know what? *I* should be a counselor."

"How did Chris take it?" she asked, ignoring my career breakthrough.

"He became a tree-hugger."

"I'm guessing you're going to explain."

I told her I found the bul over by the portables with his forehead leaned on an oak. When I took him by the arm he started spewing apologies till I ordered him to stop. Then I bought him a Nutter Butter and gave him an ear.

"I'm sick of these niggas," he'd admitted, not able to say *my brothers*. I did my best to mellow him, but an hour later Chris was back on that tree.

Miss Felton made a note to talk with him. I tried to lighten the mood. "Real rap, I don't know why they so hard on the

Watson buls. This morning some nastybul left blood in the sink."

"Good lord," she said with a nervous laugh. What went down in the dorms could shock counselors.

"Chris brothers ain't have nothing to do with that. Makes me never want to shower again. They gonna be calling me Pigpen. I don't care."

"Did you buy your interview suit?" she asked.

The change in subject threw me off. I had trouble looking her in the eyes—it made me feel small. "Look, I ain't have much time lately."

She made a face like she was trapped inside, waiting for the rain to end. She asked, "What did we say about old habits?"

"They trip us up. But—"

"But nothing. What did I say about being grown?"

"You ain't grown till you got your own." I needed her to back off. "Look. I'm doing better. I ain't drinking that lean no more. I don't smoke no more."

"Procrastination is also an addiction." Out came the calendar book. "I'm taking you to Wal-Mart on Friday. You're graduating in two months. You need a suit."

"Whatever."

She looked annoyed but I kept my eyes on hers, so's to not look shook, shamed I even felt the need to act hard. I counted fifteen ticks on the clock before I spoke again. "Don't think I ain't grateful, Miss Felton. I been seen four counselors come and go and you the realest. You know . . . it's like . . . I ain't do well in school. I'd sit in them classes thinking, I hate this. This boring. I'ma do just enough to get a C."

Her eyes went soft. "And?"

I got a lump in my throat. "I always got a F. What was enough for me was never enough for," and I circled my finger in the air.

From that point Chris had to take his three brothers to the showers and time how long they bathed. He'd count each lick of deodorant they put on they pits with military precision.

Snow came. Maintenance stuck plastic candy canes round the walkway to the front door. The gals hung glittery made-in-China snowflakes in the hall. By the welcome sign we had a Nativity with Santa standing between Mary and Joseph, which rubbed me raw cause he wasn't really there, last I checked. They put a little Charlie Brown tree in the corner of the lounge.

Second Friday in December we lined up outside Finance for our allowance. Nothing got Job Corps niggas hyped like talking bout what they'd buy in Squirrel Hill that night. I had a burner phone in mind as I signed for my check, total of sixty with my section leader stipend. Problem was the closest check-cashing spot was East Liberty. There was niggas who'd do it for you, for a fee, but I bummed ten bucks off Loom instead. He knew I was good for it.

The RAs on swing shift taped a list of discrepancies to the door: unmade beds, clothes lying round, dirty dishes. Ain't no time for that when I needed my burner. Bought it from Lil DC and called my babymoms, who still lived in our hometown, a coal-crusted navel in central Ohio. Alone, I sat on my bunk waiting for her to pick up. I noticed how the lockers never really closed, the doors curved so that one or both edges always stuck out like a hangnail.

Jadazia picked up. I could hear street noise in the background. After some catching up, I asked, "How's Abacidé?"

"She good! Her teacher say she one of the best readers in her class. I'm like, 'I know my baby's a genius.' Ha ha ha."

I gazed out the window at the air filled with fat flakes. "Can I—"

The door opened and in came Ortilani with a clipboard.

"You haven't fixed these discrepancies," he said. "Those dirty dishes are still on the sill."

"That be Loominati shit." A plastic bowl. Chicken bones and tomato sauce.

"Where's he at?"

"Probably telling the turkeys in the trash bout the Thirteen Families. Look, man, I'll get to it." That got him to leave. To Ja, "I swear, these RAs be treating us like some kids." Took me a second to find my thoughts again. "Can I talk to Abacidé?"

"She with my mom."

"So where you at?"

"Ain't none of your business where I'm at."

I pictured her with lipstick on. "Did Naquan ever get you that money?"

"No, he didn't! No, he didn't! Your brother ain't shit."

"Yo, don't get loud—"

"I'ma get loud cause I don't give a fuck! Nigga, I don't give a fuck! If there a problem, you always like talk to Naquan, talk to Naquan, and he ain't nothing but a bullshit drug dealer. He don't do shit and you out in Pittsburgh."

"Would you prefer I was still working at Burger King? I'm here for my future. For my *daughter's* future."

"*Your* daughter? Nigga, you ain't the one squeeze her out your pussy. You think I'm just a babymama. You think I'm just a ho."

"Look, I ain't tryin'a start no fight." But she went on calling me a deadbeat.

After she hung up, I sat still for minutes, my heart pinned under a boulder, like back at Burger King when I couldn't smile no more. Finally I got out my scrubs and put on jeans, a white tee, hoodie, and gold chain, though I ain't feel up to schlepping round Squirrel Hill in the cold. I wanted to talk with my moms, but the minutes was up. So I went looking for my niggas. Some of the buls said they seen Chris and Loom out by the cubicles and I'm thinking, Fuck. These dumb niggas getting marked AWOL. So I threw on a coat and went looking.

I found them between two of the Health Occ portables. The grounds looked empty, with most of the buls in the dorm. "Y'all bout to get marked AWOL," I told them.

"Really?" Chris said like the thought never occurred to him. He was using a rake to drag something wet and furry out from under the steps into a trash bag Loom was holding open. Took me a moment to realize he was raking three raccoons with they throats cut, the fur on they necks gummed with blood and snow.

"Why's y'all doing that?" I asked with a cringe. "Maintenance got it."

"Maintenance ain't here," Loom said. His gloveless fingers trembled as he tied the bag in three knots, mist puffing out his lips.

Chris spoke with urgency. "We just gonna throw 'em in the trash pile right'cher. Ain't no thing."

I saw nothing to do but help them. Loom took one end of the bag and I the other. Soon as we came from round the cubicles, and I was geared up to cuss out Loom for not fixing his discrepancies, these two Ay-Yo niggas in ski caps and Timberland coats came out from behind the shed. Both looked higher'n a motherfucker. Soon as they spotted us, the short one, yellow nigga with red stubble like fungus, came at Chris.

"What up, Duck?" He spoke friendly. "You got some money?"

"I'm busy." Chris tried to pass but the nigga put fingers on his chest. "Don't be touching me," he said in a low voice.

"And don't you be tryin'a get big, little nigga," said the lightskin, his temper ignited like a Zippo. "Your brothers ain't here. And you better not tell 'em shit or you know what'll happen. Now empty yo' pockets."

"Hold up." Loom dropped his end of the bag and left me standing there with a sack of dead vermin. The other nigga, tall dumb-looking darkskin, put himself in front of Loom.

He said, "This ain't yo' business, Loominati. Take a walk."

Loom slipped both hands in his waistband, shrugged, backed up. "You heard the man, Flex. Ain't our business." Then he pressed a hand to my chest. Took me a second to realize he was handing me his needles, and I quickly covered them up. As I fumbled them into my pocket, Loom went at the darkskin, who'd turned his back, and drove his foot so hard in this nigga balls his belt was at his waist again. He fell to his knees and Loom dropped him with a punch to the back of the head.

"They fighting!" someone yelled from an Ay-Yo window.

People came spitting out the anterior door like moths to a tasty wool sweater. Cheering and placing bets and filming on they phones and screaming so loud they had my brain on short-circuit.

"Alright, Duck! Alright, Duck!"

"Watch his left, Duck!"

"These niggas is crazy, yo!" a girl screamed in my ear. From the front of the crowd, I could see Chris with his fists up, circling the lightskin in a fighting stance. The lightskin kept glancing off, I guess for backup, though at the moment his bul was facedown on the pavement with Loominati knee in his spine. This nigga ain't come at Chris expecting no fight. He charged with wide swings that my bul ducked easy. Every time they moved, the crowd moved. Elbows and shoulders jostled me.

"Back up, niggas!" I said to no use. "Back the fuck up!"

Suddenly the crowd did as I said. I heard surprised gasps. One of Chris brothers, the marshmallow, dashed out from behind me, came and cracked the lightskin on the jaw. He crumpled. Then the two nastybul Watsons joined they brother taking shots at his unconscious head.

Chris had his hands on his cheeks, horrified. "No!" He tried to pull off marshmallow. "Stop it for y'all kill him!"

Loominati tried to restrain the brothers while Chris put his own body on top the bul they beat. I stood there, holding tight to the needles.

"Five-oh!" someone shouted. No less than five security guards came in swinging sticks. They threw my buls on the pavement. Loom had a tear in his hoodie and a cut on his fore- head. Blood stained Chris camo jacket. One of them wannabe pigs put a knee on the back of Loom's neck and ground his cheek in the gravel.

"They ain't start the shit," someone said. And, "Leave Duck the fuck alone." A glass bottle came flying from the back to smash a foot away from one of the guards. That one hurting Loom I wanted to stab in the neck with them needles, but the fire came and went. Feeling a bitch, I joined the nine or

ten spectators who was like, We ain't in it, and hurried back to
Phoenix Summit.

Rest of the night, that fight was all anybody could talk bout.
Them two Ay-Yo niggas got termed. According to some kid
who'd been in Discipline when my buls showed up, Schibetta
said they ain't do nothing wrong. The buls they beat was punks
with a dozen write-ups already, and in his mind it was street
justice. He called Loom and Chris "the good ones."

Still, they had to term Chris brothers. You can't just beat a
nigga half to death with no repercussion. Funny—any other
time them buls would of gone to jail. Three on one with lord
knows how many witnesses. But ain't nobody care if some Job
Corps nigga gets beat, just like nobody care if we get termed.
Hours passed and, seeing as I ain't seen Chris or Loom, I
assumed they was in Ay-Yo helping his brothers pack.

This nigga Tanje got so hyped he was running round the
lounge. "I'm only mad my nigga Duck ain't get his licks in.
His brothers should of let him beat that bitch. But my nigga
Loominati! It's always the niggas you least expect got them
scraps, boy!"

He annoyed me so bad I had to leave and post up in my
room. Sat on the edge of the bunk with the needles held up to
my eyes, like I was worried they'd vanish if they left my sight.
Nobody'd expected Loominati to be a tough guy, but to see
that scratched some itch they all seemed to have. I ain't never
need Loom to be no hand grenade. I liked him fine as dust on
a ceiling fan, as light from a TV, as the sound of cards shuffling.

Round six o'clock, Lindsey arrived from class looking dignified and overworked. "Was you in the shit?" he demanded to

know, gossip-hungry. But I was thinking bout my own problems, the conversation with Jadazia, the words she'd used to
pummel me.

Lindsey hugged me without another word, in the way
niggas open for each other. Deep down you ain't expect him
to have the room for you, what with all the shit he go through
his own self, but he opens his heart like a train door and you
come inside to leather cushions and rack space.

Lindsey listened to me talk bout Abacidé. He'd bought her
a Christmas card, the princess from *Tangled* in a glittery Santa
hat.

"It's like black women ain't got no respect for niggas," I
told him. "Jadazia don't see the work I do."

He nodded agreement. "It's an epidemic. They think
they don't need us. Then bitches talk shit when we get with
whitegals."

"I keep telling them bitches: we make these motherfucking
kids!" A sob wracked my chest. "It's Abacidé, man. I ain't been
there. I just don't want her to hate me."

Lindsey put both hands on my cheeks, stared me in the
eyes. "You a man. Ya hear me? When she's older, she'll understand you did what you had to do."

Not much later, his friends came in: a short blackbul who
liked wearing fresh clothes and drank too much, and a droopy-
eyed whitebul whose every reaction seemed on five-second
delay. Seeing me miserable, they passed a flask and I ain't hesitate. In some cases, being sober don't work. Like the times the
clouds open and you find yourself a fuckup trapped with other
fuckups in an institution one step up from jail. I gulped shit
whisky and waited patiently for it to kick in. At least I wasn't
staring at the wall no more.

"They'd of termed Loom if they found them needles on him," I said. "He'd be like, The RAs knew! Everybody knew! And they wouldn't give a shit."

"Loom knows you got his back," said Lindsey.

"He sure as fuck ain't act like it. Where he at now? All I want is somebody to say, That Flex, he a standup guy."

Soon the booze got me feeling happy. Lindsey played music on his phone and we got to talking stupid bout which gals we'd fuck down. And at one point I looked out the window and saw the RA from Ay-Yo drive a van to the entrance, where Chris and Loom waited, 'longside Chris brothers and they trash bags of stuff. Loom and Chris started loading up the back. From out by the dumpster came half a dozen wild turkeys, gorged on trash, they bellies hanging near to the ground. Chris brothers ran at them, not in a bully way, more like they wanted a hug. Terrified, the turkeys launched off they scaly feet and flew for the woods. I saw Loom shaking his head.

And I'm thinking, Fools. Still clowning round like nothing happened. What'll you do when you get off that Greyhound with five bucks in your pocket? And you taking the bus all day through some cracked-out hood applying to jobs that don't pay nothing, feeling like you ain't nothing, calling up your brothers at Job Corps begging for money?

"These young niggas don't know shit," I groaned.

The flask passed hand to hand till it was empty. I felt ready to throw up. Lindsey checked his phone. "We got details."

I rose to follow, but he gripped my shoulder and shook his head. Right. I hit my shin on the frame getting in bed.

Watching them two losers leave with him, it occurred to me Lindsey kept them round cause they made him feel big. Shamed me to think I needed another man to buy my daughter things or tell me I'd had too much to drink. Deciding my good deed was done, I stood on the bedpost to slip the needles under Loom's pillow. At the same time I saw that blanket he'd been working on and, figuring I had every right to touch his things, dragged it down and wrapped my whole body up. It was itchy and coarse, like my own hair, and warm.

The next morning I woke to the RA, some lightskin not much older'n me, prodding my shoulder. He wore a sky-blue dress shirt and what I assumed was his dad's skinny tie from the eighties. "What?" I growled.

He spoke calm, almost timid. "Wake up, William. It's time for details."

"Loom doing details." My brain felt like that last drop of milkshake slurped up the straw. I smashed my face down in the pillow.

"JaLondre's out there all by himself. Half the guys are on weekend pass."

"I got a headache." I closed my eyes but could feel him hover over me. "Nigga, did you hear me? I'm fucking sleeping. Best get gone cause I ain't the nigga to fuck with."

On Monday, Ortilani called me to the office, said maybe it's time I moved on from section leader.

"Everybody mess up sometime," I said from the doorway. "I'ma do better."

Slouching at the desk, he gave me an exhausted look. "You've been slacking off on details for weeks. How long did you plan on not doing the job?"

"We got a system," I explained. "Sometime Lindsey lead details, sometime Loom do it, sometime I do it."

He narrowed his eyes. "The fact that you're in Lindsey's little gang doesn't mean you get to call the shots here."

"What do that mean?" But he wasn't inclined to hear me out. I left before I could say something I'd regret. In a bathroom stall, I scolded myself. "Stupid! You stupid, stupid fuck."

Lindsey got mad when I told him. Bullshit abuse of power, he called it. Said none of them RAs knew how to do they job, so they took it out on me.

He went straight to Miss Carter in my defense. By Wednesday, I was feeling pretty good bout my chances. Thursday, Lindsey tells me he's over Miss Carter and all she cared bout was the politics. That night Ortilani gave me trash bags for my shit and moved me to a Health Occ room.

Soon as I came in, I saw three Watsons sitting on the edge of a bunk. Antelope, ninja, and the little one all in scrubs. They turned and stared at me with eyes like Chris. My skin crawled.

The other two roommates was a West Virginia hillbilly and his chubby tranny girlfriend. After lights out the tranny climbed up in his bul's bunk, right next to mine. For a while it seemed they'd never stop doing they thing. After I told them I couldn't sleep, they cut it out.

Early morning I woke up and saw the Watsons out of bed. Real rap, they was sleep standing with one leg up. I slid under the comforter.

All night I had nightmares full of lashing rain and furry creatures who appeared from the dark to whisper they knew my secrets, dreams that kept rising over me like water till I woke in a sweat.

Before I knew it, the RA came knocking on the door to wake us. My eyes was heavy. My body sounded like a glow stick cause of how much it cracked. In the thin morning light, I saw the Watsons in towels by they lockers, ready to shower.

"What's that smell?" I asked, assaulted by a rotten stench. They ignored me. Muscles aching, I climbed down off the bunk and found the source under one of they beds—a pile of roots and stems and leaves and grass. Topping it off, a dead raccoon.

"The fuck's this shit?" I yelled. "We gonna get write-ups."

The ninja jumps between me and the nest, tryin'a get big. I shouted in his face: "Seven of y'all motherfuckers! Seven! Every time I turn round there's more y'all little orphans up in here. Y'all niggas crazy like the whitebul. Why y'all killing raccoons? I can't stand y'all niggas. Fuck y'all."

The door opened and in came Chris with a basket of shower supplies under his arm. He had a Band-Aid on his forehead from security roughing him up. "Rise and shine, cadets . . ." he stopped midsentence and took in the scene with alarm.

"Man, talk to your family!" I told him.

He looked under the bed. His eyes widened. First he dumped they little nest out the window. Then he slapped the ninja in the face, hard.

"Discipline!" he roared. "Ya hear me?"

I got in his face. "Motherfucker, I'm mad at yo' ass too. I would do anything for my brother and you slapping yours in front of everybody? And you ain't say shit nothing when yo' brothers got termed over yo' ass. How you gonna treat blood like that?"

He threw up his hands like he was catching a punch. "Real rap, Flex. We Canadian—"

"The fuck do I care if you from Toronto?"

He sighed. "Canadian geese."

The story went like this: seven buls, one gal. One day, on a flight, Chris got shot by a hunter. By the time his sister found him in the cattails he'd almost bled out. She dragged him to the spirit of the forest, who healed him on condition that the males all turn human. Also, they sister couldn't honk no more and had to be silent. Soon as they turned into buls, social services found them, declared them orphans, and split up the family.

They kept birdlike qualities. Always wanting to be outside and round water. Scrapping for they food and territory. A distaste for raccoons, apparently. These past couple years they sister worked to break the curse by building a nest made of branches and bones, big enough for seven buls to sit in. Come that day they'd go back north.

Naturally, I assumed these niggas was crazy. Trauma can do weird shit to people. And ya'll know I had to tell somebody, if only to feel less crazy my damn self. Couldn't be Lindsey, so I hollered at Loom, who nodded like I'd affirmed his every suspicion.

"Magic is real," he said plainly. "The Illuminati covers it up. Same with aliens. You know what this means?"

"What?"

"You is officially the least interesting nigga in the clique. Chris had it on lock, then shit happened."

"Bird shit happened."

"Exactly."

Hindsight being 20/20, it was obvious. They even walked in V-formation down the hall. At Thanksgiving dinner, when we all gathered in the lounge, not one of them buls touched the turkey.

I decided to roll with it till everyone started making sense again. Loom got salty cause Chris waited to tell him and gave him the silent treatment all day. Round dinnertime they was cool again.

That night I went to the section leader room, where Chris sat on the grumbling radiator and Loom at the desk, the air between them charged with secrets spoke in low voices. Outside was a white world. In the parking lot, the top halves of cars broke the even sheet of snow. Flakes kept coming.

"We getting snowed in," I needlessly pointed out. Chris and Loom had the nerve to share a look, as if considering whether to include me in the conversation. I walked right in and sat on my old bunk. "I don't give a fuck," I told them. "I'm in this."

Chris said his brothers just returned from the woods—a sparrow gave the word that they sister was visiting on her way south. Some years ago she shacked up with a gander and was bringing they kids too.

"So you get to see your nieces and nephews," I said. "That's great." I had to get used to talking bout birds like they was people.

Chris looked miserable. "I don't know, my nigga. I'm afraid it might mess them up more. The more they around each other, the more they act like geese. If they see her, I'm thinking . . ."

"You afraid she might say it's time."

"She can't say nothing," he reminded me. "Her *husband* can say it's time."

I wondered: did Watson buls go on walks and randomly find theyselves in airport lobbies? If you X-rayed they stomachs, would you see worms and six-pack rings?

"It's for the best," I declared in my smartest voice. "Real rap, your brothers is fuckups as humans. Like when they ran that train on Ivonne—"

"What?" He looked sickened. "You be saying that shit, too? They was showing her a flower! The bitch say she like flowers, so they . . ." A moan of pain. Hands over his face. "Ganders mate for life. We ain't nastyass gang rapists like mallards." He stared at his sneakers. "Everybody gotta assume the worst of a nigga."

"I'm just saying—"

"Flex!" Fortunately Loom cut me off. At the desk, he was making a wreath out of pinecones, plastic figs and cranberries, potpourri, and twine. He asked Chris, "Do you wanna change back?"

"Not really. No."

Loom was skeptical. "You wanna be black. You wanna be broke and struggling. You want the cops to try and shoot your ass." When he said nothing, Loom pressed on. "You ain't had no zip code. No rent. You could go anywhere. Now you in exile. You exiled to gravity. And what you want to be is a brokeass nigga at Job Corps?"

"I like it here."

"I don't understand, personally," said Loom.

"Think about the life expectancy! In ten years we'll be dead."

"You really that afraid to die? 'Sides, geese don't give a shit about that."

Listening to them debate hurt my head in ways I never expected, cause how do you expect this conversation?

Chris was squinting at the walls, like trying to stare through them. "We all got to meet up this one time we was eight or nine. We was in different houses, three in one house and four in the other, but something worked out. We went to the zoo and got to play in Rittenhouse Square." His nostalgic smile sobered to a flat line. "There was this beautiful grass and . . . we just started eating it. That was all I could think to do. It was delicious. The foster parents broke us up and took my brothers away and . . . I cried the whole way home."

As he was talking, a voice in my head told me this made no sense, and it startled me how small that voice had become. Maybe cause of bad sleep, maybe cause I'd found distraction from a fast-approaching and uncertain future, the part of me that wanted to believe a black man could fly had its hands on the wheel. Suddenly I pictured a bird face on top of his. Flat like a mirror, gray-feathered and beautiful, unmistakably Chris.

". . . too many," I heard him whine. "Sometimes I wish I ain't had so many brothers."

Loom got a dark expression. He took care weaving the twine into a bed.

"I never knew my oldest brother," he said in a tight voice. "He got shot when I was three. My mama said she didn't want us afraid of the streets, so she sent me and my other brother out when we was little. Jay was everything to me. Then he got shot. I wanted revenge."

Chris nodded understanding. "On the nigga that shot him."

"On the world. On every nigga. Any nigga. So I see this nigga walking around and bashed his head in with a bat. I took twenty bucks out his wallet and the Jays off his feet, but it was never about that. They got me on armed robbery and attempted murder. I got in just in time to be tried as a juvenile. I did a year in Shuman, then I came here."

I did the math. Loom was round twenty. I realized I never knew his age cause he ain't celebrate birthdays.

"In juvie they taught me how to knit," he went on. "I do it cause it's peaceful. Else I think I shouldn't be alive. I think how much these white folks want us dead and I went and knocked a nigga's brains out. And maybe, some day, that nigga's people are gonna get me. And they'd have every right to. But I don't like to think about that."

I ain't know what to say. Neither did Chris, who opened his mouth to speak before he decided not to.

"I ain't got no family," Loom said into his silence. "So is you done complaining about having too much family? Cause if you ain't, I'm about to get very, very black on you." Sadly, he watched the pieces of twine unravel into a pile of junk. "We gotta do details, yo."

Unsure whether he needed space, I hugged him anyway, not too tight, like my hands was axes and I ain't want to hurt him. He hugged me back and we stood like that. "You got family," I told him as Chris joined the embrace. "What's mine is yours. Always."

Before Chris left he told us, "Thank you for not stashing my weed that one time. I needed that."

"Fo' sho," I said. Waited for him to leave before I burst out laughing. "Tell me something, Loominati: how'd we become his mentors?"

"Cause he asked us to," Loom said simply.

Saturday morning we was snowed in. The next RA never showed up, and Ortilani did his best, bless him, but by noon he was sleep sitting up at the desk. Some of us went downstairs and opened the exit door. Outside, the snow was piled high as my chest. Immediately Chris brothers dip they hands in and start flinging it at niggas. It popped off in the downstairs hall, everybody ducking and dodging, taking cover in doorways like a shooter game.

"Don't any y'all little motherfuckers hit me," I said, so course a Watson tries to assassinate me. Snowball missed me by a good foot. I ran after him and another Watson got me from the side, right in the cheek. "Y'all niggas play too much!"

Tanje congratulated the bul—"Good one, my nigga!"—cause course they was friends by then. Wild niggas found wild niggas.

For an hour or two the buls threw dance parties round the center. But after while it set in that we was stuck in this dark and lonely facility. The RAs took turns sleeping on the couch. I stayed in the section leader room playing *God of War* till my fingers cramped. We ran through smokes quick and Lindsey felt stupid cause he ain't stock up. This whitebul tried to sell me a single 'Port for nine dollars.

"Ain't nobody paying that much for a cigarette," I told him.

He grinned widely. "Somebody will." And he was right.

Sometime during that long, gray hour, the antelope Watson came in the lounge, shivering, face wet with snot. He sat on the couch and Loom wrapped him in an afghan.

"They out there," he said through chattering teeth. "I could hear 'em."

"How you know it ain't some other gooses?" I asked.

"I don't know. But we gotta go find 'em."

"Where you think they at?"

"Water. It's gotta be by water."

"The creek," I said, and Loom agreed. I ain't know how I could help. I just wanted to.

We threw on heavy clothes. Wrapped in a Pooh Bear blanket, Lindsey watched us from a chair by the window. "You going on a rescue mission?" he asked.

"Yeah," I said.

With majestic sorrow, he held up three cigarettes. "My last 'Ports," he said as he placed them in my hand.

The buls said they saw Chris go running to the gals' dorm so I headed on over and, sure enough, I found that nastybul in the stairwell, whitegal up against a wall, pants round they ankles, raw dogging.

"We gotta go," I shouted.

Startled, he staggered back and into the banister, saw me, and unleashed a scream from the depths of his blue-balls. This gal kept moaning till she realized he pulled out. Her butt gave a confused little twitch.

She glared at me through a sheath of blond hair. "What the fuck, Flexo!"

Getting his dick back in his jeans seemed to vex Chris worse'n that lock did. I wondered what to do. Scold him? Scold her? Leave? I fixed my face like I was his aunty done caught him wearing shoes inside and said, " We got shit to do before dark."

Once I'd explained the situation, Chris gal ("Fiancée," he insisted I know) offered to ask round for winter clothes. Job Corps niggas ain't much for loaning out shit—given the negative-ten-percent chance you'd get it back—but between Phoenix Summit and the gals we got a pile of mismatched gear for the Watsons. Loom rolled up his blanket ("Warmest thing we got," he said) and stuffed it in a backpack 'longside a thermos of syrupy coffee from the machine at the front desk, his needles, and a damn wood-handled hunting knife he managed to hide who-knows-where for two years. After a couple Pittsburgh winters we knew to borrow balaclavas—we was straight looking like ISIS.

Together with the Watsons we went through a downstairs hall wet with snow and muddy footprints. Out of the brothers, Chris looked least ridiculous in an overlarge plaid coat, the rest looking like a reject boy band in summertime hoodies and ball caps. 'Cept for a security guard sleep at the desk, wasn't nobody down there. We drifted by the entrance, past the counselor offices to the trash pickup in the basement, where Loom tore up pieces of hefty cardboard that he rope-tied to our feet. Ghetto snowshoes. From there we went back upstairs and out the front door. On the other side of the parking lot was buls and gals sledding down a hill on trashcan lids. Loom said he'd never been to Camp Green. I had to admit I drank cocktails at the creek once or twice.

"It's cool," Chris said. "I know the way."

Cold. Damned fucking cold. We moved at a plodding pace. Wind made the low-hanging branches batter our heads. Huddled together for warmth, hands in sleeves, the Watsons clearly missed they feathers. Passing them back and forth, we quickly burned through the 'Ports, and I was having trouble just holding them in my rubbery fingers. Every so often the branches parted just enough we could see a corn kernel called sun.

We reached a road where swerving tire tracks cut the snow into white diamonds. Down a ways we saw a Ford Focus stuck in a snowdrift. To my surprise, the back door opened, and out came none other than the marshmallow and the nastybuls, all wearing chewed-up flannel coats, looking like they'd been on the streets awhile. Chris ain't look surprised to see them; he seized them in a quick embrace before calling everyone to warm up in the car.

The eight of us squeezed in. I took the driver seat and Loom sat with ninja Watson in the passenger side. It was slightly warmer, but still chilly. Wearing gloves ain't stop my hands from going numb—I blew on them to get the blood flowing.

"Are we close?" Loom asked Chris. His arms round ninja waist, he was running the lighter flame over his palms.

"Creek's just up the hill," Chris said breathlessly. He asked me, "You okay?"

I tried to talk but my teeth kept chattering. They ain't need me there, the fact of my uselessness clear to everybody. I pictured hot apple cider and fireplaces, beds layered in blankets, all kinds of warm things I'd seen in movies. Abacidé entered my mind and I began making promises to her. After Job Corps I'd get her a scholarship to some fancy school, somewhere she could worry bout math class, gossip with friends in the library, and play sports. I promised her nothing would hold her back.

I dreaded leaving that car. Snow sparkling with ice crystals lay everywhere I looked. A white death.

We continued through the woods. Branches knit above us and everything went dark. Mist streamed from our mouths. I became aware of being fat. Trying to put one foot before the other had me competing with the sack of blubber hanging off my abdomen. The struggle got me panting like a baby trying to suck enough air to cry. My heart felt fit to explode. Before long I had to walk arm-in-arm with Loom.

Miserable as they looked, the Watsons humped long with simpleminded determination, a little like wild things, a little like pet sheep. I thought bout how niggas ain't built for the woods. The news would say, The bodies were identified as nine African-American males. Twenty African-American males. A hundred African-American males frozen solid in a Job Corps.

At first I thought I imagined the honking up ahead, till I heard another, then another, till they cries rang in the colorless wood. The antelope Watson honked so close to my ear I cussed at him. Then all of them, even Chris, started honking. Amazed, me and Loom watched them make the full-throated noises of young ganders. They redoubled the pace, and I struggled to follow in snowshoes reduced to mushy pulp.

The buls went down a hill. From the top I watched them catch hold of pines for support, submerged to they knees like a baptism. I breathed deep the bitter air, then went barreling after. Trees ain't slow me and I slid the last five feet on my ass.

Dazed, palms sticky with black dirt and sap, I pushed myself to a kneeling position. Yards away, Loom was walking down three fallen trees that made a natural stair, snowshoes off, his arms out for balance. Nimble motherfucker hopped to earth and looked round smugly. The creek was blue ice embedded with beer cans, shooter bottles glittering in the snow all round it, and the Watsons hesitated at the edge to stare in wonder.

Two dozen gooses stood on the ice, all honking 'cept one. A sleek bird with a brown-and-gray coat, she turned her diamond-shaped head our way. A gray male, her husband, I guessed, stretched his neck and hissed at us. Generations had passed in bird time. Great-nephews and great-nieces. The eight fuzzy babies slipping round might of been a fourth generation.

After testing the ice with his toe, Chris decided it best to kneel and beckon his sister. She came over, but when he reached for a hug she pecked his forehead. A lady got boundaries, I guess. He apologized. Honking happily, the brothers got on they knees to pick up the family who ran to them cross ice made shiny with reflected sun. Loom smiled from the shore. I wished I could share they joy, but it took all my energy to crawl to a tree, lay my back on the bark, and sit a while. Lord, I hoped they ain't see me, spread out like a bag of camping supplies ripped from a branch and picked at by raccoons.

Time passed. The buls' honking turned to sneezing as the chill sank in. Concerned, Loom opened his backpack to unroll the blanket, told the buls to step in. I could taste salty snot in my mouth. Cold weighed on my chest. I barely registered Chris pulling down my mask to lift the thermos to my lips. Hot coffee splashed down my throat and into my chest like Agent Orange.

I thought, Who'll believe we went on this adventure? I could barely believe myself. And wasn't I supposed to be a nurses' aid when this was done? A future that felt as unreal as Chris brothers when they vanished before my eyes. Snatched up by Santa, the Grinch, the White Witch, who knows?

Had I gone delirious? I blinked my eyes tight, opened them, and saw the blanket in the snow. Out from under it came six gray gooses.

Chris gawked as they crossed the ice to nestle they sister. He balled his fists and grabbed Loom by the coat collar. "What did you do?" he yelled.

"I don't know!" cried Loom. "I ain't mean to!"

Chris released him, shouted after his brothers. "Eddie? Mike? Keith? Albert? Dwayne? Damon?" Ain't nobody answer from the feathery mass. I remembered a movie where a gal parents get magically turned to pigs, but in the end she can pick them out of a whole pen. Somehow, she just knows. But Chris ain't have that power.

Loom took three slow steps to him, paused before he got too close. "You gotta put on the blanket," he said carefully. "You'll go crazy if you don't."

Chris hesitated. Cautious, he lifted it in pinched fingers, draped it gingerly on his back in case he needed to throw it off. Loom pulled it the rest of the way and wrapped him up. I held my breath. I waited for the change, for the goodbye.

A minute passed. Nothing. Chris dumped it off his shoulders, his face twisted with pain and anger. Loom pulled him in for a hug. The bul wept into his shoulder.

So cold, I thought. I got a daughter. I got a daughter.

Chris sister let out a triumphant honk. The flock beat wings till they had enough wind to rise in a V behind her husband, lift off the ice and fly south through the naked branches. Chasing them, Chris stepped on the ice, cracked it, plunged halfway up his shin in freezing water. I watched him fall back in the snow, clutching his leg and hissing though his teeth.

I searched for Heaven in the clouds. I saw Abacidé urging me to stand, a four-year-old with a woman's voice.

Loom seized me round the waist and struggled to lift me. Chris threw my arm on his shoulder and, grunting, they helped me up. Huddled together we walked back to the center. We walked with Loom's blanket over our heads. And every step took us to the future, vicious, exciting, but most importantly there. Waiting for us.

MINE

In the roiling dark clouds a black man waltzed all by himself.

This man wore a suit either silver or black, depending on the angle you looked from.

This man had long feet and hands. Lips together, he hummed to the tune of the thunder. His biceps bulged under his coat sleeves, and the fabric of his shirt stretched tight over his barrel chest. When he opened his eyes, they looked like gold rings.

This man Emily pictured in the clouds had nothing to do with volleyball and everything to do with a night when she was four and Daddy still seemed mountain-tall. She had run to him in fear of the lightning. "That is Sango dancing a waltz," he'd said with good humor. Sango the god of thunder.

According to Daddy, all orisha—Sango, Oshun the river, Eshu the trickster, the myriad names she read of in folklore—were avatars of God. Called Jehovah in Latin, Olorun in Yoruba, a thousand names for a singular being. No need to feel conflicted about whom she should worship. But when lightning played through the clouds, his Christianity fell before a gleeful polytheism. He pointed his thick finger out the window at the invisible dilettante.

"See?" he would tell her. "He is dancing right *there*."

◆ ◆ ◆

"It'll look like we're orphans," Emily told her sister Molly.

They were sitting on her bed, still in their pajamas. Molly had her back against the white teak headboard as she twisted Emily's hair into bantu knots. Outside, rain battered the woods at the edge of their sprawling backyard. Rotten weather for any day, let alone the day of the Division 1A Middle School Regional Volleyball Tournament.

"Mom works night shift," Molly said with a self-righteous sigh that Emily thought unnecessary. "One of her patients died from leukemia last night."

"What's that got to do with us?"

"So if she wants to sleep, she deserves to sleep."

"I deserve to have family in the stands, *not* just on the court."

Molly grunted as she finished a knot. "Uncle Osita cuts hair so he can afford to bring his children here. Uncle Odun drives a jitney and he *hopes* someday a woman will marry him. How would they feel hearing you complain like this?"

"They would say Daddy should come to my games," Emily said without hesitation. His Nigerian friends, whom they called "uncles," doted on her as much as their father did.

"Sista! Abeg you no vex me in the mawnin." Molly playfully spoke patois like their parents slipped into over wine and suya. This made Emily smile in spite of herself. With the knots finished, she admired her hair in the vanity mirror. How chic and African she looked. "It's six forty-five!" Molly said. "Make out with your reflection later. Get dressed."

◆ ◆ ◆

It had been a week since Daddy flew to Lagos to teach semi-
nars on American medicine. Emily prayed every night for his
safe return. When asked about his homeland, he often told her
funny anecdotes about accompanying his landowner father
down Ikurudo Road to the government offices. There stern-
faced British men in white wigs would give them a list of
absurd tasks to complete in order to keep their farm, because,
even in the waning colonial years, black men needed permission from the oyinbos just to fart in their own homes. What
Emily remembered most were the moments when Daddy let
his guard down. When he talked of the military junta and oil
companies and an unmistakable edge crept into his voice.

She didn't want him in Nigeria. She wanted him at the
tournament so he could see her win.

"Yinz guys's hair looks cute!" said Jessie Vessey as the sisters hurled themselves into the backseat of the Vesseys' silver
Subaru minivan. Shivering, Emily shut the door against the
elements and closed their umbrella. Jessie twisted around to
high five them. Like the sisters, she wore a blue-and-white
team tracksuit. She had been Emily's friend since first grade, a
chubby girl with red hair in a bowl cut.

Mrs. Vessey was a rotund and buxom woman, her hair an
immovable lump of microwaved ringlets dyed rubber-duck-
yellow. She wore a pink velour tracksuit, the zipper wedged
under her voluminous breasts. A cigarette sizzled in her steering hand as she drove them down rainswept hillsides. On the
back of her other wrist was a spider tattoo that danced an
arachnid Macarena as she thumbed the knob in search of a station without static.

"Can we listen to B94?" Jessie asked through a mouthful
of breakfast burrito.

"Does it sound like we can listen to B94?" her mom bellowed. "I swear, you keep complaining, I will turn this car around. I will take your friends home and we will go home."

A bolt of fear shot through Emily to think she meant it. Jessie shoved her arms across her chest in a petulant gesture but said no more. Emily could remember her as a fox-haired tomboy out of *Swiss Family Robinson*, who sang off-note in choir and played street hockey. After her dad left last spring, Jessie grew emotional and lazy; she would spend hours watching *All That, The Simpsons,* and *The X-Files* while stuffing herself with junk food. Sometimes Emily pitied her. Sometimes she wondered what she would ever do without her.

Nauseated by smoke and dysfunction, she made her face into a pleasant mask. She felt a pinch on her knuckle, glanced at Molly to exchange a droll smile. Housing developments christened with pioneer names like Verdant Trail and Pines Crossing vanished behind them as they turned onto McKnight Road. Muddy water spilled down the sheer cliffs on either side. Emily imagined the thunder god on a cloud, the pivot of his oxblood leather shoe. She appreciated living somewhere she could have such fantasies. The rambling woods, the box hedges, the stately colonials rooted her in a place of comfort. Hers was a blessed childhood, she knew.

In the squat gray-brick gymnasium, Emily watched the storm through a rectangular window set high in the locker room wall. She had to stand with one bare foot on Jessie's shoulder and the other on Tammy O'Halloran's. Outside, sheets of silver rain flattened the meadow grass. Of the trees and facility buildings between school and gym, she could make out a single centenarian oak bent under the wind, its red-leafed canopy writhing like neurons over the brain of a genius as she covered a chalkboard in formulae. The Saint Nicholas Convent School for Children, only a five-minute walk from the gym, was hidden behind the deluge.

"Is it getting worse?" asked Jessie in a trembling voice. She repositioned her hands around Emily's ankle.

"It looks like Revelation," Emily said and shuddered at the thought, her instinct to search the clouds for the seven-headed Beast.

"I almost got in an accident on the way here!" blurted Tammy.

Emily watched families struggle down the granite path adjacent to the gym. Their umbrellas whipped inside-out and hair levitated off their scalps. Some came to cheer on the St. Nick team. Others came for their opponents: North Allegheny, Eden, St. Alexis, St. Alphonsus, All Saints, Ascension, and Bishop Canevin. What caused her anxiety was seeing the North Allegheny team in their fashionably funereal black jackets, fresh off a four-game winning streak, their umbrellas overlapping like shields of a marching phalanx. When it felt like the other girls might drop her, Emily used their heads and shoulders to clamber to the floor.

The rattling glass and thunder had her teammates spooked. They talked of Bloody Mary and long-dead German nuns who supposedly walked the convent. To Emily this felt like a stupid way to start off the tournament. A way that invited evil spirits. She lightened the mood by stuffing two volleyballs under her shirt and launching herself chest-first at her teammates.

"Who am I?" She boob-punched her way through the room. "*I'll turn this car around! No, we can't listen to B94!*"

Her teammates giggled. Jessie covered her face and said "You're so mean" with such helpless passivity it took the fun out of mocking her. Molly came from behind and swatted the balls from Emily's shirt.

"You can't touch another girl's breasts, you lesbian!" Emily said in mock outrage. "I refuse to have a lesbian sister!"

Molly stood on the bench to read from a palm-sized green Bible. *"How beautiful are your sandaled feet, princess! The curves of your thighs,"* she said in a breathless whisper, *"are like jewelry."*

Their teammates' laughter offended Emily. She figured that with their upbringing Molly should know better. True, she was tall and elegant. True, a room of blond and green-eyed girls regarded her as their cool big sister. That was no excuse for stupidity.

Her finger on the next quote, Molly handed the Bible to Tammy, who was skinny and white as paper, her bright blue eyes perpetually fixed in a silent scream. With quivering breath, she read, *"Your breasts are like two fawns . . ."* and fell into a spasm of sacrilegious giggles. The cold room turned her laughter to mist.

Molly came to Emily, who ended the mirth she had started with a head shake. "People who make fun of the Bible go to Hell," she said.

It amazed her to see the gym nearly full, four sets of bleachers arranged along the inner wall to accommodate eight volleyball teams and their supporters. Aluminum seats creaked beneath the weight of moms in patterned sweaters, impatient younger siblings who climbed on every available surface, and school-mates with handmade signs. Four humorless Sisters of Saint

Nicholas had journeyed from the convent where women of their order had lived, prayed, and died for sixty-one years; a short trip, true, but given their typical indifference to school sports, they might as well have been wearing face paint. Emily made sure to thank them for coming.

"Heaven is a Place on Earth" played muddily from the old-fashioned public address system rigged in one corner, and she felt a rush of confidence that sports analysts called *home court advantage*. While she stretched her legs on the court, Mrs. Vessey returned from the concession stand where she'd been demanding the boy check the closet before telling her with such certainty that they had no Doritos. Preemptively miserable, she laid down several coats and bags of snack food to claim one quarter of the front row. Emily remembered Daddy and wished she had a science-fiction transport beam to swap the two parents.

Seated on the fourth and uppermost row, Tammy O'Halloran's dad puckered his lips to whistle at his daughter. He wore khaki shorts, a red cotton polo, and Reeboks. Tanned the color of a deep-fried thing, his slicked black hair shiny like a piano lid, he waved to Emily in his unique way—jerking his pointer finger like he was tickling someone—as he served her a smile that felt like ants crawling up her neck. Nevertheless, she waved back out of obligation.

His gaze lingered on the court, the girls, and he wasn't the only one doing so. Suddenly she felt like her shirt and shorts were too tight, adjusted them to make them looser. She noticed the ways some girls had better shapes than her. Jessie, though fat, had more developed breasts. Tammy was short and ghost-like, but her skinny legs had Emily feeling like she carried three hundred pounds of cellulite. Whenever someone whispered in the stands, she worried they were remarking on her blackness. Refusing to feel ugly, she reminded herself of Nigerians in her life, the only people whose opinions mattered, who had told her she was beautiful. Molly, lean and athletically built, was already taking on a woman's shape.

I'll look like her someday, Emily told herself.

The nun who taught Math also coached the team. She ran them through drills in the same goatish monotone she used to explain tessellation. "Tammy. Run for the ball. Jessie. Focus on the ball. Let's go. Hustle. Molly. Good job. Emily. Do what she just did . . ."

Meanwhile, their opponents from North Allegheny moved onto the court with the synchronicity of swallows. They were tall and thin, squat and thick-thighed. They had cheeks like peaches and bouncing ponytails, except for the new member—number seven, a black girl. Emily grew distracted assessing Seven, who reminded her of Molly: both had dark skin and strong jaws; both stood around five-foot-seven; both exuded dedication to their sport, even when standing still. Like the Olabisis, she wore a cultural hairstyle, her black nylon extensions as proudly Afro-American as their bantu knots were African. In the strange absence of a coach, Seven led stretches, and Emily had to marvel at her flexibility, how her spine curled with dexterous fortitude, like an oak branch holding up a backyard swing.

In line for spiking drills, she spoke over her shoulder at Tammy. "That girl wasn't there the last time we played them."

Tammy shrugged. "Could be a scholarship kid."

"Doesn't she look like Molly?"

"I don't see it. Molly's darker. She's prettier," she added.

"They probably recruited her 'cause they're scared of us," Emily mused cattily. "We beat them twice this year."

She had heard that prep schools recruited from across the globe. The girl carried herself with elegance and confidence that seemed African. Perhaps she came from Rwanda, hers a thrilling story of transatlantic survival.

"She's probably from the ghetto," Tammy said with a miserable laugh. Not funny, but Emily forced a chuckle in half-hearted solidarity.

St. Nick won the coin toss. Molly took first serve. Positioned near her, Emily imagined they looked photogenic and powerful. Molly extended her left arm with the volleyball on her fingertips like an offering to God, drew her right arm back and cocked the open palm. Like a *Post-Gazette* sports page photo, or, better yet, a Channel 11 highlight. She sent the ball over the net in a perfect parabolic arch.

"Got it!" called a stout girl on the other side, who bumped. "Got it, got it!" A five-foot-nine Valkyrie with two blond braids passed the ball. Cheers erupted from the North Allegheny stands, the dyed and rouged mothers, the crew cut boys straight out of *Dead Poets Society*.

"Mine!" In awe, Emily watched Seven leap high, a preteen Michael Jordan, and spike the ball, only to land with her knees bent and heels together, and spin back to position like Michael Jackson—the video for "Jam" embodied in one person.

Emily managed to take her eyes off Seven, whose image stayed imprinted on her brain as she searched the air for the leather sphere already rolling out of bounds. The referee—bearded Mr. Whatshisface from So-and-so Academy, the chest beneath his white polo shirt outthrust like the grill of a jeep—uncrossed his meaty forearms to gesture at North Allegheny.

Rain sounded like applause through the ceiling. Crushed at losing first serve, Emily joined the team for a quick group hug before switching positions.

St. Nick lost three sets to one.

As they lined for the hand-slapping walk of shame, Emily could feel the last drops of adrenaline leak from her bloodstream, replaced by the sting of bitter failure. She blamed Jessie for being a moose who couldn't even yell "Mine!" before she went blundering after the ball. She blamed Tammy for passing like a retard, fingers laced and elbows out like she was churning butter. Small wonder she kept sending balls into the bleachers.

Naturally their one set had been a rally by Molly, a breath of hope that her clone quickly extinguished. Seven humiliated them with her miraculous jump serve; she had St. Nick girls flopping onto their bellies like slapstick sidekicks in a cartoon.

Good game, good game. Good game, you cocky dream-crushing jerks. When she saw Seven's hand reach for hers, she almost pulled away for fear of contact. Was this girl *really* an eighth grader? She wouldn't put it past North Allegheny to cheat with a college-aged ringer.

"Good game," said Seven, braces shining.

"You too," Emily mumbled, and tapped her on her fingertips.

The bleachers were now crowded with noisome onlookers. Mrs. Vessey heaved a sigh at her daughter. "That sucked." She wrinkled her nose. "You smell, Jessie."

Disgusted at everyone, Emily made three steps toward the showers before she threw her back to the wall and wept. Molly embraced her with compassionate strength. "I hate losing," Emily sobbed.

"I know," Molly said in a tearful voice. They shared the kind of hug she never wanted to end, long enough for her to notice, over Molly's shoulder, the battery-powered clock in the center of the outside wall, seven feet off the floor, behind a cage made of slim iron bars, like a muzzled animal, its black hands still positioned at eight a.m.

After a cold and uncomfortable shower, she returned to find what appeared to be two teams having a drill session, in actuality the leisurely paced quarterfinal between St. Alphonsus and Ascension. She had changed into a pink blouse and jean shorts, but decided to keep her tube socks because they made her look sportily cute. Others deferred to her for being tall and pretty; she had Jessie sit in the third row so she could lay back with her elbows crooked over the other girl's knees. She ate freely from Tammy's bag of Cheetos.

"I want to go to the mall," she said. "I want some waffle fries and a smoothie. When my Daddy gets back he's buying me a Tiffany bracelet. I mean, seriously, who cares about a trophy?"

Dressed in a St. Nick jacket and jogging pants, Molly sat among the eighth graders in front. She pointed out a girl on the court and asked Emily, "Isn't that Lizzy from your scout troop?"

"I guess," Emily said with disinterest because they'd lost and she saw no need to care about this tournament or the runty girls still playing. Nevertheless, curiosity drew her gaze to the sidelines, to realize she had at least two degrees of separation from everyone. Girl Scout Troop #52346, the Barbara Tescarelli Dance Studio, Sister Mary Grace's piano lessons, swim classes at the "Y," Light of the Son Christian Summer Camp.

Molly wanted to stay and support friends from other schools. Eager for her approval, their teammates piped agreement. Exasperated, Emily guessed this beat staying at home in the rain, though barely.

"I understand my nephew is in that specific communion class . . ."

"Mom . . ."

". . . but that day just doesn't work for us."

"Mom . . ."

"There should be consideration for the people who really hold this parish together." Mrs. Vessey was speaking to one of the nuns, a utilitarian little woman in a beige skirt, pink blouse, and cardigan buttoned at the top. As Emily could gather, Mrs. Vessey had asked her when Jessie would attend her next confession, which the sister cheerfully provided a date for, the last words she'd spoken before Mrs. Vessey rendered upon her an involuntary vow of silence. "As much money as we invest in the church, we should get a day for communion that our whole family can attend. I have a mind to call the diocese about this . . . What, Jessie?"

"I need my stuff out your purse," Jessie said in a tight voice. She'd changed into a long-sleeved purple shirt, sleeveless denim dress, and brown leather flats.

Mrs. Vessey looked at the nun. "Being a mom," she said with flamboyant weariness. She produced from her red leather purse several sleeves of Ritz crackers, a bottle of Pepsi, a Discman, an overstuffed CD booklet, and a Game Boy. Jessie gathered it all in her arms. Before Emily could follow her, Mrs. Vessey laid a hand on her wrist. "You looked great out there."

Delivered without eye contact, still a compliment. Emily smiled graciously. "Thank y—"

"They want to win, they need more black girls on the team," she said to the nun. "I mean, not a million. But one or two more . . ."

Back in the third row, Jessie make an untidy home for herself, built of plastic and carbs and grungy hip girls singing anthems in her ears. Emily watched with morbid interest as she guzzled down crackers. As she chewed she made wet noises, strings of saliva in her teeth. Because she shared with others, it was difficult to hate her vulgarity. Jessie wanted to look cool, yes, but seemed equally motivated by a philosophy that all their ills could be solved with a diet of music and snack food. A less humble girl might display the CD booklet like a chest of polycarbonate ninja stars and, unless you bowed to her spending power, she would assassinate you with the Billboard Top 40. But Jessie let Emily pick CDs because Jessie was a kind and reasonable person, who understood that an abysmal volleyball game called for the most qualified DJ—Emily, of course.

The gym had filled to capacity. Mothers came straight from aerobics class, draped in children, Little Leaguers and pint-sized yellow belts in *karategi*. Tightly bound in denim jackets, adorned in cheap gold necklaces and rings, the women looked like they belonged to some post-apocalyptic scavenger tribe that had made their fortress in the ruins of J.C. Penneys. Raisin-faced dads in golf caps and Dockers came to sit and gaze sunglassily from the top rows and make ringing endorsements of one another. *You're a good guy, Tom. You got a good kid out there.* Hollering teenagers made the exodus from the mall. Babies shrieked from parked strollers. Everyone hungered. Into their maws vanished pizza delivery, McDonald's drive-thru, and trash bags of Halloween candy.

Having spent little time around high schoolers, Emily found herself bemused by their unanimous misery. How they described their lives as tragedies laden with false friends and loathed parents, performed on a stage made of useless classes and dismal house parties in Fox Chapel. Truly, they made her uncomfortable; the boys had a lunkheaded energy to match their oily musk; the girls exuded reckless sexuality that had them wearing short skirts in the rain, legs on display even as their sneakers reeked of mud. Talk of R-rated movies where killer dolls dismembered people sounded especially lascivious from their glossy lips.

Little kids under the bleachers knocked Emily's seat with the tops of their tousled heads. Screaming battle cries, they fought on the hardwood to the side, biting, scratching, kicking.

"Can we not just let anybody in here?" Emily moaned, then remembered the game. "Like, oh my god. This volleyball is so basic." Twelve girls without a single all-star, the teams answered each other point for point. "What time is it, Jessie?"

Jessie read off her pink jelly watch. "Eight."

"It can't be eight. It was eight an hour ago."

"Maybe I broke it. Ha! I break things sometimes. You could ask—"

"No. It's whatever." Emily sought to cure her boredom by noting how others amused themselves. Playing cards. Pogs. Crossword puzzles. Mrs. Vessey continued to assail the nun with words, a personal pan pizza and bag of chips on either side of her. Like in Father Chris's Latin class, the boredom made Emily spiteful. She sarcastically applauded whenever someone hit a net foul or bleacher ball. She fell to judging people on their appearance. *That guy looks so old, like, jurassic.* Or, *Why's she gotta walk with her butt out like that?* On the North Allegheny moms she rained particular scorn. Dressed in capris and starchy sweaters and heels, they had hair like cotton candy and cosmetically massacred faces that made her think of something removed from a stomach.

Someone's breath smelled like weed, at least according to Jessie, who pleasantly claimed that her uncle smoked all the time and it smelled like that.

"Why do people smoke it then?" Emily said. "Like, it smells like molding cardboard." She felt proud of her simile.

The timekeeper, a nondescript woman with a five-year-old monkeying around on the chair next to her, did not appear to be keeping time. After several attempts at counting fifteen minutes in her head, Emily dissolved into a heap with Tammy and Jessie, a cushion of sweaters beneath them, their legs twisted up like kindling in a woodpile.

She memorized the room. Four walls lined at the bottom with six-foot-tall blue pads, dented in spots from where kickball players had careened into them like downed X-wings in a *Star Wars* flick. Doors to the locker rooms on opposite ends of the interior wall. Two raised basketball hoops. Nine rectangular windows set high in each of the lengthwise walls. Chewing gum and shoe rubber in the bleacher tread.

Across a landscape of heads and noise, she located Seven among the North Allegheny team. She had her gaze transfixed on the game, still as a doll. No longer hating her, Emily appreciated the foreign quality she brought to this world of sameness. She pictured Seven in Classics class, one of a dozen girls in navy blue sweaters seated around a circular oak table, respectfully discussing the myth of Orpheus in Latin; she could see Seven being clever enough to not get caught sketching fashion designs in her notebook, a tight smile on her lips as she dreamed herself in prom dresses.

Sometime in that intermittent hour, Lizzy scored a point and Molly applauded. This got the other eighth graders to applaud rather than chance looking uncool.

Emily had been resting her head in Jessie's lap while daydreaming the plot for a *Dragonlance* novel where all the characters who should fall in love finally do so. Snapped to attention, her gaze shot to the scoreboard: 13-12. Lizzy's team (the one with a Native American brave on their shirts) had the lead. More importantly, whichever set this was had to end soon. The very laws of volleyball called for it. Emily bounded down the bleachers, over thickets of duffle bags and purses, to join Molly. They made up a dance on the spot, and a chant set to the Steelers chant.

"Here we go, Lizzy, here we go." *Clap clap.* "Here we go, Lizzy, here we go." *Clap clap.*

Then, from her periphery, she noticed another girl had joined them. A teenager with dirty blond hair was copying her moves. Poorly.

She cheered on Emily like they knew each other. "Go girl! Go girl!"

Mortified, Emily stopped dancing. The blunt-featured girl, who wore sweatpants and a baggy shirt, looked dumbstruck. "What?" she said.

Emily shot a smirk at Jessie, said, "Nothing," and returned to her seat. She clapped her hands as if watching a polo game. "Well done, Lizzy."

From confusion to anger, the girl took three stomps to the top bleacher, plumped down next to a white boy in an Adidas shirt. "This little girl's a bitch," she told her boyfriend.

Emily spun on them. "What did you call me?"

The guy spoke in a black accent. "Man, you gots to chill, little girl."

She now had no doubt whose breath smelled like weed. Had a cop been around, she'd have reported him for drug use. She knew these wannabes—they milled around Ross Park Mall in imitation rapper clothes, their goal in life to shoplift CDs from Sam Goody. *Mediocre white people who want to be mediocre black people,* her mom called them. She reacted like Mom would have: looked them up and down like they had a skin disease they weren't aware of, then aimed her regal Nigerian eyes at the court.

The girl kept talking. "You ain't shit, bitch. You little nappy-head bitch. And you better stop looking at my man like that."

Emily had had it. She stood to face them, clothed in her dignity like a velveteen robe. "I don't talk to people like you. I have class. And stop trying to be black."

"Oh!" said her boyfriend. "She called you *white,* son."

The girl made spastic hand gestures. "Bitch, you don't even sound black. You talk like cousin Hilary on *Fresh Prince.*"

"Do you know Dom?" the boyfriend asked her. "You look like you know Dom."

Jessie threw down her crackers in anger. "Leave her alone!"

It upset Emily to discover, against all probability, *she* was the one being bullied. To avoid escalation, she hurried Jessie to the other end of the bleacher, where they squeezed between two kids chomping Fruit Roll-Ups, their teeth stained red. The boyfriend tried to woo her back by spitting a freestyle.

The game had halted for an intermission. Hollywood Indian music played over the P.A. *Hey-a, hey-a, hey-a.* From courtside charged a dozen little boys in fake buckskin and cloth headbands, to stomp and do tomahawk chops. Embarrassed by such corniness, Emily noticed the parents around her clapping offbeat with misery in their eyes.

"Hey bitch," the girlfriend called loudly. "Over here, you stuck-up bitch. You ain't black like me. You ain't shit."

"Shut up!" Jessie screamed. "Bitch, I will slap you!"

I'm not black! Emily wanted to say. *I'm African.* Words she could not speak for fear of looking uncouth swarmed in her throat until they choked her, flies born from the trash out this girl's mouth. Seeing she had an audience, potato chips crackling between their lips as they silently judged her, she made for the referee with Jessie in tow.

He stood atop a table by the net, watching the buckskin boys with a dreamy masculine sincerity that she'd seen men adopt when reminiscing about their middle school paper routes. After she'd called his attention three times, he squinted at her as if he had poor eyesight. "Yes?"

"There's a girl harassing me. Can you throw her out?"

"Why's she harassing you?" he asked, intrigued.

"She says I flirted with her boyfriend." She chuckled at how stupid it sounded.

Jessie chimed in, "She's not even allowed to date until she's seventeen."

"If you don't want people to say those things," he said with affable dismissal, "don't dress like that."

He blew his whistle to begin the next serve.

◆ ◆ ◆

Pimply boys gathered on the third and fourth rows. None of them, as far as she could tell, had any relation to the St. Nick team. Like toads ready to leap off the pad, they spread their legs to take up space, their collective smell like unwashed laundry left for weeks in the basement.

Emily and Jessie squeezed next to Molly in the front row, a good twenty feet from the girl who'd harassed her. Ashamed, she couldn't tell Molly she'd let someone say such evil things to her. Now she had to endure these Beavises discussing what they wanted to do with girls on the court. Terms like *motorboat, eat her ass, jailbait, suck her tits, spank her, ass fuck,* and *gangbang* fell on her like effluvia from a sewer drain.

"Can you all stop?" Molly snapped at them.

They made defensive noises. One of them lifted his shirt to scratch his hairy belly. Another boy, terrified at her attention, timidly called her "Pretty black girl."

Emily felt her fists clench. Often, boys and men said things to Molly; dads at the grocery would compliment, say, her hair, as they eyed her budding breasts. In response to these particular boys, Molly stared at the far wall and fluttered her lashes as if typing sarcastic quips in Morse code. She insulted them to her friends, in a tone unlike how one human spoke of another, but as Madonna might inform a waiter that her *foie gras* was undercooked. She described their catcalls as *simian,* their appearance *uninspired,* their behavior *plebeian.*

"He really called me 'black,'" she said with contemptuous awe. "Yes, I have dark hair. I have dark skin. That is not a pickup line."

Emily was dazzled by her.

"Ain't she a peach?" she overheard Mr. O'Halloran say to another dad. "She gained a nice little bit o' weight there. She's got nice coconuts. Just like her mom."

Nervous, she snuck a backward glance like Lot's wife, to discover in horror that Tammy's dad was watching Jessie.

She had never liked him. At school functions he would seek out her dad to brag with false camaraderie about what he owned, clearly threatened by Matthew Olabisi's tax bracket. Once, at one of Tammy's Chuck E. Cheese birthday parties, the employees had to ask him to stop lifting random children by the waist to help them hit the Whac-A-Mole.

At that moment the skin-crawling sensation he gave her turned to fear. Thankfully Jessie, engrossed in the spinachy graphics of her Game Boy, had not heard him. Emily thought of her hero father, Mr. O'Halloran's opposite in every way. Pictured him in the fake leather backseat of a kabu kabu on the way between hospitals. Market stalls would line either side of the street. Daddy would be wearing a dark brown suit, brown tie and tan shirt, top button undone. Probably listening to Fela on the radio. A window cracked, he would be smoking a clove. Outside, the street would teem with pedestrians and danfo buses and okadas, noisy, but a welcome noise. A noise that made everyone into a single voice. This was how she imagined Lagos when he told her about it.

"I need to get out of here!" she said to Jessie. "I need to move. If I don't . . ."

"Yeah," said Jessie, "it sucks here." Without another word, she passed her Game Boy to Tammy's eager hands. Emily led her to the St. Alphonsus side. Not only did she hate the St. Nick bleachers, she was debating the merits of transferring schools altogether.

◆ ◆ ◆

In the Alphonsus stands, she sat surrounded by five dozen gaseous stomachs. No doubt, the greasy takeout bags and Kid Cuisine cartons piled around the footboards were to blame. People struggled to breathe as carbohydrates boiled noisily in their esophaguses. Every so often someone unleashed a cloud of methane, which she loudly complained of. Not that anyone cared.

The clock said eight. When she asked for the time, everyone said eight.

"It can't be," she insisted after the third person made the absurd claim, and said to Jessie, "Something is wrong here."

"I'm pretty sure it's eight," Jessie replied. In her hand was a slobbed-on Sonic the Hedgehog ice cream bar, Sonic's angry blue face melted with enzymes. "Not saying you're wrong. Maybe *everybody's* watches are broken."

Emily wondered if some madness had overtaken the crowd, possibly connected to the farting. But if their watches said eight—did that make her the crazy one? She decided to sit still and breathe deeply, let clarity fill her and with it find an answer. Instead she envisioned a flying saucer out of a '50s B-movie hovering over the gym with a giant magnet to ruin their sense of time and conquer the world. It annoyed her that school had made her dependent on having a working clock to neatly carve the hours.

The girls on the court looked half-dead from exhaustion. They chugged Gatorade from thermoses and awaited the next serve with their knees bent, out of breath. Full of nervous energy, Emily doubled over, clutching her stomach and groaning. "This is torture!"

That Jessie looked equally nauseous was a small comfort. "I think I might barf," she said with sudden amusement. "Do you remember that time I met Coach Cowher and I got nervous and barfed? My dad was so embarrassed."

"That's nothing!" said Emily. "When I was seven, I got really bad sunstroke in France and puked all over this glass pyramid. And guess what? The French people were mad at me because I threw up on the Louvre. So beat that."

Jessie quirked an eyebrow at her, then the two of them busted out laughing in spite of everything.

Finally Ascension beat Alphonsus three sets to two. It felt anticlimactic watching girls stagger to their benches, their shirts drenched like they'd been pulled from the ocean. Their shoelaces dragged. Their shorts sagged down their hips. The Alphonsus coach, a little red-haired woman, called them *failures in life*. Told them she only did this because the school required she lead a club. Told them that only men could play sports and girls should be cheerleaders.

Emily scoffed. "Bitch, much?"

Dismissed with a hiss from their coach, Alphonsus shuffled to the showers, past Ascension families who taunted them. *Na na na na, na na na na! Hey hey hey! Goodbye!* Even parents on the Alphonsus side joined in! Emily couldn't believe their lack of class. On instinct she looked to her home team bleachers, to the nuns. This was their gym! Their school! Certainly they would quash this display with a round of shaming such as the world had never seen . . .

Each nun looked to be enjoying it, blandly pleased, like Israelites witnessing the dogs eat Jezebel.

She heard a girl in the adjacent North Allegheny bleacher address Seven. "This is hilarious, Wanda!"

Wanda. Emily wondered why she cringed at the name. Seven regarded the subhumanity on display with a kind of tense prettiness. Her neck arched, her shoulders pinched, her flat affect speaking to unsurprised expectancy. From the Ascension crowd, a boy in a Penguins cap and untucked flannel shirt pointed at the girls and screamed, "Look at their clothes!"

Their uniforms only looked ragged because they'd been playing for seventy hours. Nevertheless, an insult rippled from tongue to tongue that these were the broke kids. It seemed everyone rose at once to pledge allegiance to Benjamin Franklin and Ulysses Grant, to Versace and Dolce, to Audi and Mercedes. Short-skirted girls threw pennies at the team. A measle-infested child in a pink princess costume dipped a wand in bubble solution to shake soapy water at them.

In the space of a few hours the parochial institutions that Emily took such pride in—Catholic, Protestant, Jesuit—had fallen apart like marble columns that crumbled to reveal papier-mâché insides. How could anyone associated with such prestigious academies behave this way?

Half a dozen Ascension students, male and female, lunged to snap towels on the girls' backsides. Like Jack the Rippers, blue veins jumped from their pale jaws as they screamed hate through anemic teeth.

Emily had to say something. "That's sexual harassment! Hey! Somebody listen—"

Suddenly a woman grabbed her by the shirt collar, snarled in her face, "How dare you!" A little round nun wearing an Alphonsus sweater; the band of her blue habit shook with anger over brown eyebrows like pinball flippers. Her pizza breath splashed on Emily like hot grease. "You better be careful with your accusations, girl."

She tried to pull away. "Let me go!"

"Do you want to ruin their futures?"

"What?"

"These boys have so much potential. You think because of O.J. you can do whatever you want!" She slapped her on the cheek. "That was for Nicole, you bitch!"

A great void swallowed up all she was or had been. A girl once called Emily Olabisi heard the toll of an infernal gong as she descended inexorably.

She snapped back to reality—the new reality. Ever since witnessing the impossibly gifted Seven, there had slithered across her mind a sense of cosmic wrongness. Like someone had forced a pair of demonic glasses on her face, the world came into lucidity: screaming, berating, jeering. Hands over ears and watery eyes. Pinching, poking, kicking. On every level of the bleachers dwelled tormentors and tormented, even underneath where subterranean elementary schoolers slathered victims with mud. Her mind surrendered to terror. All negative space in the room became home to demons wielding flesh-rending hooks, fiends from the visions of Saint Bridget. She felt the heat of the fire that never quenches and gives no light.

Wanda! Emily remembered, and sweat started on her forehead—burning sweat. She pictured Seven with a shoebox of hair and toenail clippings. She pictured her cutting a chicken's throat and drinking the blood to make herself a volleyball star.

A hand caught her under the elbow. Feeling her cheek throb, she saw Jessie had a hold of her. In her rage, the chubby girl looked wondrous and terrible. On their way to the St. Nick side, she dared glance back to see her attacker sprawled on a heap of purses. Jessie had slapped her.

◆ ◆ ◆

Wanda Jones came to St. Nick in the fourth grade. A scholarship kid from the Hill, a neighborhood Emily had only heard
about in relation to gang shootings on the nightly news, Wanda
sat in the third seat in the second row in Sister Anne Marie's
class.

Emily considered St. Nick her second home. She knew
the grounds—convent, pond, cemetery, annex, and gym—as
clearly as she knew the color of grass. She knew the driveway that branched off from McKnight Road to weave through
Bishop La Salle College campus and ultimately loop St. Nick.
She adored the age of the place: charcoal portraits of Mothers
Superior in the foyer; library books vandalized with KEEP ON
TRUCKIN' and KILROY WAS HERE; the buttressed halls
that made her feel like a girl in a storybook. She felt part of
something long and logical, her class the last ball on an abacus.

Instead of green plaid like the other girls, Wanda Jones wore
a shapeless gray jumper that hung like a sandwich board from
her bony shoulders. Neither fat nor thin, shaped like an upright
brick, she had a flat nose, her forehead high and broad, brittle
hair greased into two puffs around a Grand Canyon of scalp.
Her unplucked eyebrows stood up like bulrushes. From her
Peter Pan collar to her penny loafers, she smelled like cabbage.

At first Emily was entertained by Wanda. She would interrupt class with random outbursts like, "Theres a shark in the
clouds!" She would color in carpet fibers with marker. She
would refuse to sit crisscross applesauce on the ABC rug, but
rather in the back, where she'd busy herself drawing stupid
doodles of cartoon dogs. Infinitely patient, Sister Anne Marie
would implore her to come back.

"Make me," was Wanda's mantra. "Makememakememake-memakeme."

Sometimes, at her scariest, Wanda would sit through hours of instruction with her fingers laced behind her neck, her expression like that of someone who'd narrowly escaped a fire.

Before long some putrid boy asked Emily, "Are you two related?"

"I'm not related to retards," she told him.

That's what she called Wanda when teachers couldn't hear, *retard*. Never to the girl's face, because she'd grown a healthy fear of Wanda and her mouth. Any insult lobbed at her she could return threefold. She knew all the curse words. Moreover, when kids whispered about her it seemed she couldn't hear them, impervious behind her aura of wretchedness.

Nuns exhorted their frustration at her in long, fiery speeches about the horrors that faced bad little girls. (How Emily learned about pregnancy, come to think.) Sister Anne Marie tried to calm her with lies that the other kids wanted to accept her, if only she'd change her behavior. But it reached the point that the kindly nun withdrew a wooden paddle from her desk to spank Wanda in front of class. She had to stop on the sixth hit because the girl kept yelping like a dog.

Freak, thought Emily. *Crazy girl.*

But she seemed like something scarier. This stranger from the crime-ridden streets could turn sweet people cruel; she could make Emily feel like a stranger in her own school. She was reminded of the witches her parents said lived in Nigeria. Women who summoned demons and cursed good Christians.

A doctor was the natural enemy of a witch. Being a daughter of two physicians, it made sense she remove the stain from this sacred place.

Her plan was to frame Wanda for theft. Sneak in Sister Anne Marie's room during Music class, which doubled as her teacher's lunch break, and move her copy of *The Horse and His Boy* to Wanda's cubby. When the time came, cry about her missing book and—Bam!—get Wanda expelled.

On tiptoes, she removed the detritus from Wanda's cubby: the woefully outdated Fat Albert lunch pail, two Mad Lib books, a rotten banana, then, to her surprise, a Princess Jasmine doll. The heiress of Agrabah had lost her blue harem costume, leaving her naked, ungenitaled and identical to any Barbie except for her tan hue. The plastic jewel had fallen off the headband hot-glued to her forehead, her black nylon hair hardened into a piece of slag.

Emily stared in wonder at the skeletal bird wings jutting from Jasmine's back, probably snapped off a dead pigeon. The urgency of her crime faded as she took time inspecting this odd creation. The holes burned into Jasmine's back to insert the wings looked like miniature volcanoes, warped and rimmed with black scorch marks. In violating Jasmine, Wanda had made the most beautiful princess both stranger *and* lovelier. Emily shuddered to hold such a thing. A fetish made from death and imbued with dark power. She pictured it taking wing at night to sneak into her home and suck the blood from her and Molly's foreheads.

She told herself to leave it. Let this mad girl summon devils if she cared so little for her soul. However, as she returned it to the cubby, a cloven-hooved voice in her mind told her that she could truly hurt Wanda by taking this from her. She slipped the tiny golem down her jumper, and when the time came hid it behind a radiator.

Emily watched for Wanda to check her cubby at the end of the day. In a panic she threw everything inside it onto the floor. The mischievous smile she habitually wore collapsed into an ugly cry face. She ran to Sister Anne Marie's arms, a blubbering mess of tears and snot. Emily had to cover her mouth from laughing so hard.

That rag-doll image of Wanda was the last she ever saw of her.

But it seemed to her that the invader hadn't been truly exorcized. So, with a handful of friends, she buried Princess Jasmine under an oak tree on the playground. Dubbed Fancy Tree, it was once the place where they would sprawl in their own shadows and make up stories about themselves as medieval ladies. By third grade most had deemed such games childish, and some scoffed at Emily's ceremony. Thankfully she had Jessie there. Jessie Vessey Quite Con-tressy. Jessie Vessey Red of Tressy. Cheerfully whimsical, she showed such enthusiasm in dubbing a Styrofoam bowl of twigs and berries her *potion* that the girls happily lifted it like a talisman.

"We banish Wanda," they intoned through giggles.

"We say goodbye to the mutant Wanda Jones," Emily said as she laid Jasmine in the dirt. "You are condemned to a thousand years in the dungeon of Fancy Tree. May you never return."

"Wait here," Jessie had said, and left Emily in the lobby while she went to ask her mom if they could leave. *Hell.* The words knelled in her mind. *Fire. Damnation.* Mr. O'Halloran plopped his boombox down on the concession stand to blast Styx. "A JVC PC-X55 ghetto blaster," he informed the eighth grader doing sales, who endured this with his face buried in his arms. "Top of the line." Emily tried to wait, but terror overwhelmed her and she ran out the building.

The storm lashed her face with wind and sand. Knives of water stabbed her bare legs. Sango ripped the knots from her hair. Defiant, she took a step down the sidewalk, her head bowed, only to be picked up and thrown bodily into the tempered glass.

She found herself back inside. A sodden heap on the faux-marble floor, her mind turned to mashed potatoes, coherent thought impossible. In front of her was a pair of thin and veiny feet, like two malnourished salmon slipped inside jelly shoes. She managed to raise her head enough to see a hefty black camcorder aimed down on her. Below its cyclopian lens, the baleful smile of Tammy O'Halloran.

"Help me," Emily stammered, and attempted to touch her ankle, but the girl shrank away and made Emily crawl after. "You got it," said Tammy in a monotone. "Big volleyball star Emily," she mocked, until they'd reached the narrow hallway leading to the girls' locker room. There was something ugly about Tammy that made Emily cringe away from her on the opposite wall.

Dressed in an overlarge St. Nick sweater and plaid skirt, her skinny tormentor adjusted the lens to zoom in. "This is Tammy O'Halloran reporting for WPXI. Ma'am, why are you wet?"

"I . . ." She searched the wool of her memory. "I don't know. I think I went outside."

"Today we have an exclusive interview with Emily Olabisi, the seventh grade bitch." A piece of chewing gum careened around her teeth. "Tell me: Why do you make Jessie carry your books between classes? Why do you always have to say something if I get a higher grade than you? Why do you think you're better than everybody?"

Emily struggled to think, but Mr. O'Halloran had turned up his boombox so that seventies prog rock growled through the walls. Tammy's delight in her misery made Emily want to strangle her right there. To death. Make her dead. But the reality of their situation came back to her and with it an onslaught of comradeship, the urge to keep this petty and flawed human close, to protect Tammy's immortal soul.

"This place is cursed!" she said.

Usually, when a kid did something worth mocking, Tammy would look to Emily for permission to laugh. The conundrum of mocking Emily herself made her glance off at an imaginary ringleader. "You're being weird."

"Do you remember Wanda Jones?"

"Freaky girl from fourth grade? Do you want me to barf?"

"Do you remember what we did?"

Tammy grinned. "When you stole the Jasmine doll? You, like, really hated her. Like, borderline creepy level. What about her?"

A long-delayed spell brought on them by bad juju Emily had foolishly laid hands on.

A spell cast by a vengeful enemy.

A curse from the *ghost* of a vengeful enemy.

Scariest of all, this demonic revenant seemed to have Molly's face. Perhaps to take her place once they'd all killed each other.

"*Oooo-kaaaay*," Tammy mooed. "Wanda is Carrie White now."

Jessie returned looking outraged. "Mom says we can't leave. She's too busy telling Sister Katherine about chakra and crystals. *You have to be spiritual. You have to learn to mother yourself.* Woman, just because you listen to Yanni doesn't make you spiritual. I can't stand her!" She saw Emily and gasped. "What happened?"

The years they had known one another seemed to converge from Emily's subconscious into a palpable force that gave strength to her weary arms. Enough to take Jessie's hands in a desperate grip and protect this one certitude—a belief in the goodness of Jessie Vessey.

"Don't give in to hate," she said in reproach. "That makes it worse."

"Don't embrace the Dark Side, Luke!" Tammy laughed with gum-snapping aplomb, then deadpan, "We're not cursed because people are acting obnoxious at a game."

"This isn't the *worst*," Jessie said after a thoughtful pause. "Have you ever gone to bingo at the Elks Lodge? Those old Italian ladies are *crazy*." Remembering Emily, she admitted, "But this is really bad."

Jessie sat down to hold her. Miserable, grateful, Emily allowed herself the comfort of her arms before she spoke again. "Number seven is Wanda."

"Wanda Jones?" said Jessie, surprised. "I heard she was going to school in Monroeville."

Tammy looked imperious. "Seven's too dark. Wanda was mulatto." To Jessie, "She seriously thinks we're in Hell."

Jessie laughed nervously. "We can't be. Only sucky people go to Hell," she reasoned.

"We're not in Hell," Emily said to convince herself, and shut her eyes against the tears. In the dark she could see people snapping towels. "They'll hurt me. I can't go . . . I ca . . . I . . ." Her words staggered as she fought to keep down the gorge. She failed and threw up a purple cocktail of Cheetos and soda at Tammy's feet. Tammy screamed.

"Emily," she said after several deep breaths, "I've been putting off saying this a long time . . . but you take the Bible too seriously."

✦ ✦ ✦

"Can you please turn that down?" Molly said a second time.

The lobby reminded Emily of a toilet. Heaped raincoats and umbrellas had the floor slick with black water. Plastics and processed foods overflowed a single Rubbermaid trashcan. Most dismaying was the Alphonsus team huddled in blankets by the radiator. Cast out by families and coach and staring vacantly into space.

At the concession stand, Molly tried to reason with a sneering Mr. O'Halloran. Leaning an elbow on the counter, he rolled his eyes up into his head.

"Uh-oh. Angry black woman. Listen: don't you ever tell me what to do with my music." He gave a smile meant to look charming. "Listen, I'm a cool guy. I got black music. What do you want to hear? Otis? Prince?"

"You are being so rude right now."

Unnoticed, Emily watched this play out from behind Molly. In the back of her mind she could hear Wanda cackle.

"Who lost the game?" the self-declared king of concessions yelled with a flex of his hairy calves. "Who lost the game? Huh? *You* lost. That makes you a *loo-ser*. You made my little girl look bad."

"And you sound like a little kid."

This Hyundai salesman was addressing thirteen-year-old Molly as he would a woman he hated and desired. "When you have something that costs more than five cents, maybe you'll understand," he bellowed. "This is a five hundred dollar JVC ghetto blaster. None of that cheap-ass Chinese shit. Let me turn it up for you. You have no idea the power I have." He interrupted when she tried to speak, stressing his syllables like she was retarded. "Rich peo-ple have nice things. Poor peo-ple have no-thing. Why do you always hang around my daughter?

Why are you girls like a pimple on me? You're like a burden on me."

Within the terrible music, Emily heard strains of conversation from the gym. *Thirty thousand dollar car. Two hundred dollar watch. Five hundred dollar dress.* From her angle she could see inside at suburbanites either boasting or miserably enduring the boasting of others.

"What makes you so arrogant?" Mr. O'Halloran demanded to know of Molly.

"Our family is rich!" Emily screamed.

Molly turned and saw her, shocked at her appearance. Mr. O'Halloran smirked and said, "You're rich? You look like a mil lion bucks."

Emily shrugged away Molly's hand as she let loose her anger on this tanning-bed-crusted freak. Thirty-five hundred dollar mortgage? Try my parents own their own house. A pool in your backyard? Try imported mahogany furniture. Stuffed deer heads from your hunting trip in West Virginia? Try international travel to Paris and London.

Elevated by conceit, she became a living *curriculum vitae* of her parents' accomplishments. The asshole dad grew so flustered that he appeared to forget which ethnic minority he was gibbering at.

"I'm speaking Eng-lish!" he yelled. "Not Span-ish. Habla ingles?"

"What is wrong with you?" she countered. "I keep begging my parents to send me to boarding school. Then I won't have to be around people like—"

Suddenly Molly clamped a hand down on her mouth. Emily struggled and tried to bite her fingers. She saw that a crowd had gathered in the entranceway. They grunted the same as Mr. O'Halloran, *By what right are you so arrogant?* There in the mud-splattered cube of noise and sulking girls, she was reminded of her terrible fragility. The faces regarded her like she was a bruised banana—one they wanted to bite.

Molly spoke Yoruba to her. "They might mess with us if we call attention to ourselves."

"*Ibi yii ni eni-ẹgún,*" said Emily. This place is cursed.

"*Aran ni won.*" They are worms. "Stay with me."

They had to push through the crowd, who cast them malign looks. Tammy followed with her camera. "This is Tammy O'Halloran reporting for *National Geographic.* Here we see the Olabisi in its natural habitat. Emily's not your real name. Your name's Em-i-lo-hi. My dad calls her Ooga Booga."

Emily spit. Not in her face, like she wanted. At her feet.

Though she'd been the one to insist they stay careful, Molly almost went looking for the nun who'd attacked Emily. Terrified, Emily begged her to stay in her seat. That way she had Jessie and Molly on either side; these two girls were a reminder that she'd ever been something more than a coiled mass of fear, guilt, and hate. "Trust in God," she told her sister.

"I'll trust in lawyers," said Molly. "They don't get to beat you up. Mom's going to sue them for millions. The State Athletic Commission will hear of this."

It lifted her spirits to think of her mom in a courtroom where she would cast fiery vengeance on the nun and the hundreds in this gym and anyone who had dared give Emily emotional damage. Mom would bring Johnnie Cochran and a squad of implacable Nigerian aunties in iro and buba, and reduce their enemies to Raid-sprayed mosquitoes on a windowsill.

Trust in her loved ones and the hope for petty vengeance were her shield against absolute terror: the white people she could hear brazenly insult her heritage, or who bragged about what they owned as raindrops began to slaver from the ceiling beams and make this hell a wet hell. It brought her to the edge of madness to think the Hebrew names she'd prayed to for eternal life, the dour plaster icons whose presence she'd endured through countless masses in the belief they embodied divinity—they had forsaken her. She had no doubt the devils surrounding her would rip her to shreds at the slightest provocation.

Faced with despair, she was overcome by a protective numbness she told herself came from the Lord on high. He gave her the will to believe she would survive. So, impassive, she watched the semifinal match between St. Alexis and Bishop Canevin. From snippets of conversation she'd learned North Alleghany had made the finals after beating Ascension in embarrassing fashion. Wonderful! Everything was moving to a conclusion. Five teams were out of contention yet none had a thought of leaving. The defeated players joined their friends and family in teasing, laughing, mugging, hating, tormenting. Weeping, gnashing, cringing, diminishing.

She turned to face the puppetmaster not because she wanted to, but because she was compelled to. Shivers crawled over her skin to see Wanda—or whatever this thing was—huddled with her team on their bleachers, smiling and sisterly, giving the others a morale boost. No one had seen a coach for North Alleghany all day. North Alleghany all threw their hands in the circle and said, "One, two, three . . . Tigers!"

From there, Seven sat watching semifinals like a pro assessing her competition. If a player scored a well-earned point she would clap for them; she would wince if someone took a nasty spill. She'd laugh at her teammates' jokes and sling a few zingers of her own.

When Alphonsus tied Alexis at even sets, she clicked the heels of her white Reeboks and squeezed her knees together, excited.

Emily was forced to sit with a duffel bag on her lap as teenaged males told her what they would do with her. A few lascivious comments came from her own classmates, the same bowl-cut-wearing dorks she'd seen acting out *Mortal Kombat* Fatalities with their fingers at lunch yesterday. A thousand years ago.

A part of her wanted to snark, "Really, Dave Ricci? You're really going to do that with your one little pube-looking chin hair?" At one time, a girl named Emily would have said just that. A stupid girl who didn't know Hell was real.

As if summoned by perversity, Mr. O'Halloran returned to his seat and made his sickening presence known by cranking up the boombox. "Party time!" he yelled as groans echoed through the bleachers. Moms and dads covered their ears. Children wept. Mrs. Vessey—busy berating all four nuns about the limited parking at their school—stopped mid-tantrum to shout profanities.

"Shut up!" Mr. O'Halloran said. "If it's too loud then you're too old. Hey girl!" he called to Molly. "I'm sorry about earlier. Come here."

Emily squeezed Molly's hand to stop her from retaliating. It pained her to see Molly swallow her pride to try to ignore this man, tears in her eyes.

"I've had plenty of black women," the gross old satyr went on. "I'll pay you. Come here. Let's just talk."

Jessie gave both sisters a serious look. "He tries anything, I'll kill him."

No, thought Emily. *That's what she wants.*

She looked for Seven and found her standing to the side of her bleachers, a vision of dangerous calm within the carnival. Invisible to the crowd, she bent all the way forward and touched her forehead to her scabbed, durable knees.

The bleachers shook when Mr. O'Halloran leapt to his feet. "You won't come to me?" he roared. "Fine! I'll come to y—"

Another dad punched him in the face. Mr. O'Halloran crumpled and lay still in the footboard. The dad who put him down, a refrigerator in Zubaz pants, gave him one hard kick off the bleachers and onto the floor. Then he smashed the boombox to pieces on the cinder block wall. The St. Nick crowd cheered and chanted: "Here we go, Steelers, here we go!"

The hero spun to confront the other dads. "How long were you gonna let him do that? You're a bunch of cowards. You're a bunch of benchwarmers and I, Brad Zebrowski, am the quarterback!"

"Dad?" Tammy, who had been standing on the timekeeper's table filming a girl who'd sprained her ankle, determined to catch every moment of pain, came sprinting fast as she could from the other side of the court. Emily watched her skid to a halt beside her father and begin filming his unconscious body, giggling as she did.

Emily prayed.

She recited verse from the Book of Matthew. When she ran out of Scripture she sang hymns, Scottish and Irish and Latin translations; Keble and Tennyson; John Donne; pastoral epistles to keep Satan at bay.

Within her frenzied thoughts she heard the sins that damned her to this side of the Styx: pride, gluttony, avarice, vanity, theft. As she listened to her guilty conscience, she wondered if her life had ever been her own. What if Wanda had been guiding her all these years? What if Wanda had been controlling her since the day she'd shown up at St. Nick? What if it was Wanda who compelled her to steal the doll, her original sin the work of a malevolent hand?

She prayed to the aspects of the Almighty: Oshun; Olorun the sky-father; Eshu: Sango the thunderer, that he quell his wrath to let them out the doors.

"We just have to pray," said Emily. She felt lightheaded, a balloon sent whizzing to the sky. "We can't die here. It'll break Mom's heart. It brea . . it'a bray . . . Oh Jesus. *Lord Jesus!*"

She hated herself for causing this, but hated the unfairness as well, because no one else seemed aware of the conspiracy against them. Liberated by derangement, the puppets screamed and wept without a clue to the scalpel-wielding malignancy slicing their tissue open. Even as she pleaded with God, He refused to grant her ignorance.

Around eight a.m. St. Alexis won semifinals. A period followed in which they and North Allegheny refreshed with food and drink. Emily watched Seven make the rounds, encouraging her team. She knelt and tied a smaller girl's shoelaces.

At eight a.m. the Alexis coach wanted new finger gloves. Another coach offered to sell her a box on credit. Then began the bartering. Like thieves in the temple, they sold imitation jewelry, Mustangs, Air Jordans, skis, anything and everything of material value. Credit cards changed hands and the creditors hastily wrote numbers on the backs of their children. Debts increased by the minute.

"Daddy's gone!" Jessie yelled as her mom handed over her Visa for a new treadmill. "We need to save," she insisted, to which Mrs. Vessey told her to shut up.

By eight a.m. the accumulated trash converged toward the middle of the bleachers to form together like Voltron. Crushed soda cans and indestructible Mr. Pib bottles; Happy Meals, Kids Meals, Fun Meals emitting the plasticine odor of their toys; imminently breakable Disney figures used as projectiles; spilled bottles of Surge; plastic straws in commemorative Penguins cups; wrappers for Hershey Bars and Fruit Roll-Ups bunched in the treads like inching earthworms; leprous pustules of Bubblicious under the seats; an acidic syrup of Fun Dip; superhero comics depicting steroidal men with tiny heads and women with anti-gravity breasts; unspooled tape from overdue VHS rentals; "pearl" jewelry mixed with baby teeth; M&Ms melted to brown crust; tangled headphone wires; multicolored sprawls of shattered sand art; barrettes and scrunchies; charm bracelets torn off the wrists of former best friends, tin hearts and unicorns and half a zodiac of astrological figures that upon close examination resembled nothing at all; cardboard Sheetz coffee cups and silver Arby's roast beef foil; toothbrushes still in the plastic. This cornucopia carried the violet stench of perfume ads; pig fat off Chick-fil-A waffle fries; nail polish and acetone; pizzas rank with unrefrigerated meat; electronic games sounded hollow beeps and midi renditions of Tchaikovsky within the chorus of hate from halitosis mouths.

At eight a.m. Mrs. Vessey dropped her purse in Molly's lap. "Thanks," she said curtly then moved toward the ref like a pink barge. He appeared to have aged during the tournament, his shoulders stooped and beard gone gray. Mrs. Vessey planted her fists on her veloured hips.

"What the hell is going on?" she said to the cringing man. "Why do these teams get so long to prep for their games? You tell me now what makes them so special. I mean . . . Jesus! How lame are you?" Booed by onlookers, she addressed them with an air of infantile surprise. "I don't know why everybody's being mean to me. I'm just trying to do what's fair."

Emily heard others take up her attitude. *I want ice water. I want more M&Ms. That English teacher gives too much homework; they should fire her. Why do they let these people in here when they stink? Where is the manager?*

Tammy aimed her camcorder at a weeping Social Studies teacher. "You tell me right now why I got a B-plus and not an A-plus. You're on camera. This is admissible in court."

Emily could see the rage build in Jessie, who, after several deep breaths, handed Emily her duffel bag. "Hold this. Mom," she called as she stomped onto the court, "I want to call Dad."

Her mother looked at her with a sincerity that surprised Emily. "When we get home, sweetie. Mommy's just trying to set this right."

Jessie's cheeks crimsoned. "I want to call my dad *NOW!* None of this would be happening if you weren't such a bitch. You owe me big time."

The audience guffawed like a sitcom laugh track. "Believe me," said Mrs. Vessey in a regretful tone, "I tried to make it work with your father. It's hard being a single mom—"

"Everything's about how hard it is for you. You treat me like shit. You treat Dad like shit."

"I only wanted to make a happy home for us—"

"Everything's your fault. It's your fault I'm on meds. It's your fault I'm fat. I decree you make it up to me. I want a SNES game when we get back."

"Sure, sweetie—"

"I want a Sega!"

She refused to let her mom get a word in. Little by little, Mrs. Vessey diminished until Jessie seemed to tower over her. They found their own private corner of penance by the exit. To appease her, Mrs. Vessey offered Sega games and Huffy bikes. Dresses and shoes. She offered her junk food, from which Jessie devoured mouthful after mouthful, pausing only to belch before she demanded more of her mother.

Emily watched this unfold, grateful it was Jessie and not her.

Around eight a.m. North Allegheny took the floor against St. Alexis. Led by their captain—still no coach in sight—North Allegheny pursued the trophy with malicious force. They intentionally spiked the ball at their opponents' knees. If a North Allegheny girl fouled, her teammates descended on her like wolves to chastise. St. Alexis did their best to return in kind. Emotionless and aggressive, Seven would push her teammates out of the way to get at the ball. The thrill of the game got spectators stamping their feet. At last, some smash-mouth volleyball!

Around eight a.m., as Seven readied to serve, the middle blocker on the Alexis side collapsed. There was a hush as everyone regarded her prone body. Then the North Allegheny stands erupted. "They don't have enough players! —They forfeit! —We win!"

Emily blinked away tears. "It's over?" she asked Molly, who remained silent and tense. She dared to think about leaving. They would walk hand-in-hand through forest made wet and fragrant after the rain. They would kneel by a creek and thank God for their blessings.

Victory cries reached a pitch until the St. Alexis coach gestured them to hush. A tall, broad-hipped woman with a blond pixie cut, she wore a staff polo and capris. Amazingly, the people quieted.

The coach had a low and soothing voice. "Our prestigious academy recruits from around the globe. So I say, why not here?" Her gaze landed on the St. Nick stands. "Molly Olabisi." Fear snatched the breath from Emily. "We'll give you a full athletic scholarship," the coach promised, and waved her arms at the crowd. "Don't we want to see her play again? Mol-ly! Mol-ly!" She got them baying: "*MOL-LY! MOL-LY! MOL-LY!*"

Emotions battled on Molly's face. The desire for accolades. Fear at the consequences should she disappoint the mob. Emily clutched her arm.

"We're cursed," she said to no avail. Seven regarded Molly with serpentine calm as she rose from her seat, said goodbye to Emily with a kiss on the forehead. Emily begged, "Monisola! Stay with me!"

But Molly moved down the line of St. Nick girls to high five them. They broke the cycle of torment for one heartbreaking moment of solidarity. Tammy put down her camera to hug Molly, and Emily could feel her face grow hot with rage.

In the stands they hastily made MOLLY RULES! signs. Polaroid cameras spat out her image. Molly slipped on an Alexis jersey and took server position. A roar went up as she raised the ball on her fingertips, drew back her palm, unleashed.

As the ball soared back and forth, girls fell in exhaustion. They crawled injured to the benches. A Nordic-looking setter fell screaming in horror. A petite hitter drove her own right knee into the floor, repeatedly and on purpose, until it broke with a crack. The court grew slick with blood and excrement. Nonplussed, Seven moved graceful as a dancer over fallen bodies. Molly became outside hitter, right side hitter, opposite hitter, picking up the slack for her comrades. An iridescent volleyball angel, she dove out of bounds to save the ball. She headbutted and bicycle kicked.

Molly scored thrice in a row then dropped to one knee. Covered in sweat. Limbs trembling. A hand over her heart, her breath high and thin. Emily yelled, "Just stop! For God's sake, Molly!" But Molly rose to the sound of cheers and lightning flashes, and the roar of both sent vibrations through Emily's heart.

The whistle sounded. A step slower, Molly struggled after the ball. Seven got the three points back. Free from physical or mental strain, she looked as fresh as when they'd started.

The serve went to Seven's last teammate, a big-boned brunette with a pretty heart-shaped face. Her knees trembled and she spat insults at invisible people, sign of a shattered mind. She tossed the ball up and readied to serve, when Emily noticed an unmistakable brown substance drip from her shorts and down her left leg. It sickened her, watching the poor, gibbering girl crumple to the floor. Jeers from the stands. Laughter. As her teammate crawled away on her belly, Seven dribbled to start the next serve. At last she and Molly stood alone on either side of the net, a spaghetti western standoff that had the crowd cheering loud enough to drown the rain.

Molly laughed. "Let's go, baby! Let's go!"

Four thundering heartbeats ticked in Emily's ears. Then, silence.

She couldn't believe it. Every face had gone flaccid. In the hush her love for Molly felt like a physical thing, heavy in her arms. Barely able to see through her tears, she yelled, "I'm sorry, Wanda! It's my fault!"

Seven looked at her with confusion in her dark eyes. A moment passed where she almost resembled Wanda as Emily remembered her—a troublemaker, an artist, a loner, a little girl. Then her gaze flicked back to Molly, and Emily knew she was forgotten. She was unimportant, a faceless pawn. The beast focused her attention on the silly girl making bring-it-on gestures from across the net, her response a smile of loveless desire. Before she finished with her playthings, she would grind this girl down to nothing for sport.

Bump, set, attack. The rise and fall of the infernal sphere. It became a gray bullet. A red-winged devil with a monkey face. A world-destroying asteroid. Finally, an infinity symbol. Ouroboros—the snake that eats its own tail. Emily could see that the fiery Hell she'd feared was nonsense, a monster truck show overseen by a hot sauce mascot. In this Hell they would suffer an eternity unfulfilled, breath held for a vicarious triumph that would never come. Imbued with supernatural energy, Molly would not tire. She could not win . . . but she could not lose. She would play forever . . . or until her body gave out. Never grow up. Never find her own glory.

Emily raged at the injustice. That leech Wanda Jones had the nerve to think she'd been treated unfairly? Emily was just a kid who did something stupid and because of that she was going to lose her sister and everything else.

Her whole life they'd called her *bossy. Mean girl.* Here, in the world of tormented and tormentor, she picked a team. She breathed a prayer to Eshu and ran on court.

With mask-like faces turned toward her, she cartwheeled, did an aerial split, landed perfectly to pose before them with a peace sign at her forehead like Sailor Moon.

"Two for one!" she said.

Molly looked frightened. For the first time, Seven showed a flicker of doubt. Shaken from their fugue, the crowd roared approval for twice the entertainment. When Emily dared glance at them, their eyes were carnivorous. Emily borrowed a scrunchy for her hair. As she donned an Alexis jersey and tied on a bandanna to block the noxious stenches, she searched Seven's face for evidence of Wanda but saw no humanity. Only the desire to pluck wings off flies. Seven tossed the ball. She leapt.

Bam.

"Miiiiiine!"

Poised under the spinning orb, fingers laced, Emily brought them up . . . and pulled them apart. The ball rolled away. The crowd groaned.

Molly got in front of her. "What was that for?"

"Don't hit the ball," Emily said.

"What?"

"Just lose."

"Are you retarded? Get in position."

"They want us to play for their amusement. Let's mess with them."

"Get in position or I'll kill you!"

If this was Hell, let Emily be the demon with the pitchfork. With every net foul, she rained scorn on *You're not like the others.* Death to *You speak so well. Is Emily your real name* got a kick in the balls as she watched the ball go by without reaching for it. The sensation of denying the horde their entertainment was like stepping on all of their necks. Numb faces began to twitch in anger. They shouted scorn back at her. How dare this ungrateful girl refuse to play!

Molly tried to make up for Emily's deficiency with the innate drive of someone for whom excellence was the goal of every endeavor, but, incrementally, Seven led in points.

The ball came at Emily's face. She flinched away and threw up her hands. The crowd threw trash at this girly display. Molly dove in time to make the save. The ball somersaulted high. Molly took three lumbering steps, squatted, launched herself and, muscles rippling across her shoulders and arm, clocked it right on the chin with the heel of her palm. Seven wasn't ready. It hit her hand like a roundhouse kick and she screamed. St. Alexis scored a point.

"Can I serve?" Emily asked in a sheepish tone. Like a long-ignored little sister just wanting her turn. Seven looked wary as she sucked on the web of her thumb. After a hesitation, Molly snarled and tossed Emily the ball.

There before the crowd she posed. Like the athletes who crossed the Nyiri Desert, who trained in the fields of Dodoma, who fought through blood and sweat to the pinnacles of greatness. She dribbled, drew back her palm . . . then dribbled some more. Dribble. Fake out. Repeat.

"Are you serious?" snapped Molly.

"I'm ready." She measured the distance out the corner of her eye, spun, and hurled the ball at the bleachers where the beige hole of mediocrity called Tammy O'Halloran sat filming in the front row. Bullseye. Other than a busted lens, the camcorder was intact when it hit the floor; that crunching she heard was Tammy's face. The girl flailed and shrieked. Like a med student at the autopsy table, Emily took in her deconstructive handiwork with aloof fascination: Tammy's nose bashed into a flat triangle; a single incisor gleaming redly where her smile had been. A black bruise exploded from her lacerated upper lip to consume her cheek and swollen right eyeball and continue inexorably toward her scalp, her pale face made a harlequin mask. Ignored by the mob hurling invective at Emily, the girl flopped to the floor, drooling blood and hacking up shards of teeth.

Emily took a bow before the unworthy. "Seventh grade bitch."

Molly wheeled on her. "Go sit on the bench. I'm tired of you following me around like a puppy—"

It was then a ghoulish woman rose from the Canevin stands. "These niggers fucking suck at volleyball!"

The chorus said, "Do the tourney all over again!"

They charged the court. Immediately the sisters locked arms. Emily held her breath—she prepared to be transubstantiated. As they grabbed her face and hair, she thought of her father across the sea. Her sleeping mother. Borne aloft, she locked eyes with Seven and saw neither disappointment nor victory. Her thoughts lay beyond mortal ken.

Emily opened her eyes on a granite path speckled with desiccated leaves. Rain pattered her cheek. As if waking from a dream, she rose to kneeling. The storm had calmed—Sango taking a break. Down the path she saw flagstones disappear into nothingness.

Molly was kneeling a yard away from her, taking deep breaths and shivering. She did not look injured. She stared at Emily through her tangled hair. "Why did you do that?" she asked in a rasp.

"I had to," said Emily and lifted the hair from Molly's eyes. Through the glass doors she could see moving silhouettes, but she and her sister were banished. She threw her arms around Molly, who hesitated a moment before returning Emily's embrace. Together they walked off into the gray. Lethe fell on Emily. It seemed with every raindrop some sense of herself vanished. She struggled to remember her parents' names but knew she had to relentlessly push toward the shrouded world, so she soothed herself with thoughts of Jessie Vessey. Somewhere Jessie would leave Saint Nicholas before eighth grade and start public school in Shaler. She would listen to punk and date guys in bands. Junior year she would turn atheist, come to resent her dad and love her mom as the person in this world most like her. Jessie would enroll in a liberal arts college and become a protestor, a women's studies major, then drop out after becoming pregnant at twenty. After several years of working at Giant Eagle she would become manager. She would dye her hair and have tattoo sleeves. In her mid-twenties she would marry someone, not her child's father but a man who loved her, and visit the suburbs every weekend for coffee on the patio with her mom.

THE SON'S WAR

Dig, if you will, the picture . . .

The king's son lived to create. By an early age he had mastered botany, chemistry, all the realms of physics. Every moment he could steal from the duties of his father's house, he built automatons: insects, sea creatures, animals that walked and crawled and flew. No sooner did an idea climb down his brainstem than it found realization in his hands. So as not to waste time debating materials, he created from whatever he had on hand, be it fungus or dirt, even his own dandruff. He built like he had mercury in his blood, like he would die if he stopped, and who knew? Perhaps he would have. Soon he'd filled his father's house with inventions. Smells as green as spring and blue as winter rose to the forked-beamed rafters, all his creation. Nearly every sound and silence came from him. Foreign dignitaries visited the king's house, ostensibly on diplomatic missions, in reality to witness the wonders they had heard of.

It came time, his father decided, that the son move into his own house, one built sturdily of palm logs and mud. Before he left, however, father and son decided it best he have companions. The father gifted him a diamond stone and a jade stone, both the size of a fully grown person. For one sleepless, sweaty night, the son's chisel flashed up and down in the candlelight. Jewel shards glimmered among the rushes and a green mist thickened the air. Once he'd carved two women as beautiful as his eyes had seen, he gave them such biological functions as necessary for their purpose. He gave them advanced AI brains and ruby hearts that sparkled through their translucent breasts, the better to refract light into their cadmium veins. He sewed boots and dresses for them. Sharp in feature, lean in build and bearing the color of their jewels, they lived to serve him. These courtiers he named Diamond and Jade.

Certain tribes of his father's followed him to the new land. There the son built his house. Sleeping quarters, a kitchen, granary, and stables erected of mud reinforced with straw. Once finished, he mounted his ostrich and rode out to meet the people. He came before them in open-breasted kente robes, a veil below his eyes. The people spoke of drought. He gave them windmills and sewers and aqueducts. Aided by his agricultural innovations, their stores soon overflowed with millet and sorghum. As awed as they were enchanted, chiefs welcomed him as overlord.

The more obstinate ones refused the riches he offered. They called him a devil who offered toys with a silken glove, the better to conceal his clawed hand. These chiefs he challenged to combat, which proved none too difficult, as he'd trained Diamond and Jade in the most lethal martial arts. Champion after champion fell to them.

In time the son had a kingdom. He cooked a feast of yam and rice, goblin liver and suckled unicorn, palm wine and honeyed cider, and invited his newly ordained vassals to his house, where they supped long into the night.

Dressed in the most ostentatious robes, he held court on a teak stool, a cow-tail switch across his lap, his face hidden behind a ruby-beaded veil threaded into his adenla. His court was a beautocracy peopled by only the most splendid subjects, whom he dressed like himself, so that everywhere he looked was like staring in the waters of a clear river. They stayed as drunk on his wonders as any opiate, but to remain in his presence required they create. Art. Music. Films. Babies. Their wonders they laid before his stool, while Diamond and Jade stayed ever at his side, courtesans and bodyguards, sentinels of immaculate fastness.

One day he told the women, "You have been with me a long time. I would make you my protégés. Meet me in my Vault in the morning."

At sunrise Diamond gathered tools and descended to the tunnels beneath his house, which he called the Vault, a labyrinth carved to resemble the intricacies of his own mind. Before laying foundation on his house, he'd ordered the Vault constructed. She wondered where Jade had gone but had no time to waste in pursuing these thoughts. Diamond's crystalline legs begrimed on her passage through roughhewn tunnels, through chambers that shamed the grandest pyramid. Every embroidery on the floor and hieroglyph on the wall actualized his dreams, built to his specifications, though no one knew what became of those who'd constructed the place. Her role wasn't to ask about such things—she knew her lord had as much darkness as any ruler, and more than some.

She found him in his laboratory with a quartz leopard on the table, a panel opened on its back so he could prod the gears. So involved was he in his measuring scale—ground dragon horn weighed against a kirin horn—that he did not notice her at first. When he did, enraged breaths rattled the beads upon his lips.

"Where is Jade?" he growled.

Diamond admitted ignorance. With a brusque gesture, he bade her take jars of crushed herbs off the shelf. They would start with potions.

It so happened that Jade had stepped outside the house during the night, so she might enjoy a durian as she watched the sunrise. Moonlight illumined the pink petal trails that drifted in from the meadows. Grown indulgent with pleasure, the wondering courtesan trekked across zinc dunes to find the source of such aromas.

So it was that Jade forgot the hourglass and arrived late to the laboratory, halfway through his lesson on kinetic animation. The son scowled to see violets at her brow and her ankles. She prostrated on her ferric knees and claimed to have been distracted by a meadow which, from his chemical processes, had bloomed overnight with spring flowers. She had wandered among the yellow violet and hyacinth, seeing no fault in enjoying the fruits of their labor.

"*Our* labor?" He repeated her daring words with mockery. "You take credit for what is mine? You, who was born from my hand?" He grew furious. Like a sea lion, he bellowed until she ran from his sight.

Thus he ordered Diamond, for her first job as protégé, to shuck pearls from a hundred oysters, a gleaming heap he then tossed in a woman-shaped vat. From there began the process of animation. When they'd finished constructing Pearl, he made certain to program her with loyalty.

In the morning he brought Pearl to his amaranthine court, where Jade, who kept to the shadows, could see her replacement built identical to her in every way save coloring. Her desolate wail was met with indifference from the son, veiled and spiteful on his stool. When Diamond asked to comfort Jade, he denied her, ordered she remained standing to his right while Pearl took her place at his left. The coterie beset Jade with whispers and laughter, causing her to weep emeralds as she ran from the house in shame. A warning to all for the price of disobedience.

His spies told him she fled on her ostrich for the wild western lands, where he figured she would die. This little concerned him, as the great tinkerers and scientists of the age were coming to his house. With him, they made singing nightingales. Rain made of bark. Hills woven from human hair. Alongside alchemists and mathematicians, he rewrote the mysteries of the universe as formulae. He worked with doctors to heal diseases. He built telescopes for astronomers to view distant galaxies as easily as they could their own fingerprints. When he tired of collaborators, he sent them on their way, sometimes with gold and cattle, sometimes with no more than his thanks. Some received not even that. Everything in his land—towns, fields, his house and the caverns beneath—served his pleasure alone.

The son of the king never stayed at court for long, wishing to spend his days inventing new flowers and insects to couple with them. He rode through dream-meadows of white-stemmed and white-petalled roses, of genetically engineered purple hibiscus. People thronged the avenues to sing him songs of greeting. He held audience and listened to their problems. He bred crab-elephants for transportation and neo-trees for lumber. For entertainment he devised festivals. His people loved him.

Still, they knew little of him, because he veiled his face and his personal life. Some claimed that thousands of women had been cowed into submission by his boyish chest and sturdy shoulders, his beckoning fingers and untamed luminescence. Others claimed that he took one lady at a time as his princess (though what he did with them afterwards, no one could tell). They said women loved his touch because he could think like a woman. Some claimed he lay with men. Others said the very concept made him ill. Every story of a sweat-soaked orgy found its counter with reports of the lord's piety. Something about how he refused to be called a god, though others named him so. They said his work stole from that of a dozen artists before, yet was always something they'd never seen. They said his name was so divine it could not be spoken aloud. A rumor arose that his mother must have pale skin, given the honeyed hue of his fingers.

The parentage rumor amused him the most, because he'd started it.

It delighted him to make them guess. Another kind of creation, these controversies, stories woven until he lived a hundred lives. They were left to wonder: What man lived behind the veil? What truth dwelled within the serpentine eyes that flashed like volcanic embers when a wind shifted the beads? Eyes that caressed you, bewitched you, took all of you and gave you nothing back.

One day, after many hours of hearing petitions, he could take no more. He yearned to return to the clanking and odors of his lab. As he announced court adjourned, Diamond swept through the beads in travel-stained robes. She prostrated herself.

"Long may the crown rest upon your head. Long may the slipper touch your feet." Without further formality, "The reports are true. The land on our western border is in chaos and disorder."

This troubled the son. For as long as he remembered, the western lands had no ruler, peopled by fiercely independent nomads. They would not trade with him—not only did they refuse his gifts, they would send his emissaries back with missing appendages. Rumor was a strong and terrible king had wrested control after much bloody conflict.

"Speak," he told her.

"The crops will not grow," said the scintillant woman. "The rivers are brown with refuse. Babies are born dead. This new king has brought them famine and despair. The people call out your name! I heard this with my own ears. They pray you will liberate them!"

Her insolence to propose such a thing vexed him, as he cared only for his own realm. It irritated him that his courtiers were staring his way like they expected him to perform a trick. Ever enigmatic, he lifted a hand to raise the veil from over his mouth, a mischievous smile the only answer they would get. Without a word he left for his chambers. The next day he decreed that none were to speak to him about the western lands.

The son of the king made creatures that were half woman, half kiln. One-third goat, one-third worm, one-third vinyl record. Half man, half dragon, half cat, half bat, half velvet. Timidly, an advisor told him he could not do this forever. He had the advisor banished to the west.

He learned of the Mountain Queen and her great beauty. Infatuation sent him into the mountains on a flying carpet, at the head of a caravan bearing such gifts that befit her stature. He seduced her. They married in a ceremony only witnessed by their trusted servants. For half a year he stayed at her court, then for half a year she at his, until their marriage grew volatile because neither could be tamed. The queen returned to her house in the sky and there she remained. For some time afterward, the son cast a brooding figure.

And the people wondered: Was he son or daughter? What lay under the feminine walk like curtains swaying? What lay under the wolfish growl? When he rode through the streets, they genuflected and called, "Omo Oba! Omo Oba!"

A farmer, past the age of holding his tongue for anyone, asked: "When will you refer to yourself as king? After all, kings bow to you."

Normally he would suffer no such questioning from a commoner, but the musicality in the farmer's rusty voice compelled him toward diplomacy. His response: "Tell me of one king whose name causes hearts to tremble like mine. Whose name commands fear and love like mine. I will challenge him, slay him, and burn his house to the ground."

They could name no one.

"Every nation has a king," he said. "I abhor to do as others do."

On the solstice of the eternal sun-swell (he'd determined the word *day* boring, and none could utter it under pain of death), he held court. Pearl came before him. "Long may the crown rest upon your head," said the nacreous woman, "long may the slipper touch your feet. Omo Oba, the western lands are bleeding. Their king's secret police, called the Green Fourteen, kidnap people in the night. Thousands are tortured and murdered. The people fear even to think thoughts against him, but when they dare speak out, they call for you to annex them! They wail and gnash their teeth to be as happy as we."

He barely heard her, entranced in his new litter of narwhal-leopards. He would toss lava rocks from a bowl and watch the sharp-toothed kits snap them out the air. To please him, they rolled on their backs and belched fire. This continued until the son had fully amused himself. Hunched on his stool, he fell to tedious business.

"I am not interested in conquest," he said. "Conquest is for those who have no resources, who can think of nothing better to do than take. I have an abundance. Even as I speak, my aqua-machines make rivers in the southern marches. My neo-trees grow into forests I have gifted to the monkey kings. I wish for no more than I can make with my own bone and dreams, which should be more than enough for any of you." He gave his robes a flourish. "We are done."

He brooded on the matter in his chambers. In truth, he feared to spend time on anything other than creation. That it made others happy mattered nothing to him. (The satisfaction of his subjects had always been windfall for his personal happiness.) War meant destruction and, as of yet, he knew not how to make destruction beautiful. To think on it made him feel less like royalty and more like a crustacean, immobilized in a shell. To wage this campaign would depress him, drain him, kill him.

It seemed his courtiers required some response, so he built a machine that echoed his own voice and programmed it to howl in torment all night. The baleful noise found its way through chinks in the wood, filling the compound until neither seer nor servant could rest. None save the son of the king, who slept well.

After all, his greatest creation was the mystery of himself. They knew of his obsessions. They knew him for a princox, a popinjay, a ponce, a prick, a playboy, a putz, a puck, a piece of shit; they knew that his narcissism equaled his talent. The rest was theirs to guess.

He would have nothing to do with death. He didn't even believe in such a thing.

In a mania, he made wonders no one had conceived of. Purple ladders. Fruit you could wear as a hat. Recipes for starfish. Twenty-three sex positions. Daisies with petals so bright they blinded. Entire cities devoted to the erotic. Lakes that purified. He made the most beautiful girl in the world, so beautiful he nearly abandoned his duties to run away with her. He made so much that he gave it away to others. Thus he built alliances among the kings and queens. And once he'd created to the point of exhaustion, he wasn't done. Not nearly.

But when he went out among the people, he found them disgruntled. Over the years, they'd grown certain of their superiority to those in the west. Theirs was a civilized land, they said, while those people lived in barbarism, savages ruled by a dictator. Conquest of the west seemed to them a birthright, one that he, as their leader, should supply. So when he supped with his vassals, the seers cast palm nuts in their trays and recited the mysteries, all pointing to a victory that would live in song.

"No song that I will ever sing," he scoffed.

To compound the outrage, his subjects questioned him to his face. *What will you do?* chiefs would ask of him, scowling with deferred ambitions.

He cursed himself for his blindness. Of all gifts, he'd neglected to give them enemies. Their nationalism disgusted him. Only *he* deserved to think so highly of himself.

"The malcontents have a point," Diamond told him that night in their pavilion. She sat spread-legged on a stool, her naked body mottled with candlelight. Pearl sharpened her spear in the shadows. "The western king is a monster."

"And I am not a monster?" he asked. "This afternoon, I executed a chief, and his son, for daring to question me." He swallowed a lump in his throat. "And the three pages. I still smell their burning flesh."

"They gave you no choice," said Pearl in a low voice. "They said they would never bow to you."

"I am not sad I killed them," he said, though the tightness in his throat remained. "I just don't understand. They were mere pages. Why die for him? Or any chief?"

The boys had so impressed him with their courage that, when Pearl lit the kindling beneath their soft feet, he'd expected them to burn in silent condemnation. To become lions with manes of flame. But in the end they screamed like chickens being slaughtered. Though he wished to love their memory, he hated those arrogant brats. He'd have killed them a thousand times if he could.

"Too many songs around the fire," said Diamond with typical calm. "They thought it their time to be warriors. Omo Oba, you are only partly a monster. And I would say your higher nature balances your monstrosity. The western king is all monster. As long as he breathes, he shows the world your way isn't the only way. How long before he attacks us, as he's attacked his own people?"

The son poured two cups of wine for them, coconut milk for himself. He passed them the cups and lay on the furs to stretch his naked body. "What do you think?" he asked Pearl.

Grim existentialism coruscated her square-cut features. "We will have to fight. Either the western king, or these malcontents who believe you weak. I will go where you tell me to go. I will kill who you tell me to kill."

Such confusion! He loathed to show indecision before even his two most trusted, which would look like weakness in a king, let alone the son of a king. To clear his mind, he lay with them. Naked—as clothed—they held no secrets from him. They had served as spymasters, explorers, treasurers, priestesses, champions, and emissaries—now they wished to be his generals. It became clear to him that they chafed at the long peace he'd cultivated; thinking their edges dulled, they sought battle.

Nevertheless, their words plagued him as he lay awake beneath the humid air. Diamond worked her crystal tongue up and down the serrated plane of his ribs. Maybe she could hear his heart ache for those in the west. At last he recognized this foreign sensation as sympathy. To save the helpless on such a grand scale would be a new experience.

In the morning he came before his people naked and unveiled, and it seemed in his nudity they knew less of him than before. "To war!" he said.

He set about building an army such as the world had never seen. He made tanks, siege engines, and swords. Machine guns and racks and iron maidens. Cat-o'-nine-tails and thumbscrews and atom bombs. Hovercrafts that flashed like silver-winged birds in the sky. Chemical bombs that exploded pheromones; they would make the enemy's cats supremely amorous, to overrun his temples and marketplaces with mongrel felines. He programmed marksmen who could strike a beetle from the air with one shot. Afterward, he bred mermaids born with the lower halves of women and upper halves of trout; having no arms to hold weapons, they would fling themselves at the enemy until his bullets were spent.

He made a suit of quilted armor that would enhance his strength tenfold. He sewed a turban to keep the sun from his eyes and carved a black wooden helm horned like a ram.

On the night before they marched, he took to his room to make his ultimate weapon. His nervous courtiers waited outside as night swelled the belly of the hourglass. In time they slept.

Later, they startled awake at the sound of rattling beads. They saw a shivering hand emerge from the curtain, followed by the dawn-limned visage of their lord, who appeared to have aged ten years overnight. Sweat coated his bare chest. He collapsed into their arms. They fanned his valleyed cheeks with palm leaves and dabbed his dry lips with water. The orange gourd strapped to his back seemed altogether unremarkable, which only emphasized its dread portent.

That morning the son drove in a tank carved from a titanic gourd to greet his army on the grasslands. Foot soldiers and vassals stood in all their panoply, sunlight glinting off their spearheads. His hippo-lions and ostriches wore battle armor. His organic men dressed in robes slit up the side to provide for movement, and each one hailed him with their bronze sword. The admiration of his troops approached fanaticism. For these young men, his slightest wish outweighed every ambition they'd ever had for themselves. They would sacrifice anything and everything. He told himself to love this.

Diamond led the vassals, Pearl led the suicide mermaids, and he personally generaled a thousand thousand automatons, warriors of steel and iron. Their flesh inlaid with jewels, they stretched over the meadows like a rainbow-hued river, and in their thousand thousands appeared more numerous than the blades of grass they flattened on their westward march.

Along the trek he beheld shining cities arisen during his reign, where fat merchants thronged the avenue to soften his tread with chrysanthemums. There rose jade ziggurats where philosophers debated the mysteries. In sun-skewering towers made of quartz, astronomers read the stars. A haze fell upon his

senses like the veil he had cast off. Moments had arisen where
he would look on his army and see only colorful insects, hear
only the militarized drone of bees. His old confidence returned
when dazzled by the wonders of his realm.

They traversed swampland. Crocodiles ate his men while
others died of airborne pathogens. Around the fires, they said
their lord would devise a pump to drain the poisoned water
from this bog and turn it to bubbles on which they would float
to safety. And though he wept when Diamond gave him the
tally of dead, he did nothing.

After the swamp came a mountain range. The narrow passes
funneled their army to a train of stumbling and exhausted
bodies. Some men died in avalanches, others from fatigue. *He'll
turn the rocks into food,* they said, but he didn't, so they starved.
Suspicious whispers rose around the fire. They questioned if
they followed a cruel lord to their dooms.

Then came the village. The odor of devastation pierced the
walls of the tank to lodge in his throat and gag him. Strapping on a gas mask, he opened the lid to survey hovels built
in disarray. Above him the vultures made circling dots. Gray
peasants clung to their doorways, all bone and eyes and fear.
Because Pearl had prepared him with intel, he was unsurprised,
yet nonetheless disgusted, to see the villagers had holes in the
shape of figs where their noses had been severed. Their king
had decreed that only he may smell. The wind belonged to
him, as did all dreams, all truth. The villagers stared at the army
of liberation like it was a scent in the grass—something they
longed for but could never have—and despite his nausea the
son pitied them. Such wanton cruelty steeled his resolve to
decapitate this villain. On the dismal plod through the village
he kept one hand wrapped under the gourd upon his back.

With the village behind them, Diamond reported that urchins were following. Five dozen mangy, potbellied creatures crying out for food. Sustained by the despair in their broken bodies, they showed no sign of quitting pursuit.

"All must earn their keep," the son said gravely. The children were given machine guns and made soldiers. Diamond had to take each one individually and twist their fingers, gnarled as apple cores, around the triggers.

Stretching between the border towns and the enemy's black-walled capital were miles of savannah, monotonous bushes and stunted trees. The corpses of disease-ridden gazelle and starved lions littered the plain, their blood so befouled even the flies avoided them, with scant cover for an army of his size. The son delighted in knowing the enemy would see him coming in all his majesty. His scouts reported burning villages on the road ahead. He called halt. He emerged from his tank with a megaphone.

"Noble warriors," he addressed his army. "The jackal wants to send us a sign. Are you scared?"

"No!" they roared.

"Will we win?"

"Yes!"

"Stake tents. I have led you well these last three years. But do not think you have seen all the gifts I will give. My reign has only begun," he said to cheers that shook the heavens. "With you at my side we will create a new age. It starts with this victory! Tomorrow we take his city!"

Their cheers continued unabated until their throats were raw. That evening he retired to his tent, relieved to find freedom from their adoration. He'd brought his ostrich mount for companionship, though she did little more than provide witness to his agitation, her feelings of neglect coached in a low squawk as he paced the reeds. Much could go wrong and, though he loathed his own weakness, he knew without Diamond and Pearl he would lack for strategy. He voiced his fear of failure, cursed the enemy to a thousand deaths, and drank liberally from a gourd of goat milk.

Diamond and Pearl arrived to report. Each carried three calabashes of gunpowder atop her head, held with netting like wives bearing water to the village. Their faces bore the white chalk markings of priestesses, a role they acted nightly to get the soldiers' blood up. Confidently, they said his TV-headed propagandists had infiltrated the villages to seduce the farmers and fishermen with utopian visions of his lands. They told the peasants that the great lord had come from the east to rain freedom. The Creator. The Problem-solver. The Giver of Gifts. It would be only a matter of time before they rose against the tyrant.

During the report, a scout entered to say the enemy had arrived to parlay.

Only a fool would not see the ambush coming, but his scouts reported no soldiers for a league, only villages put to torch. Thus emboldened, he rode out, flanked by Diamond and Pearl, to show the enemy his teeth. He dressed as a warrior in armor, horned helm, two necklaces made of cork, and a hippo-lion's tooth.

Three women waited for him in the open savannah. By the torchlight he made out their ostrich mounts, their antelope masks painted with long teeth and carved with slits for eyeholes. The one in the center wore silk robes corseted at the waist, a heavy woolen scarf raised to her cheeks, silk breeches and calfskin boots. She lifted her mask and he could hear a choked gasp from Diamond at the green face beneath. That the son shivered to see her did not escape Jade's notice; nor would much escape her notice, he learned, as she pulled down her scarf to reveal the entirety of her sardonic face. Her new lord had taken her nose but given her new eyes—one in each cheek. The green orbs regarded him with contempt after so many years.

"A sculptor is summoned and the woodpecker shows up," she said.

"You need a long spoon to dine with the devil," he proverbed in retort. He moved the gourd from his back to his lap. "Jade, fine clothes will never conceal what a disappointment you are. Tell your master to surrender and I will spare his forces. That is the best he can hope for, as I intend to execute him."

"Our master is a god," said Jade.

"It is the great privilege of my life to serve him," said the woman to her right, her voice hollow behind the mask.

"He has accomplished more than any king in history," said the woman to her left.

The son shouted, "I will make his head an ornament on my saddle. His heart will be eaten by lizards. His skull will be a home for rats. Tell him that I will kill him piece by piece and the thing I will make of his body will be my masterpiece."

Jade tapped her fingers on her lips with a theatrical yawn. "It was you who taught me cruelty when you banished me to this place. But my master taught me cruelty as an art. I sat at his feet and read the infernal scrolls. He taught me the ecstasy of murder."

"Which qualified you to be his errand girl," Pearl spat.

The eyes on the left of Jade's face stayed fixed on the son. Those on the right swiveled in Pearl's direction. The son felt a chill. "And you are *his* whore," Jade told Pearl, who snarled and reached for her sword. Immediately Diamond laid a hand atop hers. The son noticed them struggle, a test of strength that the shell-shucked woman quickly lost. With Pearl suppressed, Diamond turned her attention back to Jade.

"I cannot speak for Omo Oba," she spoke with affection, "but you were my sister once. If you would come back to us, all is long forgiven."

"I never said that!" the son snapped.

Upon Diamond's offer he could see the conflict ripple across Jade's face, before he interrupted and hatred flared once more in her quadrupled gaze. A cold hand of fear squeezed the back of his neck, traveled down his spine to sink fingers in his gut. Worse was the certainty he'd lost Diamond. That poisonous drop of disobedience had infected her and, no matter the outcome of this war, she would never be his again. Incensed, he banged the flat of his sword on his elephant-hide shield.

"Shut up already. Damn." To Jade, "Those are my terms and you will deliver them."

In a dispassionate tone, she addressed Diamond: "You were my sister, true. I shall weep when I kill you. And I shall always hate him for the rift he tore between us. The nuts have been cast and we all have our roles. But know until I die you will always be my sister." With a sudden smile, she cast her green eyes on him, their facets lit with vengeful triumph. "Know this, princeling. In reward for my loyalty, my king has allowed me to witness your shock and terror. Doubtless your scouts told you about the burning villages on the road ahead. Soon your army of ticks will smell the sweet fumes of petals I grew myself. I imagine half of your rabble will die within the hour."

The surprise must have registered on his face, because she howled with sadistic laughter. Her desire won, she wheeled her ostrich to turn. He saw four eyes in the back of her head as well, all of them hateful. Swift and silent, Diamond threw her spear at Jade, but she easily deflected with her shield. Aiming for the women as they galloped away, Pearl loosed an arrow that took one masked rider through the back of her neck, and had the next arrow nocked when the son stayed her hand.

"To camp," he said in horror. With a kick to his ostrich's flanks, he made haste for the fires of his host. On the gallop across the hard land, his creeping distrust of Diamond compelled him to ride at a distance from her. For now he needed her, more than he cared to admit, but after this war he would scrap her. Replace her with a woman of gold.

Jade did not bluff. All through camp his flesh-and-blood men clutched their throats. He wandered among the sick, a hand over his nose, to discover he could still breathe. The antidotes he'd brewed to build tolerance to poison had made him an atom of life in the massacre, the pointlessness of which struck him with melancholy that nearly consumed him, before Pearl's voice snatched him back from the pit. She was rallying doctors from their tents to administer healing balms.

He had lost many troops, not the half Jade had gloated of. Overcome with relief, he needed his soldiers to hold him up, else he'd faint away. When he crossed paths with Diamond he said nothing to her. Let her know he considered her a broken machine.

The reprieve left him unprepared when the earth trembled, opened, and erupted forth carnivorous snails the size of elephants. The war began.

As bloody as a battle could be, as long as a battle could be, this was. Hippo-lions rammed their catapultian skulls into snails. Hovercraft fighters dueled to the death with bat-winged salamanders. Two evenly matched armies of automatons clashed, the rending of metal a terrible song as night greyed to morning. The son didn't know by what means he survived; a dozen times he should have died, before some stroke of chance caused an arrow to miss or a mounted foe to fall gurgling on his own blood before he could spear his regal target. Something about this battle seemed familiar, like a memory of the future. He thought only of survival as he slew from atop his mount. Everywhere he looked were acts of heroism from men whose blood and names would dissolve into the soil.

His bodyguards made a perimeter of gunfire to push back the enemy that seemed to spring from the ground like hell-demons. They bought time for Diamond to climb a siege tower. The son looked through a spyglass to where the enemy gathered on the high ground. Dust plumes nearly obscured a figure who must have been their king. Dressed in heavy furs and a leather hood, he reminded the son of a ghost from the underworld, his face hidden by a mesh veil decorated with seashells. He stood on the back of a crocodile, reins in one hand, the other clutching the switch with which he lashed his steed.

The son passed the glass to Pearl and heard her suck her teeth, the sound like two stones clacking. Only now did he see his foolishness for letting someone amass such an army. Glutted on prosperity, stupefied by his own magnificence, he'd failed his people and himself. He looked to the siege tower where Diamond stood shining on the precipice in all her glory. He gave a nod.

A flute to her lips, she blew a long and buzzing note that rang over the battlefield like the last song of a dying god. The doors on the tower burst open and there emerged swarms of murmuring wasps. They unfurled like a great cape toward the enemy lines, in numbers that extinguished the sun.

Exhilarated by the darkness he'd created, the son snatched the spyglass from Pearl to behold his bio-weapon. When it seemed like they might spear the heart of the foot soldiers, the phalanx split in half. As one thrumming unit they stretched to make a *V* around the army. He rejoiced in watching the masked king jerk his mount back and forth, unable to hide his fear. Noseless foot soldiers sounded horror and confusion, stabbed futilely at the bugs that inexorably closed their two ends together like a shaving razor. The son and Pearl howled gloating laughter. The deadly pincer engulfed his enemy with a cacophony of rending metal and screams that filled the air for minutes. When the wasps cleared, their numbers vastly depleted, they left in their wake a third of the enemy destroyed.

Pearl clapped with joy. "Yes! You are a genius, Omo Oba! The greatest genius this world has seen!"

Diamond appeared at his side, having swiftly descended to mount her ostrich. The son hoisted his spear to catch sunlight on the blade. "Charge!"

The earth thundered. Dust billowed under their mounts. Ancient war-cries sounded from their throats, as if they were possessed by bloody ancestors who had forged empires. Her skin impervious to dust and arrows, Diamond outdistanced the son. Wielding a spear in each hand, the incandescent angel of oblivion, she raised her blades high to bring them down in a scything motion. Her every blow made a cripple, a widow, an orphan. Pearl undid the netting atop her head, lit the bombs, and threw them at the enemy. Explosions blasted the savannah. Flesh rained on the parched earth. Automatons at his back, armor pumping vitality to him, the son hacked limbs and cleaved skulls to the teeth. Made tumultuous with blood and corpses, the terrain grew difficult. Still he pushed his mount past fatigue. He, the son of hate, would redden a kingdom to stab at his enemy's throat.

Soon his mount fell in the tangled bodies and in doing so hurled him down in the morass of gore. He wallowed helplessly like a sow in the slaughterhouse. He rose, fell, crawled, rose, stumbled, retched, and rose, his armor spurring him to stand. Dust swelled his throat. He could see an ostrich decapitated at the base of its neck. Its body was coated in thick black feathers, its scaly legs tangled in a way that resembled a sage sitting crosslegged, and blood spurted from the stump. He found himself marveling at how the head that lay yards away looked like some slithering bird-snake hybrid, how its beak kept opening to try and speak.

As if in a dream he saw Diamond, her robes tattered, calm amidst the horrors. She removed a bomb from her headdress and lit it with her lighter, and it was then he saw the dozen enemy soldiers charging, closing the fifty yards between them. "*No!*" he yelled, but the incendiary flew from her hand. The earth flowered dirt. The son went airborne. Debris and twisted metal clotted the sky. Heavily, he struck the earth.

Blind. Strangled. For a desperate minute he floundered in airless dark. When he finally knuckled the dirt from his eyes, he found Diamond on her knees, pinioned by half a dozen spears. He knew she was dead, and he wept. Some would have called her an artificial person, but he knew nothing was more real than that which he created.

Bearing a dozen cuts from enemy bronze, Pearl rallied her mermaids in a charge at the king, so close to them the son could hear his seashells rattle as he hollered commands. Five antelope-masked bodyguards surrounded him.

"Follow them!" the son roared to his remaining forces, a clutch of automatons and ostriches and what remained of his vassals. The shout of the battlefield drowned his words. They charged.

By the time he arrived, breathless and hacking up saliva, the mermaids had died to the last. Most perished assaulting a snail that had moved to shield its master. They lay among its shattered shell, green ichor oozing from holes their spears had made. The sight of their delicate legs severed and crushed gave the son pause. More pitiful were the mutilated fish faces already starting to ripen, a dinner for the flies. Among them lay Pearl, who had speared the snail through its throat even as it flattened her under its belly, a smile on her lips.

A spear flew at his face. He dodged to the right. Another moment and the blade would have gored him. He thrust his spear through the antelope-masked woman's belly, the force of which jarred his arm to the shoulder. Blood spewed from her mouthhole. Even as he jerked the blade free, the rest of them charged, wolf-eyed women bearing spears and cudgels. Behind them he saw their mounted lord, Jade at his side with shield and sword.

Mad with bloodlust, the son met them with bronze. Strength pumped from the armor into his exhausted limbs. For Diamond and Pearl, he hacked and dismembered.

Five lay dead at his feet. Jade vaulted over their bodies. It seemed as if she moved through water, so clearly did he see the blade stab for him. His shield-arm refused to rise. Metal punctured his breast and kept driving until it exited his back. In terror he saw his blood gush down the quilting. Four eyes glimmered down on him, soaking in the kill. With his left hand he gripped the pommel and stopped her from twisting the blade. With his right he squeezed her neck. She had time enough to register shock before he crushed her throat to green shards. Her head landed at the foot of her lord's scaly mount.

The veiled one regarded the head only a moment before turning his masked visage to the son. Unarmed, he extended both hands with the dusty palms turned upward.

"Come!" said the enemy. "Come!"

The son's armor was rags. Knees buckled, he cast aside his broken spear and hefted the sword of a fallen soldier. In the din of battle, a hush fell over them. He saw dead bodies everywhere and sorrowed for all he had wrought. He tried to banish this weakness but it grew roots in him. It seemed there would be no end to the bloodshed, that it would sweep them all in a tornado of corpses until the world was dead.

The son let drop the sword. Because he still had his ultimate weapon strapped to his back.

Instead of running for his enemy, he made for a hovercraft that had crashed but remained intact, quickly started the engine. As he flew heavenward, he heard a roar from the veiled one.

"Coward!"

The son clung desperately to the handholds as the air grew cold and thin. Below he could see the bodies of his subjects clog the savannah, pieces of jeweled skin blowing like tumbleweeds. His legendary army turned to leaves in a gutter pipe. The shouts of triumph or defeat grew faint. Wind and sorrow brought tears to his eyes. He flew far and away from the battlefield, only to find, when he looked down, the relentless enemy following on his steed.

He was pursued over savannah and field to the murmuring coast, where the ghosts of mermaids sang to fishermen and gulls dreamed of when they were princes. Where the tallest palm in the kingdom grew atop a precipice. The sun had begun its descent as the son angled for a landing. The smell of destruction still clung to his nostrils, the smoky scent of regret. The wound in his chest bled. His vision dimmed.

"You'll be glad to know you finished me, Jade," he rasped. "I am left without my kingdom, my stool, my art. I am nothing." Too weak to operate the controls, he could no longer decelerate. The nose of the machine slammed full force into the earth and sent him airborne. Only the remains of his armor protected him as he rolled several feet. Battered and bruised, he rose unsteadily, stripped off the torn armor so he could move freely in his breeks. Gingerly, he touched the wound in his chest and came away with fresh blood on his fingers. He hugged the tallest palm and began to climb.

Every inch he gained drained the strength from him. Not even halfway up, he glanced over his shoulder and saw the dust of the approaching king. He kept climbing.

A deep voice called from below, "Hold!"

The son stopped. "Why should I?" he called to the hooded one. "While I still have my weapon, I can win."

The enemy stood at the roots. "First you must know who I am."

He lifted his hood and lowered the seashell veil. In astonishment the son stared upon the same beautiful features he'd first beheld staring into the lake. Unexpectedly, this revelation brought peace to his beleaguered mind.

"Of course," he said to the enemy, himself. "You were always there. The part of me I rejected."

The enemy nodded. "When you were born, your father saw the demon in you. He called his priestesses. They shook the calabash rattle and said the prayers until I was exorcized. You were able to pursue greatness without my dark words in your ear. I was expelled to wander the world seeking my place." He extended his hand. "Give me the weapon. I call a truce."

"Why did you attack me?" the son demanded to know. "We could have *always* called truce."

"Because I wanted an end to it," said the side of him that hurt and maimed. "There was no other way to exercise my passions but through cruelty. I have crushed all opposition and the people live in fear of my whim, which is capricious. I hate everyone and everything. I chafe at my reign because I know it to be chains. My people despise me."

"I would say you've earned it," the son rejoined, even as he admired his shadow, for he recognized one who shared his obsessive nature.

"You feel chained too," said the shadow. "I know because I am you. But unlike you, I never wanted to rule."

"Neither did I!" snapped the son. The outburst left him lightheaded, and for a heart-stopping moment his hands slipped down the hairy trunk. He dug fingernails into the wood and clung, waiting for his body to stop shaking. He knew, at last, that he spoke the truth. Great as it was, his realm had ever been a byproduct of his artistry, his stool an inheritance he'd grown to loathe with passing years.

His shadow extended a hand. "Let us be brothers."

The son noticed the trail of blood down the trunk. Cold sweat beaded his brow. He knew that he would never reach the canopy. The effort of lifting the gourd off his back caused his shoulder to throb with pain. "There will be an end," he panted.

Seeing his intention, the shadow dove to catch the gourd as it fell. It shattered at his feet. From it came the son's greatest possession: his imagination. His brilliance took wing to fill the downtrodden western lands, then every land. All he'd once hoarded now belonged to the world.

"So you fall," he told the shadow who, in his haste, tripped and impaled himself on the shards. With a last startled gasp, the king died.

There between heaven and earth a sense of peace came upon the son. Unable to hold on, he plummeted to the waters below.

Blue enveloped him. He watched the light waver above. Was this death? If so, he did not fear. He absorbed the consoling silence. A school of fish braided between his legs, reminder of his poor mermaids. Let the ocean be my pyre, he thought.

From the dark emerged a silhouette that took shape as it grew larger, then coalesced into the image of his father, a giant of a man, faceless after all these years.

"There are worlds beyond this one," he had said. "Places where the curtain is thin. I won't see them, but perhaps you will." A true memory. It had been long since he'd thought of his father, and he knew this would be the last time.

Finally he felt sand through his torn sandals. He had no idea how his body had righted itself, yet he stood on his feet, upright before a cave from which a shadowy figure approached with patient gait. He still bled; in the dark his death was the color of mulberries. The son sank to his knees with no strength left to fight. Not after battling himself.

The stranger was an old man with a beard to his toes. "You come from the sunlit lands," he said. "You smell of battle."

"Because I was in a battle," the son replied shamefully. "Many died, including two women who loved me."

"I smell jade on your hands."

"Because today I killed a woman who'd loved me."

"Yet there is also happiness in you."

"Because I killed the side of myself I hate."

"Have you? That seems a hard task. You mourn not for the people who died for you, nor by your hand."

"I do mourn the dead," said the son, "but I mourn for myself most of all. I gave my creativity to the world, and because of this I have nothing left to give. I cannot live in a world where I am like everyone else."

The elder's thick lips tightened in a smile. "Fish tell me they sing of you in the sunlit lands. They have erected shrines to your memory. They say you descended to the ocean but shall one day return to lead them."

He shook his head once. "I die. Even if I could return, without my talents it would be worse than death."

"And if you were able to go elsewhere? Be someone else?"

"I would *not* have a kingdom. I would be joy itself. I would give the people life and make them dance."

"I have a feeling," said the old man, "that you have much left to give. And much battle still to do with your shadow."

In his mind the son heard his own voice say, *Take me with you.* Dark crept in from the corners of his eyes. He welcomed it. In darkness there was discovery.

He let go.

When the light returned, he found himself holding some type of weapon. A bludgeon made of rosewood, shiny as a scepter. The moment he put fingers to strings he started experimenting with sounds. He stood on a stage in front of an empty theater. He saw five people, men and women of brown and white hues. Each had an instrument. A breathtaking sight! All the people united. This was the world he wanted to live in. He turned to one of them, a black man in a headband.

"Yo Dez," he said, "I'ma riff and you throw in when you ready." And he played.

AMONG THE ZOOLOGISTS

In loving memory of Jean Giraud, Carl Macek,
Ernie Chan, Gary Gygax,
and all the pioneers

It was the spring or summer or fall of 1983 when I was sprawled in my seat on the Chinatown bus, under the heavy black fabric of my wizard robe, while the driver beat the traffic by cruising several miles on the highway shoulder. We were deep in the Catskills, an hour outside of Ithaca. Blue clouds frothed around the snow-capped peak of the mountain ahead. No picture could have done it justice. I opened a crackly old Asimov paperback, savoring its perfume of glue and wood pulp. First I read the order forms in the back, their one-sentence descriptions taking me to Barsoom, Riverworld, and Karhide. After that I read the publishing info in the front, then the fan club membership card. It made me nostalgic for my days writing and distributing fanzines. The cover, one tug from coming off, showed Earth rising moon-like over red desert dunes. Once I'd explored every inch of book except the story, I began to read.

Oh, Isaac. How I loved his brain. This would be the fourth time I'd read that particular novel and I always found something new. I was deep in some philosophical quandary when I looked up to find we hadn't yet passed the mountain, but were circling the mossy cliffs at its base. To my right the earth dipped into a valley where the pines thrust like arrowheads. I imagined a cyborg battle on the beaver dams. Surrounded by such beauty, the destination was bound to disappoint.

I was on my way to a comic book trade show upstate, my third such gig in a month. I worked for Matrix, LLC, creators of *Ravenblade*. At that point I would have been assistant game editor and editor-in-chief of *High Elf Quarterly*, though I've advanced since then, thank you very much. Luck had it that no one was in the seat beside me, a rarity for the Chinatown bus, so I filled the other cushion with monster manuals and player guides, dungeon maps folded into cardboard boxes illustrated with dragons, and drawstring pouches of 10-sided die. Matrix, LLC still operated from the same messy little office on 23rd Street where the founders developed their first miniature wargames in the seventies. But we were growing. We sold five hundred thousand units a year and had ads in Marvel comics. We were in negotiations with Hollywood for a syndicated cartoon series and were developing a new, Oriental-based campaign setting.

Our weak spot was the tie-in novels that we published at a velocity the Edward Stratemeyer machine would have envied during their height of churning out Nancy Drews. The writing was rote. Elves. Dwarves. Dark lords. The good guys win. Our covers could be embarrassingly sexist; if not a demon or mullet-haired badass, it was babes in chainmail two-pieces whose breast sizes had increased incrementally since the original *Doom of Kar-Tath!* module in '77.

Certain that my line of novels could change this, I'd proposed it to the company's two-man leadership that week—a series based around unicorns. Good and evil, magic and might, love and war. Something like Marion Zimmer Bradley, with what I imagined would be nuanced characters and real conflicts.

After grimacing through my presentation, one of the co-chairs opened a pop can. "Unicorns?" he'd said. "Isn't that kind of nerdy?"

His dismissal was a toxic memory. The comic show would likely be eight dealer tables in a cramped room, a hotel without cable, and a bar that closed too early. To tell of the fantastic world of Aerelania and the mysterious Ravenblade, I'd brought a 20-minute promotional tape to play on loop and a wizard robe that felt like wearing a bearskin. My job paid well enough, though nothing equal to the work I did, and for the months prior I'd been earning extra cash writing pornographic sci-fi under the pseudonym James J. Quasar. After five years without promotion, I was considering moving back to Chicago and becoming a librarian.

The bus was packed with drifters and babies hitting high notes, while the odor of the driver's cigarette itched my nostrils. It seemed disrespectful to be doing so under a sign that said PLEASE FOR NO SMOKE, followed by the same instructions in Mandarin. I approached him. "Excuse me," I said, "the sign says no smoking."

His sunglasses were twin abysses. "Driver!" he said.

There was nothing to be done with people like that. I sat and watched the sheep graze until we pulled off at a truck stop. Ten minutes, and God help you if you were a second late. Some passengers made a beeline for the log cabin convenience store. The rest of us stretched in the parking lot: the young backpacker couple; the Chinese parents with four-year-old quadruplets; the Punjabi appliance salesman who'd seen my being alone as invitation to talk to me, who yammered at me for twenty minutes before he got the point of my silence.

I tried on the robe. The bell sleeves felt like bowling balls hanging from my shoulders and the hood obscured much of my vision. I cinched on a rope belt decorated with paper herbs, rubber chicken feet, and empty leather pouches. Next came the Wyvern's Gauntlet on my arm, the Dragonlord Wand in my belt, the Staff of Malyss in my hand. Matrix had paid a good deal for these props. Half-blind and sweating, I nevertheless felt like a sorcerer. My fellow passengers touched the velvet and remarked on its softness. I took a Polaroid with the quadruplets, spinning my staff over their heads as their mother grinned behind the camera. I was reminded of college when I would roleplay an elf in the Society for Creative Anachronism. If I had real magic, I'd have summoned a sunset no different than that moment—silent fireworks of yellow, purple, and pink exploding behind the mountain.

"There's one!" A decidedly strained, decidedly Cajun voice. Across the parking lot were three people in robes like mine, their individual statures bringing to mind an ogre, a dwarf, and an elf. They wore black leather instead of cloth and struggled with a chest that looked like it belonged in a sultan's treasure vault. Each person held a wooden lion's paw.

"Will you help us?" the elf asked. She had an English accent that could be called posh.

I assumed they were fellow nerds going to the comic show, dressed as Melnibonéan sorcerer-priests. But as I hurried over, I saw their robes were beyond what the average cosplayer could sew in their living room. And it wasn't the weight they struggled with, but the violent rocking of the chest, like a trout caught in a boy's hands.

Gripping the fourth claw, I helped them guide the belligerent box into the trunk of their Crown Vic station wagon. Along the solid gold inlay were bas-reliefs of orgiastic bodies coupling. As I looked closer, a side panel burst open on the box. Whatever was inside of it snarled and I siezed with terror. In quick succession, the largest robed person pressed down on the lid, the stocky one injected a syringe half as long as his arm into the panel, and, just right, the smallest inserted a dead sparrow. From inside came a growl that made me think of bloody boils, then a contented purr, or the sound bloody boils would make if they could purr.

"That was almost disastrous." The woman unsnapped the leather mask over her mouth. She looked young, even girlish, and was frowning. "There was nothing in its morphogenetics or semiotics to indicate this behavioral shift?"

"Maybe aposematism?" the ogre asked in a Bronx accent.

"I should have known," she continued berating herself, "but the phenomena proper were aligned for a gestational hibernetic period. Olfactory, tactile, behavioral," her eyes widened in worry, "what if I missed acoustic?"

"All I know is the little damn bastard almost got away from us," said the stocky one, wiping his bearded face with a hanky. His grin was a half-moon cratered with coffee stains. "He's just a puppy, after all. Think of it this way, Sajeewa: How often do we see *anything* take on the causational characteristics of *Bos primigenius?*"

Her scowl flipped into a piratical smirk. "I was going to say *Panthera leo leo.*"

They weren't going to the comic show. What intrigued me was the understated genius in the southerner's bulging brown eyes, his irises like chocolate donuts. His manner awkward and self-deprecating, even among friends. Some might have seen his paunch under the leather as middle-aged deterioration. To me it spoke of pleasure. He could probably slurp down a basket of crawfish. Shave off his gnomic beard and he'd have looked like any sun-deprived white man. He charmed, disarmed, and attracted me.

"We missed opening ceremonies." The big one had stripped to his waist. He was a sandy-skinned man in a wifebeater that rode up to his navel, muscular almost to grotesquerie.

I thought I'd been forgotten. Then the southerner shook my hand. His bobbing knuckles had a sharp medicinal smell that made me dizzy. "Thanks a bunch, mutualistic symbiote. Nice to meet'cha. I'm Brady. You need a ride to the conference?"

A choice, like in those kids' books. To go with them, turn to page 9. To stay on the bus, turn to page 11. Though a voice in my head told me never go with strangers, I looked to the bus and saw only failure. I saw speed limits and addresses and artificial light. The banality of *E. T.* and music videos and modern rock records. Aging and death.

The Bronx man was called Gino. He sat in the driver's seat, Brady in the passenger side, while I took the backseat with Sajeewa. She had her hands in her lap and, when her Ophelian gaze met mine, affection dug into my heart like a worm into an apple. The Chinatown bus pulled onto the interstate at exactly the eight minute and five second mark, my *Ravenblade* promotional kit inside.

As Gino drove toward the mountain, I grew fearful yet couldn't help smiling. Whatever emotions showed on my face, Sajeewa remained oblivious as she drowsed her fingers down the Staff of Malyss, admiring the grooves and runes. I shuddered from the energy of her small body. Her hair smelled as if she wore antique books for hats, and her skin made me think of beautiful things: dawn over the Hudson turning the waters red-gold, the sun an artist, like Frazetta painting the sensual curves of a warrior woman. Sajeewa threw down the staff, placed her hands on the leather seat, and leaned toward me with such quickness I jumped. She removed my pants and, seeing my arousal, grabbed my ankles to lift up my knees, then lowered her savage mouth to lick my asshole.

They were zoologists, I realized. They had a look to them, like they told time by the shadows on the grass and ate their meat to the marrow.

The sky was bloated with stars. Ice crystals flooded my lungs and a ninth level elf cleric floated before me, dressed in white, the tip of her pretty pink tongue between my legs. The orgasm flooded me and I went limp, worthless. My body sagged and a necklace of pain wrapped my larynx. At some point, she'd put me in a dog collar tied to the hanger hook.

I arched my back to stay upright. Sajeewa came into focus, lips glistening in the watercolor blur of her face. My every drop of sweat pointed to her. Every cough bore her name. The Crown Vic was parked on a night-girdled mountain plateau, and I had a foggy memory of Gino careening up the turns like some Gothic hero fleeing a haunted manor in his carriage.

Sajeewa's voice descended from Heaven, or maybe Barsoom. "That'll do for a start."

The four mouths of my heart were gulping blood greedily. Bright light stung my eyes. It faded into the rectangle of a marquee. WELCOME, it said, INT'L ZOOLOGY CONFERENCE.

"Truss the runt," said Sajeewa.

The men dragged me from the car and dropped me with no undue gentleness on the pavement. They placed the chest upon my back and tied it around me with rope. The lightbulbs in the marquee cigarette-burned my vision, making the world a grindhouse movie. I saw silhouettes of my companions leaving toward the hotel cluster, their departing backs in shortest to tallest order. I heaved myself onto hands and knees and crawled after.

Mere seconds later, I sprawled on the ground, fighting for breath, their leather shoes aimed accusingly in my face. "Terrible," said Gino.

"The runtiest of runts." Brady.

"Poor duck." Sajeewa. "Gino, carry it. Brady, help me with the zygote."

By himself, Gino was the muscle. Brady was a cheerful intellectual. Sajeewa was the leader. Once, I'd been an elf or wizard; now I was the runt. I wanted nothing more than to play that role. I would be the monarch of runts. Kwisatz Haderach of the shat upon. An orifical heroine from one of those depraved French space operas. I thought of the zoologists not as a triangle (like you might) but a yin yang: Gino and Brady half-circles, Sajeewa the flat-ironed *S* in the middle, and myself the two dots they engulfed. Oh, to feel such love!

Gino carried me. Dimly, I heard attendees drag squeaky-wheeled luggage across the lot. The zoologists traveled in groups of three. On first sight, they could have been court stenographers, retail managers, or any such group of middle-aged professionals. We passed through a brick and marble porte-cochére to a courtyard of manicured rose bushes arranged in parterres like spokes on a wagon wheel. Decorating the resort grounds were polystyrene sculptures of Olympian gods, marble benches built for the tiny butts of nymphs, silver fountains trickling by the batten shutters of the suites. Sajeewa and Brady stopped several times to rest from carrying the chest.

Inside a lobby walled with artificial wood, red-clothed bellboys pushed luggage carts filled with animal carriers, navigating the crowd like a tribe of harried ringmasters. The air was cacophonous with pigs oinking, raccoons trilling, and a dozen other sounds I couldn't place. The concierge was a Native American in a burgundy corduroy vest that looked like it could deflect a knife. His sideways oval pin said he was Manfred. He checked in my companions and gave them room keys. Though I felt protected in Gino's arms, I asked to be let down. The moment my foot touched the floor, I swam with vertigo, lay my palms on the edge of a glass coffee table to keep from falling.

Brady laughed softly. "I think we might have broken our new symbiote, Sajeewa."

"Nonsense," she said. "It's obviously the mountain air causing this case of the wobblies."

Muddy paw prints showed our way to the lower level. I smelled hair, feathers, and shit. We dodged marmosets to enter the conference area where zoologists mingled with llamas, meerkats, and cheetahs. Vultures nested in the chandeliers. Skinks clambered up tables to dip their blue tongues in water pitchers. A baby elephant charged back and forth like she was attacking Roman legions, only to caress friendly scientists with her trunk. The racket grew so loud I had to hum in my throat to drown it out. An old iguana of a man in a white cowboy hat smiled from behind a registration desk draped in red cloth. To his right, a tawny lion sat on his haunches.

"Brady, you *Taxidea taxus!*" the man greeted in a Mesquite Bar-B-Que accent.

Brady hugged him over the table. "L'Enfant! It's always good to see the, ah, country boys in this superior position and locality."

"Hope you remembered to bring that bourbon from last year." One by one, L'Enfant hugged them. "Sajeewa! Great to see you, dear. I really respected your last article. Doctor DiScala! I am sorry for your loss. I miss him too. We need to cross-pollinate before this nesting is over. And you are?"

I found an empty slot on the registration list and signed that person's name. They worked at the Chicago Zoological Society. Making sure the accent matched: my one bit of stealth.

L'Enfant raised his eyebrows. "That's you?" He piranha'd my limp hand in both of his. "I greatly enjoyed that paper on diurnal Chiroptera. You said what needed to be said."

The lion knew I was false. He fixed me with a feline stare and I knew with dread that he smelled my unease. Lucky for me, like all cats, he found human affairs boring, which he showed by unleashing a meat-flavored yawn. I got my badge, lanyard, and goody bag. The others put on their badges. Dr. Brady Thibodieux of Loyola University. Dr. Sajeewa Vibushi-naya, Oxford University. Dr. Giovanni DiScala, the Smithson-ian Institute.

I was drawn to a corner where stood a six-foot-high, gold-framed portrait of a bearded and slope-browed man. Flowers and notes and picked bones lay in a heap under it. The plaque read: TO OUR GREAT FATHER, THANK YOU FOR LIGHTING THE CANDLE. REST IN PEACE CHARLES ROBERT DARWIN. 1809-1982.

At first, I thought I'd misread his year of death. Then I felt the weight of Gino's paws on my shoulders. "I know," he said with tears in his voice. "If you need to salinate, let it out." A half dozen zoologists were kneeling before the memorial, moaning and weeping, and I saw nothing to question in the face of such sincere grief.

We joined the groups that clustered in the hall like bunches of grapes. "Are you on the pachyderm panel?" "I loved your article about quadrupeds." "There is so much we can learn from marsupials." "Meet me at the bar after this next panel." "This is what Darwin (praises be to the great ancestor) would have wanted." Slowly, I got used to the fecal smell, like a hundred zoos in one room. Every few seconds a wingtip brushed my nose or someone furry slipped around my ankles. I received compliments on my article, to which I mumbled thanks, and managed to engage in pleasant conversation without specifics. They were interested in the chest, to which Sajeewa either replied coyly ("All will be revealed at the Sunday panel, dearie") or disdainfully ("I *said* Sunday"). Gino gulped cup after paper cup of water. Cigarette in his teeth, Brady did up his polka-dot necktie in a mirror while Sajeewa flipped through the hefty program book.

"'New Discoveries on Tropical Invertebrates' with Erica Braun." She flashed her canines. "And the Society for Cultural Zoology is reviewing this poppycock? This will *not* stand."

Brady blew into his eyeglasses and wiped them on a sleeve. "I guess we *could* begin a predatory sequence. But don't you think it might be best to find our nesting site?"

"'Find our nesting site,' he says. One day, history's going to judge us. And the historians are going to say, 'Where were you? You were deciding who gets the bed and who gets the couch while that monogenic kleptoparasite destroyed zoology with pseudo-science.'" Her ecstatic flurry of gibberish made me want to lick her toes. She passed us stacks of paper from her suitcase. "They're in the Witherspoon Room. Let's migrate."

Brady put out his cig in a tray. "Rock 'n roll!"

He and Gino hoisted the chest. Sajeewa pointed to me. "Runt, bring up the rear."

Above the door to the Witherspoon Room was a wood-whittled bust of a roaring elephant. Polo-shirted badge checkers scattered at our coming. Seeing a suit of armor, I gripped the mace it held and twisted until I freed it from the gadlinged knuckles. I struggled to heft it in my clammy hands. I felt like Bilbo Baggins tagging along on the quest to Mt. Doom. Mostly, I felt superfluous.

With a roar, Gino kicked the doors open. Three panelists sat behind a table at the end of the room. The woman in the middle was thin and wore her hair in a bun—the type of woman you might see in profile on a brooch. Upon our entry she turned as pale as the wall. "Oh, Doctor Vibushinaya," said the man to her right, as if we were expected. "Please, take a—"

Erica Braun shot to her feet and waved her arms like an air traffic controller trying to guide a malfunctioning plane to landing. "Sajeewa, you protozoa! You are not going to politicize this! Where is security?"

Smooth as fire on a log, Sajeewa advanced on her opponent. Brady and Gino moved on either side of her, passing copies of her study to the awestruck audience, while I followed three steps behind. "Your research is flawed," snarled Sajeewa. "The Oxford Zoology Department, of which I am dean, has been conducting invertebrate research in the Amazon for *five years!* I led the expeditions myself. First of all, you used the same data set to study differing taxa. You have an obvious bias for agricultural, medical, and forest entomology—"

"Shut up, Sajeewa! You will not push your liberal agenda here!" Erica Braun aimed a dried-up finger at me. "I don't know what lies she told you, but this female will inject you with neurotoxins." Pointed at Sajeewa. "You—"

"Your data concentrates only on specific taxa," Sajeewa purred, "with no attempt to engage species richness. And you're going to sit in front of these people and honestly say you've discovered the distribution of the major arthropod orders?" She waved her paper in the air. "Oxford's discoveries of variance far outstrip any study at this conference!"

I pitied the woman, who turned red with fury. "You . . .You . . .You can't just migrate here and start adding *Homo sapiens* to your subphylum!"

I didn't know what they spoke of, but I wanted to defend Sajeewa as if she were my lifelong mistress, holding the rear in case anyone tried to stop her. Our champion Gino strode behind the table and, with a knife thrust that set the crystal chandelier chiming, pinned trifold paper to the wall. On it were equations and formulae. He turned and folded his mighty arms, the bastard son of Conan the Cimmerian and Martin Luther.

"Though you tried hard to keep it secret," Sajeewa said with contempt, "Oxford intercepted your infrasonic auditions. Our research teams dispatched to eight tropical regions *eight months* before yours. During which we discovered distressing levels of sulfur in the algae ingested by cnidarians and flatworms, by means of a thorough ethnomethodological analysis of zooxanthellae densities. This is a crisis of biodiversity that requires immediate attention, and it was only discovered through a variance of data sets for one hundred different taxa. So I'm afraid, my duck, that your research is obsolete." She faced the audience. "It's nearly the twenty-first century. Do we remain eukaryotes or evolve? Are we not zoologists?"

"Zoologists!" they roared.

Sajeewa looked at Erica Braun like a Pamplona bull eyeing a white-trousered backside. "Do you wish to compare studies, or do you yield?"

Afraid Erica Braun would dive over the table to throttle Sajeewa, I inched toward my mistress, surprised at my readiness to swing the mace. This didn't come to pass, as Braun scooped up her trenchcoat and the remains of her dignity to storm off down the aisle.

Sajeewa, Gino, and Brady took their seats. Unworthy to join them, I sat on the carpet with the Komodo dragons, where their genius could splash me. "Now, my lambs," said Sajeewa, "shall we begin?"

Listening to her talk about the poor, poisoned arthropods of Micronesia made me feel like a thermometer filling with mercury. The world-changing implications of her study had the audience baying that we needed to protect them, except for two people in the front row, androgynous waifs minimally dressed in what looked like black electrical tape. Their expressionless faces made me shudder.

Brady, who had helped on Sajeewa's study, added his calm insights. Such a bland man. Had to have been a hippie in his day. I adored his android-like delivery that his students must have hated. How he self-consciously trimmed his Southern drawl. They ended their panel at exactly 9:30. Flush with victory, Sajeewa surged past the worshipful throng to roll on the carpet with timber wolves.

"Oh, I love animals so much!" she said.

While Gino gathered the defeated panelists' notes, wrist-watches, and money—the spoils of victory—Brady took my hand and led me inside a shadowed drawing room. Aristocrats hunted foxes across the china.

"It's amazing." His beard scratched my cheek as he nibbled my neck. "Watching Saji's research pay off like that . . . My left prefrontal cortex is *aflame* . . ."

"It's your research too." I laid my hands on his chest, surprised to feel lumps under his shirt—he was wearing bondage gear. I unzipped his pants and his modest cock sprang out, his balls tightened into a pink apricot. Taking him in hand, I could feel the blood rush beneath his skin. My pulse was a fist punching its way up my throat. "I want to suck your dick."

"*Fuck* what you want." He spun me around and pushed me facedown on the pinewood table. Grunting in pain, I saw the tip of a bronze candlestick float into my periphery.

"Here's *my* erectile organ," he said through heavy breaths. "Yes?"

Inside, I was laughing. It was Brady, I would tell them. In the drawing room. With the candlestick. I nodded and, ever the gentleman, he obliged. The cruel metal slid in and out of me, quaking me with pleasure. Ripping me in half.

"More!" I begged. My wish granted, a shadow fell on me and I was staring up at abdominal muscles that rolled like a seismic chart. Gino wore gear made of criss-crossing leather straps, his cock thrusting through a hole in his black Speedo. I felt larval, cocooned, and envisioned him as a mutant moth like Godzilla would battle, voluptuously furred, wings wafting a smell of paper and earth. The insectoid vision passed and I saw him drop his dick on the table. At first I hesitated, scared of the size. Then I fixed my expression into one of grateful vacuity. I engulfed him. Someone who smelled of dog sat their narrow ass on my spine and I knew it was Sajeewa, who tongue-kissed Brady while Gino filled my mouth with dick-fire.

Time passed. I found myself staring at the calm rise and fall of Sajeewa's chest, her breasts standing straight up like dollops of fudge. I lay in the press of bodies, the oniony stink of skin, my jaw slathered in fuck. In the nearest corner stood the chest, the thing inside awake and purring. A nervous feeling plucked my guts like deft fingers on harp strings to think it could hear us, even, impossibly, see us through the oak and gold. See us spent, nude, and merely human. Sliding my fingers in Brady's, I made a a barrier reef with him. We kissed like high school sweethearts.

That's what I miss the most about him. The kisses. I think of him often. Even now, I can't bring myself to think of Sajeewa. When she enters my mind, the panic spurs me to replace her with thoughts more pleasurable, mundane, or excessive.

"You're right. I was a bit of a hippie. I was opposed to the war but, ah, I went to 'Nam. I figured if I didn't go they'd just send some other poor bastard. 'Nam was where the army taught me to train *Rattus rattus* to kill Vietnamese larvae. Those lobe-finned tetrapods said, 'If we take out the young generation, in twenty years there'll be no one to fight us.' How sick is that?

"Yeah, I'm crying. That was my lowest moment. Hrm? What kind of question is that? Course I did zoology before that. You ain't learned herpetology 'til you shot an eight-foot *Alligator mississippiensis* in your backyard. Me and the larvae made a terrarium for our *Lepus marinus* from an old pickup

truck. We held the glass in with glue. Now, I don't mean profes-
sional glue. I mean Elmer's Glue.

"You ask too many questions, runt. Get back in your
corner. Bark three times. Good. Sajeewa is my mate and has
some damn high fecundity. We have two progeny. Oxford took
'em right after they were born to train in paleontology. Sure,
I'd like to see 'em more, but, y'know, I can't wave a magic stick
and change the rules. Our progeny'll grow up to be alphas, no
doubt."

We had a room on the second floor. Sajeewa rope-tied my ankle
to the leg of a dresser drawer, with just enough slack to crawl to
the windowsill. Awash in starlight, I felt full to bursting, pregnant with their brilliance. Was this the power of pheromones?
This attack of rosy-red chemicals that had me rolling on my
back in lovelorn frustration? I watched Sajeewa convulse at the
precipice of the bed, screaming "Appa!" over and over. An arm
flung across his face, Gino would periodically punch the headboard. Whatever nightmare troubled Brady made him hyper-
ventilate. I wanted to possess them. Wanted to embrace their
tumultuous bodies and frolic there like a tick bird on a rhino.

They'd deposited their chest in the bathtub. The thing was
silent. The spongy gray shit it deposited through a hole smelled
noxious. Closing my eyes, I saw animals. Tigers in the Seren-
geti. Wolves prowling the city streets. I opened my eyes and saw
animals. Insomniac seals splashed in the fountain they'd chosen
for their glacier. Zoologists were still up, their beery chatter
sparkling in the dark like ingots of sound. Beyond were the
lush green Catskills where Rip van Winkle slept. Beyond was
a violet sky.

In the morning Sajeewa woke everybody with INXS on the tape player. Gino ironed his suit, a black pinstriped skyscraper fitted to his frame. Sajeewa painted her lips with Revlon No. 5 in front of the bathroom mirror and a palisade of cosmetics. Powdered her brown skin beige, buttoned her red blazer with shoulder pads like a naval carrier landing strip. Half-dressed in a shirt and boxers, Brady sidestepped her wingspan to sit on the tub rim, open a hidden panel in the chest, and write observations of the sleeping creature in a yellow legal pad. Like a human computer, he scrawled data as fast as he could mutter to himself: "Cellular processes on par with embryology of comparable known species. No significant variance in macrobiology . . ."

Sajeewa sat in his lap and grinned down on the thing with equal parts affection and madly scientific glee. Still smiling, she told me, "Don't think of bathing, runt. Or changing your camouflage. Cleanliness isn't for the likes of you."

Good, as I had nothing else to wear, anyway. By then the wizard robe had me filmed in the wet and stink of myself. Two or three flies danced across my naked skin. Still Sajeewa disappointed me. I wanted her for my de Sade and Sada, her pithy comments doing little to satisfy that early-morning-empty-belly craving for an artistic kind of cruelty. Could she make me dispose of the thing's shit with my tongue, perhaps? Gino adjusted the brightness on the TV. When it settled, there was Reagan rasping and squinting at a press conference.

"Can you believe that male used to practice mimesis?" said Sajeewa. "I mean, cowboy movies. How could they make him president?" While she groused, I crawled to the window. Below another trio of savants passed through the garden to the lobby, each shrouded in a leather hood. When they noticed me I waved to them. They waved back.

My memory burst with violet and emerald. Mizzou. 1968. Crossing the campus green, I carried a box of *Galactic*, the science fiction fanzine I edited. I printed them on the ditto machine in the library basement, under the supervision of an ancient archivist, and I was sore-eyed, purple-handed with a green heart, giddy from ink fumes. Those copies I would mail to our five hundred subscribers, and I was particularly excited because this issue (#5, a collector's item!) had a story of mine, as opposed to my usual reviews.

I saw a man on his way to the microbiology building. His not-too-pristine lab coat didn't draw attention, but the students gawked at the leather gauntlets and catcher's mask he wore. At the time, I simply thought him odd, and loved him for it.

The man had to have been a zoologist. I felt a fool for ignoring him. On that day, my path led to the edge of the quad where stood six Ionic columns in a row, to meet the Society for Creative Anachronism. In my roleplaying life, we called ourselves a *guild*. Dressed as lords and ladies, my guildmates eagerly paged through *Galactic*, careful not to smudge the ink. As the persimmon sun sank into the mouth of evening, we planned our next weekend of medieval recreation. We recited "Lament for Boromir" and toasted cheap wine to the fallen son of Gondor. I had *Return of the King* in my back pocket, like a totem, like The One Ring itself.

Had I met Sajeewa before? Had Brady been a droning professor I'd crushed on? My heart raced to think: maybe I'd been a zoologist the whole time. Life diverted me but I was where I belonged.

◆ ◆ ◆

Sajeewa demanded we skip the continental breakfast to attend our first panel, "Musionomy of Mammalias." I would have to stay hungry. The Hancock Room had a painting of an ostrich over the door. The Spanish mammalogists had heard of our coming and left their cash, papers, and cassette tapes of orangutan-made piano concertos stacked politely on the table. Then, "Frontiers in Ornithological Psychology" in the Lynch Room. The Canadian ornithologists tried to argue for a minute and a half—we left hauling three birdcages of canaries typing Morse code with their beaks. Brady and Gino lent their intimidating presence when Sajeewa rebutted "Marginalization in the Wake of Domestication" and "Conflicting Representations of the Treatment of Dispersing and Raiding Male Baboons on South Africa's Cape Peninsula" with her superior Oxford acumen, and I was ecstatic as she tied an Apple Macintosh to my back. Brady and Gino had wheelbarrows for the spoils. Crawling behind them through a hall clotted with scientists and piss smells, I could hear monkeys cackle above. I was nearly bowled over by a pack of naked children. They spoke in high grunts and climbed atop the ice machine to laugh with the monkeys.

"Frontiers in Cross-Hybridization." The Huntington Room had an amphitheater design, eight tiered rows encircling the stone altar where the panelists sat. We arrived early to get second row seats. The French parasitologist was a tall man of North African descent. On either side of him sat the waifs from the day before. The Frenchman displayed his photo on the cover of last June's *Zoology Monthly*, as proud of it as he was the toddler-sized egg on the altar. Part shell, part petrified wood, it was antifreeze green and gleamed with fungal moisture. Beneath the membrane, I saw the imprint of small teeth.

"You don't see anybody else put their project on the table like that," Sajeewa whispered to Brady. "Some of us have tact."

"The Paris Zoo will be as they are," he replied, sounding impossibly neutral. "It's the nature of zoology."

"Nature of wankery," she said. Our presence caused a discernible tension in the room, glances from those in the crowd, occasional stares from the waifs.

The Frenchman got his audience weeping from the tragedy of the Haitian Creole Pig. "They had nothing to do with swine influenza, but America did not care. The United States ordered the extinction of a noble species." By keeping a blank expression, I pretended for Sajeewa's sake that I wasn't stirred. "Captive breeding has not worked! Hybridization is the way to save endangered species!" He gestured to the egg. "Our little amniote might be wonderful when he hatches. He might be a monster. If he is, we will love him. We will love that monster. To those of you who share our phylogenetic tree: we salute you. To those invertebrates who oppose us: go fuck yourselves. There are no hard feelings. That's just the way it is. You can sit *on* a bottle of wine."

The audience cheered. Then Sajeewa rose from her seat. Reverent murmurs sounded among the crowd and I readied for the rebuttal, sensing that every panel we'd usurped had led to this. Their eyes shining, the waifs were quick to unfolder their studies, while their alpha smiled with all twenty-some teeth.

"Yes, Sajeewa?" he greeted. "What might you say about taxa variation? Or will you propose we develop our cell theory before interspecific hybridization?"

His underlings laughed with their mouths closed. I thought I saw doubt in her thrust jaw.

What she did was throw down four issues of *Zoology Monthly,* each bearing her face. "Boring," she said, and made us leave.

A jade altar had been erected by the kidney-shaped pool. From listening to the zoologists' conversation, I learned it depicted the classes of animal: gorilla for mammal, cobra for reptile, spikefish for fish, beetle for insect, eagle for bird, and jellyfish for whatever they are. They twisted around each other until they seemed a single entity. The Monterey Aquarium organized the reception and I was disappointed in the snack selection. Airy crackers and ham circles served along with a hot, cabbagey dip that had the texture of saliva. Like eating a particularly ambitious elementary school lunch. The Monterey trio wore shirts that said PINNIPEDS ARE THE SEALIEST CREATURES. Zoologists splashed with dolphins. They lobbed beachballs and chanted odes to their colleges:

"Harvard! Harvard! First in zoology! The monkey's friend! And the penguin! H-A-R-V-A-R-D!"

Dressed in a queenly white one-piece, Sajeewa sang from her symbiotes' shoulders. "*Sumus omnibus animalibus!* Oxford! Oxford!"

At the cabana, I sipped a margarita that tasted half strawberry, half gasoline, at the same time enjoying the company of a beautiful Nigerian lepidopterist. "I understand all the criticisms against the conference," she was saying, "about how expensive it is and how it shills for the universities. I think that's valid but there's still nothing like it. Where else could you find

something like 'Explorations in Cephalopod Mimesis'?"
Nowhere I've been, I thought.

"You know," she said conspiratorially, "the Paris Zoo is telling everyone they're going to be kings of the conference. How silly is that? I bet Sajeewa has something planned for them."

In my heart I sighed—of course everything came back to their rivalries. All around zoologists were having disingenuous conversations, same as game designers did at our conferences, their ingratiating tones a giveaway that they hated one another.

"Tonight my kaleidoscope is going to forage at the hotel feeding area," she continued. "We'll roost and engage in mimicry." As I tried to suss out her words, she grinningly added, "My song is 'Wuthering Heights' by Kate Bush."

"Karaoke!" I replied too quickly. "I mean . . . I'd have to ask my alpha."

I adored her wonder for it all, because I was noticing how certain zoologists checked their watches and stared vacantly into martinis. For me, everyone was a marvel made flesh and fur. I recalled my past like a story I'd read. Dedicated to the phantasmagorical, I'd sought to stretch that moment of Christmas presents under the tree into adulthood. Before Tolkien, I had read *Weird Tales,* lured by the covers promising crimson-lipped women in black masks shaped like flying bats; pin-up girls tied to sacrificial altars; Conan the spitting image of Johnny Weismuller. Inside, C. L. Moore spun word-pictures of pagan hells; H. P. Lovecraft dreamed up new dooms; into my adolescence the newsstands seduced me with violent and sexy fantasy, before their rack space was usurped by the four-color gosh-wow of comic books.

No comics could supplant those wild pulps in my heart. My bookshelves bulged with over a thousand classic paperbacks, though I wouldn't call myself a collector. I didn't collect them—I absorbed them. To follow in my forebears' ink-prints, I made worlds. I learned cartography, linguistics, costuming, and a teaspoon of astrophysics. Maybe someone found escape in my games. Maybe a twelve-year-old girl discovered her desires through the basketball-sized tits on the covers. But the closeness of the Nigerian woman reminded me how little of that joy had returned my way. I wept. She asked if I was okay. Staying in character, I said my love for the conference had me overwhelmed.

She hugged me and patted my back. "Salination from the vision organs can be a stimulating part of the courtship ritual," she said brightly.

"Are you trying to interbreed with my symbiote?" said a voice over my shoulder. Sajeewa. I shuddered.

The lepidopterist broke the hug. She looked alarmed. "No, Sajeewa. You know I wouldn't dream of such a thing."

"You'd best not." Fresh from the pool, she lifted wet hair from her eyes to stare at me in revulsion. "Does it love the goddess? Does it worship the goddess?"

I dropped to my knees. "It does!"

She sneered. "Fucking loser. The goddess doesn't feel its love. The goddess thinks it's not even *Equus ferrus caballus*. It's Brachyura."

"What?" I asked, and regretted it. The lepidopterist looked startled by my ignorance. Sajeewa, never dreaming of infiltration, mistook my confusion for defiance.

"Brachyura," she repeated, pointing to the tiles.

My heart was racing. They would rend me limb from limb. My pieces would be thrown to their red-toothed children. Then the lepidopterist forced her heel into my spine and I fell on all fours. "Don't be disobedient, whore," she said. "Where are your chelae? Your mandibles?" She looked to Sajeewa for approval as she arranged my body in various positions. Made me point my knees up and hold my hands like pincers.

Object, abject, I turned Cancerous, squatted on my haunches and circled my claws in the air like a cruisegoer as the ship pulls from port. I was a mindless animal, food to be cracked open and dipped in butter sauce. "Lick the perspiration from my phalanx," Sajeewa intoned. I needed no translation. My tongue an antenna, I tasted the chlorine on every toe.

That wasn't the end of my punishment. Sajeewa made me strip naked and dress in a lobster costume comprised of a headband with plastic eyestalks, a puffy pink vest that buttoned up the back and fit so tight I couldn't raise my shoulders, a foam tail around my waist, foam claws that rendered my hands useless. She allowed a Swedish cryptozoologist to butt-fuck me in the fifth row of the Carroll Room because he'd asked politely. Getting fucked in front of dozens got me so excited I nearly fainted on his cock. I craved more sex so, to be cruel, Brady leashed me and walked me on all fours to the bar, where I squatted under a table as he drank beer with L'Enfant. They used me for a footstool.

At the next table over, two beardless men in lab coats were writing furiously on legal pads. "Hurry up!" said one of them after glancing at his watch. "Our panel's in fifteen minutes!"

Their earnestness made me twitch my lobster tail affectionately. Brady drove the heel of his loafer into my rib. "Buckle down, down there," he said and poured whisky on my open cuts. They laughed as I writhed in pain. My back, arms, and legs ached from carrying spoils. Bug bites were itching me intolerably.

But I was a slut. A little slut without limits. I kept telling myself this when the subphylum went to get booze and left me tied to the dresser, in the dark. Acquired canaries and marmosets shrieked from their cages. On the armchair lay an antlered, doggish skull I thought could be the mythical kirin. The minutes crawled. Unfulfilled love swelled inside of me until it ached like a ruptured appendix below my ribs, the begrimed skin of my chest pocked with newborn zits. Frustration had me gnawing my own arm.

I was startled by the sound of the shower curtain falling. Pincers pointed down, I thumped to the bathroom, concerned for the thing in the chest. I pressed my claws together to lift the plastic sheet and gaze upon the box with a lump in my throat. When I touched the side, I could feel the thing move, like the purr of a cat under its fur. It wanted out. It wanted to feel the sun unblind its eyes.

A statuette of a large-breasted mermaid with arms upraised crowned the chest, some type of lid. Curiosity overcame caution. I squeezed my wrists against her waist and twisted my shoulders to lift her. The rush of dank wind from the hole made my eyes smart. Then the wind sucked back in. Out. In. Breathing.

Made daring by loneliness, I stretched my legs to stand up. The rope bit into my ankle. Gasping at the pain, I stretched farther. Claws on the bathtub wall, I lowered my crotch to the golden lid. At first discomforted by the unyielding metal, I found my rhythm, rolling my pelvis, fucking the box. There were points I could swear the thing shifted, ready to buck me off. Fear brought urgency to my grinding, but it didn't buck. Indeed, its breathing sped up, a partner in my pleasure.

After climaxing, I lay debased among Sajeewa's panties. "Thank you," I said. "Thank you, honey."

I had rescrewed the lid and returned to the dresser by the time Gino entered, an indomitable leather belt in hand. His face was flushed with drink. "A quickie," he said. I climbed to my knees and clapped my claws in excitement.

"I also have a kid with Saji. Name's Donatella. Oh, she's at Oxford right now learning cryptozoology. Who introduced me to Saji? Darwin. (Praises be to the great ancestor.) He spoke to my class when I was a zygote. I didn't think much of it. But that day I established my dominance on the playground by breaking this little punk's mandible. Darwin (praises be to the great ancestor) came up and said I'd make a great zoologist. So I migrated to England.

"In person? He's much sexier than Einstein. Don't get me wrong, Einstein's got the follicle protein filament. But Darwin (praises be to the great ancestor) had a squama frontalis like he had more cranial capacity than any *Homo sapien*. And this far-seeing gaze. You could tell he was an explorer. He was my pair-bond and mutualistic symbiote. He filled my neurochemistry with serotonin.

"One day he pulls me aside and he says, 'Gino, my boy, this is bullshit. Modern zoology is all about ego. Everybody wants their face on the magazine. We're losing two hundred species a day. Did I discover all these animals just to watch them die?' And he says he couldn't fight like he used to, getting older and all. But there's this female Sajeewa who wants to rebuild ecosystems from the ground up. From then on, I was her mate."

◆ ◆ ◆

Bartlett Hall was filled to capacity for "A Conversation with Wilbur Strakslayer." The sound of screaming birds echoed off the mauve walls that slanted outward from the stage to accommodate more than a thousand dapper scientists. Two dark green wingback armchairs stood on center stage. Wearing heels and a gold-lamé gown with diamonds on the chest, Sajeewa held my leash to crab-walk me down the aisle. I watched the war for perching rights being waged in the UFO-shaped chandeliers. Shadows through the glass, they pecked and clawed and beat wings. An eagle pursued a myna bird from one chandelier to another until the smaller bird dropped dead of exhaustion. A robin and owl fell at our feet as we took our seats in the second row. It seemed a perfect analogy for the feuding zoological societies. The stares of the rebutted felt hot on the back of my neck. I wanted to hide. In this way I differed from Brady, placid as ever, and Gino, who smiled condescendingly on his lessers. Hundreds regarded us in reverence as well, acknowledging Sajeewa as a vineyard from whose wine they had been enriched.

Her tone of voice like a red rubber ball bouncing around a playroom, she told me Wilbur Strakslayer's accomplishments. A noted researcher on obscure amphibians, he was the first black man to study zoology at Oxford, later instrumental in making the International Zoological Society come out against apartheid. She built my anticipation as I crouched on my haunches in the seat beside her. It was hard to sit comfortably—my chest and back stung from where Gino had beaten me. I had a stitch in my right side. Two men walked onstage and I could hear her breath catch. She began to masturbate me.

The interviewer was none other than L'Enfant. Across from him lounged Wilbur Strakslayer, a portly man with a handlebar mustache, his hands folded over his belly. If he were a fantasy creature, he'd have been a hobbit content with a pipe and warm fire. L'Enfant smacked his microphone until it turned on and his voice boomed over the auditorium. "Howdy howdy hey! Please give a warm welcome to professor emeritus Wilbur Strakslayer."

From there, the ancient herpetologist told us a story that began in 1863. He was born of the Khoikhoi tribe. The year he became a man, he went to battle. His warrior training didn't help him see his enemy's feint, landing him with a spear through the thigh, a week in a stockade, then sold for six rifles and a cask of whisky to British zoologists who intended on displaying him as a specimen of Negro inferiority.

Shackled in the ship's hold among the fish and freshwater barrels, his only companion was a lobotomized gorilla who sounded chillingly humanlike when she cried. Wilbur accompanied them north to find evidence of *Serpentis glacies*, or Strak the Ice Snake. Periodically, white men came to poke at his teeth and measure his skull with what looked like a metal wishbone. They wrenched a molar out of his head with pliers. They measured the length of his penis and fondled it. They sketched demeaning pictures of him. They drew his blood. He despaired of seeing home again.

Many hopeless days later, the boat got trapped in ice. They brought him up to help pick the floes. He recalled being afraid of the cold, yet the moment he walked on deck and saw the northern sun, he filled with wonder. He said the sky looked like water. Then the ship's mermaid figurehead came alive and bit the captain in half. It turned out the ice serpent had found *them*, and infected their vessel with hydra heads. Days of battle followed. Maddened and desperate men fought room to room, a head waiting for them in each one.

Only Wilbur survived. He figured out that every part of Strak, every organ, had an individual life. ("Brilliant!" Sajeewa whispered as she suckled my ear.) For thirty days he killed the beast piece by piece. Afterward he guided the crippled boat south. By the time he sailed into London Harbor on a ship of the dead, he was the world's foremost expert on Strak, awarded a commission by the queen.

All things considered, it was the most amazing story I'd ever heard. Then the old man gave a rambling speech wherein he mainly criticized Thatcher for invading the Falklands. I grew bored.

Brady whispered to Sajeewa, "I have something to tell you."

"Tell it, then."

"I got a collect call from Oxford," he said, "about our progeny. Let's talk in the hall."

She hesitated a second, then stood to squeeze by Gino, Brady following behind. At my questioning look, Gino shrugged, reached over to affectionately caress my hair. I tried to focus on Wilbur Strakslayer, still going on. Apartheid was an abomination, he said. Where was the United States in all this? I struggled to stay awake.

After a long time standing in the eaves, a young woman stepped forward to politely tell him that they had to end for the next panel.

"But I am not done!" he said, sounding pleased with himself. "For I have decided to give my own corpus in pursuit of biodiversity."

An astonished murmur rippled through the crowd. From stage right, the French alpha and his waifs came running. One of them carried what looked like a car engine with eight syringe-capped tentacles. The other hauled their egg. "Depechez-vous!" the alpha screamed. They shoved the needles in the herpetologist's back. Wilbur Strakslayer sat still and ready, tubes bristling from him and trailing like spilled spaghetti to the machine, then from machine to egg. L'Enfant knelt before him to hold his hands.

"Witness cross-hybridization!" said the French alpha. "As Darwin (praises be to the great ancestor) would want!"

"No!"

Everyone turned at Sajeewa's scream. Zoologists climbed on their seats to whoop and jeer as she made her way down the red carpet. Barely able to see above the crowd, I glimpsed Brady grab her elbow from behind. She spun and slapped him across the cheek.

"You fucking liar!" she said.

Noticing her, Wilbur Strakslayer gave a melty smile. "My corpus is old, my dear!" he shouted. "Why not take a healthy young one? This is for science."

She tried to run for the stage but Brady had her around the waist. She screamed and kicked. I thought maybe the French had bought him. If they had, the money was a mere bonus because his eyes showed euphoria. A thrill-seeker witnessing the most exciting scenario he could imagine.

A howl, high and baleful, resounded from the throats of *Homo sapiens* and other mammals. My love for Sajeewa lost the battle with scientific curiosity and I was riveted to the stage. Gino, too, rose to watch Wilbur. By hauling up and down on levers inserted in the egg, the waifs drew wine-red blood from the old man.

I heard Brady through the din. "Look at it! It's beautiful!"
"Let me go, you traitor!" said Sajeewa. I looked in time to
see her bite into his eye. He cried in pain. Zoologists cheered
as she threw her head back with an eruption of blood, to spit
the eye on the carpet like a pulped, inedible cherry.

Brady fell on all fours, grunting and screaming. Sajeewa
stepped over him to try and push through the crowd that jostled for space in the aisle. I lost sight of her in the ebb of lab
coats and hands and fur and hair. In the roar of the mob, pain
and happiness became one melody.

Onstage, the Strakslayer's face collapsed in around the
mouth. His eyes clouded. I lost interest in him or the drama of
my subphylum when a hoof punched through the egg. Next
came a snub green snout. Before my eyes, it grew from a slime-
covered baby to a pig twice the size of a man, with a black-
and-green mottled hide.

The French zoologists dropped to their knees. "Wilbur!"
they hallelujahed. "Wilbur!"

Shoeless and disheveled, Sajeewa ran onstage in time to
catch the Strakslayer before he hit the floor. He was mumbling,
half in, half out of his body. The auditorium swelled with a joyful
noise that drowned out her cries, or all sorrow, for that matter.

Back in our room, I asked her, "How can I help?"

She leaned back in the La-Z-Boy and massaged her forehead as if trying to wake her brain. She dunked her nose to
the armrest and sucked three fat worms of cocaine off a hand
mirror. Frightened of her and for her, I found my gaze returning to the wooden chair by the bathroom, strewn with Brady's
suits like confetti on an empty stage.

In a voice that sounded amputated from her brain, she said, "You're an exemplary runt, you know that? Best we've had in years."

Were everything not so tense, I might have felt flattered. As it was I could only dread what came next and cringe at the sounds of revelry that battered our drapes. Sajeewa took several minutes to regain her stiff upper lip. I could hear Gino punching holes in the bathroom wall. His barking sounded barely human.

Elbows on her knees, she leaned forward and stared into space. "There were three major developments that led to my evolution," she said. "The first was when I migrated to England from Sri Lanka as a girl. The second was when I tracked the genome-wide evolution rate among all known species. And the third was meeti—"

Something thudded against our window. Parisian monkeys taunting us.

Sajeewa sighed heavily. "The third was meeting Wilbur Strakslayer."

"He was your mentor," I said.

Her voice constricted with pain. "He wasn't just a father to me. There was *synchrony* in our behavioral interaction. He was a *mother,* too. He taught me the *beauty* of animals. And he turned out to be a bloody fool. Would that I had been there to steer him from their lies and save him from himself." She set her jaw resolutely. "But I can't dwell on his foolishness. The further existence of species is more important than my petty wants. Yet I think: my own field turned my mentor into a *Sus Linnaeus.* Every amino acid in my DNA wants revenge! And Brady . . ." She choked back a sob before it betrayed her. "The vengeance we'll exact on that one-eyed seditionist will serve as a warning for generations."

Gino stepped out of the bathroom, sweaty and shivering.
Sajeewa shot him a glare and said, "Are you quite finished?"

Brady's betrayal had injured him worse than it did her. His
mouth hung open, his entire face slack with a look of startled
innocence that suggested his abilities of comprehension had
been left in Bartlett Hall. His delayed answer of "Yeah, I'm
okay" made it clear he was running on instinct. I saw in him
the guilt that I wished I'd felt for not stopping Brady.

Sajeewa hugged Gino, tiller to his storm-tossed ship. I
would have, too, but seeing as I was weighed down by pearl
necklaces and earrings and dollar bills strapped to me with
masking tape, I struggled enough to lift my feet. I felt like an
enormous beetle.

The window rattled again. Sajeewa gazed on my treasure
outfit.

"What's the use?" she sighed. "They can have it all." She
picked a tablecloth off the floor and whisked it over a dining
trestle with the chest on the bottom, hid it from sight. "I know
what they say about me. 'Little Paki git.' I hear them in my
sleep! But I'll be dead before I let that cullionly barbermonger
touch our embryo!"

"We don't have to do this, Sa," said Gino. "We can rebute
'em. I say, if we're going down, we go down fighting."

She smiled without mirth. "That will guarantee they get
him. No. We'll let them think they won." The coke had her
pacing, ready to lose with aplomb. "As long as we have him we
can come back. No. Let's go out there and shag the bollocks off
these tetrapods." To me, "Take him now!"

Beyond a doubt, I was the third. Sajeewa got greedy but the
universe corrected her in substituting Brady for myself. Somewhere in the cosmic cesspool of terrible possibilities, there was

a universe where the South won the Civil War, one where the Nazis conquered Britain, and one where I stayed on the bus. Such thoughts had me grinning despite the dourness of my subphylum, who cut the jewels and currency off me and dressed me in my wizard robe. Shoving the Staff of Malyss into my hand, Sajeewa kissed me so hard she drew blood. When we embraced I could feel her body quiver against mine. I told her, "I'll be back soon."

"And I'll be waiting," she said for my ears only.

I peered at the pool through the floral drapes. Blue, white, and red lights covered the altar, hotel room, balconies, anywhere they could string neon. Wilbur the pig sat before the luminescent altar. While the Parisian zoologists guzzled burgundy from the bottle and lounged across their divan like a trio of engorged ticks, subphyla offered their goods and research to the ever-growing pile encircling Wilbur. Then they disrobed and joined the heaving mass of bodies, fucking, fucking, heaped in the pool and spilling onto the deck. Their moans were a choir. Languages mingled into one gurgle of breathless pleasure. I perceived the heap as a great and hideous woman; so much flesh packed together voided the males and gave birth to a new fertility goddess, to my eyes. I resisted the urge to hurl myself mindlessly into her embrace.

On my way out the door, I looked back. Sajeewa and Gino held hands, naked at the window where the French could see them. Presenting themselves to the idol.

"We're almost there," I whispered to the chest on our way down a hall decorated in soulless landscape portraits. Destination: Crown Vic. "I won't let anyone hurt you." Animal noises sounded behind the doors. The air smelled of blood and sex. I took the elevator down.

A sound that I first mistook for muzak grew louder, coalescing into screams from unhuman throats. The elevator stopped at the lobby, and I could hear roars and death-rattles on the other side of the doors. My breath came quick. I took a moment to lift my sweating palms off the trestle and wipe them on my robe. The doors opened.

A bloodsoaked hunting ground. Frozen with fear, I watched L'Enfant's tawny lion gnaw a deer it had laid on the sofa. Like they'd swapped prey, a grizzly bear killed a hyena by bashing its head on the coffee table. Baby zebras were hoofing a carnivorous turtle to death behind the check-in desk.

Something broke in me and I ran through the lobby, a terrified Midwestern nerd. Gold-framed mirrors reflected the trestle and my horrified face. I saw gibbons mating, eagles nesting, aardvarks pissing, doves flying, and a she-tiger eating Manfred. Half the animals hunted the other half. Fear carried me out of the resort and onto the lunar surface of the parking lot.

Six inches of snow coated the concrete. When had it snowed? At the sound of growling, I turned to see five wolves stalking me, black as shadows. The outlines of their ribs told me they were starving. Had they been sent by the French? I put all my weight behind the trestle to shove it through the hindering frost.

The wheels slipped side to side. The scrabbling sounds of the wolves' paws grew closer. In my haste to escape I did not see the steel guardrail until the trestle collided with it and I watched in horror as it flipped upward, end over end, to plummet off the edge of the plateau. Shocked and horrified, I dropped the Staff of Malyss only to trip over the wood, step on the hem of my robe and tumble toward the rail. I hit my knees on the edge, spun, grabbed desperately at empty air before I fell backwards, screaming, into nothingness.

Wind roared in my ears. My eyes stung. Through the terror and blurring world, I could see the trestle hurtling down and away from me. Then all went black.

I awoke to find myself facedown on a snowy precipice. Surprisingly, I was more banged up than injured. First, I blew the snow off my lips. Next, I lifted my hand, placed it palm down to push myself up, and to my surprise closed fingers on the Staff of Malyss. It had stayed by my side. Feeling invigorated by its loyalty, I used it to rise to my knees, where I took stock of my surroundings.

The box had fallen a good fifty feet below, then tumbled further to crash through a wrought-iron cemetery fence. I saw the path it made through the snow, a brown trail of grass congealed with coffin liquor. It had settled among the moss-furred graves of the ancient Dutch. Though dented, it had landed upright, lid busted off, a cloud of mist rising from within.

Behind me, I glimpsed a path leading down the mountain, nearly hidden from sight, beneath the snow. A sheep path, I thought. As I imagined climbing down to rescue the zygote, I saw myself falling and smashing on the rocks. My courage quit me and, tugging my hood over my face, I walked away.

Come morning the mountain breathed a chill wind into the valley. Sitting on a log pile outside the convenience store, I huddled in my robe and stared at the highway. I could only think of how I'd failed my first—my only—adventure. When the Chinatown bus arrived, I saw a new driver at the wheel. Surprisingly, my gear for the comic show remained where I'd left it. It occurred to me that this could be the same bus come dieseling back after making a full round to New York City. I turned my watch back to account for the time change. I slept.

I woke to calendar-art beauty: a twisting road, barns, corn-fields, and the occasional little white chapel. A road sign with a silhouette of a man on a tractor. Melancholy, I read the new George R. R. Martin book. I slept.

I woke. I got off in a village of white clapboard build-ings. A farmer's market stretched down Main. Aging hippies perused the stands while teenagers darted between the park and soda shop. I stepped onto the porch of the Voodoo Child Inn, a plantation-style hotel, where a ponytailed manager was painting the words COMIC CONVENTION on the wooden plank beside the door.

It turned out that the inn *did* have cable, as well as a bar that stayed open until two in the morning, plus a decent Italian restaurant. I slept. I woke, showered, made my way to the show room. Matrix, LLC had a table reserved between a computer programmer selling disk games and a '60s sitcom star. She laid out glossy 5x10s of her younger self sporting a bouffant hairdo, which, in search for the most eye-catching pattern, she kept rearranging on the table like a shell game. She regarded my table with the same disdain in which she looked on her own iconography.

"One of *those* games," she said as I set up. "Like . . . whatever it's called."

Rather than reward her condescension with response, I mentally practiced my sales pitch. Yes, we had much in common with *Dungeons & Dragons*, among other things. We had ninjas because kids liked ninjas. The Scanvanian Berserkers were Vikings. The Plains People were our Native Americans. Falana Elves lived in trees because Ewoks lived in trees.

We categorized fantasy. Turned magic into easily mastered statistics. But Baptist churches in Florida burned our games in belief they turned children to witchcraft. Every time I played my elf ranger, I took revenge on the enemies I couldn't touch in real life. My company chairs? I'd murdered them a thousand times.

Dressed in my robe, I yelled of Aerelania like the crassest carny in Coney Island advertising the dog-faced boy and 12-inch woman. In three hours, I sold half my merchandise.

I circumnavigated the room. Had a long conversation with a young woman who looked like a Golden Age Hollywood starlet cosplaying a Midwestern spinster. She wrote, illustrated, published, and distributed an erotic intergalactic science fiction comic. At that point her book was only available in deluxe editions sold through specialty shops. We both loved Darkover novels. She agreed to join me for dinner.

The comic book seller had Betamax bootlegs of *Dr. Who*, *The Twilight Zone*, *The Prisoner*, and the *Planet of the Apes* TV series. Golden and Silver Age displayed on the top rack, pornography on the bottom in black plastic bags. Seeing the comics filled me with affection. Between their covers, worlds. Despite my pledge to make no purchases until the last day, when prices fell, the new *Sword of Cerebus* anthology snapped my resolve.

I tried one of the programmer's games, furiously swiveling the joystick to pilot a polygonal knight through a maze; I met a television producer who bought Japanese animated shows and edited them together for an American audience; I talked about *Prince Valiant* with a handsome British journalist who'd stopped by while researching a story about the legacy of Woodstock. He dreamed of writing "literary" comics.

In a back corner, *Ravenblade* players had three folding tables strewn with figurines, boards, Pepsi, and Pringles. The rune master wore a purple pointy wizard hat hand-sewn with felt stars. Upon seeing my robes and staff, he ceded me the chair with a princely bow.

We played into the evening. Afterward, I spoke with the two most enthusiastic players. They said my game *had* gotten them into witchcraft. I asked if they were interested in game design, and if they'd ever been to New York City.

I was reading *Cerebus* in my room when my young men knocked on the door. Cheekily, I named them by their shirts: Maiden and Priest. As an experiment, I told them to beat each other.

At first it was fun, the enthusiastic youngsters diving off furniture like pro wrestlers. Gradually it turned pathetic, fascinatingly so, because I'd never known I liked seeing others suffer. Only when they were bruised and weeping did I allow them to beat me.

"Not the face," I said.

I slept. I woke to the telephone ringing. Looking down, I found the blood on my chest had dried into flakes of brown leaf. I blew it off. Disentangling from the sleep-heavy limbs of my lovers, I crawled across the carpet to the nightstand, reached up to swat the handset once, twice, until it clunked down on the floor next to my head. I mumbled into it, "Yeah?"

A collect call from New York City, said the concierge. Most likely some nonsense from the chair, I figured. I donned my robe and limped my sore body downstairs. By the desk, someone had erected a life-sized replica of the Robot from *Lost in Space*.

Over static that roared like a wind tunnel, the Matrix co-chair shouted happy news. Most of the authors I'd queried were excited about my shared universe.

"There was no way in hell I thought you'd get 'em," he said, "but you did it. I mean, fucking *unicorns!*" Matrix was going to publish my series, with myself as primary author.

I had to sit down. Who should I call first? My parents? My grandpap who always gave me a dime at the drugstore to buy *Amazing Stories* and Ace Doubles? Then it dawned on me that I might not control the series. The co-chair fancied himself a writer. He had his own books based on a character who was obviously him, an ultra-powerful wizard who slept with hot elf babes. I pictured him in the office, cookie crumbs in his yellow beard, touching himself to thoughts of himself. He'd want his hoofs on my unicorns.

Half an hour later, I sat brooding in the ruby-lit restaurant. Johnny Carson was doing his fortune-teller routine on the TV over the bar. The cartoonist sat across from me. She wore her curls in a ponytail, the knot of her calico scarf moved stylishly to the side. "Why are you still in your robe?" she asked.

"It feels like a part of me," I said.

"You look deep in thought."

"Thinking of a story." She asked what it was about. "Unicorns. Elves. Dwarves. Dark lords. The good guys win."

Such a concept! Virtue is rewarded. Darkness doesn't last. From the depths of despair one could find joy and peace, spring made all the sweeter by the winter endured. My thoughts must have shown on my face, because she had a suspicious look.

"That's not all you're thinking about," she said.

"I'm also thinking how much I'd *really* like to do a hostile takeover of my company."

I didn't mean to say it out loud. The artist flashed her white canines. So I showed her the wounds on my chest.

Did I ultimately run the company? Of course. It just took a little imagination and a whole lot of talent. I'm a legendary fantasy writer.

On the way to my room, we gigglingly devised a scenario involving an elf, a wizard, and two orcs. Unlocking the door, I was slapped senseless by the smell of excrement. All amusement left the cartoonist's face and she backed up until she reached the other side of the hall. She clutched her fingers to the wallpaper like she could hold on to the illustrated vines. Once I could think straight, my belly tingled with fear and curiosity. Remembering the cartoonist, I told her I'd protect her. She didn't believe me. Taking her wrist, I forced her to follow.

On the table by the window, closed when I'd left but now wide open, stood the battered chest. Its lid was back on, the mermaid's neck twisted so her ear touched her shoulder. The cartoonist clapped her hands over her mouth to keep from vomiting. Piss and shit smeared the carpet beside the bed. Something told me I didn't want to see inside the chest.

Maiden was standing on the dresser drawers, so pale that at first I mistook him for his own ghost. He raised a trembling finger to the open bathroom door. Picking the Staff of Malyss off the floor, I held it before me as I stole forward.

It all made sense when I thought of it. I'd been greedy. Four was too many.

At the doorway I halted. I smelled spice and mud and snow and death. A low growl greeted me, affection that I would return tenfold.

"You came," I said in wonder. The silence spoke of a million tomorrows.

THE PIPER'S CHRISTMAS GIFT

"Rat!" he found breath to whisper, shaking. "Are you afraid?"
"Afraid?" murmured the Rat, his eyes shining with unutterable love. "Afraid! Of HIM? O, never, never! And yet—and yet—O, Mole, I am afraid!"
— Kenneth Graham, *The Wind in the Willows*

Atop the sewers and cobblestone, Herald Square was. Under the thickening snow, Herald Square was. Mary was. Sara was. The girls walked West 34th Street with a pace born of necessity, dodging the pointed-toed shoes that lunged their way. The men who loomed above wore bowlers and overcoats, their carpet-bags bulging with gift-wrapped boxes, and the snow that adorned their fur-clad shoulders made them look little different from Yetis; the beleaguered expressions the women must have worn as they hitched their walking skirts over slush puddles were concealed behind veils pulled down from their feathered hats. More and more of them came, stepping off horse-drawn streetcars that moved single file down the street, to add their energy and money to the overflowing cup of commerce. Mary clutched the small sack holding her precious cargo to her chest, as tightly as Sara held the porcelain baby doll that was her constant companion.

You my girl, Cedric had said. *You guard this with your life.*
He'd entrusted her with the sack. He'd entrusted her with
an address and a number. If she came back empty-handed he
would ball his fists and curse at her. This time he might make
true his threats to leave them. A twinge of panic hit Mary's
guts whenever she glanced to the side and could not see Sara,
but then she would hear the sound of labored breathing from
behind and remember the diligence with which Sara accompanied her in all tasks, the unguessable stamina within her small
frame. It was the year when the fires consumed San Francisco,
although our protagonists knew nothing of this, and would
not have cared, overmuch. Mary was just north of ten, Sara just
south of eight.

Sara whispered something to the doll she held in both
arms. It was buttoned up in a grime-stained red peacoat, its
blue eyes glimmering over a tartan scarf. Even on an important
mission, Sara wouldn't leave the other Sara—Sara the doll. It
amazed Mary how Sara could be such a *girl* sometimes—fanciful, soft-hearted, distracted by pretty things—yet she never
failed to follow her big sister's lead, and she never complained.
She was tiny for her age, hardly bigger'n a johnny plug, with a
physical frailty often mistaken for worse ailment. Besides that,
her reluctance to speak to anyone except Mary led some to
think her dull. A necklace made from string, keys, and bits of
colored glass bounced around her scrawny neck. Her sooty
dress had grown so sheer that Mary could see the skin beneath,
and, in place of her ruined stockings, she wore the Sunday fun-
nies. Little Nemo had adventures all the way up her legs. Mary
pulled her by the hand through a line of chattering patrons
outside a box office.

"What're they going to see?" Sara asked.

Mary sighed. Here it came. The flood of questions. "They going to see opera," she replied. "It's rich people music made by dagos."

"I ain't never met no rich dagos," Sara said with a wondering tone.

Mary had to ignore her and keep aware of their surroundings. She stared up at chins and the underbellies of umbrellas. Far grander than buildings in the Tenderloin, the theaters rose until they vanished in the yellow dust of their own electric light. The crowd talked excitedly in German, Italian, and clipped New York dialects.

Sara tugged on her coat sleeve. "What about the theaters where we live? Is that what they go to see? Opera?"

"Don't talk about them theaters. Them's bad places and only pagans go there." Bad places that Cedric liked to stay around, playing dice with other boys by the rathskeller. Once in a while, a prostitute would step outside and, like a divine messenger, bless the chosen boy with a half-dollar to get her cigarettes or chop suey. Music would drift out in a bawdy breeze, until Mary knew the melodies to all the popular rags: "In the Land of the Buffalo," "The Dill Pickles Rag," "Do Re Mi Fa Sol La Ti Do."

"What's a pagan?" Sara asked.

"A pagan's a person who don't like God," said Mary. "They like the Devil. That's why they go to Hell."

"Have we ever met a pagan?"

"Why?" Mary shot back. "Do you wanna be a pagan? You wanna never get to Heaven? Keep talking that wickedness. See if the Devil don't hear you."

She didn't notice the Salvation Army bell ringer until the bell was clanging in her face. With propulsion that would have

drawn applause from the elevators in the Standard Oil Building, she hopped to the right and spun around the woman.
Everywhere she looked were hostile faces. Despite their but-
ton-hole-flowered coats and silly oiled mustaches, these white
people shared the same disgust at her presence as the disheveled immigrants in the Tenderloin. They might call her a nigger
or kill her. At first opportunity she went into the street, away
from the bulk of them. A sharp wind made the thinly glazed
snow on the cobbles pinwheel around her toes. She had to
tuck her chin to her chest for warmth. Goddamn, it was cold.
Nice night for Cedric to send them out while he stayed warm
beside the Herald Building. When they met up again (a "ren-
dez-vows," as he called it), Mary had a mind to tell him to go
dip his skinny yellow ass in the Hudson, balls first.

"Do kids still get born in mangers?" asked Sara, who, now
that she had begun, approached meaningless interrogations
with the same devotion that helped her keep pace with Mary,
deterred by neither the chill nor her sister's annoyance.

"Ain't nobody born in mangers no more," said Mary. "And
ain't nobody born in mangers back then. Nobody 'cept Jesus,
'cause he the son o' God. He special."

"But they got stables. Can't the storks drop the baby there?"

"Did you say *storks?* Girl, you strange."

Suddenly her foot turned on a patch of ice and she landed
hard on one knee, the pain lancing up her leg to carol in her
hip. The sack flew from her hand and into the street. Within
seconds it was obscured behind hooves and carriage wheels.
Her leg was heavy and throbbing, like someone had poured
cement in the bones; still, she grit her teeth and limped after
the sack. The moment she grabbed it, she saw two white lights
bearing down on her like a pair of Medusa eyes above the

icicle-fanged grill of the automobile. She tried to run but her leg refused to move. A policeman's whistle burst the air like fireworks and the girl was suddenly airborne, flung backwards to land in a heap on the sidewalk.

Snowflakes tickled her eyelids, and, when she found the strength to open them, she was confronted with a spiraling gray sky, swaying right, left, right, until it came to a stop. Her stomach clenched in a painful attempt to vomit its empty contents. The figure of a lanky man grew clear in her vision. His face was the color and texture of a skinned orange peel. He smiled.

"This must mean a lot to you," he said, "to risk your life."

To look at, her rescuer could have been a dusky white man, or a Negro, maybe even an Arab or Oriental. Against the clouds his full red beard blazed livid as a storm. His eyebrows had the color of a roaring fireplace. The eyes that scintillated beneath them were far apart, similar to a horse or goat, and changeable in color, either amber or emerald depending on which angle she looked. He clothed himself in December: a Norfolk jacket and derby of jolly russet, his waistcoat mossy green, the pocket watch attached by a slender chain like tinsel. A cream- and silver-striped silk scarf puffed out from his vest collar. At his southern pole, he wore leather ankle boots, the white pearl-buttoned spats stained from travel. Entrancing in his overstated way, yet frightening. When he grinned at Mary, it was with teeth the whitest possible color, the white that newborn snowhares saw in their dreams. His long arm extended like a coast toward her, and, holding it in nails manicured to foppish and perfect points, he offered the sack.

Feeling grateful, relieved, and furious in equal measure, she snatched it from him and clutched it to her chest. Cedric had given her an address, and a number, and she meant to carry out his orders. Grownups didn't do nice things for children who weren't their own, not unless they wanted something. Probably something dirty. As she readied her legs to bolt, she saw Sara standing in front of the man, at eye level with the tops of his knees. Mirthful curiosity suffused her face as she smiled for him, unafraid.

"You want to look at the toys?" he asked her in a voice dry as dust on an attic chair. His accent held a hint of the Bronx.

Sara nodded all too happily.

"Yes!" he boomed. "Come, ye pip!" Turning on his heel, he strutted under the swinging wooden sign that said ANDER-SON'S TOYS, his chest thrust like a rooster ready to sing down the dawn, and Sara skipped after him. Mary's first thought: this Oriental swami had hypnotized her sister!

Panicked, she followed them into the store, where the sight of toys scattered her thoughts like shards of a broken hand mirror. Within the chocolate-brown walls lay a treasure trove. Upon her entrance the three white families surveying the toys all turned and stared, their silly smiles replaced with expressions of disbelief and worry. This called for caution: keep her distance and make no sudden movements. She turned her attention to the menagerie of exotic animals on the central table: wind-up tigers, string-pulled zebras, simple tin recreations of chimpanzees and elephants. Wooden aeroplanes hung from the ceiling beside the ice skates and sleds that brought to mind *Hans Brinker*, beside the pop-guns, feather headdresses, bows and suction-cup arrows. Hung on the corner Christmas tree were nutcrackers, candy canes, angels, gingerbread houses, and baubles whose reflective surfaces stretched her head into a cucumber shape. The scented soap smell of the store made her dizzy like the time she'd nipped some of Cedric's brandy. Mary recognized certain characters, such as the Yellow Kid on a pin. The dapper-dressed insect on a board game had something to do with Oz; then there were stuffed toys, paper dolls, and tin figures depicting scarecrows, sawhorses, and lions with bows in their hair. To her dismay, Mary saw far too much Buster Brown. Few things unsettled her like the product mascot with the pageboy haircut. No cocaine fiend leering from the alley, nor Baba Yaga in a fairy tale, nor boogeyman underbed could make her shudder as she did at Buster's blue eyes like wagon wheels, or his toothsome dog that looked like something that would greet you at the gates of Hell. Quickly, she averted her gaze to four doll babies within a glass case, painted and glazed, all of whom paled in comparison to the battle-worn bisque doll in Sara's arms.

No doubt, Sara-the-doll was an expensive toy. If her scarf had come undone in that moment, the patrons would have seen valentine lips parted over a ruler-straight ridge of upper teeth, painted yellow brows and a button nose between which glimmered radiant green eyes. She had long, sharp lashes and real human hair like marigold petals descending to her shoulders, made stiff and heavy with dirt. Mary kept one eye on the white people, who no doubt harbored suspicions about where they'd found such a doll.

After all, it had literally belonged to a white girl.

Two summers ago, on an outing with the orphans, Mary had stolen it from a child in Central Park. She'd seen the yellow-haired girl place what looked like a miniature version of herself on a bench, snatched Sara-the-doll while her mistress played on the maypole, and smuggled it under her uniform to the asylum, a gift for Sara. Her proudest moment.

Sitting at the counter, his elbows bent beside a gold-plated music box, was a bald, bespectacled, and unsmiling old man. He watched Sara as she ran between displays. Mary knew he wanted to protect his turf, like the little Irish boys who threw rocks at them. When their eyes met, the geezer lifted his nose like she was dirt on his shoe. Not to be outdone, she sneered like he was vomit.

Grown used to seeing Sara in the gloom, Mary awed at her beauty as if for the first time, the gas-lamps exalting what the shadows so evilly buried. A sand-colored angel, nearly white, nearly starlight. Bold with toy-lust, her sister gawked at the model train zipping around its track as one might gawk at sausage in a butcher's window. *Stupid*, Mary thought. *We can't eat toys.* Then her stomach growled, and she imagined the train as a sausage link going around, and told herself not to think of food. The mysterious stranger, who shared in Sara's excitement, produced an opera-glass from his coat pocket so as to inspect the Lilliputian village. He couldn't have looked odder if he were walking on all fours.

Didn't anyone ever tell him grownups weren't supposed to like toys? Mary wondered if he was one of those "fairies" she'd heard of. The kind who liked boys and wore women's clothing for no money. When Sara reached to touch the engine car, the toy-seller gave a cough.

"Will you be purchasing anything today, sir?" he asked the stranger.

In reply, the goatish man grinned, his teeth a diamond bracelet across the red fur. Approaching the counter in what Mary could only describe as a prance, he handed the geezer a business card. "Professor J.M. Nesbitt, of the Church of Antiquated Theology!" he bellowed. "Also Chair of the Yonkers

Spiritualist Society, High Priest of the Hermetic Order of Supplicants, and President in Absentia of the Knickerbocker Intemperance Society." His chest expanded. "I have returned from my spiritual journeys in the Orient to oversee the affairs of my New York flock. I am the apostate of the Kabbalic mysteries, an adept of ancient Sumerian texts, and the one earthly connection to Godhead. In short, a wizard. Pleased to make your acquaintance."

The man returned his handshake with blunt formality.

"Perhaps you would like to attend one of my gnostic demonstrations," J.M. Nesbitt proselytized. "It is our most sacred time of year, I say. And tonight, my friend, my wards will be purchasing a gift of *their* choice. Say, could you let me have a look at that?"

He pointed to a board game on the top shelf. The toy-seller had to climb a ladder for the wood-sided box and grunted with exertion as he carried it down, much to the stranger's amusement. "Cabin Boy," said the toy-seller, showing him the box. "'A rags-to-riches game of adventure on the high seas.'"

"How do you like this?" J.M. Nesbitt asked Sara.

She stood on tiptoes to inspect it. "Is there one for girls?" she asked.

"No," said the toy-seller.

"Don't want it," she concluded. "It's too big, anyway."

Mary found the whole thing absurd. Turning down toys as if she did this every day! They could sell that board game, or at least pawn it. Nesbitt's nonsense about being a wizard was obvious flimflam, but the part about him belonging to a church raised her hackles. Memories of the orphanage came to mind. How the children would gather in the auditorium, their skin in colors of tan, brown, and black, like canned beans all dumped in one pot. Dr. Chambers would shout Bible verse at them in a Tennessee drawl, determined to save their wicked souls. The good doctor loved them the way a hammer loves a nail, and she'd often gone to bed with the bruises of his love.

Nothing she endured in her current life of empty stomachs and cold nights would convince her to return to the Destitute Negro Children's Asylum. In her mind's eye, she stepped through the door and into the foyer. The floor beneath the thin rug creaked like a cry of pain. A painting of a brown-skinned angel hung over the parlor entrance, the Lord's Prayer etched in the canvas with raspberry stitching, and the room was a shadow-flooded chamber of dour portraits nailed above divans that squatted on animal paws like chimeras. She could see the wooden knob on the banister. She could see Dr. Chambers atop the stairwell. "You stink!" he roared with a mono-grammed handkerchief pressed over his nose.

The thought of him was like a knife at her throat. Months had passed since she'd escaped his presence, and still she feared his childish rages, his delicate sense of smell.

On the streets Mary learned her lessons quick, the first being to trust no one. *Only Cedric,* she thought, though lately she found that hard. The liquor made him wild and mean. Cautious, she followed her sister to a teak bookshelf, where she placed her body between Sara and Professor Nesbitt. Ready to punch, kick, bite, or run, as the situation called for.

Illustrated covers faced out behind the glass. Light ran up and down a dust jacket depicting an automobile on a country road, driven by three children with cherubic faces. Mary figured that books, unlike people, didn't need coats to keep warm, and wouldn't that make it difficult to read, anyway? On the next book over, a girl in a high-backed red chair glowered across the table at a banana-nosed man in an absurdly large bowtie. Between them sat a rabbit with a most rabbity look on his face. Mary recognized Alice. The visiting nurse at the asylum had read them her story. Alice went to a tea party, and met the Queen of Hearts, and had her head cut off, and that was as much as Mary remembered.

Next, Sara pointed to a book with St. Nick on the cover. "The reindeer don't actually fly," she informed J.M. Nesbitt. "They just jump really far. And they don't belong to Santa. They belong to another man, and they made a deal that he can only take 'em out once a year."

"Is that so?" The man chuckled. "Where did you learn this?"

"A book," she said matter-of-factly. She came to a cover depicting a country boy with his hands in the pockets of his overalls. "Tom Sawyer!" she said to the stranger's delight.

Naturally, Sara cooed over the book with little white girls flouncing around in bonnets. She held up her doll baby so it could see. The girls on the cover looked not unlike the one in the sailor collar who, at that moment, was staring at Mary like she would the Congo pygmy caged in the Bronx Zoo monkey house. *Stupid girl*, Mary thought. She stuck out her tongue at the girl and had the satisfaction of seeing her drop her book of paper dolls in fear.

A stocking stuffer caught Mary's eye. Holly berries decorated the cover, and the illustration showed a black, black boy with a red, red smile. *Sambo.* Reflected in the glass, Mary saw her own inky skin, flat cap, wooly hair, peacoat, and knee pants. Less girl than boy, less orphan than oxen; big boned and squat, though her clothes sagged from weight loss. Of all the characters, only Sambo resembled her.

Once, she'd tried to make characters look like her and Sara. She colored the illustrations in a boarding school book to turn every white girl brown. She recalled how happily Sara laughed when she showed her. A phantom ache came to her cheek, remembering the clout from Dr. Chambers.

Is that me? she thought in the presence of Sambo. A wild child in the wilderness, the tiger-beguiling pickaninny brought to life.

Then again, she didn't trust books. She trusted stories. Stories were the hearth-rug and the warmth of other children pressed close. Stories made her happy. It was another thing to go around with your nose in a book, your mind in some fantasy, until you walked into a wall.

Sara threw her palm on the glass, which caused the toy-seller to wince. She indicated a doorstop of a book with rubber-faced characters on the cover.

"*Wizard of Oz!*" said Sara.

"It's not an Oz book," the toy-seller interjected. "Maybe wait 'til next year when he puts one out. We got *Little Black Sambo.*"

The insult had Mary gnawing her bottom lip. But Sara persisted. "Mister, I want Oz!"

Then, by chance, Mary noticed a book with a purple cover. The author's name on the bottom gave her a thrill she only found from something which had the potential to give Sara pleasure. "They got Frances What's-her-name Burnett!" she told her sister, who ran to the case in excitement.

"She wrote *Little Princess!*" said Sara.

Mary couldn't help smiling like a dope. *A Little Princess* was Sara's favorite book, from where she got her name. J.M. Nesbitt asked the toy-seller, "Is that her new one?"

"Yep," the man droned.

"We the people from the books," Sara told Nesbitt. "Sara Crewe, Mary Lennox, and Cedric Fauntleroy. Them's our names. Just the last names is different. But I don't like Cedric no more."

Mary hissed in her ear, "Don't tell him all our business!"

It came down to the new Baum and the new Burnett. Ignoring the toy-seller's hostility—or perhaps oblivious to it— Sara sat Indian style on the floor, the books in front of her. "Pick one," said Nesbitt, not unkindly, though he glanced at his watch as he did. The choice had her frowning with indecision. She asked Mary for an answer.

Mary, knowing one way to swiftly determine quality in a book, looked at the illustrations. The Baum had the same Sunday funny style as the Oz books, comical characters with bodies cobbled from this and that. It intrigued her to see an androgynous child, a six-foot-tall gingerbread man dressed as a dandy, and a host of people with onions for heads. The pictures of fairies in the Burnett book, though undeniably pretty, left her cold.

"We want to read fairies!" Sara said, meaning she and the doll.

"We always read about fairies!" said Mary, surprised by the passion in her voice. "I mean, all them books the nurse read us was fairy tales. The Oz book is new." She felt she needed to make her case. "I like Frances," she mumbled the hard-to-pronounce middle name, "Burnett's other books. But them books was about girls, right? So this ain't really like the books we like. I'm just sick of fairies!"

Nesbitt's massive, hairy noggin lowered from the sky to settle at eye level with them. He was squatting like a frog and smiling impishly. "Is that your choice? The Baum?"

Sara nodded.

"Yes! Well done!" said J.M. Nesbitt, and gave Mary a hearty pat on the back. She grit her teeth, as she hated being touched. And he said to the store, "She's made her choice!"

As the toy-seller rang up the book, Nesbitt regarded him warily. "You disapprove of my wards?" he asked.

"Nothing of the sort, sir." The man refused to look at them.

"Nah, you won't say it," said the professor. "That's fine. 'Cause I think, whether you like my wards or not, you know why I buy them books. I think you woke up early when you were a kid, and crept so as not to wake up your siblings on the floor. And you ran to the dock. You could barely see through all the men, that's how small you were. Your heart gave a trill to see the Union Jack waving in front of the sun, enough to make you scream, 'For England!' Before the sailors were even in earshot, you piped up, 'What news of Little Nell?' Am I wrong?"

The clerk's scalp reddened. Mary had no clue what Professor J.M. Nesbitt was saying, only that it struck a nerve in the man. Like they were playing the dozens in some secret white folk language. Silent, the toy-seller thrust a handful of coins at the professor.

"Oh," said J.M. Nesbitt, "and could you gift wrap that?"

The teacher at the asylum, Miss Dinah, had spoken of the founders in admiring tones. Descended from the New York branch of a notable abolitionist family, they had dedicated their lives to uplifting the Negro, the asylum being their greatest gift to the blacks of Manhattan. When Mary thought on this, it only stood to reason they would release Dr. Chambers once they learned of his excesses. It was Christmastime, a year before she escaped.

She resolved to tell the founders everything. When it came her turn to sit on the stool before Miss Dinah, she reminded herself it all served a purpose, the searing pain as the teacher combed lye into her hair with a butter knife. Miss Dinah said, "Hold still. You'll look just like a girl in *McCall's*," as Mary squirmed and wept, her scalp a burning effigy.

On Christmas Day, the orphans formed a line in the court-yard, in fresh-laundered uniforms, to beam smiles and sing "Jesus, Lover of my Soul" as two elderly white women stepped from their carriage, wrapped in furs and complaining of the cold. One ancestress took singular pleasure in walking down the line to touch them upon their heads; when she weighted her fingers on Mary's curls and the brittle skin beneath, she stared the woman in her small bright eyes.

"He beats us," she said in a low voice, but loud enough that her intended target registered shock.

Without another word, the woman returned to her car-riage, where she waited with her sister as their driver emptied a sack of spinning tops and rubber balls onto the cobblestones. The founders departed to Washington Square, looking glum. Mary hoped for something to come of her risk, but a week passed, then another, and with each week the presence of Dr. Chambers seemed more enduring, inescapable as gravity. Thus, she learned beyond doubt that the rich undertook "charity" as a vanity, a momentary action of foremost benefit to themselves.

Outside the store, Sara struggled to hold on to her new treasure, the book bound in string and green-and-red paper, and at the same time carry her doll. Two things for her to covet and fawn over, to weigh her down as she showed Nes-bitt her gratitude with a sheepish grin that broke Mary's heart. Sara believed the stories. She thought herself the heroine in a book about a girl adopted by a rich man and taken to live in some limestone chateau on Fifth Avenue. The clearness with which Mary could see dream-castles building behind her gray eyes made the distractions of this uptown huckster seem all the crueler.

Up close, J.M. Nesbitt smelled earthy, like a massive potato pulled from the garden. His breath made feathery plumes of mist as he spoke. "Remember," he said, "you can't look at it until the twenty-fifth."

The way his gaze lingered on her sister made Mary picture ugly things: brown and dried bloodstains, rotting mouse corpses, black mold. This one didn't seem to like girls, but he had to want something.

Men'll come up to you, Cedric had told her. *He'll want to stick his thing in you. If you make a fuss he'll just take what he wants. Close your eyes if you gotta. Then you bring me the money. A nickel for you, the rest for me.*

What if he try to hurt me? she'd asked.

That's why you got me. He hurts you, I'll cut his fuckin' throat.

Though Cedric had yet to put Mary on the street, she guessed he would when her tits grew in, if not before. Like most things, it seemed inevitable.

"That'll be a quarter-dollar," she told J.M. Nesbitt to get it over with. Better her than Sara.

His red eyebrows rose. "For what?" he asked.

"For"—she swallowed the lump in her throat—"whatever you want to do."

The man turned speechless. Much lip-pursing and tongue-clicking ensued. His eyes spoke pity, which annoyed her, because she needed his money and nothing else. Then a clamor interrupted the moment; a carriage driven by two chestnut colts charged down the street toward them, between the range of shoveled snow and the sidewalk, dangerously close to shoppers. As it neared, Mary was shocked to see two women at the reins, their skin like marble, smooth and pale. One had a very long nose, the other had close-set eyes. Both clad themselves in fur coats and hats shaped like cornucopias emptied of food, under which they wore their hair in stylish bobs. They made grand gesticulations, Horsewomen of the Apocalypse careening and hurling clots of slush in all directions.

Professor J.M. Nesbitt heaved a misty sigh. "My dear," he told Mary, "I am here to see the new sun. That is all." He doffed his bowler. "Evening to you, ladies. Happy solstice." Arms out like a scarecrow, he turned to the approaching madwomen. "Bring me flesh and bring me wine! Bring me pine logs hither!"

One of them snatched up his left hand. Still holding the reins, she lifted the tall man onto the seat with little effort. The feat of strength took Mary's breath away. She remembered where she'd seen women like his beautiful comrades. Magazine advertisements. Perfume boxes. There in real life, they sent red ribbons of laughter into the night as their carriage darted like a jackrabbit among the slower conveyances.

Creep, she thought.

"I think that man was a pagan," said Sara, gazing after him.

Mary pinched her ear hard enough to make her squeal. "Never run off like that again! What if that man was gonna kidnap you? Say you'll never do that again!"

"Never!" cried Sara.

"C'mon!" She had an address, and a number, and they were late. Having had her fill of digressions, Mary suppressed her awe at the fabled intersection of West 34th, Broadway, and

6th Avenue. The crowd thinned, and the girls stared up at the department store across the street, its red star a beacon through the snowfall. It took up the whole block, a palace bristling with buttresses and flags, terraces and lampposts, doors and pillars, windows and awnings. A boy about Mary's age heralded from the thoroughfare: "Extra! Extra! Harry Thaw stands trial! Jealous husband stands trial for playboy architect's murder! Jezebel actress at the center of it all!" Sara might have gaped at Macy's forever if Mary didn't tug her into the street. This time she took caution before crossing around the vehicles that ambled both directions like cattle at auction. A street-sweep leaned on a broom handle to push slush into the gutter. Not far from him a patrolman blew his whistle at someone, before he turned attention to an advancing streetcar that he waved along with his club. The police who weren't busy directing traffic were chasing away the bums under the 6th Avenue elevated tracks. Customers hailed hansom cabs from the curb.

The girls kept under the Macy's awning for a minute, to stay out of the snow, then trudged resolutely down the sidewalk until they reached the address Cedric had given. It was an attractive opera house whose patrons clustered beneath a gaily colored awning, but her destination led them down the side alley. Soot-blackened bricks, dirty snow, the moonlight extinguished, it seemed to her that she walked inside a piece of coal. Rather than discomfort, she felt like she finally had her bearings. Under her flat cap and thatch of hair existed a mental map of fire escapes and rathskellers, fences and rooftops: paths charted in the cartography of stray cats.

In the alley behind the theater, she knocked five times on the iron door before it pushed heavily outward and a tall white woman emerged. With her corseted waist and neck like an ivory tower, she resembled a violin, while something in her expressive eyes told Mary she could, like the instrument, inspire joy and sorrow equally. A glittering grin sprang to her lips, but not for them; she was staring at the sack. Mary had an inkling the woman's patched-up skirt and brown bodice with red stitching was supposed to look common, though her clothing appeared finer than any she'd seen on a Negro woman, her face garish with makeup. From behind her came the sound of many people scurrying and yelling. The woman said, "*Les jeune filles!* Is this from the West Indian?"

"Yep," said Mary. "Money."

As she giggled and scratched the back of her neck, the woman, with one hand, opened her coin purse and passed Mary the payment, then clutched for the sack. First, Mary counted. Three dollars in coins—the number. She gave her the sack. From it the woman removed a small wooden box that she flipped open with a thumb to scoop white powder on her fingernail. Sara lingered to watch what she would do, but Mary hurried her back down the alley. Whether rich or poor, fiends were trouble. Sara walked with an awkward gait, as she had the book stuffed under her dress, held in place with the doll over her stomach.

Back in the thoroughfare, carriages and automobiles had stalled going uptown. Men in silk top hats leaned out from under folded covers to yell and shake their canes, drawing Mary's gaze to the source of the calamity: a horse trying to stand on its broken leg, tangled in its own reins, young theatergoers toppled in the snow. The cloud of electric light from the opera house illuminated the animal's wild, rolling eyes. Mary felt for the creature. It lived its whole life blinded to every direction but straight, and now they would kill it. Didn't seem right.

This was Herald Square at Christmastime. Lit up, decked out, perfumed. Let the fairies and fiends have it, she decided. Carriages continued downtown toward the darksome silhouettes of skyscrapers, under the disembodied light, into the mist.

Every day the memories became dimmer, like a thrice-told story. Grits drenched in melted butter; Miss Jane leading the choir in the auditorium; pages of a tattered hymnbook balanced between her knees; the nurse's splotchy brown ankles; an oak tree flowering with girls.

Sara was the link between memories. They had been together since the time Mary's teeth grew in, curled up like pups on the same mattress. Mary didn't know if she was her real sister, and it didn't matter, especially since the Lord saw fit to give them the same name. Both had a piece of paper that registered them in the third month of the year and, being utterly parentless, given the surname March.

Her affection for Sara grew in part from the fact that she was beautiful, and the other orphans ugly, frog-eyed boys and girls with crooked teeth. Mary considered herself an ugly child; her shoulders and chest too broad, her eyes too small, her hands and feet like spatulas. Ugly and smelly, as Dr. Chambers reminded her. Soon the Jezebel Hole between her legs would start to stink, he warned, the sin within her bleeding like stigmata. Mary came to know of her body as a walking heap of shameful parts.

Sara never got such a lesson, because even the doctor loved her black curls and intuitive eyes. The dimples in her cheeks like thumbprints in toffee fudge. Sometimes he took her in his study to sit his "little dove" on his lap, and the cruelty would dissolve from his face until he looked almost kindly. Watching them through his open door, Mary would tremble at the hulking man's enjoyment of her sister.

Whether Sara was born an Esther, or Jane, or Eulabell, nobody knew, her birth name collecting dust in a ledger while everyone from Dr. Chambers to the cleaning woman called her "String," inspired by her twig body and runt status in the orphan hierarchy, a name she grew to hate as the years went by. Shortly before her seventh birthday, when she stood on the precipice overlooking the rest of her life, and, perhaps seeing the prospect of journeying that unknown country with String around her neck, she chose a name for a beautiful light-skinned girl. She would be Sara like the impossibly kind, impeccably cultured, gothically suffering heroine of *A Little Princess*.

This marked a change in the universe that took the other orphans some getting used to. Imperious Sadie—who thought herself better than the others because she knew her parents— saw opportunity for cruelty. "Hurry up, *String*. What? You don't like your name, *String?*"

"She said her name's Sara," Mary remembered a boy chastising. "Call her Sara, maybe she'll hurry up."

That boy was Cedric October, a handsome child the color of maple sap. The strongest and most respected boy—"lawdly," they called him. In the end, his admonishment failed to stop Sadie. It took Mary's offer to push her down two flights of stairs to make her learn the name. A few more well-intentioned threats and String became a relic of the past.

Ever playful, Sara came up with Pioneer Girls. In the enclosed garden behind the asylum, she and five others would pretend they were a family of Kansas settlers baking bread and fortifying for Indian attack. Mary would play the pioneer man who mined gold every day. Eventually the pioneers took a transatlantic steamer, then a train from London to Paris, then a hot air balloon that had Sara climbing to the highest boughs of the oak, where she encouraged the others to follow, until the laughter of March and February and July lit up the canopy. Then one day the visiting nurse, having found no books to read to them after their checkups, read from an old Barnum & Bailey program, and the Pioneer Girls became cartwheeling Circus Girls. Sara's stories had no end, only and then, and then, and then . . .

Often Mary wondered: Was it possible that the Queen of Sheba's enemies kidnapped her daughter and hid her in the Tenderloin? Or, while on a steamer to New York, the Pharaoh's newborn was swept away in a thunderstorm and washed ashore? Sometimes she thought of herself as the mother and Sara the child, this beautiful and helpless creature bestowed on her by Heaven, a duty she took with stern seriousness and doubt in her ability to fulfill such a charge.

These memories she treasured, a handful of silver coins, and it seemed that every day she spent one, while the others faded, turning from silver to copper to brass to buttons.

After an hour spent riding the backboard of a streetcar to the Tenderloin, the three runaways climbed a fire escape to the water tower they'd been camping under for two weeks. Sara fell asleep having successfully hidden the book from Cedric. In the dark, Mary helped him build a fire from sticks and newspaper, the hum of Herald Square still in her ears. "West Indian owe me good now," he muttered. "No more scrapin' for Cedric, no sir. That Frenchy nigger gone give me work." The looseness of his overalls and increasingly skull-like aspect of his face caused her to mourn his lost beauty. After they had finished, he rolled up in a horse-hair blanket and fell asleep without a word of thanks.

Glad to take the weight off her heels, both of them ashen and hard like the rims of ceramic mugs, she held the ends of her blanket tight around her shoulders and lay close to the flames. Across the fire, Sara appeared warm under her filthy woolen rug; still, Mary noted the hollowness of her cheeks, the thinness in her lips. Hopefully she dreamt of Nesbitt, not of hunger. Mary searched for a memory to lull her mind, but couldn't sleep with Dr. Chambers crouching over Sara, a ghost made of soot and smoke. One perfumed hand dangled between his knees, the other held the handkerchief to his nose. However she called him a figment, he seemed real enough, perched to claim Mary's most precious thing when she closed her eyes.

So it wasn't pleasant memories, but tears, that carried her to that elastic reality Little Nemo discovered under his white bedsheets. She found herself in front of the Herald Building. With a sound of grinding metal, the statue of the white man on the fountain pedestal came to life, shook the pigeons off his shoulders, and stepped heavily into the snow. Minerva came alive on the rooftop and scaled down the face of the Herald like a spider, followed by the two tough little men who swung sledgehammers to ring the hour. With a bird's eye, Mary saw bronze lions come roaring to life; William Tecumseh Sherman trotted his metal horse down the sidewalk; Lady Liberty herself ambled neck-deep through New York Harbor. Upon reaching the teeming streets, the statues shrank to human size, although they retained the bronze hue on their metal skin. Mary saw ghostly spirits rise from buildings across the city to mist through New York like low-hanging clouds. From livery-stables and blacksmith shops, from newspaper offices and operas, the buildings sent their spirits into the statues. Blushing with vitality, the concrete forefathers took on the aspects of those buildings: for those bearing older spirits, they grew beards of thatch and reddish skin like brick, and donned stained glass eyewear. Meanwhile, the younger spirits stood tall, very tall, with limestone skin, their eyes shaped like the gothic buttresses popular in newer architecture. In basalt boots they strolled the nighttime streets, men in stovepipe hats, women in straw hats plumed with tiny American flags. Soon the theaters, dance-halls, and saloons resounded with their crass ballads. Excited, the spirits said *winter* the way others might say *Christmas.*

A booming voice shook the stars from the sky: "Wake up!"

At the edge of thought, she heard their voices: like cracking frost, like burning coal, like the sound of skin unsticking from metal.

"Wake up!" said Cedric.

Blinking the sleep away, she saw a fresh coat of sparkling powder piled into a two-foot wall around the support beams; smooth and even, it made her yearn for a fleece blanket. No sooner did she sit up than hunger hit her belly. She thought it would eat a hole right through her.

A foot away from her knelt Cedric, and he had the unwrapped Baum book raised above his head like he intended to swat a fly with it. "Where did you get this?" he said accusingly.

She grabbed for it, but he held it out of reach.

"Where'd you get this?" he repeated. His New York accent was being replaced with a Southern drawl like the other street boys.

"I . . . I . . ." She thought quick. "I stole it. From somebody's bag."

The roughness with which he flipped through the pages alarmed her, like watching him pet a kitten too hard. "If you was gonna steal something," he said, "why a damn book? Why not some money?"

"I just wanted something to read to Sara. You know she love books."

Reminded of Sara, he glared at the sleeping nymph as if disappointed to discover her still there. "Yeah, I know. She love books and that doll. We should sell 'em both."

"No," Mary said. "We won't."

"She don't do shit and I'm sick of it. Sun's out, so why's she sleeping?"

"She shouldn't be sleeping." Sunlight off the snow illuminated the girl's prone from. Protruding from the rug was Sara-the-doll's porcelain head like a living baby atop a pile of rags. Fear rained from Mary's stomach to her feet. So great a panic that she not only pushed aside Cedric to reach her sister but swatted the sunlight as if beating away Jesus's hands. Gently, she lifted the girl's arm to pick up the doll and place it on the concrete. The movement made Sara-the-doll bat her eyelids. Mary lifted Sara's chin and gazed on her, quite like a doll herself. Pink coloring rimmed her wide nostrils, the skin beneath damp from sniffling. Mary put a hand under her nose and heartened to feel warm breaths. She breathed a silent thank-you to God.

Sara coughed, woke with a shiver, greeted Mary with a thoughtful expression that invigorated the big sister like hot coffee. Immediately Sara's countenance changed to one of horror.

"Gimme my book back!" she yelled.

"Go get it," Cedric said with a bored tone, and tossed it in the snow.

Heedless of the cold, Sara ran after it, and her arms and legs vanished as she clambered up the white hill. Mary lunged at Cedric's throat with her hands. They grappled, equally matched in strength, before he employed his long legs to kick the rear of her knee and drop her on her back.

"The hell's wrong with you? Is you crazy?" He cocked his fist. Even as she waited for the blow, she thought, *He look pitiful.* The effort of holding up his arm tired him.

Sara returned with her book, which looked minimally damaged. Sara, on the other hand, had the aspect of an explorer just returned from the arctic, snow-clotted and beleaguered, her dilated nostrils sizzling with angry breaths. "Get away from her!" she shouted.

The anger-born strength seemed to melt from Cedric, and he collapsed onto his rump. "Frig it," he said. "Let's just go. We gotta get the West Indian his money."

Mary waited for her heart to stop racing. "We can't bring that book," she told Sara. "Other kids'll try to take it."

She gave the would-be bibliophile a look that would tolerate no argument. Sara started to cry but nonetheless concealed the book under her rug. She lifted the doll to signal that she was ready. Morning sounds could be heard from the streets:

"Laces! Gotcha buttons and shoelaces!—Gotcha milk, here!—Pork, beef, chicken!—Siga! Siga pou vann!—Coal and firewood! Warm your apartment!"

And the time for dreaming had ended.

Instead of a hand to help her up, Cedric offered Mary his whisky. She took a long drought that burned down her throat and dropped into her belly like a stone. So warm, so glorious. Like invisible hands cracking open her ribcage to build a campfire from the bone shards.

Stick to the streets you know, Cedric often said, a maxim he'd borrowed from a beggar on 40th who'd lost both legs to "a yellow monkey with a machete" while on duty in the Philippines. Negroes lived on 25th through 58th Street, between 6th and 9th Avenues. Between 26th and 58th were barbershops, groceries, and restaurants. Cafes were on 37th, pimps and dope pushers on 41st. Fifty-third was home to Bohemians looking for sex and music, and the theaters that catered to both. There were churches to go for food and forgiveness, saloons for odd jobs. Go too deep in the 50s and the micks'll get you. The coppers are micks too, so don't trust 'em. The black Spaniards on San Juan Hill will beat you bad as a mick.

Like a prey animal, Mary March had to stay keen of her environment. Keep one eye on the man in the soiled coat spouting Bible verses. Keep another eye on the two beggars pretending to be blind and lame. Keep a third eye on Sara so she kept up. *Don't call too much attention to yo'self* was another Cedric maxim. It seemed that Sara remembered this because she took glee in breaking the rule with a relentless torrent of jibber-jabber.

"Is we there yet?" she asked on their way down the street.

Mary held a rag over her nose. Awful and awfuller smells kept threatening to make her throw up. "Girl, you quit with that sass mouth. You wasn't never so sassy back at the asylum."

"We ain't at the asylum no more."

"Ooh, I'm sick o' you."

"You ain't sick o' me!"

"Shut up," Cedric called back.

"Hi!" Sara called to a homeless tramp, who waved back. To Mary, "How come in 'The Twelve Days o' Christmas' the one person keep giving the other person birds?"

"'Cause birds is sacred to white folks," Mary said with a solemn tone, to hide her amusement.

"How come the foreign man who sell bread got them curls on his hat?"

"He Jew."

"What's Jew?"

"Them's funny immigrants. They dress like that 'cause they like playing dress-up."

Cedric grunted. "Y'all both some yappin' bitches."

"Why can't we live with the Kentucky lady?" Sara asked.

The question gave Mary pause. The Kentucky woman on 50th Street had let them stay at her apartment awhile. "'Cause she got enough kids and she don't want no more," she finally said with nostalgia for those days.

"I wanna have lots o' kids," said Sara.

"Wonderful. You can get on charity too. And having kids ain't like taking care o' no doll." She pointed at Sara-the-doll's dirty coat. "That doll getting nasty. If the relief people saw her, they'd say, 'That girl Sara's an unfit mother. She must be idle, letting her daughter get dirty like that.' Then they'd throw you in jail and put your doll in an asylum."

Suddenly upset, Sara hugged the doll to her chest. "I wouldn't let 'em put her in the asylum." She brightened. "Maybe Kentucky lady'll take us in if we talk like we from Kentucky."

"You just being stupid now."

"Ah kin toke lahk dis, if yew wont," Sara said. "I mean, if yew all wont. Yewwwww allllllll. Yyyyyy'alllllllll."

"You sound just like Doctor Chambers," said Cedric. At the poorly concealed pain in his voice, Mary felt a twinge of sympathy.

Sara said, "Yew sow'n jus' lahk Doctuh Chambuhs."

"Enough!" he roared.

By then they'd reached Cedric's crew, who called themselves the Seventh Street Gang, though they qualified as a gang by the loosest standard, only five scab-kneed, worn-shooed, bloody-knuckled, dull-eyed, big-headed boys with names like Bruiser and Half-Dollar, who all dreamed of someday being "toughs" for the West Indian. For now, it was scavenging and petty crime. When Cedric showed them the money from last night's sale, they cheered him like a conquering hero.

"Didn't we really do that?" Sara asked Mary with theatrical innocence. "He must have trouble with his memory."

The kids made their way across unshoveled streets to the West Indian's saloon. Called the Merry Maiden, it sat on the bottom floor of a two-story brick edifice that, due to a poor foundation, leaned to the side like the drunks who would stumble out the weatherbeaten door at dawn. The first floor hosted rags and gambling, the upper floor reserved for the West Indian's "girls." At night, sounds of sin and tragedy blared from the walls.

At the moment it stood mute, an altogether sad-looking place. When they'd first come to the streets, Mary feared to go there because the Lord cast judgment on drunks and gamblers. That was in October, when she was a leaf fallen from the orphanage window. Winter came and put ice in her veins. Leaning one shoulder on the sodden wall, she bemusedly watched Cedric strut to the doorman, a tall and broad-shouldered islander in a peacoat, who accepted the three dollars.

"Ya be wantin' any more jobs," said the doorman, "wait awhile in de alley."

So they did. Mary's job was to sit at the bottom of the rickety wooden stair leading to the West Indian's second floor office and watch the door while Cedric played dice with the boys. She became aware of how she stank, wished more than anything for a bath. As she smoked a cigarette, she listened to the boys' frost-thickened, stuttering conversation about Wild West cowboys and the gruesome, romantic ways they died. Did you know Jesse James was shot in the back of the head by his own flunky? Did y'all niggers know Billy the Kid took a bullet outta Joe Grant's gun to win their shootout?

Mary felt like she'd lived this day before; all that changed was she grew hungrier and her feet grew sorer. Looking to the sky, she longed for the sun: the nappy-haired gentleman who warmed her face, now shorn of his red-gold locks, his smile hidden behind dismal clouds. The blue realm he reigned over bleached gray. Come spring, she might tie ribbons in her hair and turn a somersault to celebrate, damn what Cedric had to say about it.

She was distracted by the high, henlike chatter of three "charity girls," twelve- and thirteen-year-old hussies who came around the Seventh Street Gang looking for a date. Under the excuse of running errands for their mothers, they would smile at Cedric and talk about dresses they couldn't afford. Since she was Cedric's girl, they hated her, not like she cared. Her concern was her sister might fall under their vapid influence, so she felt grateful they paid her no mind. Probably felt threatened by her beauty. Unvexed, Sara made her own company. She poured a bowl of water on the cobblestones and watched it freeze, and in that moment Mary admired how the soot that marked them all seemed like ground-up black diamonds on her skin. Once the water hardened, Sara waltzed with her doll on their private ice pond.

"What is going on, Ozma?" she said to it. "Snow in Munchkin Country? Who ever heard of such a thing?"

Mary felt herself smile. Sara played Dorothy, Sara-the-doll was Ozma, and they were on a journey to see the Scarecrow. Again, Mary was struck by her strangeness. She seemed older than she was, mentally attuned to a neverending stream of tales. Sara slipped and fell on her butt. Instantly Mary rose, then paused, because Sara didn't cry. Yes, her eyes grew dewy, but instead of bawling she drew into herself, staring bewilderedly on the wide and cold world like a yellow squirrel. Clutching the doll to her chest, she whispered something in its porcelain ear.

That wasn't good. Jim Douglass the dope fiend used to talk to people who weren't there. Last month, he got into such a heated argument with himself he lost attention and stepped in front of a horse-drawn wagon. He didn't have much of a head at all, after that. Mary wondered if it wouldn't be kinder to flag down the visiting teacher, a weary-looking woman who visited Negro houses to check on truant children, and ask her to return Sara to the asylum. Dr. Chambers would be furious, but he loved her in his own way. He only hit her the one time.

Then, for some reason, she thought of Nesbitt the humbug wizard. She wondered if he might come to the Merry Maiden with his beautiful friends. After all, white people visited the black-and-tan saloons. Come nightfall, a herd of stockinged Gibson girls would disgorge from their hansom cabs and descend into the rathskeller for another round of slumming.

Then again, Nesbitt wasn't white, as far as she knew. She wished he didn't loom so large in her mind, but his manner had been so queer, the toy shop so warm. She blamed him for her thoughts. Surrender Sara to the visiting teacher? Never in a hundred years!

Still, she was compelled to check on her sister, who had yet to leave that spot. As she approached, Mary found her sitting with Sara-the-doll's mouth to her ear. Nothing indicated she noticed Mary standing a yard away from her.

"Rubbish," said Sara in a prim English accent. "I do quite like the story of how Ivan stole the magic lamp from Aladdin, and you, rude girl, insist on interrupting me."

"Tell me later," Sara said sharply in her normal voice. "Right now we need to find food. You need to help, especially since you ain't paying me for the serial."

"You wound me, young lady," said Sara in the accent again. "That you would speak to me so *crassly* after our long friendship."

"Sorry," Sara apologized to herself. "But things are real bad. So let's put our heads together and come up with a way to help Mary. *Then* tell me the story."

"Hey," said Mary, and Sara gazed at her with alarm in her eyes. *Pretty eyes,* thought Mary. Like two chips of ice. Cautiously, she knelt and took her hand. "You talking to the doll."

The statement of fact made Sara stare at the ground. Afraid she'd made her feel guilty over an honest bit of make believe, Mary said, "It's really okay—"

"She our chronicler," Sara stated.

Mary felt sick. "Huh?"

Sara rocked her porcelain comrade in her arms and spoke of the past. "I kind of liked the asylum sometimes." Said in shy apology, because she knew how Mary felt about the place. "We was always learning or going on trips and there was always something going on. Like when Evelyn July told everyone I was a tattletale and no one liked me and then you figured out it was Evelyn August doing the tattling. Like you was a detective! It was like a book so I made Sara my chronicler," she said with conviction in every word. "She watch what we do and take notes and when we sleeping she send the stories to England and they read it every day. 'The Adventures of Mary and Sara.' 'Cept now things got hard she complain all the time and just wanna tell fairy tales," she added with equal amounts fondness and impatience for her flighty, imaginary friend.

Heartsick, Mary held her close, gulping back tears and hugging her like she could not bear to stop. After all, Sara had never asked to leave the asylum.

"Mary!" At the sound of Cedric's voice, she snapped to attention and saw him racing to the stair, where a massive black man stood at the top. Cedric shook his fist at her. "You had one job!"

When she returned to his side, prepared for him to threaten her, it came as a relief to find his anger replaced with nervous excitement, his reason being the new sack in his hands. "It's for the Lady of New Orleans," he said, ecstatic.

Mary wondered if she shivered from the cold or the infamous name. Bombarding her with the smell of whisky, he pressed his dry lips to hers. She saw nothing to do but kiss him back. The other boys made gagging noises.

Night cloaked the Tenderloin in purple and gray. Cedric stayed at the water tower while Mary and Sara made a trek to the

50s, the tenements on either side like large, flat paintings. Mary kept an eye out for robbers, never knowing who might try and take the package. While the first sack had been light, this one weighed almost nothing at all. For that reason she let Sara have the satisfaction of carrying it. Mary had a name, and an address, which led them up a fire escape at the back of a building. She knocked on the window, repeating the speech she'd prepared in her mind. At the fifth knock, it slid up with a groan. The lace parted and there appeared a woman's face like a granite block set on muslin. The obese Negress squinted through her spectacles with small, piggy eyes.

Mary stood to her full height, held up the sack. "From the West Indian," she said. "For the Lady of New Orleans. Five dol—"

A woman's voice rang from inside. "I am not ready for company! Theresa! They will wait until I am ready!" Her Southern twang reminded Mary of Dr. Chambers, making her cringe.

"You will have to wait," the husky-voiced Negress repeated in weary resignation. *Slam.* Mary's speech flopped pathetically to the rails, a broken-winged bird.

Wait, then. The ironwork under her butt was hard and rimmed with ice. She had enough experience sleeping on fire escapes to know she distrusted them. She always felt like she would fall. Three stories down, silver grass glimmered in a small backyard. Feeling her stomach lurch, she looked across at Sara. Her sister had insisted on bringing the book, which she wasn't even reading. One arm around the doll, the other on Mr. Baum, Sara drifted in and out of sleep.

Dizziness called Mary's attention to her empty belly. She knew she wasn't dying. It just felt like dying. Good*damn*, it was cold. Bone-splitting, fingers-falling-off cold. She closed her legs and rubbed her thighs together to make warmth. She thought of Little Black Sambo, and of herself, children in the woods. All he wanted was to go for a walk, when the four tigers threatened to eat him if he didn't give up his clothes and umbrella. Their greed backfired on them when they fought over who was the grandest tiger, and Sambo recovered his belongings while the tigers chased each other in a circle. They ran so fast they became syrup for his pancakes.

Her stomach moaned. *Don't think about pancakes*, she told herself. Still, if she could have one of Sambo's treasures, she would choose the purple shoes with crimson soles and crimson lining. Her feet hurt so much.

Someone, the nurse, maybe, or Cedric, once told her that the world outside the city was forest. Endless green hills where eagles nested and Iroquois stalked the brush. Mary had never seen a real tree, only the flowery and girlish ones in Central Park. The only birds she knew were pigeons and the bronze owls that blinked the hour from the cornice of the *Herald*. Forest trees couldn't be as tall as buildings. Buildings shadowed all, saw all, knew all, and to look up for too long made her breath clutch as she pictured the view from those heights. She tried to envision springtime pastures—what she imagined New Jersey looked like—and saw *him* walking barefoot through the forest in a blue robe embroidered with gold, threads of sunlight in his beard, his body shaped like the blond tree trunks that thrust up like spears of a buried army. The pure, invigorating air seemed to her at one rhythm with his breathing. She saw a tiny red-breasted bird land on his shoulder and a fawn lick his open palm. A man of the city *and* the woods, where her world ended and another began. This, for Mary, was the height of indulgence: daydreaming of J.M. Nesbitt in the freezing cold.

She struggled to stay focused. Sometimes she could be as fanciful as Sara, letting her imagination grow like jasmine and orchid and hollyhock, though hers was a garden she tended in secret. She could hear the chiming conversation of icicles. Unable to look up or down, she had to look straight at Sara, and her stupid doll, and the stupid rich man's book.

"Gimme that!" She wrestled it from Sara. Swatting away her sister's hands, she ripped out the frontispiece and ate it, imagined it as bread filling her belly. Sara cried like a spoiled brat. Mary tore a handful of pages and stuffed them in her mouth, only to pause at an illustration of the gingerbread man, the male or female child, and an obese dog being conveyed through the sky by a flying flamingo. *Flamingos can't fly*, she thought, and struck a match. The pages burning in the middle of the gantry illuminated Sara's tearful face. Warmth! The book was a beating black heart feeding the flames with its life.

"The wizard gave me that!" said Sara.

"If he a wizard, why ain't he do something useful?" Mary shouted. "Like take us away from here? Why ain't he stop us from starving? He just a stupid crazy white man!"

The window flew open. There appeared a white woman as shriveled as the Negress was fat, bug-eyed with terror. Her hair was a wreath of yellow smoke around her scalp.

"Vandals!" She emptied a tea kettle on the book. The water hissed and steamed and melted ice. The sound echoed off the tenement walls behind them, becoming massive, a warren of snakes. Mary and Sara put their backs to the rail. The woman grabbed their wrists, hauled them into the apartment, and dropped them on the hard wood floor.

Before Mary could think to flee, her abductress slammed the window shut. It took Mary a moment to adjust her eyes to the darkness. They stood in a small bedroom cluttered with ramshackle furniture and several dozen articles of clothing, some hung on laundry lines nailed in the walls, much of it lumped on the floor in reeking piles. In the middle of the floor, a gas-lamp cast light on the thin, expressionless faces of six small girls seated around it. The place smelled of damp earth and fried fish.

"Theresa!" said the white woman. As she pushed them from the room, fingernails like eight daggers at their backs, Mary watched the girls. They had question-mark spines, head scarves tied under their pointed chins, deep-set eyes downcast as they mechanically sewed lining on coats and trousers. Having never known what made the Lady of New Orleans famous among thieves, Mary was surprised at the simplicity of it. Thugs needed clothing too.

"Ther*esa!*" said the old woman. "These *van*dals lit the fire es*cape* on fire!" Mary saw one of the girls had a crate nailed together around her scrawny ankles.

They were led into a kitchen that smelled of sweat and burnt hair. Seated at a round table was the Negress and five girls making flowers from scraps of red and green paper. Their finished bunches filled an ever-growing pile in the center. Swaying ponderously in her rocking chair, the Negress wore the blue dress, head wrap, shawl, and once-white checkerboard apron of a Southern mammy. She stopped in mid-rock, shot glass poised on her bottom lip. "You brought them in here?" she said with alarm.

The white woman thrust the kettle imperiously at the Negress, splashing a fat drop onto her thigh. Theresa closed her eyes and murmured deep in her throat. The kitchen smelled of mildew and cooked meat. Its illumination came from brass-holdered candles placed on the various furnitures and cupboards. From the walls came clanking, stomping, scream-ing, water sputtering from a sink, a baby's cry: the gruesome sounds of the tenement. Despite the chill in the air, Mary felt her palms grow slick with sweat.

The white woman screamed. "These two little monkeys were lighting our fire escape on fire! Oh, you two will be punished!"

Fear clenched like a fist in Mary's gut. She took note of how many people there were, the available exits, how quickly she could reach the knives and scissors on the table.

On the ironing board sat a cage that was too small for the live rabbits stuffed inside. They writhed in a furry mass, a living ball of sickle teeth and drooling pink eyes, and Mary felt for them. *What kind of people keep rabbits?* she asked herself, and as quickly answered herself, *People who never leave.* Every so often, the rabbits screamed their suffocation. In the corner of the room stood a gas stove that looked like the bottom half of an egg perched on three legs, and Mary knew what the rabbits were for. Her mouth went dry. She took her sister's hand and readied for whatever would come. Sara shivered so terribly her knees knocked together but had too much dignity to cry. *Good girl.* They could still make it out of the tiger's den.

"Miss Evangeline"—the Negress wiped her hands on her apron—"these is the delivery boy—uh, girls with the package. You wasn't supposed to bring them inside."

Her mistress's eyes went wild. She dropped the kettle with a clatter and turned this way and that, dressing-gown sweeping the floor, her hands out like lobster claws. Finally, she clamped them on the shoulders of the nearest girl, as if she might stran-gle her. Instead she stroked the child's head. The terror never left the girl's face.

"Oh, silly me," said the Southern woman in a singsong lilt. Her furious expression turned to one of dead-eyed pleasantry. "Welcome, little darlings. I am glad to have your company, as are my granddaughters." She waved a hand at the dusky girls. "Why, Theresa, what a goose you are. You could have brought our company inside if you knew they were going to light our fire escape. Tell me, what if there was a fire? Where would we escape to if the escape is on fire?"

Flies buzzed around the ceiling cracks. Mary shifted from foot to foot, rather than give them a stationary target. She hated flies worse than ants or rats.

Theresa lowered her eyes. "I'm sorry, Miss Evangeline."

"I said I was not ready. I never said they could not come inside. Having a conflagration on the side of your house does seem a bit conspicuous, does it not?"

"Yes, Miss Evangeline."

All the while, the children kept their eyes on their work. They coughed and scratched at rashes on their arms. Mary worried she might catch something. Two things became obvious: these kids were not the Lady's grandchildren, and the title "Lady of New Orleans" was not meant in respect.

"Now," said the Lady, "as I am still not ready for company, you two arsonists will entertain Theresa for a minute."

While the Lady spruced up in her bedroom, Mary and Sara put their backs to the wall. Theresa rose from the wicker chair and moved as if the years of her life were shackles. Kneeling, she picked up the tea kettle and, with great bovine steps, placed it on the stove. The woman started a pot of oats mixed with a can of Borden's Evaporated Milk. Where she walked, the flower-makers cringed at the touch of her shadow. Mary didn't know whether this sweatshop or the giant black woman frightened her more. Theresa settled her bulk back in the chair. She poured a shot of John Jameson's and drank it noisily, her throat pouching in and out like a frog's. Swallowing took her several moments of gritting her teeth and screwing up her face.

"Nnngggg," she grunted. "Mmm. That's good whisky." She wiped her lips with a plump forefinger and fixed her stare on the girls. "How much the West Indian asking for them photographs? That's what in the bag, by the way."

"Five dollars," said Mary, with bass in her voice. Cedric had entrusted her with a number, and she meant to collect.

The woman flicked her finger like there was dirt in her nail. "You get three."

"Huh?" said Mary. "That ain't right."

"How do you figure, child?"

Three was enough for her, if it meant getting out of there. But Cedric said five.

"West Indian gone be mad," she reminded the woman in a serious voice. She'd hoped Theresa would flinch at his name, but the Negress burst with hearty laughter that set her huge body quaking like a doomed palace in Atlantis.

"Oh, child." She wiped a tear from her eye. "I'm sure that old black Fagin got you and the other little Thirty Street pickpockets thinking he the devil hissef. But in New York, Theresa St. Clare is a *name*." She taunted Mary. "Do *you* even have a name, let alone a *name?*"

"I'm Mary March," she said in defiance. A small name, one the world afforded neither fear nor honor. But it was hers, and she would demand respect for it.

Mary wondered if she could reason with the woman. She thought fast. "How much do your girls make on flowers? Five cents a gross? Well, it takes an hour just to go from the Merry Maiden to—"

Theresa's groan sounded like it came from deep inside a cave. "Quiet, child," she said. "You trying to haggle? That's good you got some brass in you." She poured another shot. "The West Indian been getting his garments done here for a long time. Longer than you been on this Earth. And I want you to tell him something." Her eyes narrowed. "Long as we know'd him, he never cheat us. Now he send us street rats like y'all asking half a month's rent for a bunch of photographs. I know he thinks Miss Evangeline's going dull in the head. You tell him she ain't dull, and she ain't idle. Just like you got your master, Mary March, I got my mistress, and I won't see her took advantage of."

Mary clamped her lips together. She fought to hold back tears. With a clatter, Miss Evangeline's door swung open, and there posed the woman in chinchilla.

"Smile, child," Theresa whispered to Mary.

The Lady's room reminded Mary of a hearse, its cramped confines decorated in lace and Shuttlesworth plates, candles and saints; its grandest accoutrements were a toilet-table crusted all over with spilled cosmetics, and an antique wardrobe of dresses turned to moth hives. Like black leaves, photographs lay in whorls on the shelves and floor. The Bible on her night-table was opened to Jonah. The Lady dumped her newest photographs on to her bed and sprawled among them like she was taking a warm bath. "Bourbon Street," she sighed. "Canal Street. Lake Pontchartrain." Her hand fluttered to her chest. "Taken by a true Louisianan. Theresa, do you remember Louisiana?"

"I do, Miss Evangeline." Theresa stood by the door, a grimly smiling sentinel.

"Theresa's been with me my whole life." Her voice went thin with reminiscence. "She was just the wildest thing you ever saw. Those were our golden days, down on the plantation. A regular Arcadia."

Now Mary saw the little girl lying behind the Lady on a corner of the bed. Hands clasped prayerfully under her cheek, her eyes were vacant. Red lip prints trailed down her throat and under her collar. This fresh horror had Mary's heartbeat pounding in her ears, demanding all her composure to keep her fear from showing. Beside her, Sara hugged the doll tight.

"Your family was good people," she heard Theresa say. "Christian people."

"You are a terrible liar," said Miss Evangeline. "My mother was a bitch from Hell."

Good people don't run sweatshops, Mary thought. They didn't deal in flies and fear, sick children and paper blossoms. Beating weak beneath that scrawny freckled chest lay a heart rimmed in frost. Mary loathed the both of them.

The Lady threw up the photographs to let them fall like feathers. With a gesture to Sara, she said, "You. Baby Doll. You look ready to freeze to death."

"I-I am cold, ma'am." The words came shivering out of Sara.

"You look right wretched. Just like the Little Match-Seller. Do you remember that children's tale?"

Mary said she did. As she recalled, a Little Match-Seller was forced by her father to sell matches in a blizzard, had a bunch of hallucinations, and froze to death. Awful goddamn story.

Propping her stubbly chin on an elbow, the Lady looked at her wardrobe. "Theresa, correct me if I'm wrong, but are those two children's coats in the wardrobe? Bring them to me."

The fat woman's bottom lip quivered. "Miss Evangeline, it ain't right."

"Please don't be willful, Theresa. There's two girls' coats right there. The Good Lord has seen it right to take my eyesight day by day, but for the nonce I see what I see. Here we have two girls and they are cold. It's the Christmas season. Let it be said the Lady of New Orleans is a charitable soul."

"Miss Evangeline, them coats . . ." Theresa choked on the words. "Do you 'member . . ."

"Shut up and bring the fucking coats, please."

Another gift, more sinister than the last. Made of red velvet, the coats flared down from the neck like tea-bells. White fur lined the hood, cape, and cuffs, and the cape tied at the throat with white lacing. On the lady's instruction, the girls put them on. For all their wear, they were the finest clothes to touch Mary's skin. As she slipped her hands through the sleeves, the goose down on the inner lining felt like a soft-furred animal brushing against her knuckles. Clasping her hands together gave the appearance that she wore a muff. Heavy and light at the same time, the coat enveloped Mary in warmth.

"Lovely as two winter roses," said the Lady. "I bet the most you hoped for was a tip. Well, I would say you got a great deal more. Just like a Christmas story. Farewell, my turtle doves. Now"—she turned to her bed warmer—"give them their five dollars, Theresa."

"Yes, Miss Evangeline." The fat woman ushered them, none too gently, from the room.

"Oh, Topsy," the Lady muttered. "Topsy, Topsy, Topsy. I do wish you could still do a summerset."

Theresa closed the door behind her. Finding her shot of whisky filled with drowned flies, she dumped it on the floor, poured another. One of the girls wrapped her a cigarette from a bag of JOB brand tobacco. The former slave sat, all the while staring at the sisters with a mix of admiration and envy.

"Where's our money?" said Mary, her voice betraying anger. The woman had no right to keep them any longer.

"Shut up," Theresa said. "Her father was good Christian people. Never beat nobody." Her eyes glazed over. "When she was 'bout your age, she got sick. I climbed right into that bed with her. I wanted to take the sickness into me. Better I die than she. *She!* As close to an angel to be seen on this horrid world. She lived. Was my love brought her back from the Gates. You wanna hear 'bout them coats?"

"No!" Sara piped up. Her voice sounded very small.

"You shut yo' mouth, quadroon," said the woman. "Because I came back for Miss Evangeline. I already lived up north with Miss Feely. I had a life in Vermont, freedom papers and every-thing. But Miss Evangeline's sainted father, God rest his soul, got stabbed to death by some ruffian. Now her mother, she was a piece of work. Stole her own daughter's inheritance and put her out on the street." She pursed her lips. "I found her work-ing as a cleaning girl in a brothel in Nawlins. She still had the most beautiful golden hair. Like an angel in Hell," she choked out the words, a moment's sorrow. "I took her up north with me, but our train crashed and we had to go it on foot. Them coats you wearing was blessed by the Almighty. Them coats got us all the way from Louisiana to New York. All them crackers between here and there, ain't a one know'd there was a little white girl and nigger girl under there. No money to speak of when we got here. But we got through." She glugged down the shot, narrowed her eyes on them. "Don't you lose them coats. Else I'll find you. What did you see here, girls?"

"Nothing," they both said.

"Damn right, you didn't." For a moment she stared at the wall, as if she could see the plantation through the cracks and fading vines. The white girls folded paper. "You know, when I was a girl—"

"Can we please leave?" said Mary.

"When I was a girl," she repeated louder, lighting her cigarette with a match, "nobody know'd where I come from, so they say I just sprung up out the ground." She laughed wretchedly. "I could vex the white folks. I really could." A pause. "There ain't no such thing as a child just sprung out the ground. Tell me, girl, what do they call a little nigger child ain't no black man to say he the daddy?"

"O-orphan?" Mary stammered.

Anger flashed in the woman's eyes. "I ain't no orphan! My family come from good stock! There's pure blood in these veins!"

Mary recoiled in horror. "Your . . . *sister?*"

Now the woman turned contemplative. She tightened her shawl around her shoulders. "Sing, granddaughters," she instructed the girls at the table.

They weren't from America. Trying to pronounce the words, they sounded like they had grass in their mouths, but they sang. Lord in Heaven, they sang.

"*O holy night! The stars are brightly shining. It is the night of our dear savior's birth.*"

Theresa's brooding gaze pierced through the smoke. "We was born so close together we might as well be twins. Would you let anybody take advantage of your sister?"

"No," Mary squeaked, and took Sara's hand.

"*Long lay the world in sin and error pining . . .*" One of the girls broke down weeping, tears on the flowers. Momentarily, the others faltered, before resuming their song louder than before.

"Please!" Mary begged. "Please let us go. We ain't done nothin' to you."

The woman sat upright, truly incensed. "Nothing? *Nothing?* You seduced her!"

Mary set her feet to bolt for the door. Theresa shook like a woman possessed, overwhelmed with a dark passion. "Chillun can't never keep their mouths shut. Y'all's raggedy asses is orphans. I can tell. Ain't nobody gonna miss y'all. Ain't no mama to clutch her breath for you." She flung her cigarette in a flower girl's face. The girl screamed like a mouse getting stepped on, unnoticed by Theresa, who shot to her feet like a piece of popping popcorn and grabbed a carving knife off the table. "Don't run. The door's bolted. Don't move."

"A thrill of hope, the weary world rejoices. For yonder breaks a new and glorious morn."

The world slowed. The floor shook as the woman advanced like a steamer into harbor. Mary threw herself in front of Sara. Light flashed along the blade, and above it she saw starbursts of frost on a window.

"Think you can take what is mine?" said Theresa, the tears on her cheeks shining like the blade. "Take 'em off. Take 'em off, I say!"

"Okay!" Mary started to untie the collar. "You can ha—"

"Faaaaalllll on your kneeeeees . . ."

Theresa lunged for them. Mary dove to the right, pushing Sara with her. Theresa's momentum caught her knife in the wall and brought a rack of dishes clattering down. Tangled in the coat, Mary struggled to stand. Sara tried to pull her up by her sleeve. With astounding quickness, Theresa hurled a pot at them. Mary brought up her arm to shield herself. Her arm went numb, then burned with pain.

She retreated until her back hit the wall. Nauseated with hurt, she no longer saw the woman, only the knife, the twitching wrist. She felt Sara's hands on her shoulder. One-armed, she braced herself before Sara and flashed her teeth. She searched for Jesus's mercy. And she saw *him*.

They should have died that night they grew so hungry that she and Cedric were eating mud, forcing Sara to gag it down. On that night a Kentucky woman, on her way home from the laundry, offered a place to stay. For two nights, they lived and ate with Mrs. Ruggle, her nine children, and the boarders who slept in the lofts. The Ruggles hung stockings on their wall. Mary braided the girls' hair. It felt like having a family.

Mary should have been arrested when she stole the doll in Central Park. But no one saw her, and Sara got her little princess. Over a year, they hid it in the walls during the day, cuddled with it at night, no one the wiser. Even Cedric couldn't force them to pawn it.

Or when Sara asked Dr. Chambers if she could play a little longer. She was getting sassy, as a beautiful girl might, an affront the doctor corrected with the back of his fist. It wasn't like when he hit Mary. The bruises sank into her soil, and, because no one could see them, she could pretend for Sara's sake it didn't hurt. However, Sara's cheek was a purple shadow on the moon, a demonic eclipse Mary could not ignore. Only a monster would hurt someone so beautiful.

That same night, she'd lain awake and plotting escape when she heard the floor creak, and saw one of the boys sneaking around the girls' dormitory, long-limbed and nimble, like a shadow moving on its own. Wondering why Cedric had come in her room, she saw him unlatch the window and push it open, poised in the moonlight.

She didn't waste another second. "Let us go with you!"

"You'll just slow me down!" he told her.

"We can help you!" she said, and added, "The both of us."

Orphans were beginning to stir from sleep. "Then keep up," he said.

They poised at the ledge, a steep drop and four-foot jump to the next roof. Beyond that, freedom. The curses and yells of drunks became one din. Cats screamed their valentines. A train hollered. Cedric leapt and landed on the other side in a roll. Sara froze on the ledge, crying and fighting to stay put, and Mary had to push her into his arms. From that high, she saw the city as Jesus did. Factory smoke concealed the stars. Chimneys and unfinished brick walls sprang from the rooftops like neck hairs on edge. Big-shouldered bridges held up the sky. The buildings kept multiplying until the end of sight. She said a prayer and jumped. She flew.

Mary and Sara should have died in the streets, but someone watched over them. Now the rabbits in the cage were squealing and baring their long teeth. Mary could die in the tenement, or she could become like the little rabbit in the story. Spotted by the farmer, he hid in the watering can, upset the potted plants, dove under the fence and was gone.

Little Sambo was wild and black like her, but he still beat the tigers.

Sara threw her doll at the woman's face. The sudden act startled Theresa, stalled her. The missile missed her by a good foot, but Sara-the-doll's coat collar stuck on the latch to the rabbit cage, pulling it open as it dropped. Emancipated vermin dove onto the table, into the center of the flowers. Paper petals filled the room like ticker tape. The girls' singing turned to screams as they dove under the ironing board. Swatting the petals, Theresa heard her sister yell to know what the matter was. Those horrible children were vanished in the red and green. Enraged, she charged their direction, slashing the air like a butcher. Her toe hit a small hand and she stabbed down, heard the satisfying sound of her knife punching flesh. Before it had time to scream, she stabbed again. Evil nigger girls. Why did they come to disturb her happy home?

Flowers settled on the floor, aftermath of a plaid blizzard. The rabbits were gone. Smooth, small, white fingers touched her foot, and she feared she'd killed one of her own girls. It turned out to be the doll, her belly ripped open, her face placid and beautiful among the cotton fluff. Theresa couldn't believe her hands had killed a white girl, even a fake one, and they wouldn't stop shaking. From the hall came the sound of her drunk neighbor stumbling home. And under his clamor, the weeping voices of girls she knew.

This is how the story ends.

Two girls in beautiful coats made their way to a water tower, where they told a boy who waited they didn't have the money. When he yelled at them, the tall one pushed him into the snow, and they left.

Or this is how it ends. The eldest delivered the youngest to the visiting teacher the next day.

Or this is how it ends. The American abolition movement never gained enough traction to threaten the planters of the South. When rebellion broke, it was slaves, not slavemasters, who set Dixie ablaze. For the armistice, the Negroes received their own nation in the center of the country, where they sowed barley and battled the remaining indigenes for land. Surprised to find money in their coat pockets, the hooded girls bribed their way onto an orphan train out west. After intermittent days in the boxcar crowded with other children, they were greeted by the sight of black people working their own fields, riding horses, living content in their own towns. Dropped off in one such village, they waited at the station, and waited, until a black Creole gentleman arrived in a horse-drawn carriage. He'd been expecting a boy for the farm and instead found two girls, named for the third month, whose charm and toughness convinced him he'd found the joy of his latter years.

Or they stayed to familiar places. A newspaper boy in Herald Square would swear he saw two girls in velvet hoods step into a hotel, where the concierge was expecting young ladies whose coats matched that description, and without looking at their faces offered them a canvasback dinner.

Maybe the actors at the opera house saw girls with shrouded faces walk hand-in-hand into Macy's. Before taking in the many wonders, they went to the doll case to say a prayer, as if for a dead family member.

Or maybe their story *was* like *Anne of Green Gables,* only set in New York. We will never know. No one would swear these girls found their way to Greeley Square, where they stepped onto a wagon whose driver clothed himself in December, for if they saw such a thing, they forgot.

And of the Negroes taking the trolley car home—the waiters and porters, the hackmen and draymen, the cooks and bellhops—some claimed they saw two such girls making the long and wearying trek through the colored neighborhood.

And then, and then, and then . . .

ACKNOWLEDGMENTS

These last few years have been long and hard. They have been years of movement. Thank you to all who have supported me. For offering critique on the stories in this book. For telling me "It will be okay" when I couldn't tell myself. For the love you have given to me.

Denver: Patty, Steven, Mairead, Courtney, Pavlos, Hanna, Sarra, Tyler, Landon, Jessica, Bonnie, Olivia.

Louisiana: Khadijah, Jules, Charlotte, Dan.

Philly: Oki, Alex, Lou, Jenn.

Pittsburgh: Toni, Carlin, Charlie, CJ, Nate, Jess, Dan, Liz, Annie, Molly. My father Dr. Elwin Cotman, O.D.

Toronto: Stephen, Claire, Kelly, Emma.

New York: Henry, Audrey, Madeleine, Christine, Sammy.

The Bay: Marisa, Spenser, Danielle, Melinda, Vernon, Brian, Krystal, Dorien, Hanna, Joel, Wendy, Mega, Christine, Kara, Dan, Josh.

Nisi Shawl, for being an inspiration as a writer and human, and giving me the character of Teetee.

Liz Hand, for friendship and support and the beauty of her writing. Alissa Nutting, for being an ear when I needed one. John O'Neill. Jeff VanderMeer. Kelly and Gavin.

And everyone in the fight against fascism and white supremacy. In these dark days, you are the candle.

PUBLICATION HISTORY

"The Piper's Christmas Gift" was first published in *Quail Bell Magazine,* 2013. "Dance on Saturday," "Seven Watsons," "Mine," "The Son's War," and "Among the Zoologists" are published here for the first time.

ABOUT THE AUTHOR

Elwin Cotman (elwincotman.com) is a native of Pittsburgh, Pennsylvania. He is the author of *Dance on Saturday* and two previous collections of short stories, *The Jack Daniels Sessions EP* and *Hard Times Blues*. In 2011 he was nominated for a Carl Brandon Society Award. He has toured extensively across North America and Europe. He is at work on his first novel.